LiFE WITH Archie®

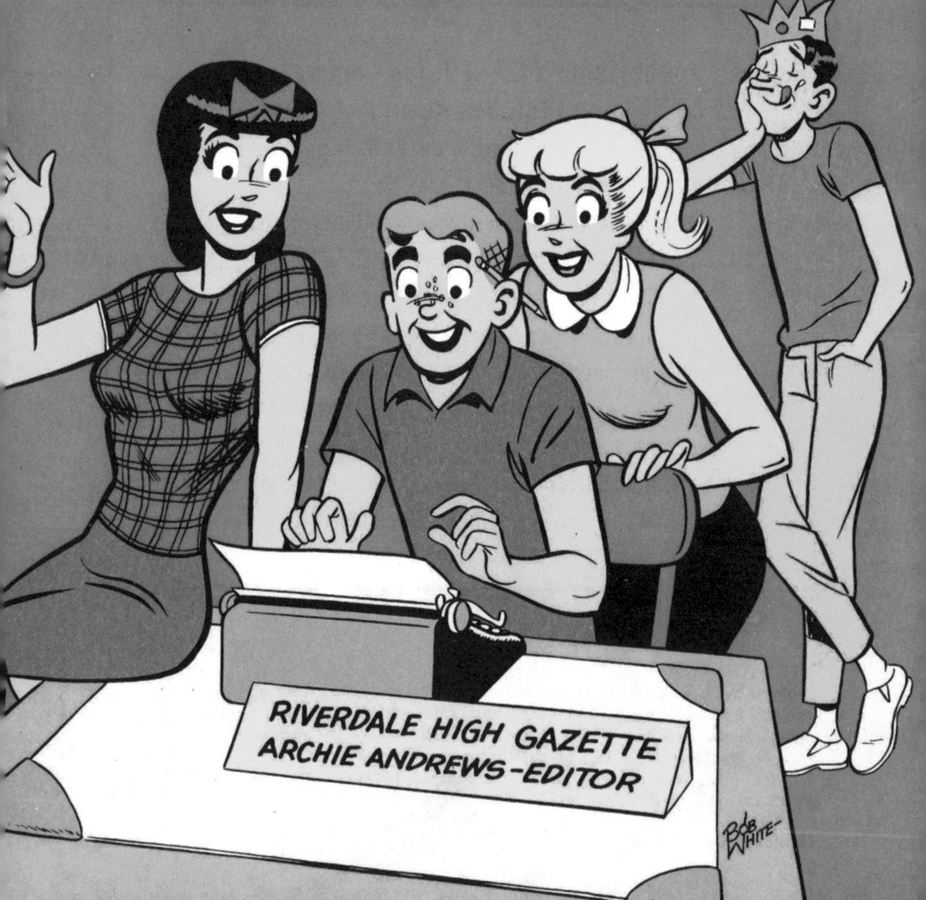
RIVERDALE HIGH GAZETTE
ARCHIE ANDREWS-EDITOR
BOB WHITE

LIFE
WITH
Archie

Publisher / Co-CEO: Jon Goldwater
Co-President / Editor-In-Chief: Victor Gorelick
Co-President: Mike Pellerito
Co-President: Alex Segura
Chief Creative Officer: Roberto Aguirre-Sacasa
Chief Operating Officer: William Mooar
Chief Financial Officer: Robert Wintle
Director of Book Sales & Operations: Jonathan Betancourt
Production Manager: Stephen Oswald
Lead Designer: Kari McLachlan
Associate Editor: Carlos Antunes
Assistant Editor / Proofreader: Jamie Lee Rotante
Co-CEO: Nancy Silberkleit

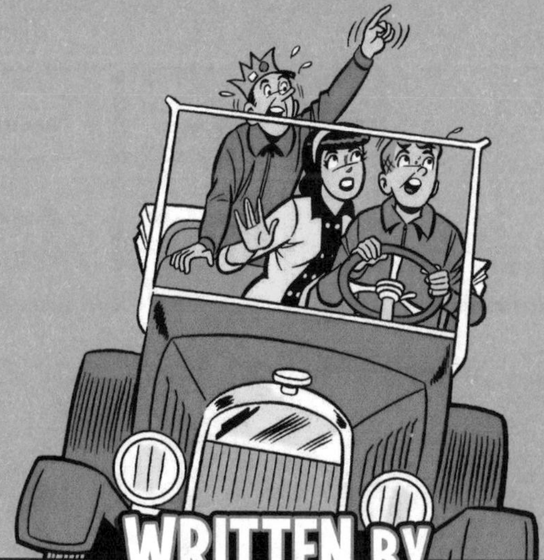

WRITTEN BY

Sy Reit, Geoge Gladir, Frank Doyle,
Bob White & Bob Bolling

ART BY

Samm Schwartz, Bob White, Harry Lucey, Dan DeCarlo,
Bob Bolling, Marty Epp, Barry Grossman, Rudy Lapick
Mario Acquaviva, Victor Gorelick & Vince DeCarlo

This book contains some material that was originally created in a less socially sensitive time in our society and reflects attitudes that may be interpreted as being unacceptable today. The stories are reprinted here without alteration for historical reference.

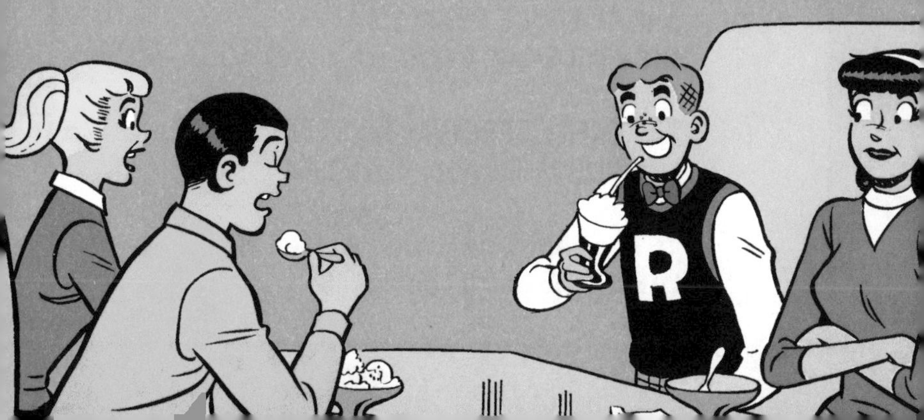

LiFE WITH Archie®

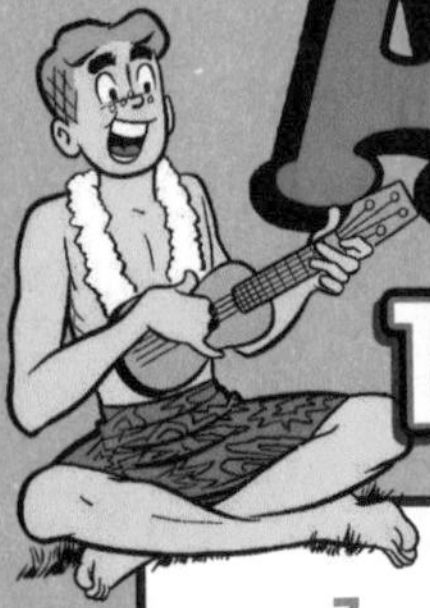

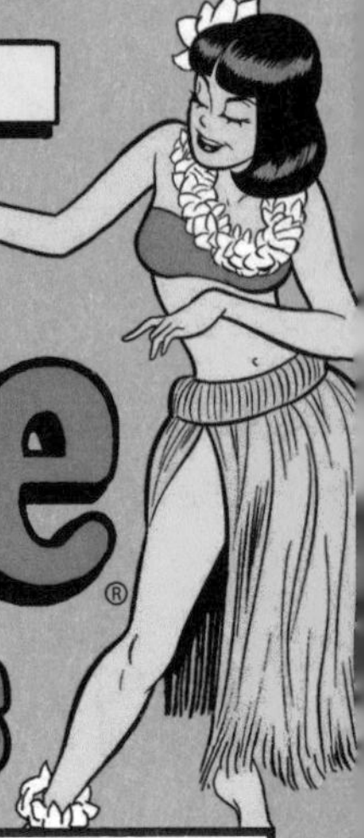

TABLE OF CONTENTS

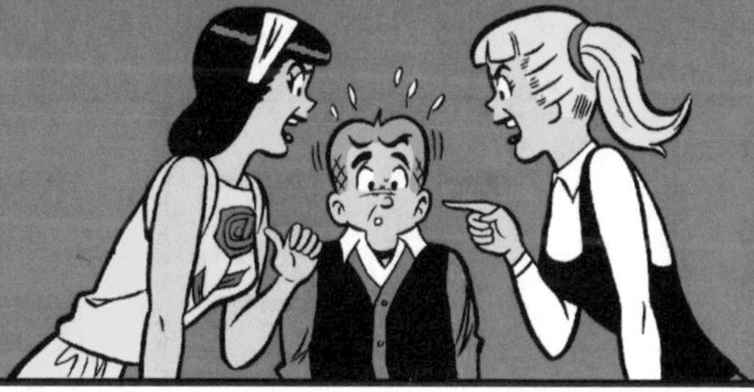

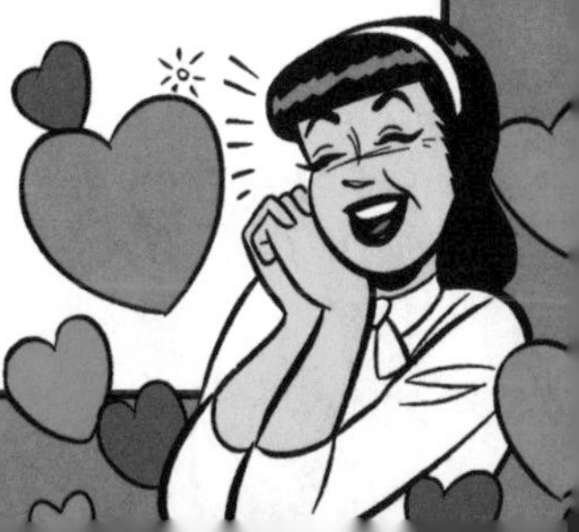

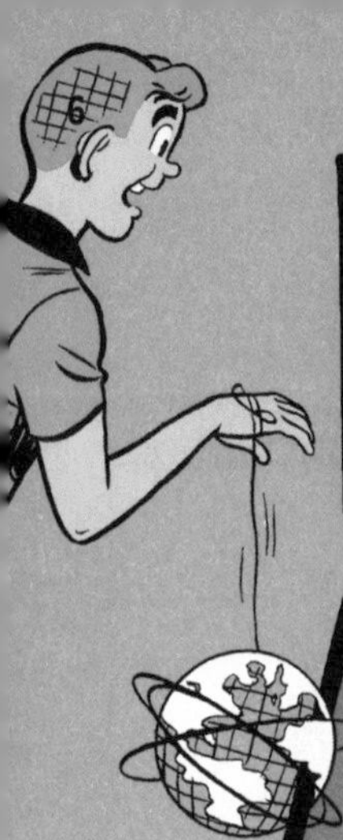

LiFE WITH Archie®

The *Life with Archie* series originally ran from 1958 to 1991 and featured Archie Andrews in adventure stories that were longer—and more dramatic—than the standard Archie tales. Most often, the stories were of escapades experienced by Archie and the gang, as they thwarted thieves, smugglers, ghosts, monsters and the like. As the series progressed, more "alternate universes" were featured, like the gang being secret agents and superheroes. Many years later, in 2010, the series would return as a magazine-sized comic devoted to stories that spun out of the headline-making "Archie Wedding" storyline.

In this collection, we explore some of the earlier stories which featured zany adventures and saw the gang come face-to-face with criminals, discover forgotten lands, and solve crazy mysteries—PLUS some regular ol' high school hijinks just for fun!

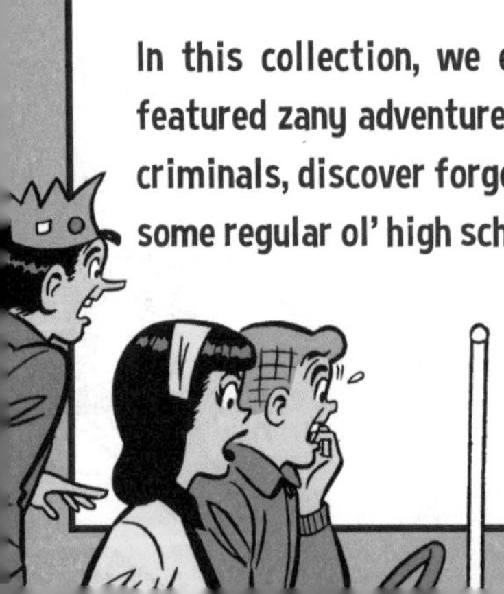

Welcome to the wild world of America's not-so-average teen and experience LIFE WITH ARCHIE!

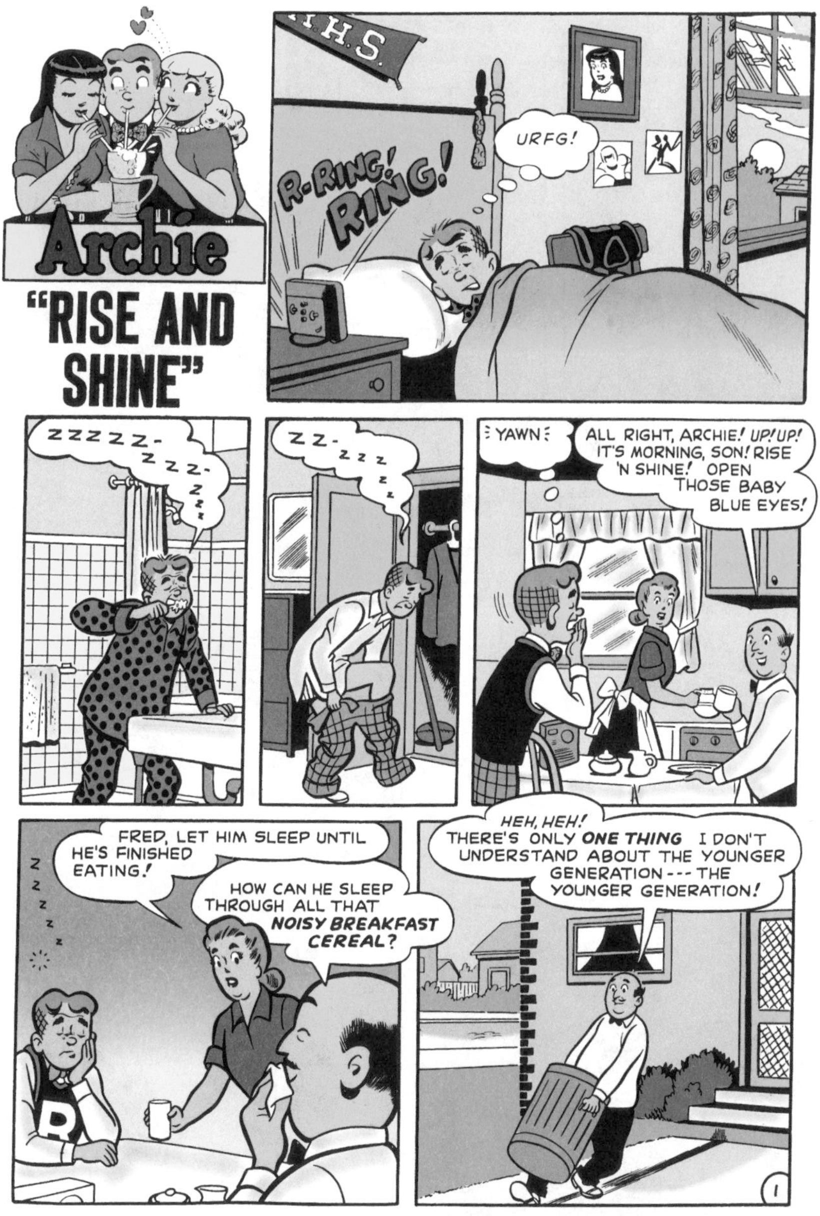
Archie
"RISE AND SHINE"
R-RING! RING!
URFG!
ZZZZZ-ZZZ-ZZZ
ZZ-ZZZZZ
YAWN
ALL RIGHT, ARCHIE! UP! UP! IT'S MORNING, SON! RISE 'N SHINE! OPEN THOSE BABY BLUE EYES!
FRED, LET HIM SLEEP UNTIL HE'S FINISHED EATING!
HOW CAN HE SLEEP THROUGH ALL THAT NOISY BREAKFAST CEREAL?
HEH, HEH! THERE'S ONLY ONE THING I DON'T UNDERSTAND ABOUT THE YOUNGER GENERATION --- THE YOUNGER GENERATION!
1

Story: Sy Reit Pencils: Samm Schwartz

Originally printed in LIFE WITH ARCHIE #1, September 1958

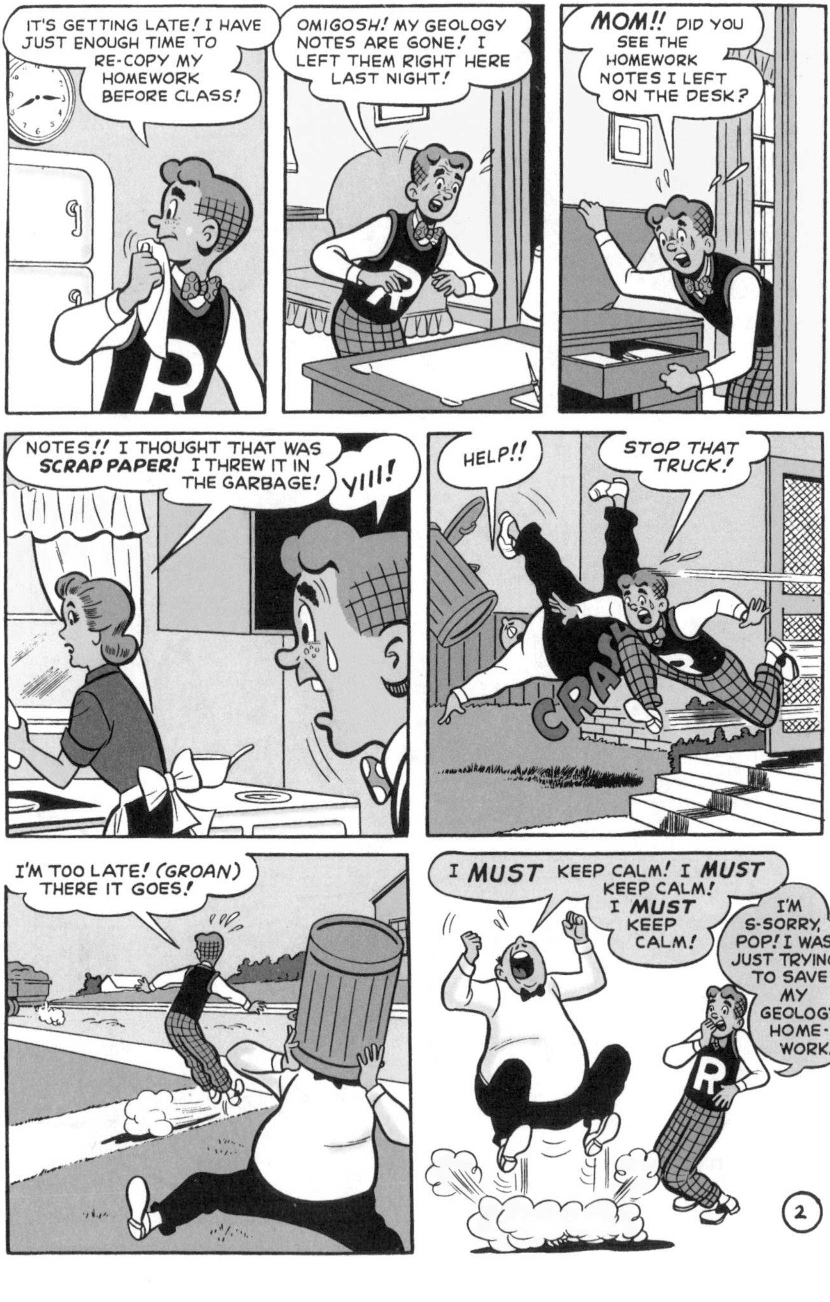
IT'S GETTING LATE! I HAVE JUST ENOUGH TIME TO RE-COPY MY HOMEWORK BEFORE CLASS!
OMIGOSH! MY GEOLOGY NOTES ARE GONE! I LEFT THEM RIGHT HERE LAST NIGHT!
MOM!! DID YOU SEE THE HOMEWORK NOTES I LEFT ON THE DESK?
NOTES!! I THOUGHT THAT WAS SCRAP PAPER! I THREW IT IN THE GARBAGE!
YIII!
HELP!!
STOP THAT TRUCK!
CRASH
I'M TOO LATE! (GROAN) THERE IT GOES!
I MUST KEEP CALM! I MUST KEEP CALM! I MUST KEEP CALM!
I'M S-SORRY, POP! I WAS JUST TRYING TO SAVE MY GEOLOGY HOME-WORK!
2

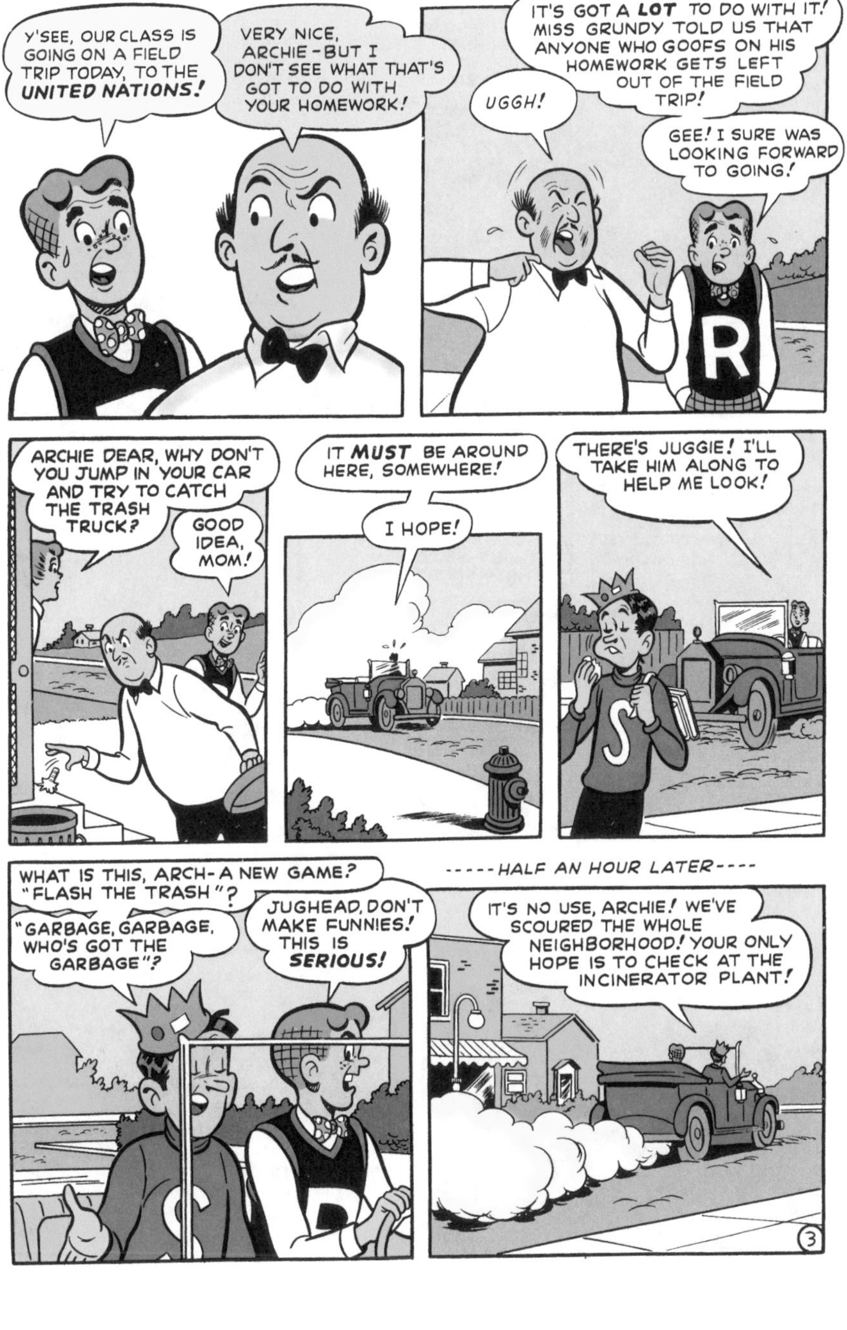
Y'SEE, OUR CLASS IS GOING ON A FIELD TRIP TODAY, TO THE UNITED NATIONS!
VERY NICE, ARCHIE - BUT I DON'T SEE WHAT THAT'S GOT TO DO WITH YOUR HOMEWORK!
IT'S GOT A LOT TO DO WITH IT! MISS GRUNDY TOLD US THAT ANYONE WHO GOOFS ON HIS HOMEWORK GETS LEFT OUT OF THE FIELD TRIP!
UGGH!
GEE! I SURE WAS LOOKING FORWARD TO GOING!
ARCHIE DEAR, WHY DON'T YOU JUMP IN YOUR CAR AND TRY TO CATCH THE TRASH TRUCK?
GOOD IDEA, MOM!
IT MUST BE AROUND HERE, SOMEWHERE!
I HOPE!
THERE'S JUGGIE! I'LL TAKE HIM ALONG TO HELP ME LOOK!
WHAT IS THIS, ARCH- A NEW GAME? "FLASH THE TRASH"?
"GARBAGE, GARBAGE, WHO'S GOT THE GARBAGE"?
JUGHEAD, DON'T MAKE FUNNIES! THIS IS SERIOUS!
-----HALF AN HOUR LATER----
IT'S NO USE, ARCHIE! WE'VE SCOURED THE WHOLE NEIGHBORHOOD! YOUR ONLY HOPE IS TO CHECK AT THE INCINERATOR PLANT!
3

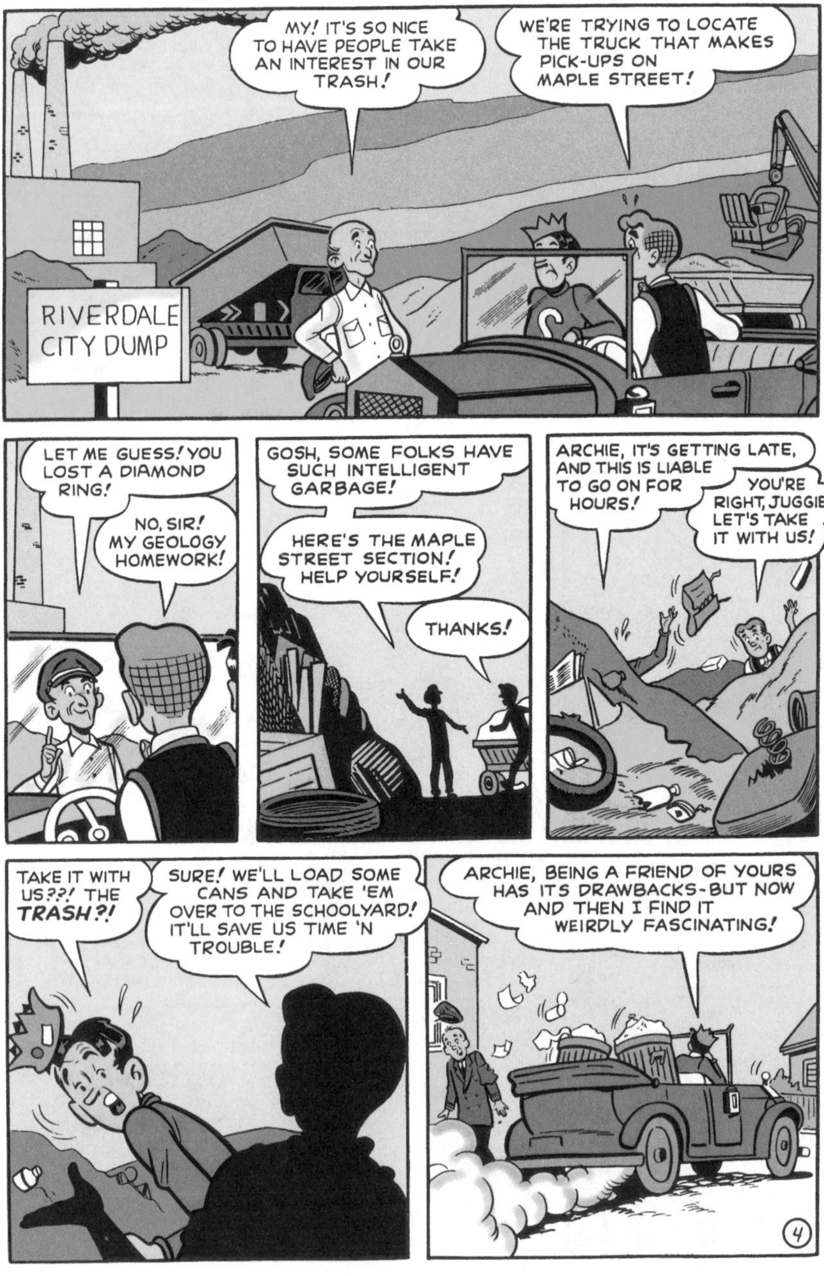
MY! IT'S SO NICE TO HAVE PEOPLE TAKE AN INTEREST IN OUR TRASH!
WE'RE TRYING TO LOCATE THE TRUCK THAT MAKES PICK-UPS ON MAPLE STREET!
RIVERDALE CITY DUMP
LET ME GUESS! YOU LOST A DIAMOND RING!
NO, SIR! MY GEOLOGY HOMEWORK!
GOSH, SOME FOLKS HAVE SUCH INTELLIGENT GARBAGE!
HERE'S THE MAPLE STREET SECTION! HELP YOURSELF!
THANKS!
ARCHIE, IT'S GETTING LATE, AND THIS IS LIABLE TO GO ON FOR HOURS!
YOU'RE RIGHT, JUGGIE! LET'S TAKE IT WITH US!
TAKE IT WITH US??! THE TRASH?!
SURE! WE'LL LOAD SOME CANS AND TAKE 'EM OVER TO THE SCHOOLYARD! IT'LL SAVE US TIME 'N TROUBLE!
ARCHIE, BEING A FRIEND OF YOURS HAS ITS DRAWBACKS-BUT NOW AND THEN I FIND IT WEIRDLY FASCINATING!
4

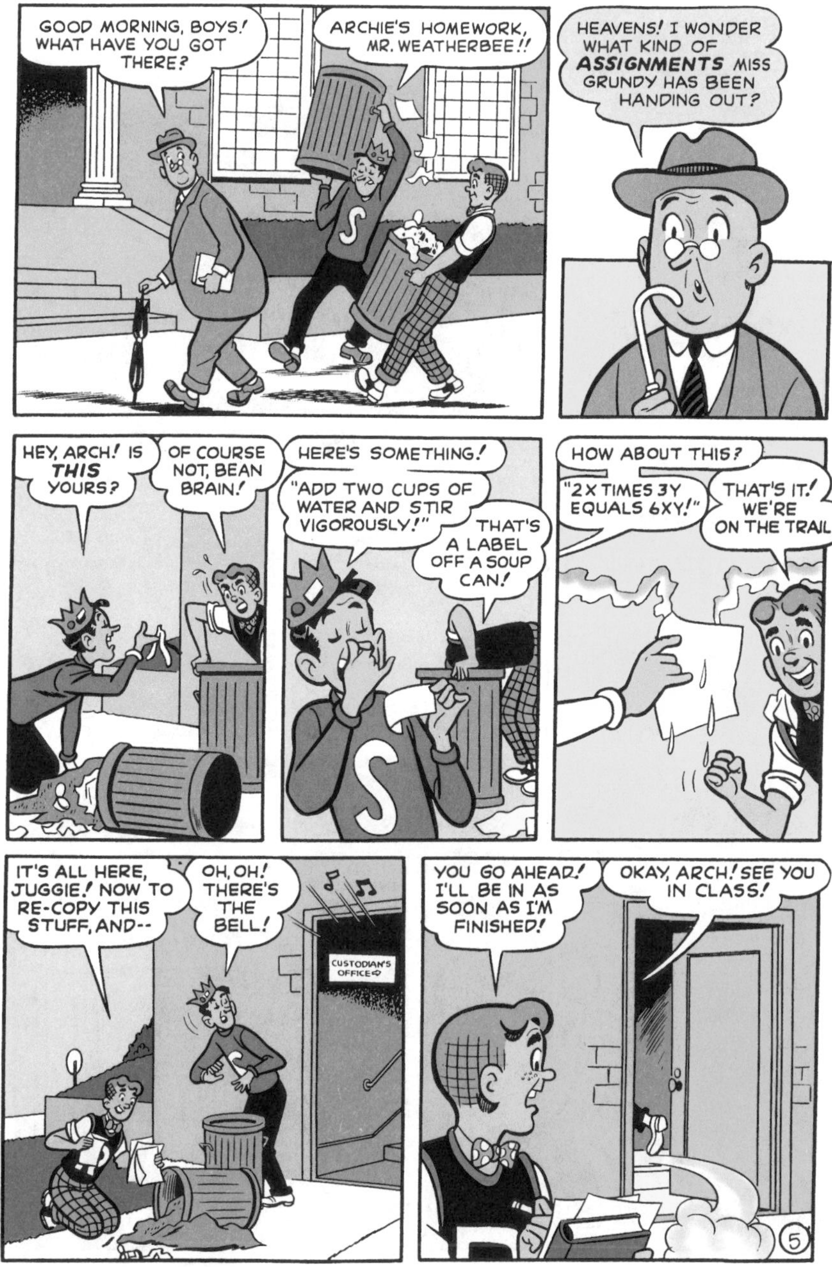
GOOD MORNING, BOYS! WHAT HAVE YOU GOT THERE?
ARCHIE'S HOMEWORK, MR. WEATHERBEE!!
HEAVENS! I WONDER WHAT KIND OF ASSIGNMENTS MISS GRUNDY HAS BEEN HANDING OUT?
HEY, ARCH! IS THIS YOURS?
OF COURSE NOT, BEAN BRAIN!
HERE'S SOMETHING!
"ADD TWO CUPS OF WATER AND STIR VIGOROUSLY!"
THAT'S A LABEL OFF A SOUP CAN!
HOW ABOUT THIS?
"2X TIMES 3Y EQUALS 6XY!"
THAT'S IT! WE'RE ON THE TRAIL!
IT'S ALL HERE, JUGGIE! NOW TO RE-COPY THIS STUFF, AND--
OH, OH! THERE'S THE BELL!
CUSTODIAN'S OFFICE
YOU GO AHEAD! I'LL BE IN AS SOON AS I'M FINISHED!
OKAY, ARCH! SEE YOU IN CLASS!
5

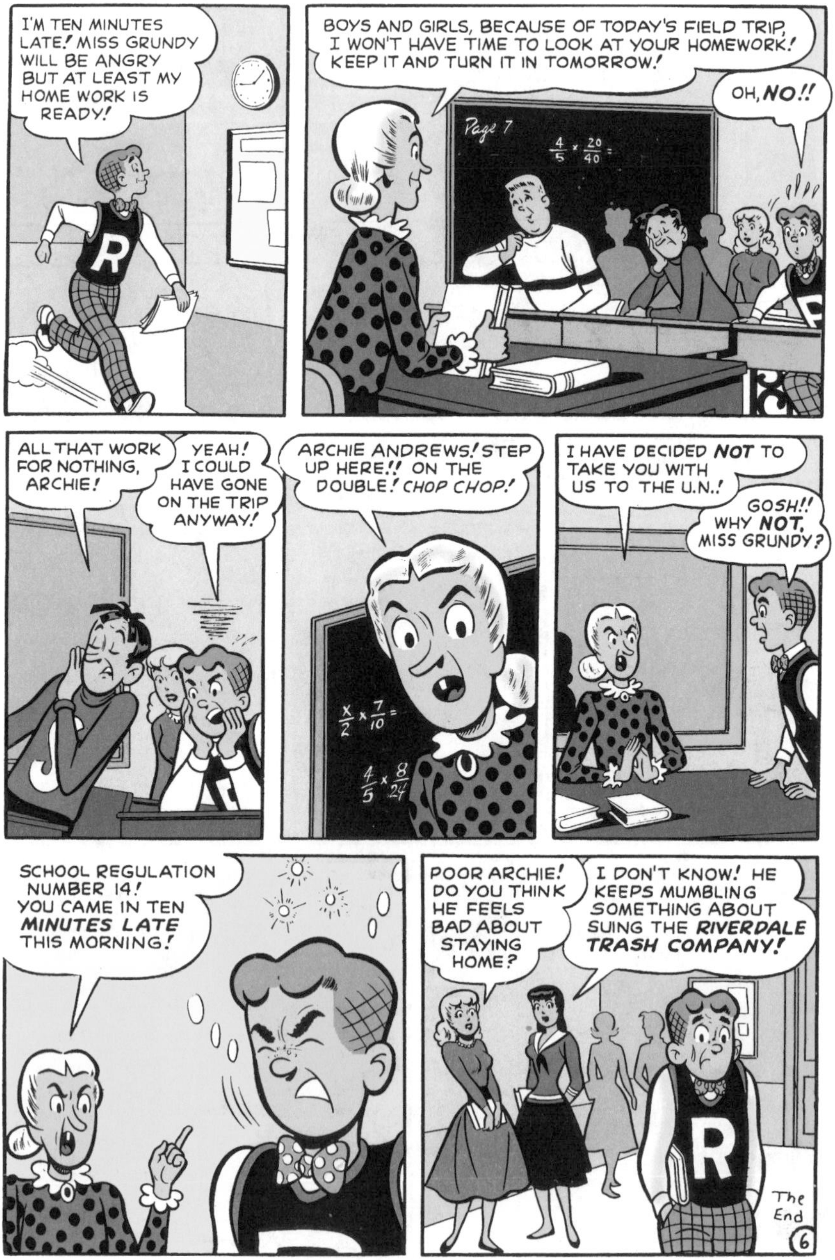
I'M TEN MINUTES LATE! MISS GRUNDY WILL BE ANGRY BUT AT LEAST MY HOME WORK IS READY!
BOYS AND GIRLS, BECAUSE OF TODAY'S FIELD TRIP, I WON'T HAVE TIME TO LOOK AT YOUR HOMEWORK! KEEP IT AND TURN IT IN TOMORROW!
OH, NO!!
Page 7
4/5 x 20/40 =
ALL THAT WORK FOR NOTHING, ARCHIE!
YEAH! I COULD HAVE GONE ON THE TRIP ANYWAY!
ARCHIE ANDREWS! STEP UP HERE!! ON THE DOUBLE! CHOP CHOP!
x/2 x 7/10 =
4/5 x 8/24
I HAVE DECIDED NOT TO TAKE YOU WITH US TO THE U.N.!
GOSH!! WHY NOT, MISS GRUNDY?
SCHOOL REGULATION NUMBER 14! YOU CAME IN TEN MINUTES LATE THIS MORNING!
POOR ARCHIE! DO YOU THINK HE FEELS BAD ABOUT STAYING HOME?
I DON'T KNOW! HE KEEPS MUMBLING SOMETHING ABOUT SUING THE RIVERDALE TRASH COMPANY!
The End
6

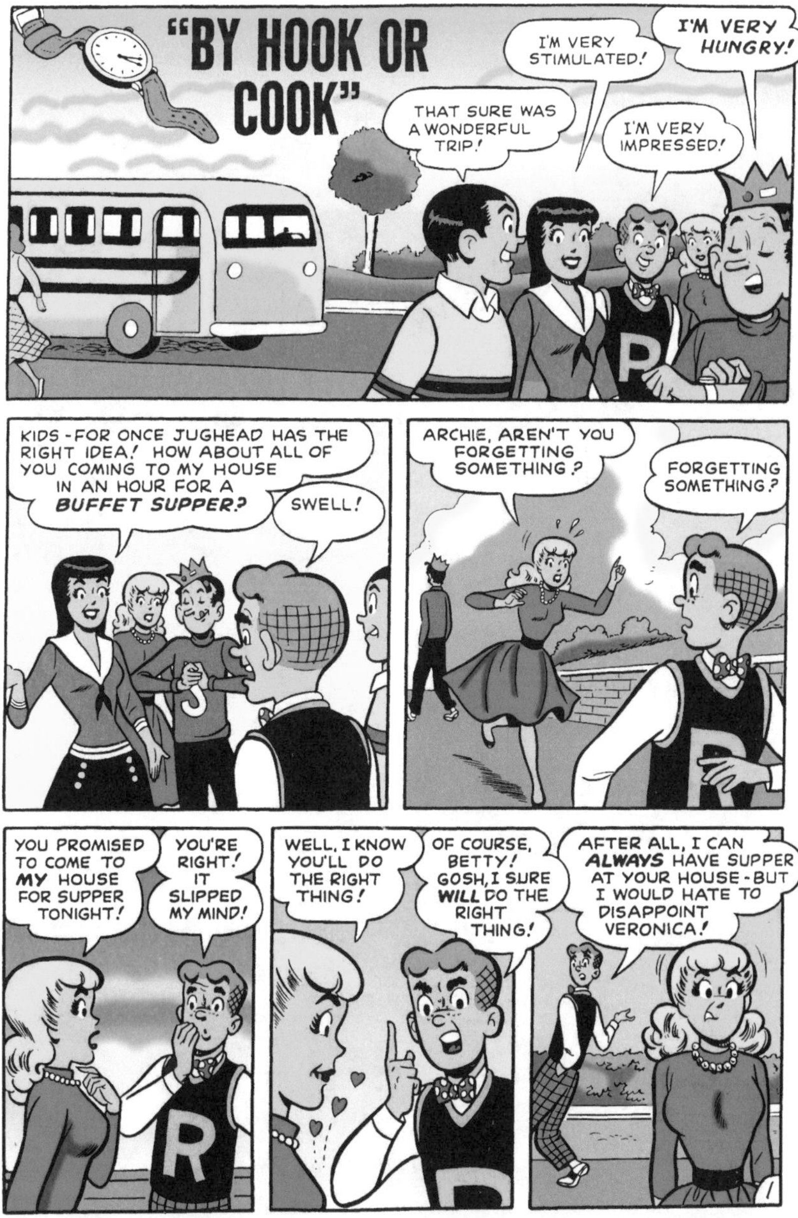
"BY HOOK OR COOK"
THAT SURE WAS A WONDERFUL TRIP!
I'M VERY STIMULATED!
I'M VERY IMPRESSED!
I'M VERY HUNGRY!
KIDS - FOR ONCE JUGHEAD HAS THE RIGHT IDEA! HOW ABOUT ALL OF YOU COMING TO MY HOUSE IN AN HOUR FOR A BUFFET SUPPER?
SWELL!
ARCHIE, AREN'T YOU FORGETTING SOMETHING?
FORGETTING SOMETHING?
YOU PROMISED TO COME TO MY HOUSE FOR SUPPER TONIGHT!
YOU'RE RIGHT! IT SLIPPED MY MIND!
WELL, I KNOW YOU'LL DO THE RIGHT THING!
OF COURSE, BETTY! GOSH, I SURE WILL DO THE RIGHT THING!
AFTER ALL, I CAN ALWAYS HAVE SUPPER AT YOUR HOUSE - BUT I WOULD HATE TO DISAPPOINT VERONICA!
1

Story: Sy Reit Pencils: Samm Schwartz

Originally printed in LIFE WITH ARCHIE #1, September 1958

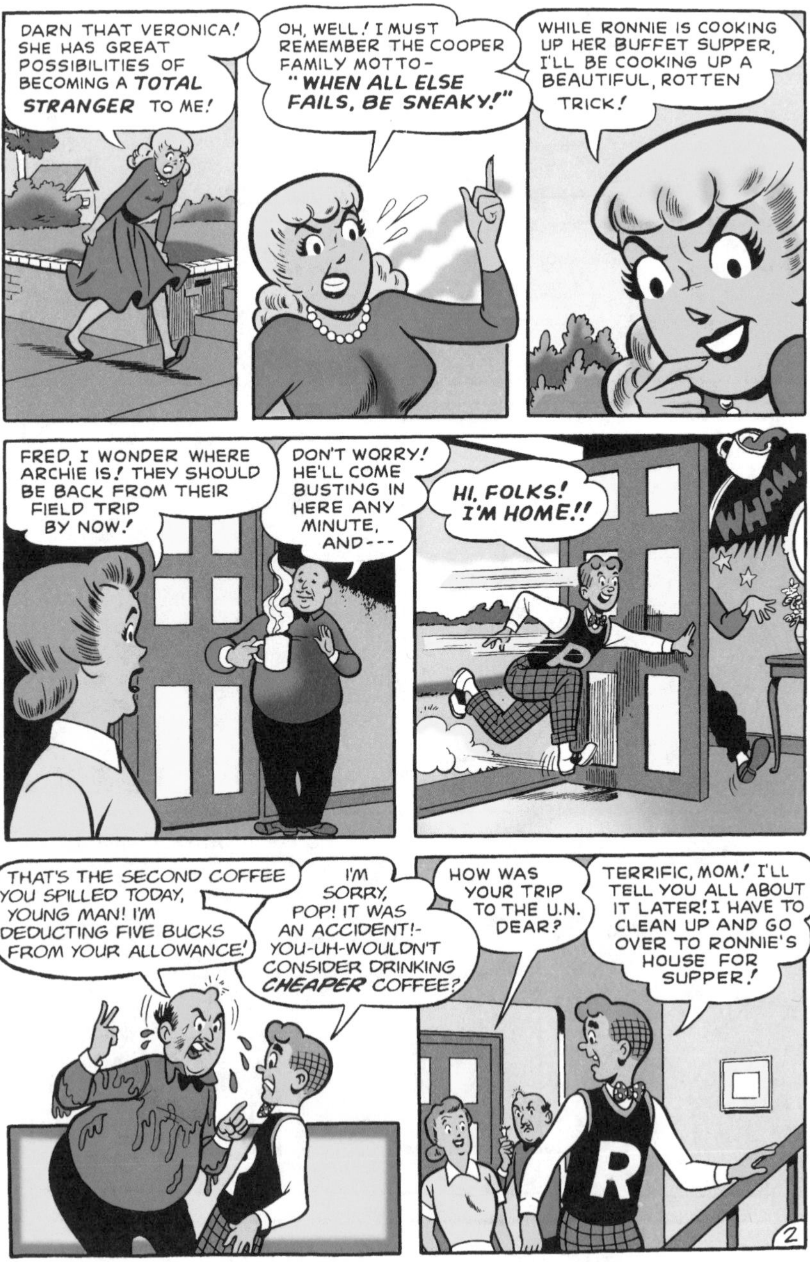
DARN THAT VERONICA! SHE HAS GREAT POSSIBILITIES OF BECOMING A TOTAL STRANGER TO ME!
OH, WELL! I MUST REMEMBER THE COOPER FAMILY MOTTO- "WHEN ALL ELSE FAILS, BE SNEAKY!"
WHILE RONNIE IS COOKING UP HER BUFFET SUPPER, I'LL BE COOKING UP A BEAUTIFUL, ROTTEN TRICK!
FRED, I WONDER WHERE ARCHIE IS! THEY SHOULD BE BACK FROM THEIR FIELD TRIP BY NOW!
DON'T WORRY! HE'LL COME BUSTING IN HERE ANY MINUTE, AND---
HI, FOLKS! I'M HOME!!
WHAM!
THAT'S THE SECOND COFFEE YOU SPILLED TODAY, YOUNG MAN! I'M DEDUCTING FIVE BUCKS FROM YOUR ALLOWANCE!
I'M SORRY, POP! IT WAS AN ACCIDENT!- YOU-UH-WOULDN'T CONSIDER DRINKING CHEAPER COFFEE?
HOW WAS YOUR TRIP TO THE U.N. DEAR?
TERRIFIC, MOM! I'LL TELL YOU ALL ABOUT IT LATER! I HAVE TO CLEAN UP AND GO OVER TO RONNIE'S HOUSE FOR SUPPER!
R
2

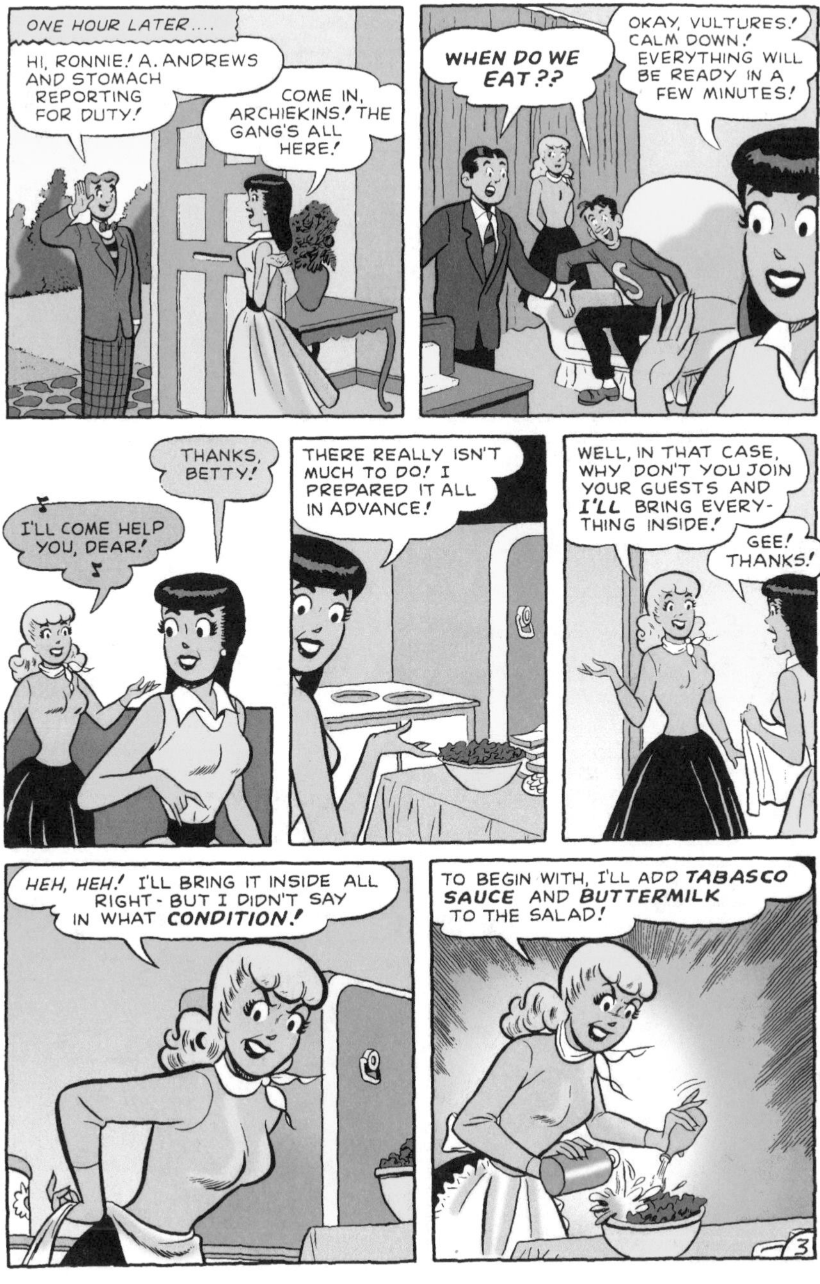
ONE HOUR LATER....
HI, RONNIE! A. ANDREWS AND STOMACH REPORTING FOR DUTY!
COME IN, ARCHIEKINS! THE GANG'S ALL HERE!
WHEN DO WE EAT??
OKAY, VULTURES! CALM DOWN! EVERYTHING WILL BE READY IN A FEW MINUTES!
I'LL COME HELP YOU, DEAR!
THANKS, BETTY!
THERE REALLY ISN'T MUCH TO DO! I PREPARED IT ALL IN ADVANCE!
WELL, IN THAT CASE, WHY DON'T YOU JOIN YOUR GUESTS AND I'LL BRING EVERY-THING INSIDE!
GEE! THANKS!
HEH, HEH! I'LL BRING IT INSIDE ALL RIGHT - BUT I DIDN'T SAY IN WHAT CONDITION!
TO BEGIN WITH, I'LL ADD TABASCO SAUCE AND BUTTERMILK TO THE SALAD!
3

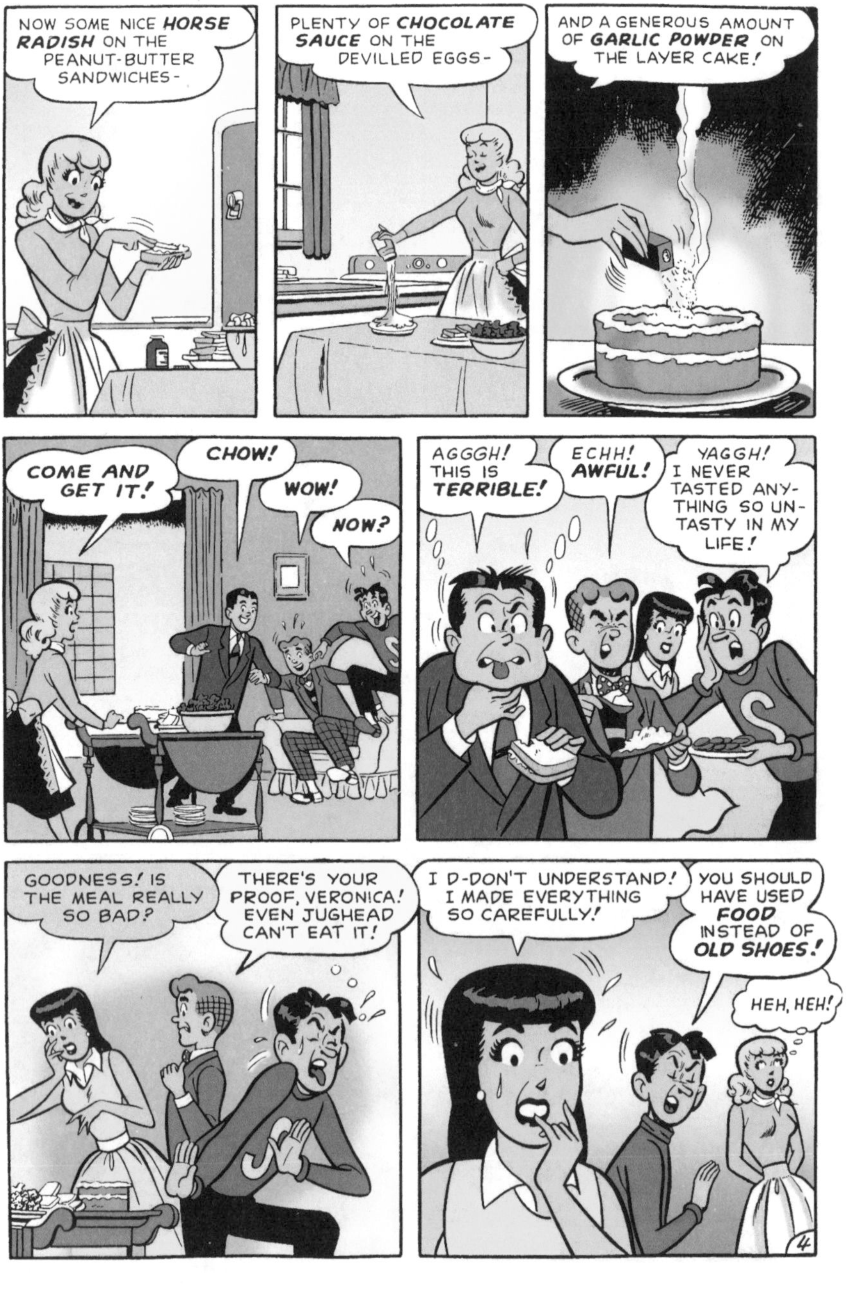
NOW SOME NICE HORSE RADISH ON THE PEANUT-BUTTER SANDWICHES -
PLENTY OF CHOCOLATE SAUCE ON THE DEVILLED EGGS -
AND A GENEROUS AMOUNT OF GARLIC POWDER ON THE LAYER CAKE!
COME AND GET IT!
CHOW!
WOW!
NOW?
AGGGH! THIS IS TERRIBLE!
ECHH! AWFUL!
YAGGH! I NEVER TASTED ANY-THING SO UN-TASTY IN MY LIFE!
GOODNESS! IS THE MEAL REALLY SO BAD?
THERE'S YOUR PROOF, VERONICA! EVEN JUGHEAD CAN'T EAT IT!
I D-DON'T UNDERSTAND! I MADE EVERYTHING SO CAREFULLY!
YOU SHOULD HAVE USED FOOD INSTEAD OF OLD SHOES!
HEH, HEH!
4

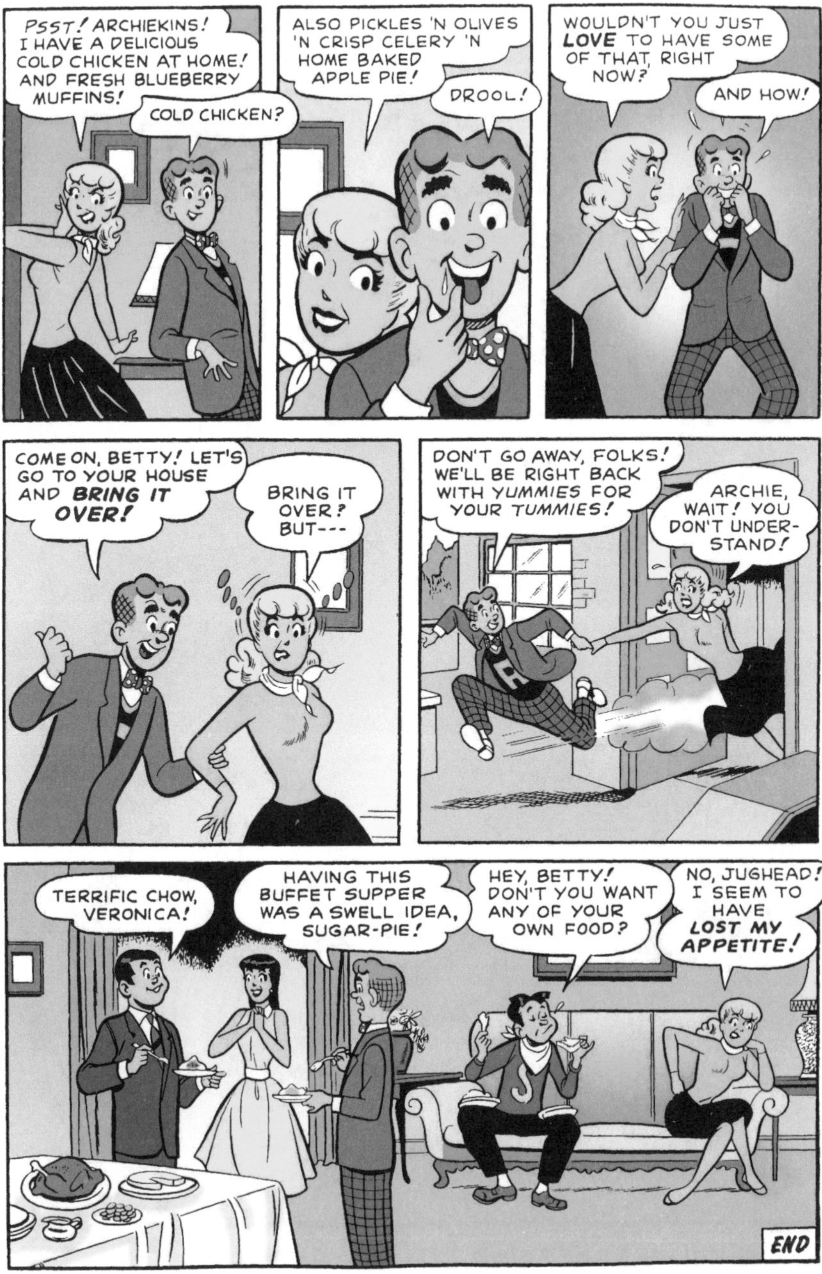
PSST! ARCHIEKINS! I HAVE A DELICIOUS COLD CHICKEN AT HOME! AND FRESH BLUEBERRY MUFFINS!
COLD CHICKEN?
ALSO PICKLES 'N OLIVES 'N CRISP CELERY 'N HOME BAKED APPLE PIE!
DROOL!
WOULDN'T YOU JUST LOVE TO HAVE SOME OF THAT, RIGHT NOW?
AND HOW!
COME ON, BETTY! LET'S GO TO YOUR HOUSE AND BRING IT OVER!
BRING IT OVER? BUT---
DON'T GO AWAY, FOLKS! WE'LL BE RIGHT BACK WITH YUMMIES FOR YOUR TUMMIES!
ARCHIE, WAIT! YOU DON'T UNDER-STAND!
TERRIFIC CHOW, VERONICA!
HAVING THIS BUFFET SUPPER WAS A SWELL IDEA, SUGAR-PIE!
HEY, BETTY! DON'T YOU WANT ANY OF YOUR OWN FOOD?
NO, JUGHEAD! I SEEM TO HAVE LOST MY APPETITE!
END

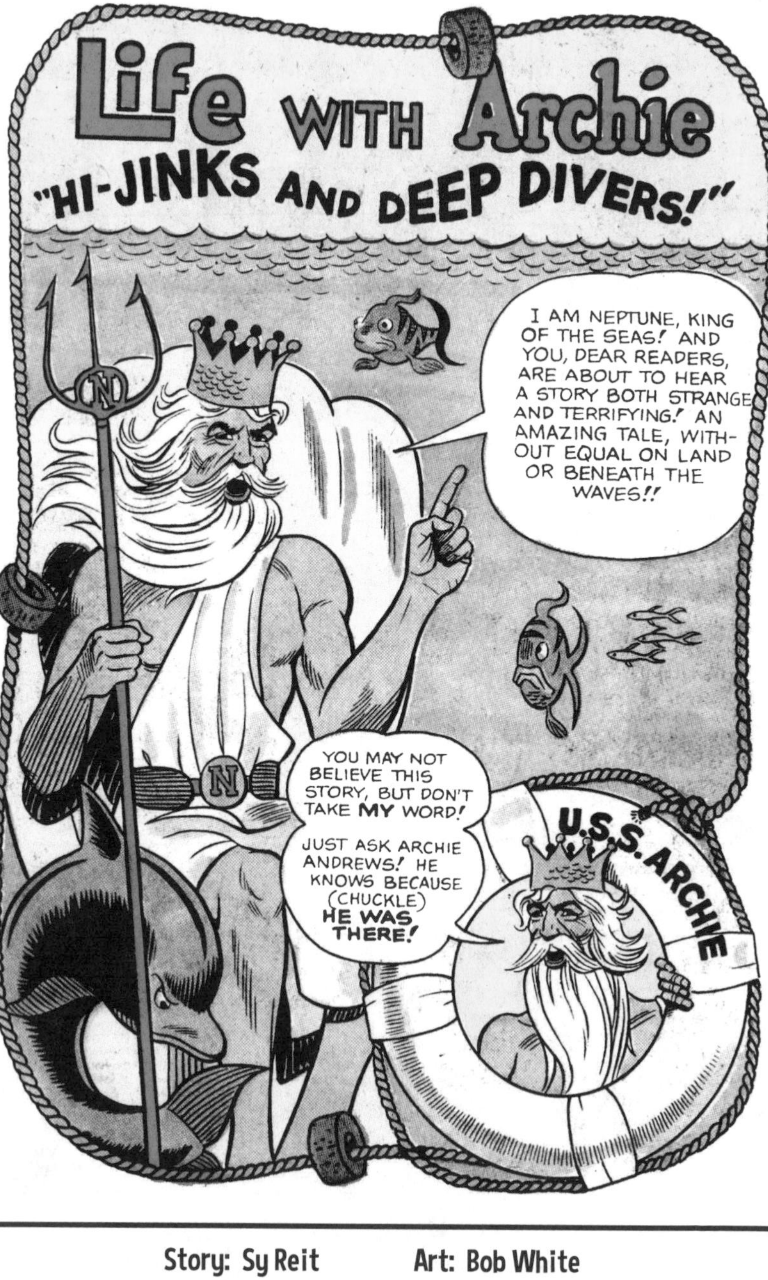
LIFE WITH ARCHIE
"HI-JINKS AND DEEP DIVERS!"
I AM NEPTUNE, KING OF THE SEAS! AND YOU, DEAR READERS, ARE ABOUT TO HEAR A STORY BOTH STRANGE AND TERRIFYING! AN AMAZING TALE, WITHOUT EQUAL ON LAND OR BENEATH THE WAVES!!
YOU MAY NOT BELIEVE THIS STORY, BUT DON'T TAKE MY WORD!
JUST ASK ARCHIE ANDREWS! HE KNOWS BECAUSE (CHUCKLE) HE WAS THERE!
U.S.S. ARCHIE

Story: Sy Reit Art: Bob White

Originally printed in LIFE WITH ARCHIE #16, September 1962

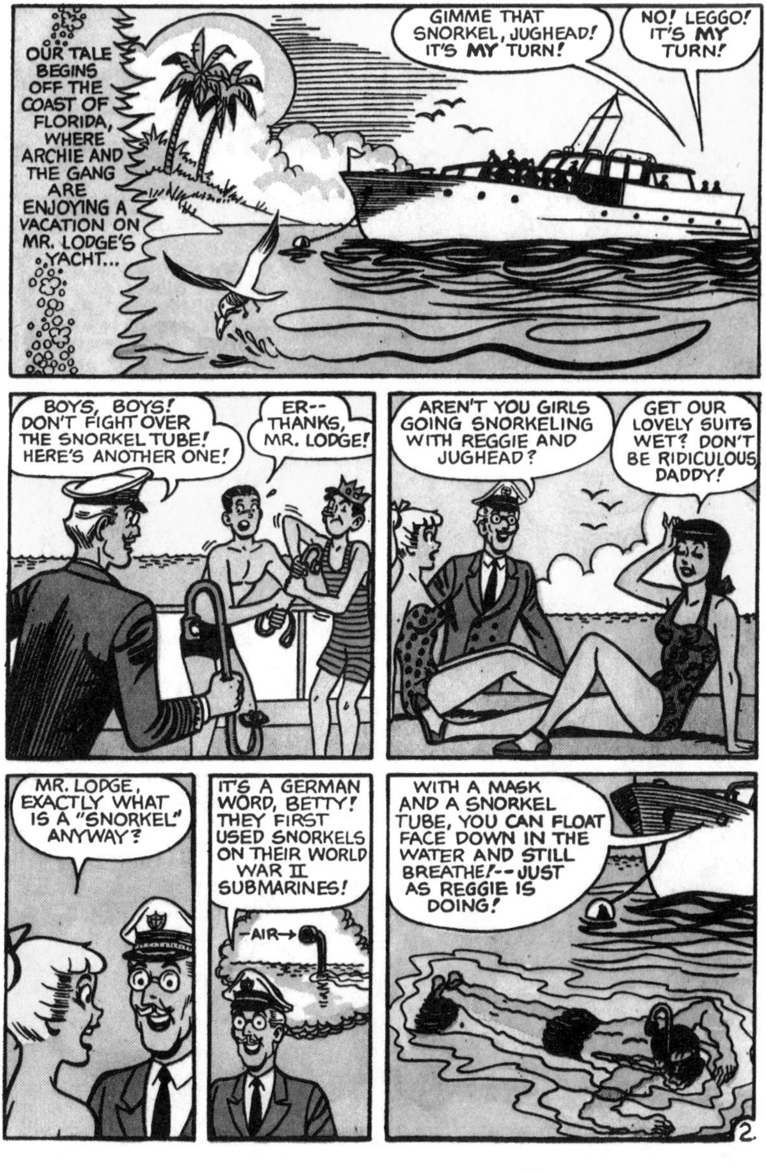
OUR TALE BEGINS OFF THE COAST OF FLORIDA, WHERE ARCHIE AND THE GANG ARE ENJOYING A VACATION ON MR. LODGE'S YACHT...
GIMME THAT SNORKEL, JUGHEAD! IT'S MY TURN!
NO! LEGGO! IT'S MY TURN!
BOYS, BOYS! DON'T FIGHT OVER THE SNORKEL TUBE! HERE'S ANOTHER ONE!
ER-- THANKS, MR. LODGE!
AREN'T YOU GIRLS GOING SNORKELING WITH REGGIE AND JUGHEAD?
GET OUR LOVELY SUITS WET? DON'T BE RIDICULOUS, DADDY!
MR. LODGE, EXACTLY WHAT IS A "SNORKEL" ANYWAY?
IT'S A GERMAN WORD, BETTY! THEY FIRST USED SNORKELS ON THEIR WORLD WAR II SUBMARINES!
-AIR→
WITH A MASK AND A SNORKEL TUBE, YOU CAN FLOAT FACE DOWN IN THE WATER AND STILL BREATHE!-- JUST AS REGGIE IS DOING!
2.

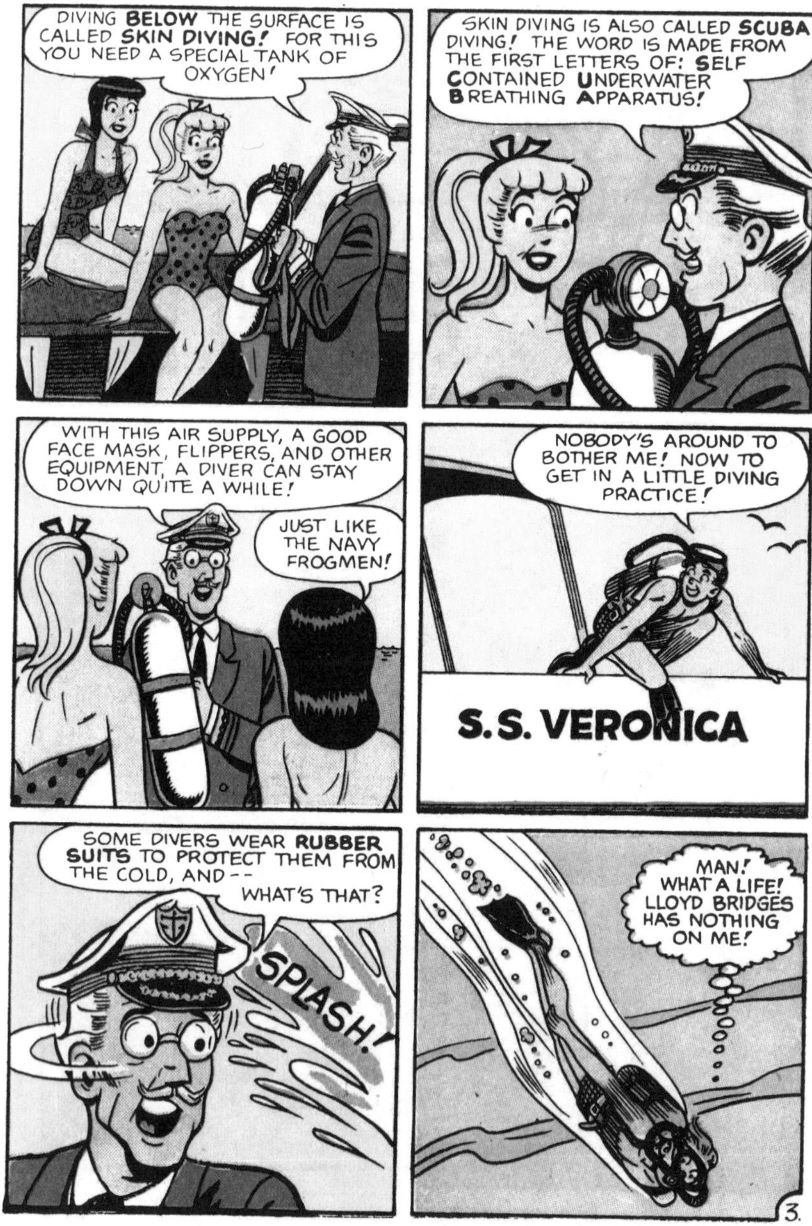
DIVING BELOW THE SURFACE IS CALLED SKIN DIVING! FOR THIS YOU NEED A SPECIAL TANK OF OXYGEN!
SKIN DIVING IS ALSO CALLED SCUBA DIVING! THE WORD IS MADE FROM THE FIRST LETTERS OF: SELF CONTAINED UNDERWATER BREATHING APPARATUS!
WITH THIS AIR SUPPLY, A GOOD FACE MASK, FLIPPERS, AND OTHER EQUIPMENT, A DIVER CAN STAY DOWN QUITE A WHILE!
JUST LIKE THE NAVY FROGMEN!
NOBODY'S AROUND TO BOTHER ME! NOW TO GET IN A LITTLE DIVING PRACTICE!
S.S. VERONICA
SOME DIVERS WEAR RUBBER SUITS TO PROTECT THEM FROM THE COLD, AND--
WHAT'S THAT?
SPLASH!
MAN! WHAT A LIFE! LLOYD BRIDGES HAS NOTHING ON ME!
3.

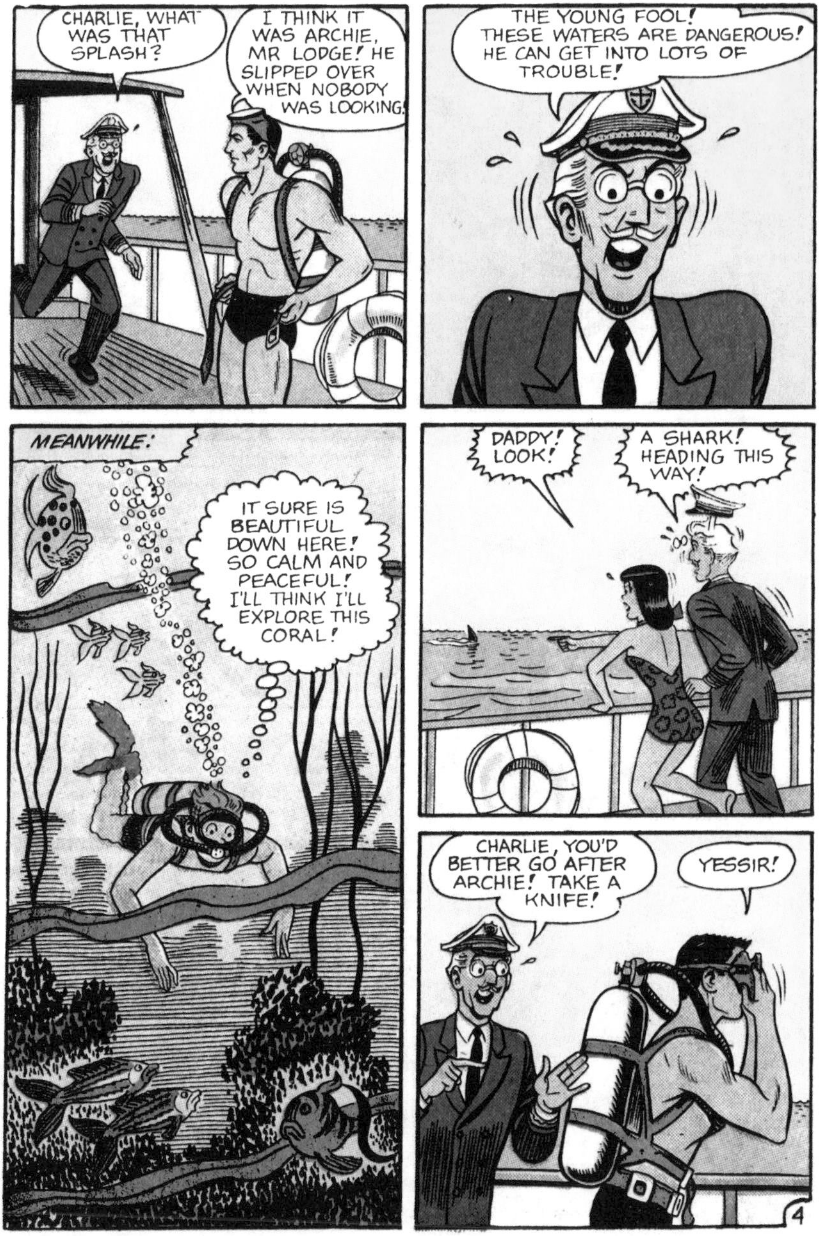
CHARLIE, WHAT WAS THAT SPLASH?
I THINK IT WAS ARCHIE, MR LODGE! HE SLIPPED OVER WHEN NOBODY WAS LOOKING!
THE YOUNG FOOL! THESE WATERS ARE DANGEROUS! HE CAN GET INTO LOTS OF TROUBLE!
MEANWHILE:
IT SURE IS BEAUTIFUL DOWN HERE! SO CALM AND PEACEFUL! I'LL THINK I'LL EXPLORE THIS CORAL!
DADDY! LOOK!
A SHARK! HEADING THIS WAY!
CHARLIE, YOU'D BETTER GO AFTER ARCHIE! TAKE A KNIFE!
YESSIR!
4

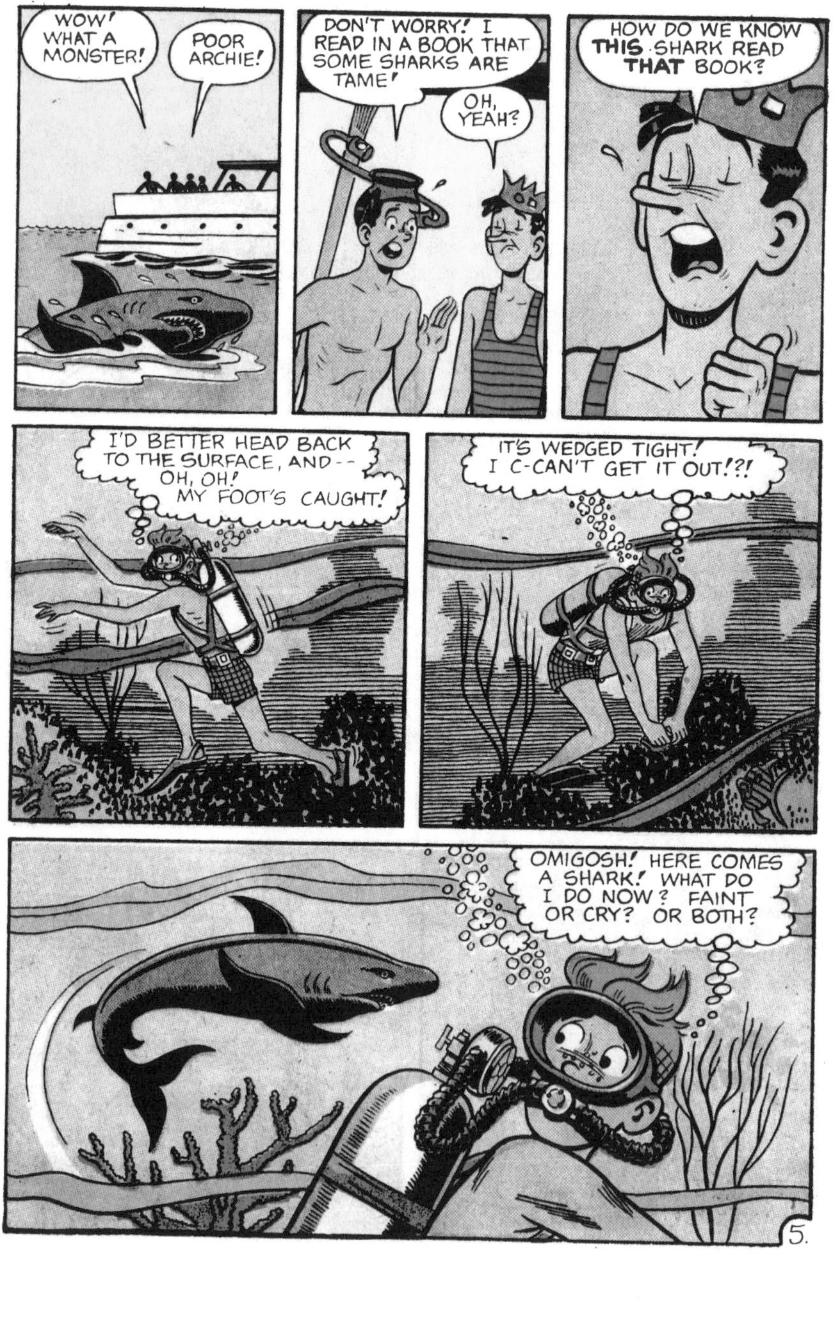
WOW! WHAT A MONSTER!
POOR ARCHIE!
DON'T WORRY! I READ IN A BOOK THAT SOME SHARKS ARE TAME!
OH, YEAH?
HOW DO WE KNOW THIS SHARK READ THAT BOOK?
I'D BETTER HEAD BACK TO THE SURFACE, AND-- OH, OH! MY FOOT'S CAUGHT!
IT'S WEDGED TIGHT! I C-CAN'T GET IT OUT!?!
OMIGOSH! HERE COMES A SHARK! WHAT DO I DO NOW? FAINT OR CRY? OR BOTH?
5.

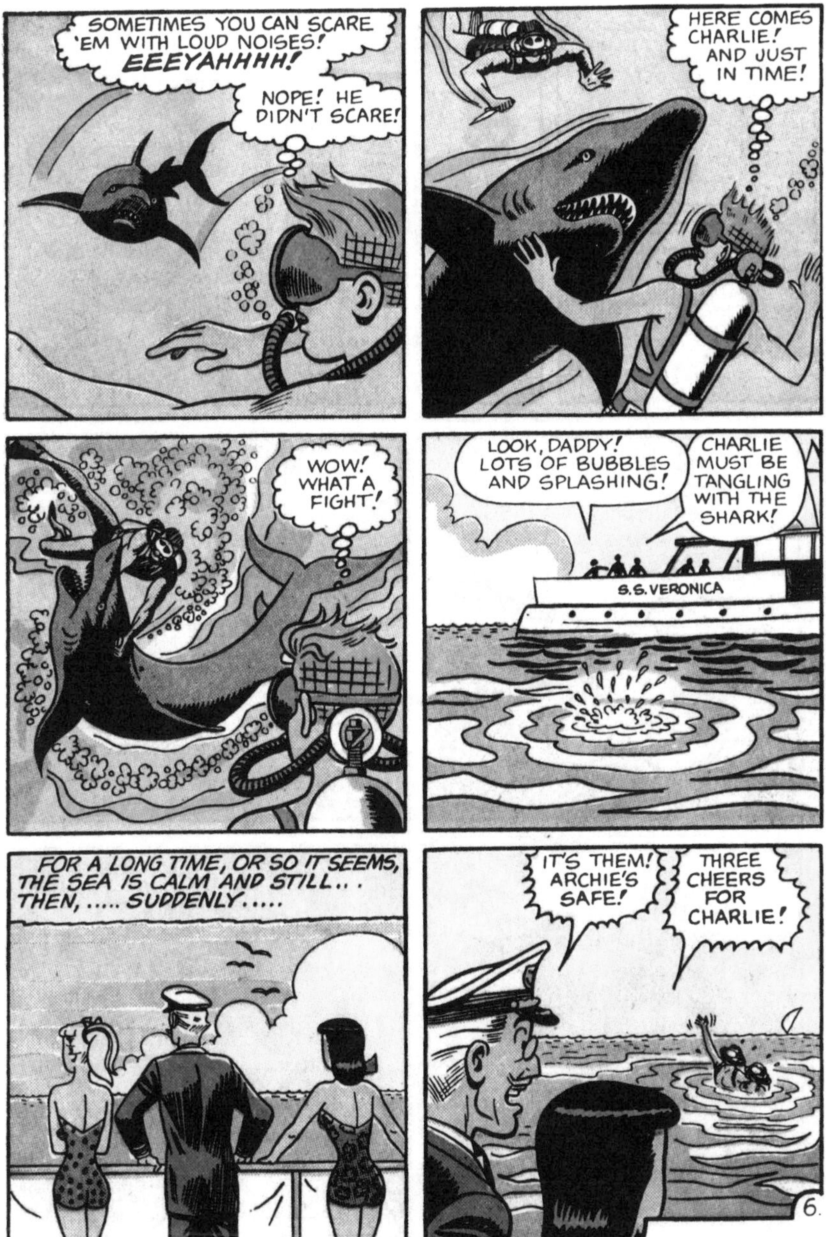
SOMETIMES YOU CAN SCARE 'EM WITH LOUD NOISES! EEEYAHHHH!
NOPE! HE DIDN'T SCARE!
HERE COMES CHARLIE! AND JUST IN TIME!
WOW! WHAT A FIGHT!
LOOK, DADDY! LOTS OF BUBBLES AND SPLASHING!
CHARLIE MUST BE TANGLING WITH THE SHARK!
S.S. VERONICA
FOR A LONG TIME, OR SO IT SEEMS, THE SEA IS CALM AND STILL... THEN, ... SUDDENLY.....
IT'S THEM! ARCHIE'S SAFE!
THREE CHEERS FOR CHARLIE!
6.

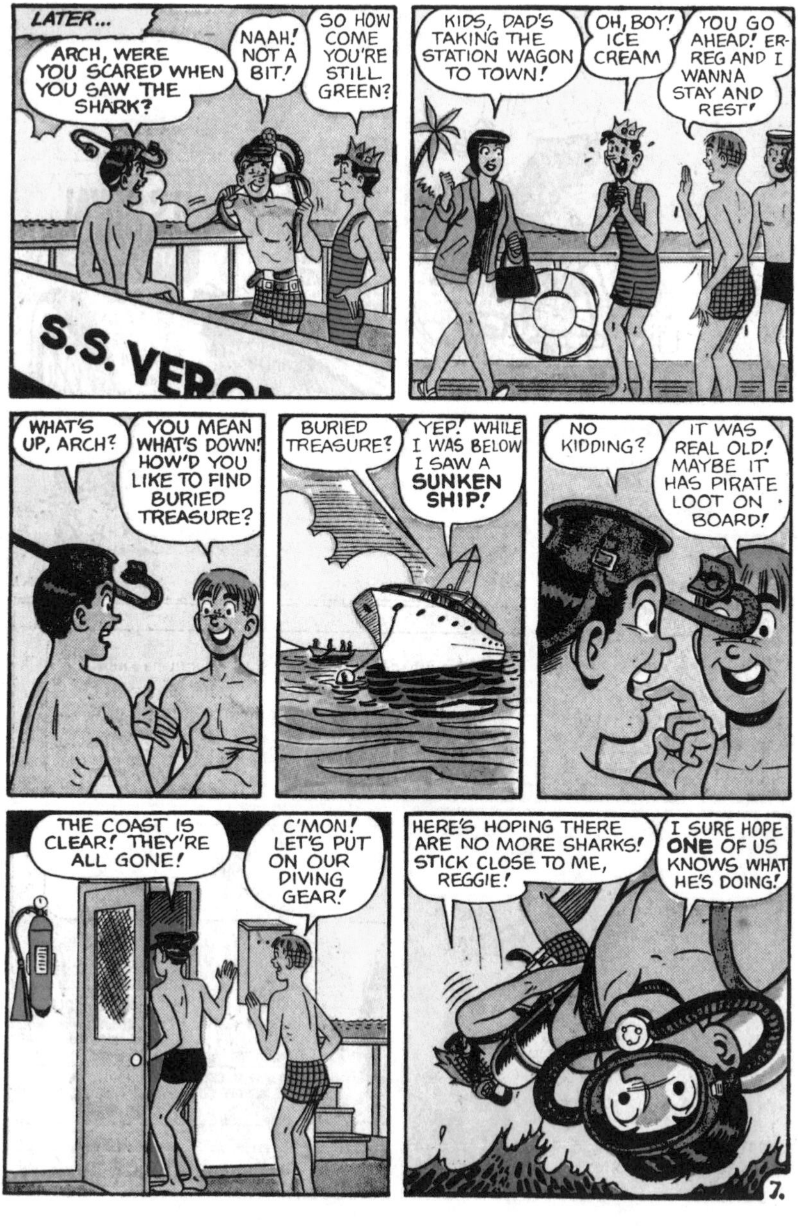
LATER...
ARCH, WERE YOU SCARED WHEN YOU SAW THE SHARK?
NAAH! NOT A BIT!
SO HOW COME YOU'RE STILL GREEN?
S.S. VERO
KIDS, DAD'S TAKING THE STATION WAGON TO TOWN!
OH, BOY! ICE CREAM
YOU GO AHEAD! ER-REG AND I WANNA STAY AND REST!
WHAT'S UP, ARCH?
YOU MEAN WHAT'S DOWN! HOW'D YOU LIKE TO FIND BURIED TREASURE?
BURIED TREASURE?
YEP! WHILE I WAS BELOW I SAW A SUNKEN SHIP!
NO KIDDING?
IT WAS REAL OLD! MAYBE IT HAS PIRATE LOOT ON BOARD!
THE COAST IS CLEAR! THEY'RE ALL GONE!
C'MON! LET'S PUT ON OUR DIVING GEAR!
HERE'S HOPING THERE ARE NO MORE SHARKS! STICK CLOSE TO ME, REGGIE!
I SURE HOPE ONE OF US KNOWS WHAT HE'S DOING!
7.

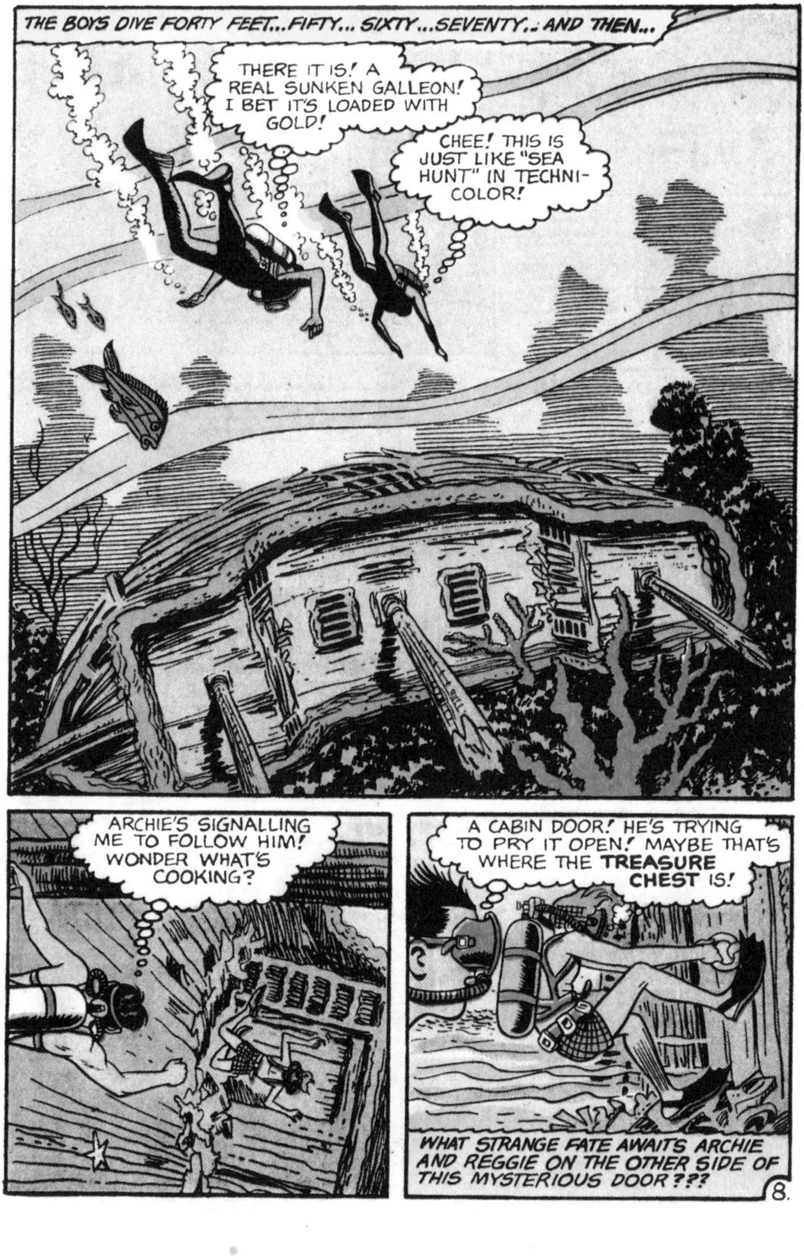
THE BOYS DIVE FORTY FEET...FIFTY... SIXTY...SEVENTY...AND THEN...
THERE IT IS! A REAL SUNKEN GALLEON! I BET IT'S LOADED WITH GOLD!
CHEE! THIS IS JUST LIKE "SEA HUNT" IN TECHNI-COLOR!
ARCHIE'S SIGNALLING ME TO FOLLOW HIM! WONDER WHAT'S COOKING?
A CABIN DOOR! HE'S TRYING TO PRY IT OPEN! MAYBE THAT'S WHERE THE TREASURE CHEST IS!
WHAT STRANGE FATE AWAITS ARCHIE AND REGGIE ON THE OTHER SIDE OF THIS MYSTERIOUS DOOR???
8.

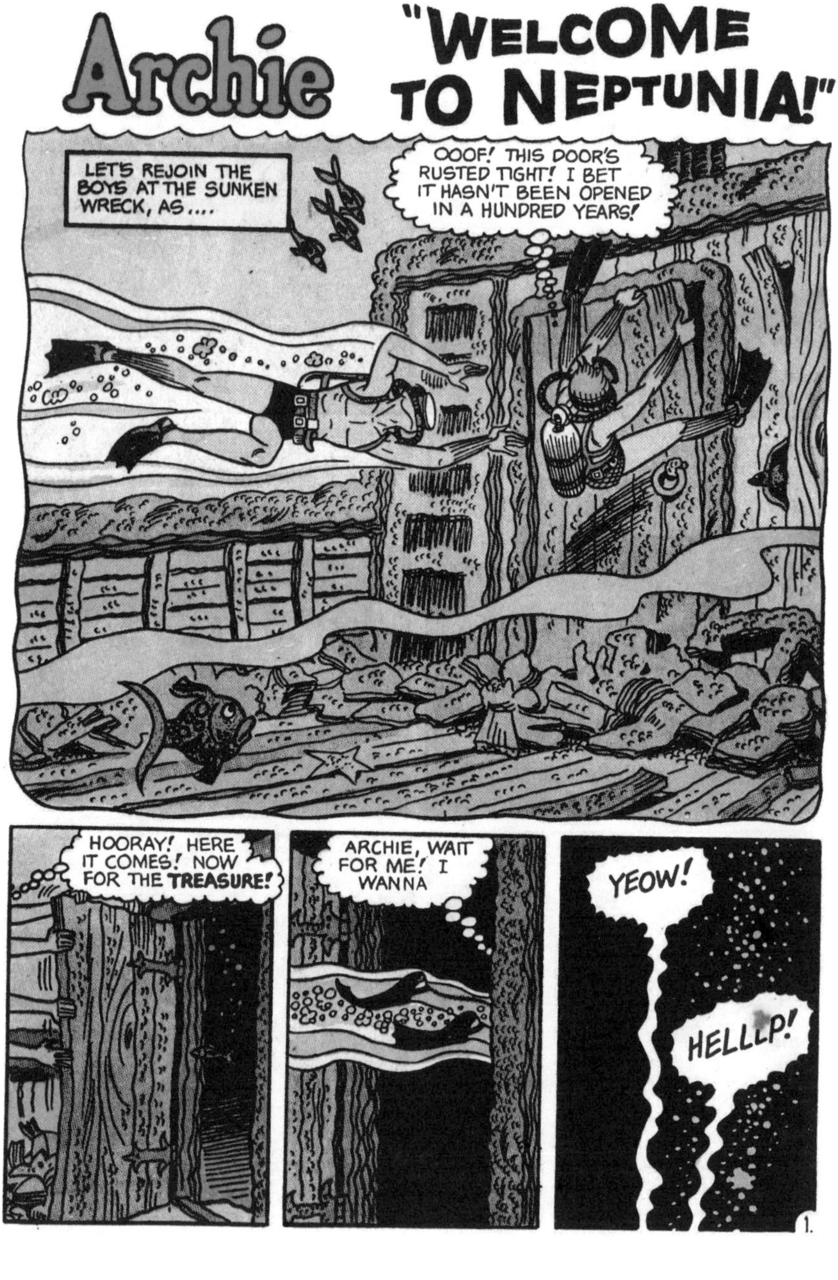
Archie
"WELCOME TO NEPTUNIA!"
LET'S REJOIN THE BOYS AT THE SUNKEN WRECK, AS....
OOOF! THIS DOOR'S RUSTED TIGHT! I BET IT HASN'T BEEN OPENED IN A HUNDRED YEARS!
HOORAY! HERE IT COMES! NOW FOR THE TREASURE!
ARCHIE, WAIT FOR ME! I WANNA
YEOW!
HELLLP!
1.

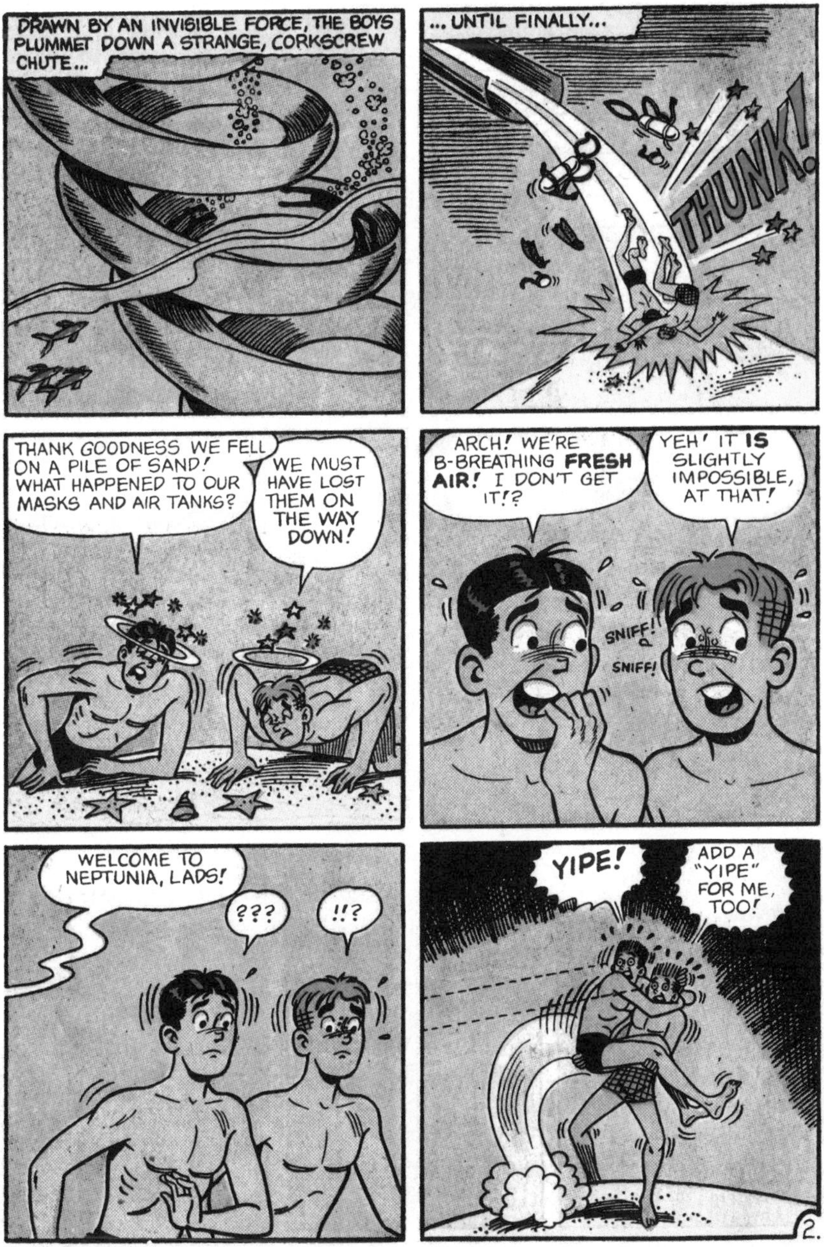
DRAWN BY AN INVISIBLE FORCE, THE BOYS PLUMMET DOWN A STRANGE, CORKSCREW CHUTE...
... UNTIL FINALLY...
THUNK!
THANK GOODNESS WE FELL ON A PILE OF SAND! WHAT HAPPENED TO OUR MASKS AND AIR TANKS?
WE MUST HAVE LOST THEM ON THE WAY DOWN!
ARCH! WE'RE B-BREATHING FRESH AIR! I DON'T GET IT!?
SNIFF!
SNIFF!
YEH! IT IS SLIGHTLY IMPOSSIBLE, AT THAT!
WELCOME TO NEPTUNIA, LADS!
???
!!?
YIPE!
ADD A "YIPE" FOR ME, TOO!
2.

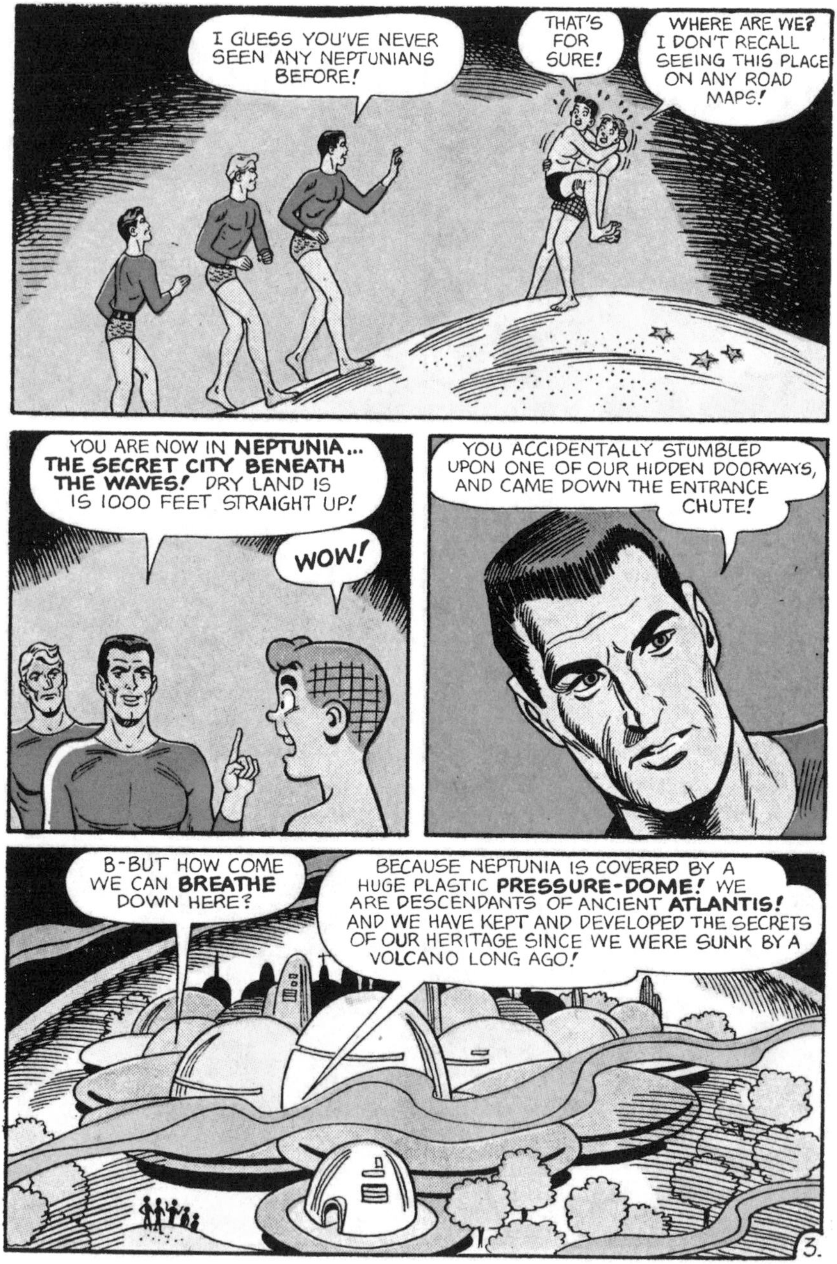
I GUESS YOU'VE NEVER SEEN ANY NEPTUNIANS BEFORE!
THAT'S FOR SURE!
WHERE ARE WE? I DON'T RECALL SEEING THIS PLACE ON ANY ROAD MAPS!
YOU ARE NOW IN **NEPTUNIA... THE SECRET CITY BENEATH THE WAVES!** DRY LAND IS IS 1000 FEET STRAIGHT UP!
WOW!
YOU ACCIDENTALLY STUMBLED UPON ONE OF OUR HIDDEN DOORWAYS, AND CAME DOWN THE ENTRANCE CHUTE!
B-BUT HOW COME WE CAN **BREATHE** DOWN HERE?
BECAUSE NEPTUNIA IS COVERED BY A HUGE PLASTIC **PRESSURE-DOME!** WE ARE DESCENDANTS OF ANCIENT **ATLANTIS!** AND WE HAVE KEPT AND DEVELOPED THE SECRETS OF OUR HERITAGE SINCE WE WERE SUNK BY A VOLCANO LONG AGO!
3.

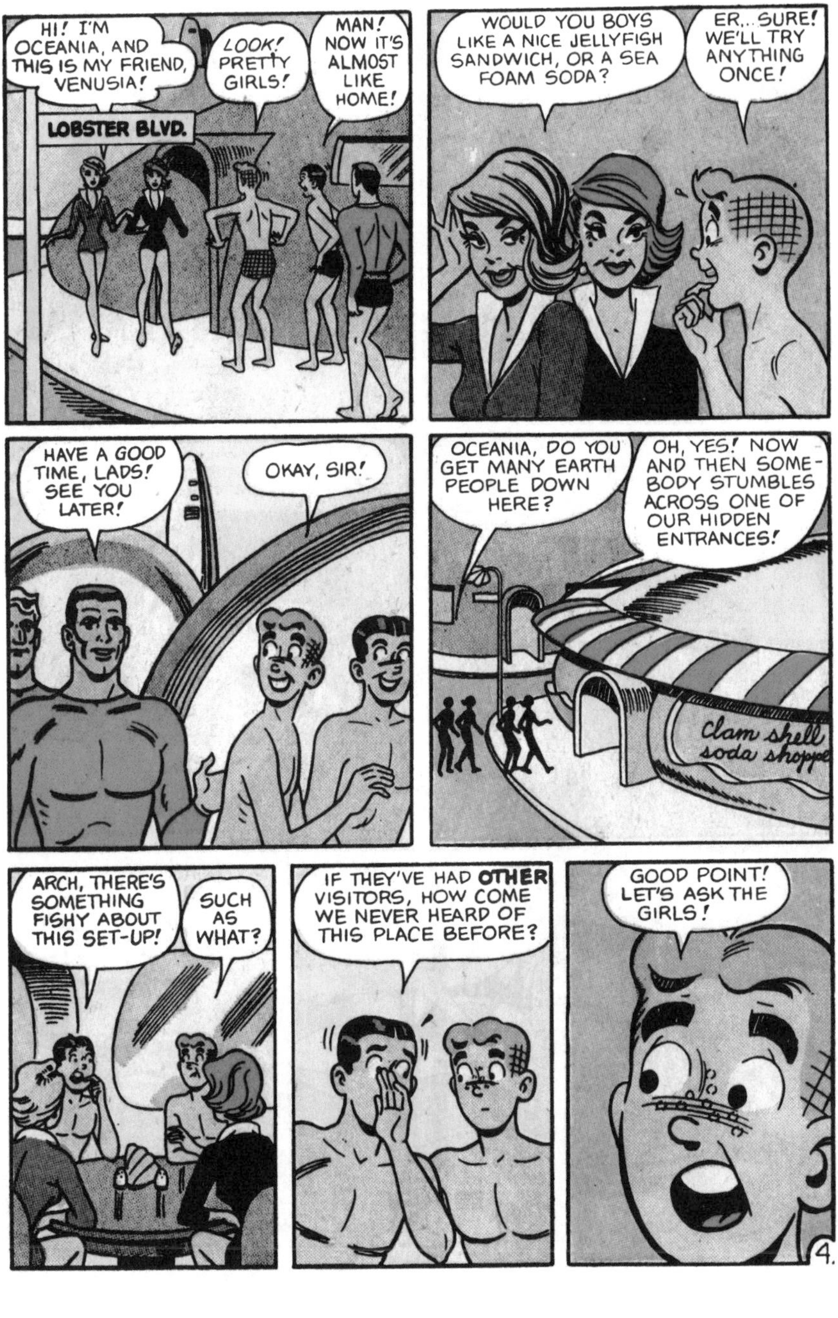
HI! I'M OCEANIA, AND THIS IS MY FRIEND, VENUSIA!
LOBSTER BLVD.
LOOK! PRETTY GIRLS!
MAN! NOW IT'S ALMOST LIKE HOME!
WOULD YOU BOYS LIKE A NICE JELLYFISH SANDWICH, OR A SEA FOAM SODA?
ER... SURE! WE'LL TRY ANYTHING ONCE!
HAVE A GOOD TIME, LADS! SEE YOU LATER!
OKAY, SIR!
OCEANIA, DO YOU GET MANY EARTH PEOPLE DOWN HERE?
OH, YES! NOW AND THEN SOMEBODY STUMBLES ACROSS ONE OF OUR HIDDEN ENTRANCES!
Clam shell soda shoppe
ARCH, THERE'S SOMETHING FISHY ABOUT THIS SET-UP!
SUCH AS WHAT?
IF THEY'VE HAD OTHER VISITORS, HOW COME WE NEVER HEARD OF THIS PLACE BEFORE?
GOOD POINT! LET'S ASK THE GIRLS!
4.

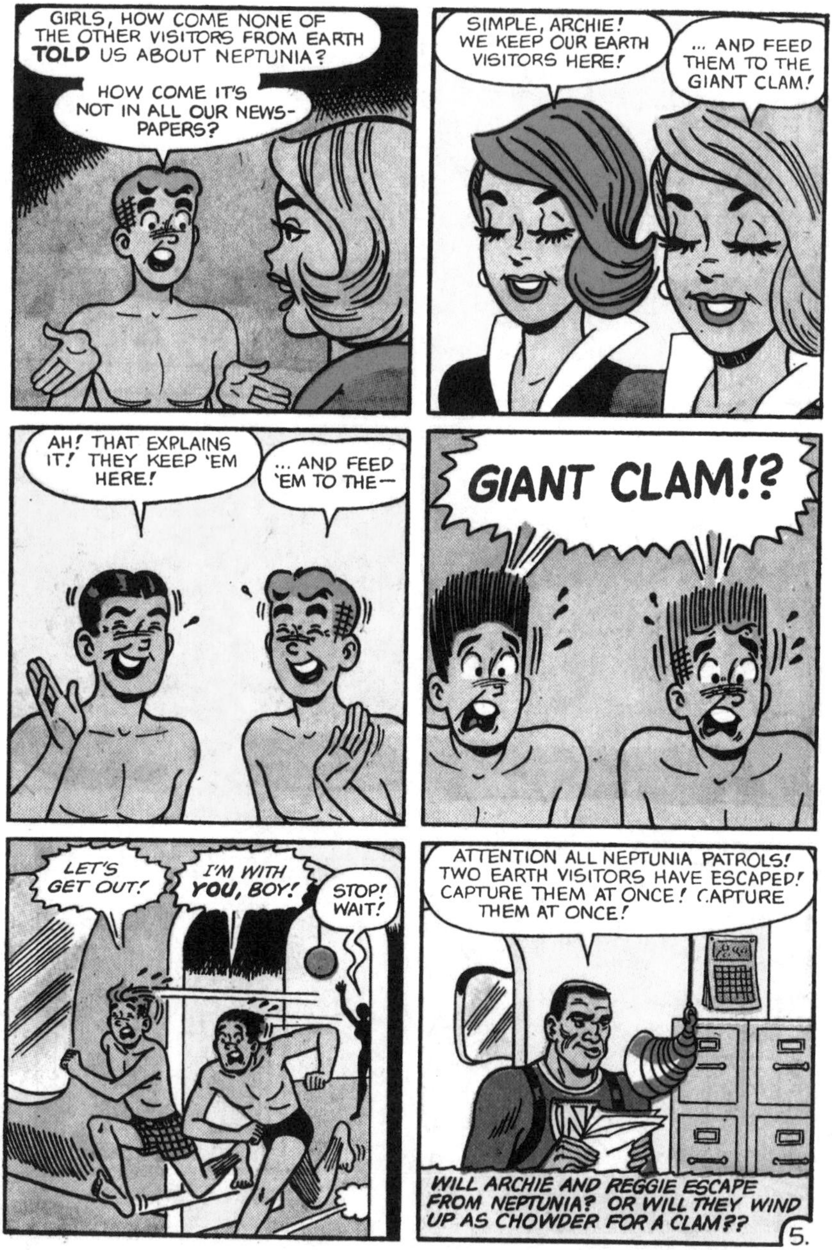
GIRLS, HOW COME NONE OF THE OTHER VISITORS FROM EARTH TOLD US ABOUT NEPTUNIA?
HOW COME IT'S NOT IN ALL OUR NEWS-PAPERS?
SIMPLE, ARCHIE! WE KEEP OUR EARTH VISITORS HERE!
... AND FEED THEM TO THE GIANT CLAM!
AH! THAT EXPLAINS IT! THEY KEEP 'EM HERE!
... AND FEED 'EM TO THE—
GIANT CLAM!?
LET'S GET OUT!
I'M WITH YOU, BOY!
STOP! WAIT!
ATTENTION ALL NEPTUNIA PATROLS! TWO EARTH VISITORS HAVE ESCAPED! CAPTURE THEM AT ONCE! CAPTURE THEM AT ONCE!
WILL ARCHIE AND REGGIE ESCAPE FROM NEPTUNIA? OR WILL THEY WIND UP AS CHOWDER FOR A CLAM??
5.

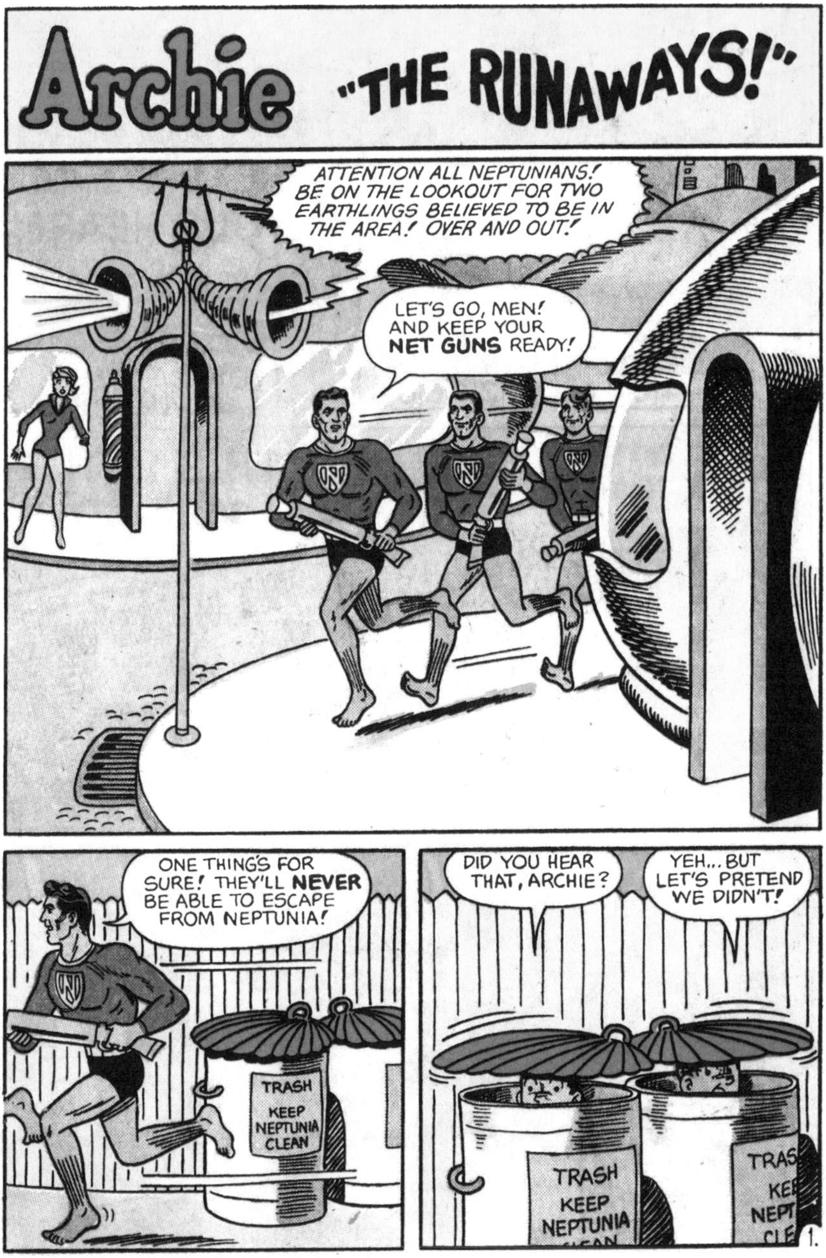
Archie
"THE RUNAWAYS!"
ATTENTION ALL NEPTUNIANS! BE ON THE LOOKOUT FOR TWO EARTHLINGS BELIEVED TO BE IN THE AREA! OVER AND OUT!
LET'S GO, MEN! AND KEEP YOUR NET GUNS READY!
ONE THING'S FOR SURE! THEY'LL NEVER BE ABLE TO ESCAPE FROM NEPTUNIA!
TRASH
KEEP NEPTUNIA CLEAN
DID YOU HEAR THAT, ARCHIE?
YEH... BUT LET'S PRETEND WE DIDN'T!
TRASH
KEEP NEPTUNIA
1.

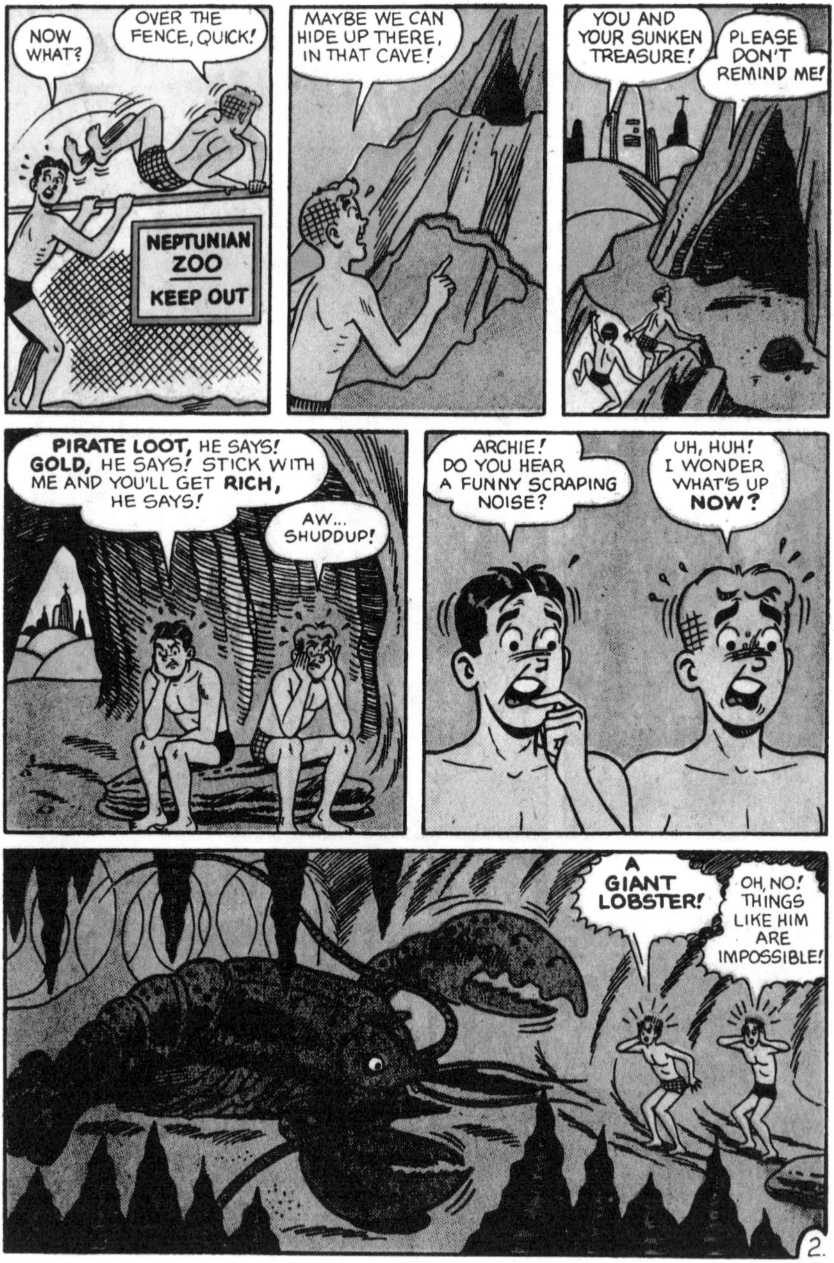
NOW WHAT?
OVER THE FENCE, QUICK!
NEPTUNIAN ZOO KEEP OUT
MAYBE WE CAN HIDE UP THERE, IN THAT CAVE!
YOU AND YOUR SUNKEN TREASURE!
PLEASE DON'T REMIND ME!
PIRATE LOOT, HE SAYS! GOLD, HE SAYS! STICK WITH ME AND YOU'LL GET RICH, HE SAYS!
AW... SHUDDUP!
ARCHIE! DO YOU HEAR A FUNNY SCRAPING NOISE?
UH, HUH! I WONDER WHAT'S UP NOW?
A GIANT LOBSTER!
OH, NO! THINGS LIKE HIM ARE IMPOSSIBLE!
2.

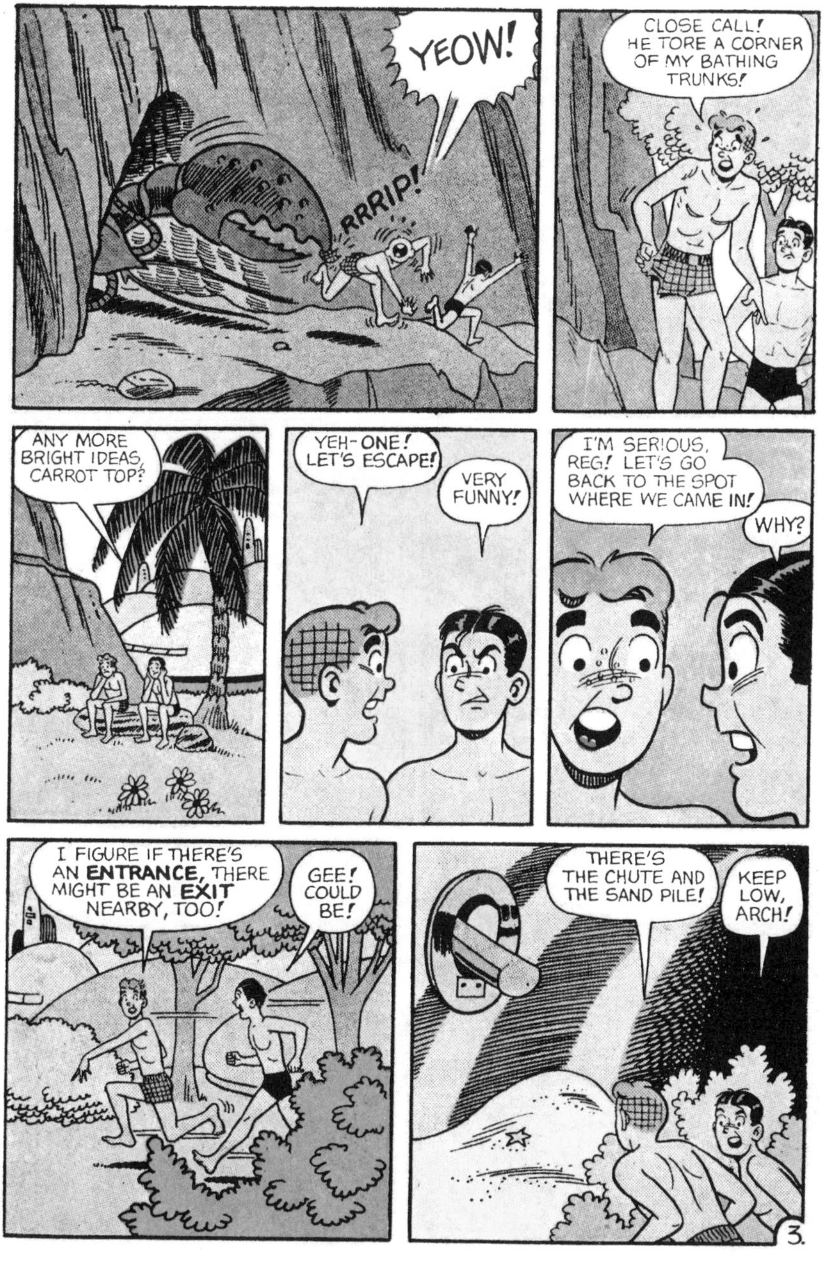
YEOW!
RRRIP!
CLOSE CALL! HE TORE A CORNER OF MY BATHING TRUNKS!
ANY MORE BRIGHT IDEAS, CARROT TOP?
YEH-ONE! LET'S ESCAPE!
VERY FUNNY!
I'M SERIOUS, REG! LET'S GO BACK TO THE SPOT WHERE WE CAME IN!
WHY?
I FIGURE IF THERE'S AN ENTRANCE, THERE MIGHT BE AN EXIT NEARBY, TOO!
GEE! COULD BE!
THERE'S THE CHUTE AND THE SAND PILE!
KEEP LOW, ARCH!
3.

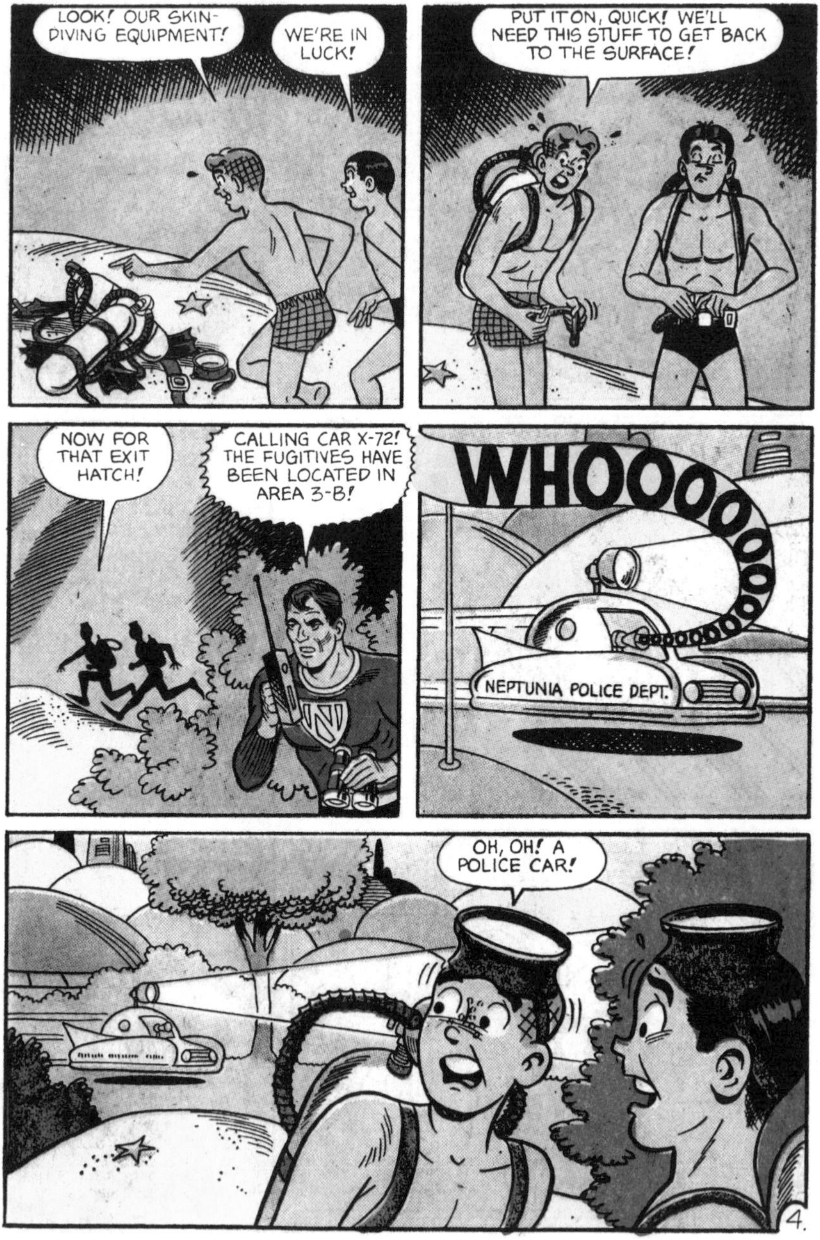
LOOK! OUR SKIN-DIVING EQUIPMENT!
WE'RE IN LUCK!
PUT IT ON, QUICK! WE'LL NEED THIS STUFF TO GET BACK TO THE SURFACE!
NOW FOR THAT EXIT HATCH!
CALLING CAR X-72! THE FUGITIVES HAVE BEEN LOCATED IN AREA 3-B!
WHOOOOOOOOOOOOOO
NEPTUNIA POLICE DEPT.
OH, OH! A POLICE CAR!
4.

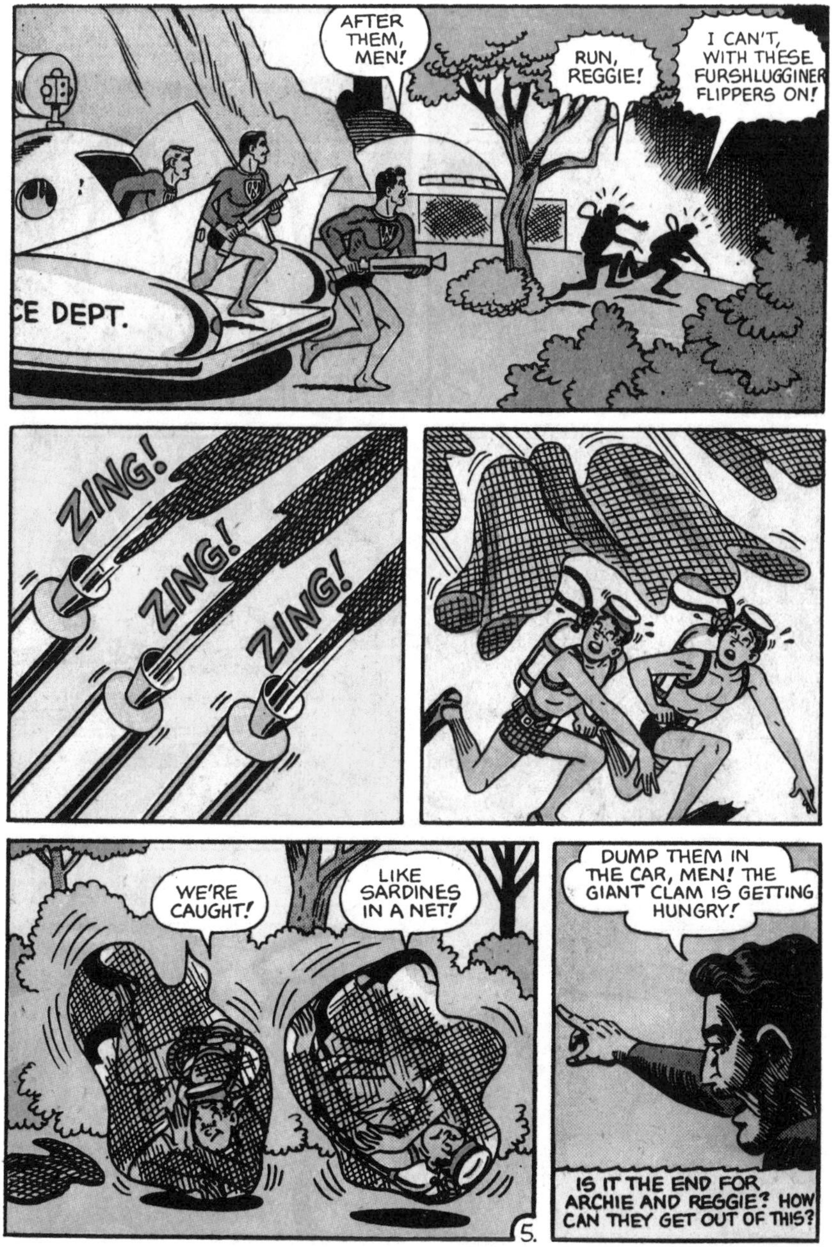
AFTER THEM, MEN!
RUN, REGGIE!
I CAN'T, WITH THESE FURSHLUGGINER FLIPPERS ON!
CE DEPT.
ZING!
ZING!
ZING!
WE'RE CAUGHT!
LIKE SARDINES IN A NET!
DUMP THEM IN THE CAR, MEN! THE GIANT CLAM IS GETTING HUNGRY!
IS IT THE END FOR ARCHIE AND REGGIE? HOW CAN THEY GET OUT OF THIS?
5.

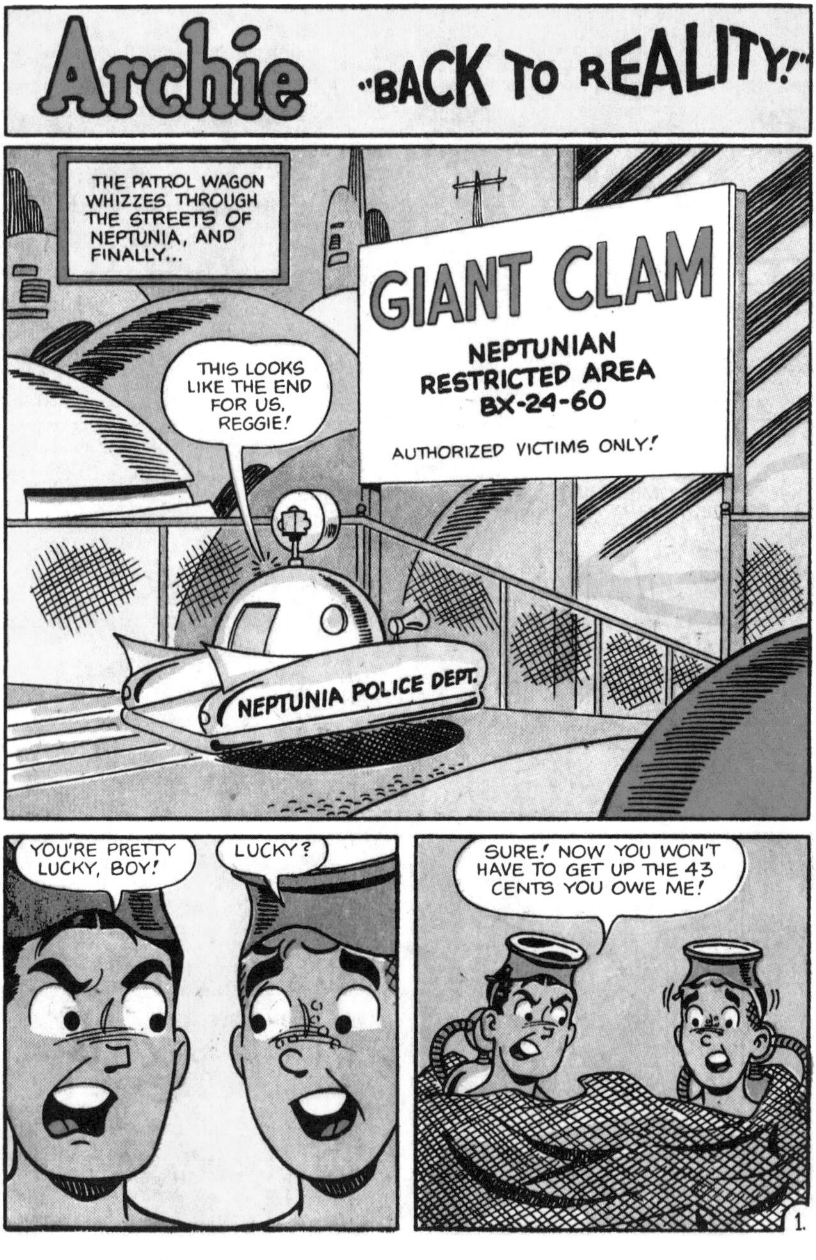
Archie
"BACK TO REALITY!"
THE PATROL WAGON WHIZZES THROUGH THE STREETS OF NEPTUNIA, AND FINALLY...
GIANT CLAM
NEPTUNIAN RESTRICTED AREA BX-24-60
AUTHORIZED VICTIMS ONLY!
THIS LOOKS LIKE THE END FOR US, REGGIE!
NEPTUNIA POLICE DEPT.
YOU'RE PRETTY LUCKY, BOY!
LUCKY?
SURE! NOW YOU WON'T HAVE TO GET UP THE 43 CENTS YOU OWE ME!
1.

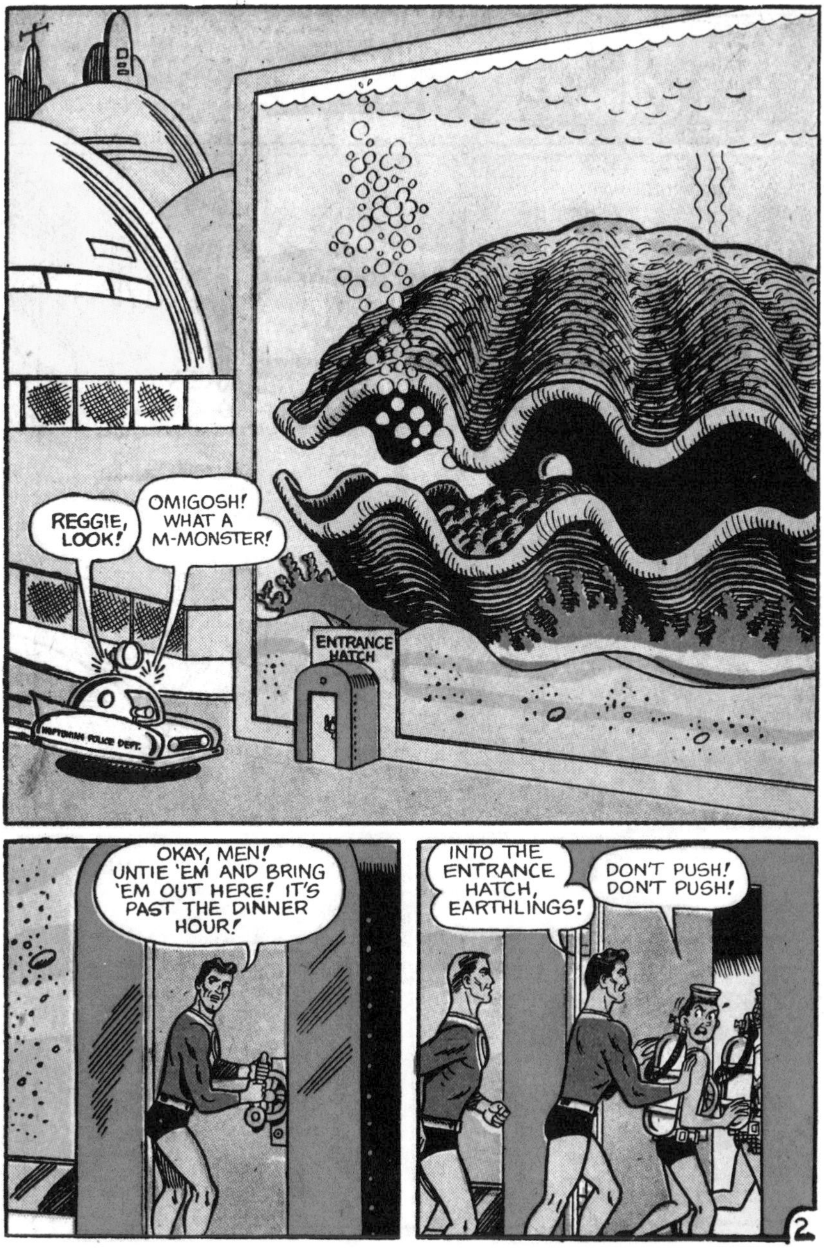
REGGIE, LOOK!
OMIGOSH! WHAT A M-MONSTER!
ENTRANCE HATCH
OKAY, MEN! UNTIE 'EM AND BRING 'EM OUT HERE! IT'S PAST THE DINNER HOUR!
INTO THE ENTRANCE HATCH, EARTHLINGS!
DON'T PUSH! DON'T PUSH!
2

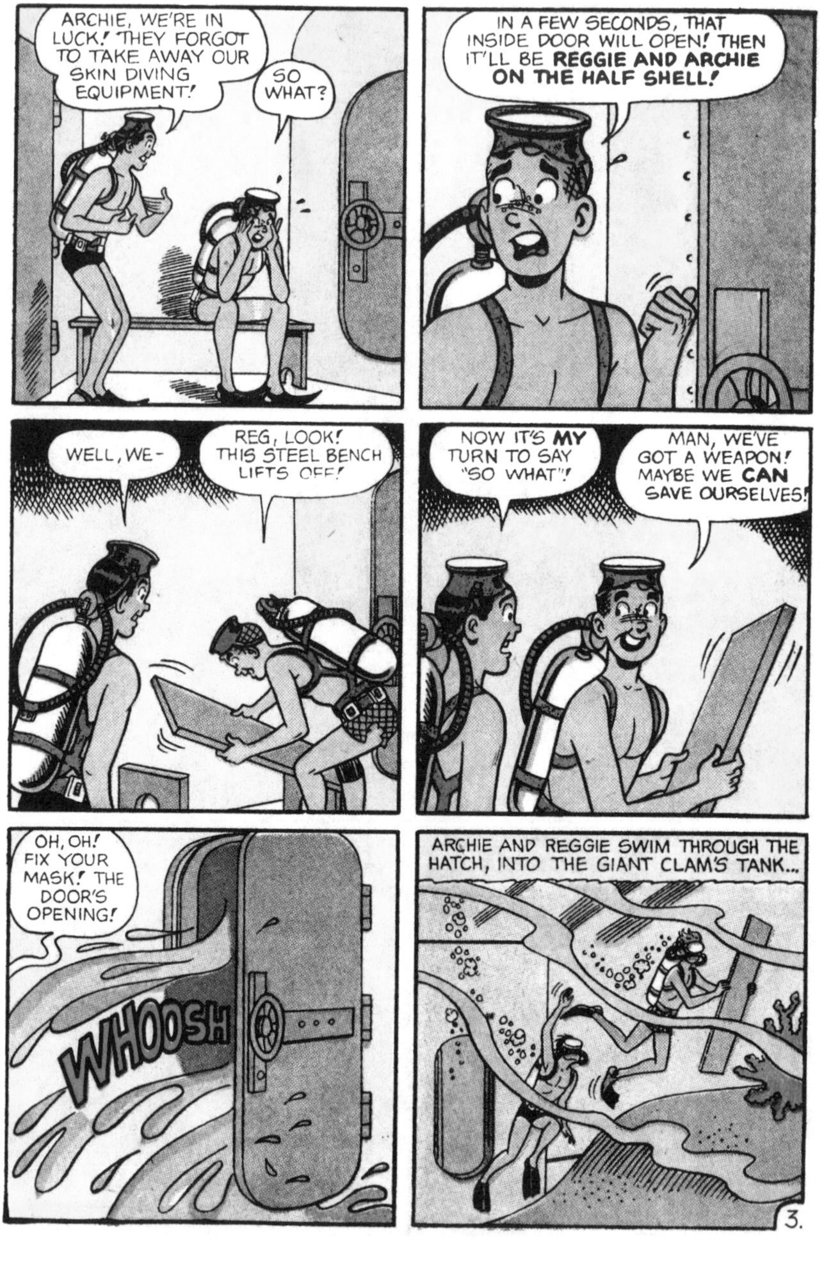
ARCHIE, WE'RE IN LUCK! THEY FORGOT TO TAKE AWAY OUR SKIN DIVING EQUIPMENT!
SO WHAT?
IN A FEW SECONDS, THAT INSIDE DOOR WILL OPEN! THEN IT'LL BE **REGGIE AND ARCHIE ON THE HALF SHELL!**
WELL, WE-
REG, LOOK! THIS STEEL BENCH LIFTS OFF!
NOW IT'S **MY** TURN TO SAY "SO WHAT"!
MAN, WE'VE GOT A WEAPON! MAYBE WE **CAN** SAVE OURSELVES!
OH, OH! FIX YOUR MASK! THE DOOR'S OPENING!
WHOOSH
ARCHIE AND REGGIE SWIM THROUGH THE HATCH, INTO THE GIANT CLAM'S TANK...
3.

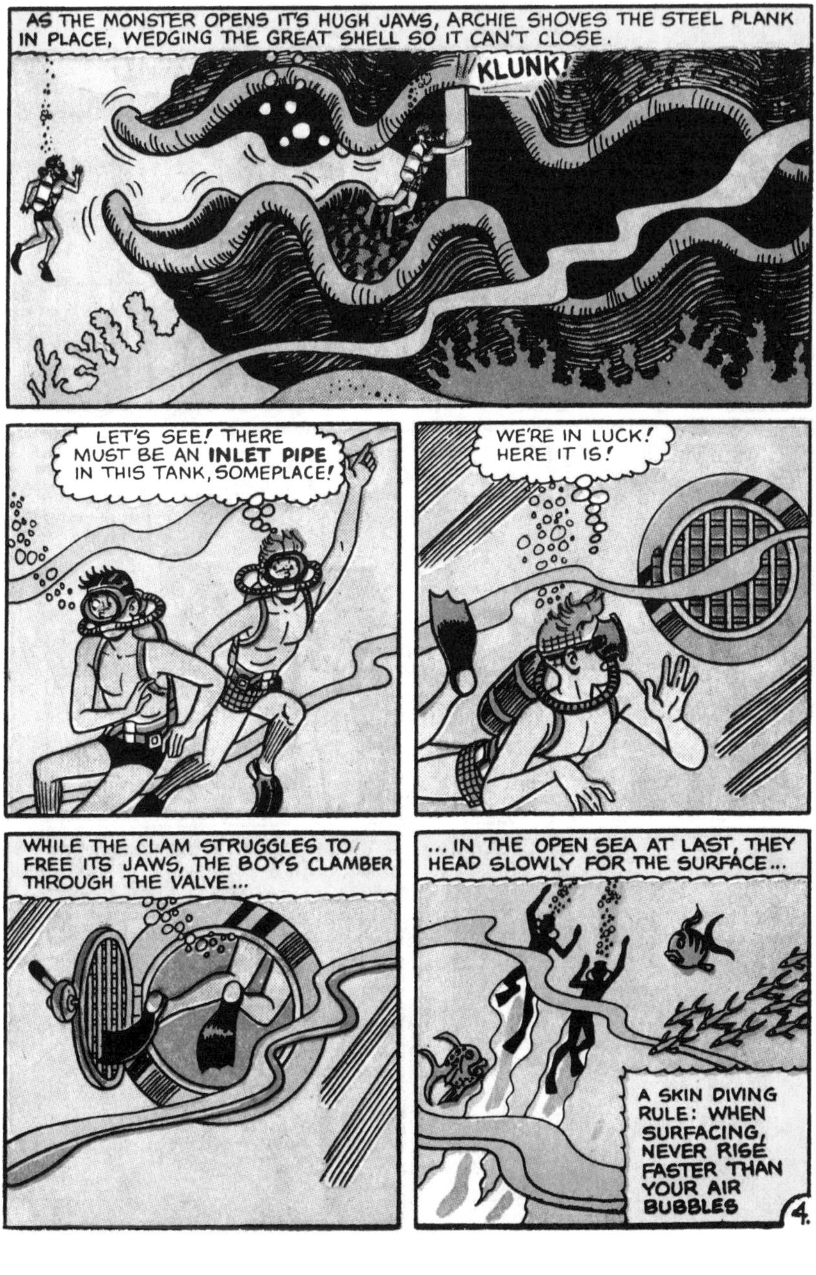
AS THE MONSTER OPENS IT'S HUGH JAWS, ARCHIE SHOVES THE STEEL PLANK IN PLACE, WEDGING THE GREAT SHELL SO IT CAN'T CLOSE.
KLUNK!
LET'S SEE! THERE MUST BE AN INLET PIPE IN THIS TANK, SOMEPLACE!
WE'RE IN LUCK! HERE IT IS!
WHILE THE CLAM STRUGGLES TO FREE ITS JAWS, THE BOYS CLAMBER THROUGH THE VALVE...
... IN THE OPEN SEA AT LAST, THEY HEAD SLOWLY FOR THE SURFACE...
A SKIN DIVING RULE: WHEN SURFACING, NEVER RISE FASTER THAN YOUR AIR BUBBLES
4.

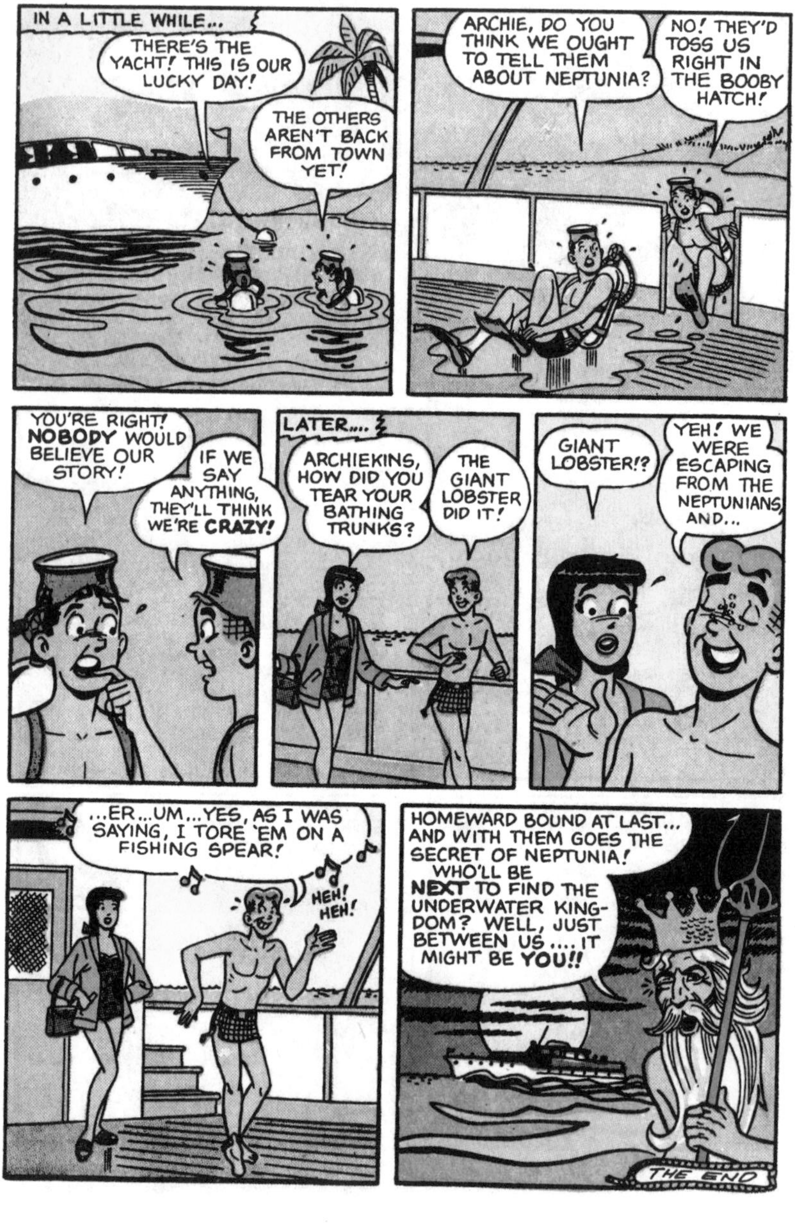
IN A LITTLE WHILE...
THERE'S THE YACHT! THIS IS OUR LUCKY DAY!
THE OTHERS AREN'T BACK FROM TOWN YET!
ARCHIE, DO YOU THINK WE OUGHT TO TELL THEM ABOUT NEPTUNIA?
NO! THEY'D TOSS US RIGHT IN THE BOOBY HATCH!
YOU'RE RIGHT! NOBODY WOULD BELIEVE OUR STORY!
IF WE SAY ANYTHING, THEY'LL THINK WE'RE CRAZY!
LATER....
ARCHIEKINS, HOW DID YOU TEAR YOUR BATHING TRUNKS?
THE GIANT LOBSTER DID IT!
GIANT LOBSTER!?
YEH! WE WERE ESCAPING FROM THE NEPTUNIANS, AND...
...ER...UM...YES, AS I WAS SAYING, I TORE 'EM ON A FISHING SPEAR!
HEH! HEH!
HOMEWARD BOUND AT LAST... AND WITH THEM GOES THE SECRET OF NEPTUNIA! WHO'LL BE NEXT TO FIND THE UNDERWATER KINGDOM? WELL, JUST BETWEEN US .... IT MIGHT BE YOU!!
THE END

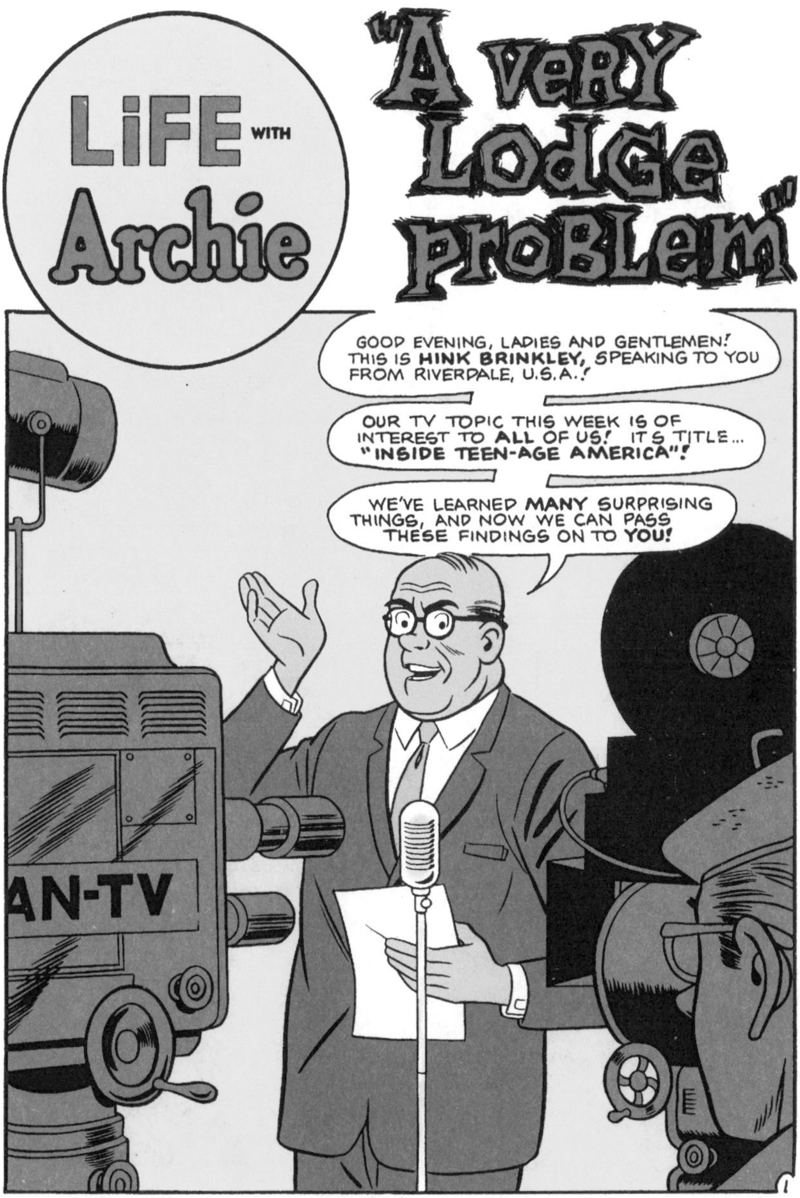
LIFE WITH Archie
"A VERY LODGE PROBLEM"
GOOD EVENING, LADIES AND GENTLEMEN! THIS IS HINK BRINKLEY, SPEAKING TO YOU FROM RIVERDALE, U.S.A.!
OUR TV TOPIC THIS WEEK IS OF INTEREST TO ALL OF US! IT'S TITLE... "INSIDE TEEN-AGE AMERICA"!
WE'VE LEARNED MANY SURPRISING THINGS, AND NOW WE CAN PASS THESE FINDINGS ON TO YOU!
AN-TV

Story: Sy Reit Art: Bob White

Originally printed in LIFE WITH ARCHIE #23, October 1963

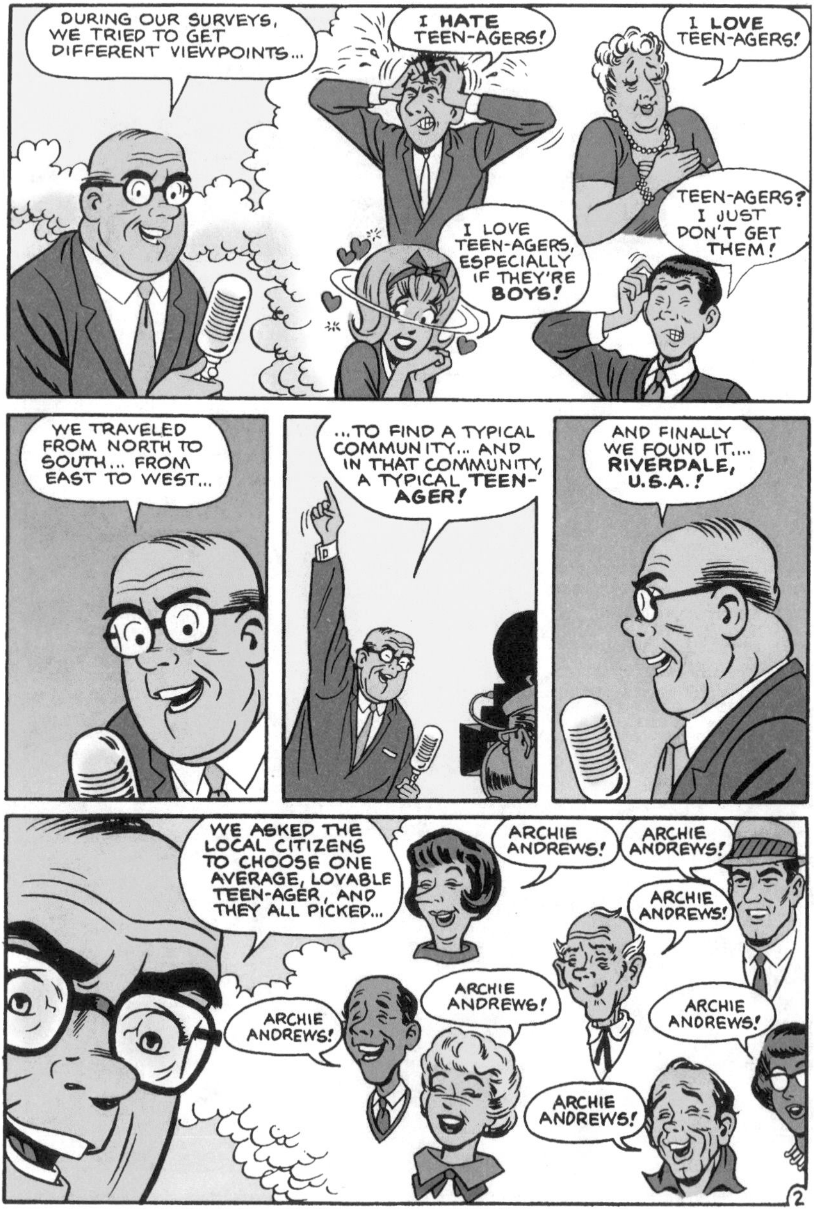
DURING OUR SURVEYS, WE TRIED TO GET DIFFERENT VIEWPOINTS...
I HATE TEEN-AGERS!
I LOVE TEEN-AGERS!
I LOVE TEEN-AGERS, ESPECIALLY IF THEY'RE BOYS!
TEEN-AGERS? I JUST DON'T GET THEM!
WE TRAVELED FROM NORTH TO SOUTH... FROM EAST TO WEST...
...TO FIND A TYPICAL COMMUNITY... AND IN THAT COMMUNITY, A TYPICAL TEEN-AGER!
AND FINALLY WE FOUND IT.... RIVERDALE, U.S.A.!
WE ASKED THE LOCAL CITIZENS TO CHOOSE ONE AVERAGE, LOVABLE TEEN-AGER, AND THEY ALL PICKED...
ARCHIE ANDREWS!
ARCHIE ANDREWS!
ARCHIE ANDREWS!
ARCHIE ANDREWS!
ARCHIE ANDREWS!
ARCHIE ANDREWS!
ARCHIE ANDREWS!
2

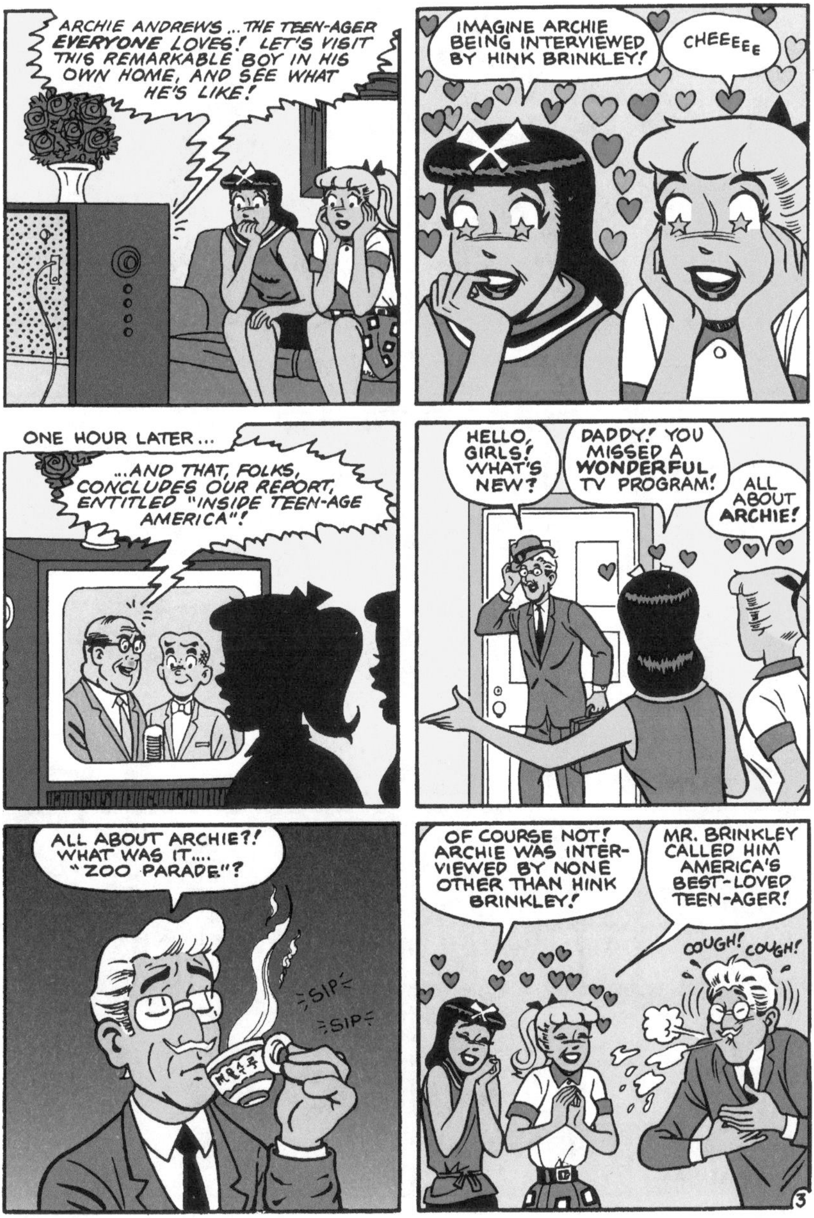
ARCHIE ANDREWS ... THE TEEN-AGER EVERYONE LOVES! LET'S VISIT THIS REMARKABLE BOY IN HIS OWN HOME, AND SEE WHAT HE'S LIKE!
IMAGINE ARCHIE BEING INTERVIEWED BY HINK BRINKLEY!
CHEEEEEE
ONE HOUR LATER ...
...AND THAT, FOLKS, CONCLUDES OUR REPORT, ENTITLED "INSIDE TEEN-AGE AMERICA"!
HELLO, GIRLS! WHAT'S NEW?
DADDY! YOU MISSED A WONDERFUL TV PROGRAM!
ALL ABOUT ARCHIE!
ALL ABOUT ARCHIE?! WHAT WAS IT.... "ZOO PARADE"?
SIP
SIP
OF COURSE NOT! ARCHIE WAS INTER-VIEWED BY NONE OTHER THAN HINK BRINKLEY!
MR. BRINKLEY CALLED HIM AMERICA'S BEST-LOVED TEEN-AGER!
COUGH! COUGH!
3

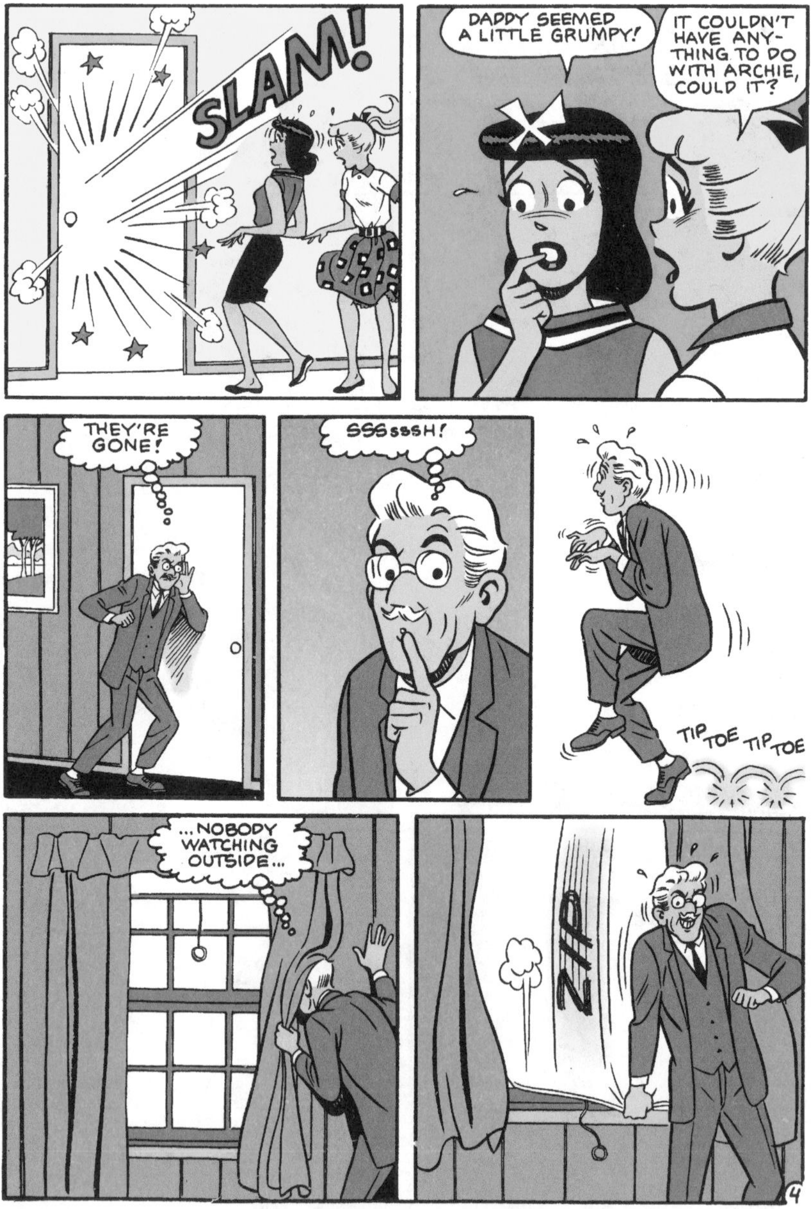
SLAM!
DADDY SEEMED A LITTLE GRUMPY!
IT COULDN'T HAVE ANY-THING TO DO WITH ARCHIE, COULD IT?
THEY'RE GONE!
SSSsssH!
TIP TOE TIP TOE
...NOBODY WATCHING OUTSIDE...
ZIP
4

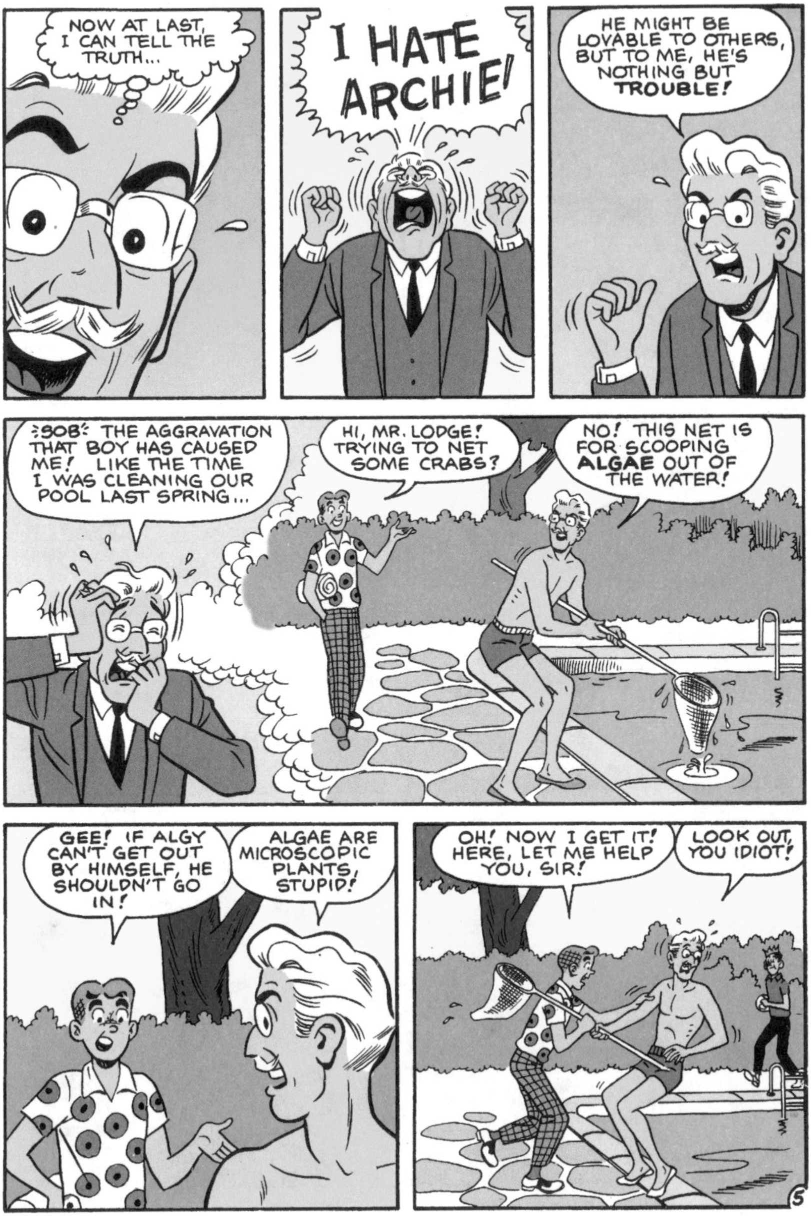
NOW AT LAST, I CAN TELL THE TRUTH...
I HATE ARCHIE!
HE MIGHT BE LOVABLE TO OTHERS, BUT TO ME, HE'S NOTHING BUT TROUBLE!
:SOB: THE AGGRAVATION THAT BOY HAS CAUSED ME! LIKE THE TIME I WAS CLEANING OUR POOL LAST SPRING...
HI, MR. LODGE! TRYING TO NET SOME CRABS?
NO! THIS NET IS FOR SCOOPING ALGAE OUT OF THE WATER!
GEE! IF ALGY CAN'T GET OUT BY HIMSELF, HE SHOULDN'T GO IN!
ALGAE ARE MICROSCOPIC PLANTS, STUPID!
OH! NOW I GET IT! HERE, LET ME HELP YOU, SIR!
LOOK OUT, YOU IDIOT!
5

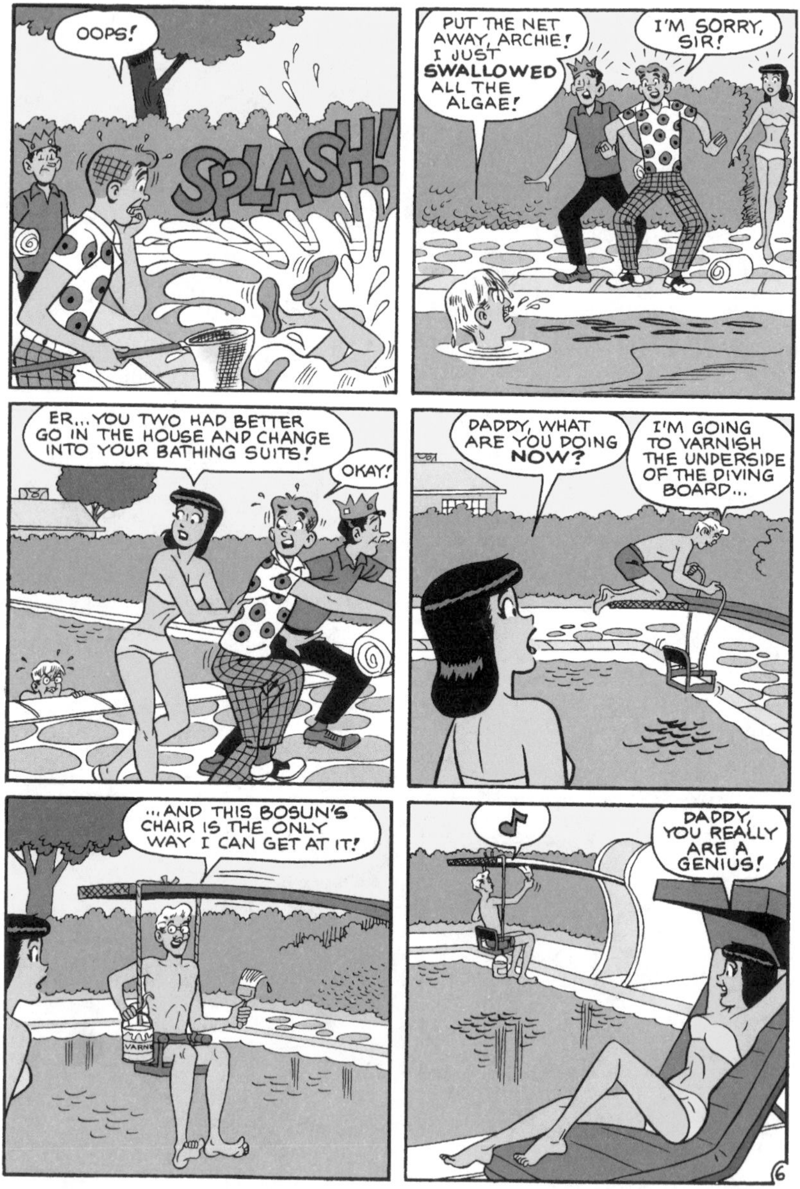
OOPS!
SPLASH!
PUT THE NET AWAY, ARCHIE! I JUST SWALLOWED ALL THE ALGAE!
I'M SORRY, SIR!
ER... YOU TWO HAD BETTER GO IN THE HOUSE AND CHANGE INTO YOUR BATHING SUITS!
OKAY!
DADDY, WHAT ARE YOU DOING NOW?
I'M GOING TO VARNISH THE UNDERSIDE OF THE DIVING BOARD...
...AND THIS BOSUN'S CHAIR IS THE ONLY WAY I CAN GET AT IT!
VARN
DADDY, YOU REALLY ARE A GENIUS!
6

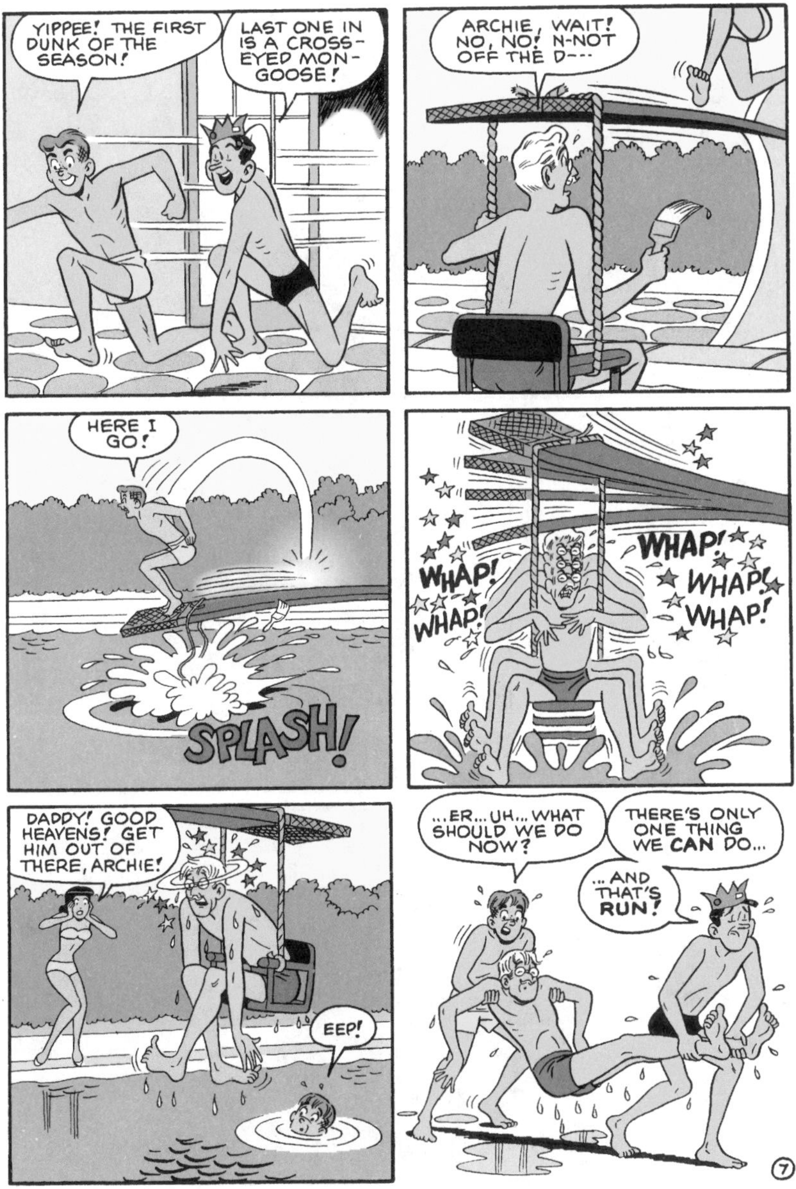
YIPPEE! THE FIRST DUNK OF THE SEASON!
LAST ONE IN IS A CROSS-EYED MON-GOOSE!
ARCHIE, WAIT! NO, NO! N-NOT OFF THE D---
HERE I GO!
SPLASH!
WHAP!
WHAP!
WHAP!
WHAP!
WHAP!
DADDY! GOOD HEAVENS! GET HIM OUT OF THERE, ARCHIE!
EEP!
...ER...UH...WHAT SHOULD WE DO NOW?
THERE'S ONLY ONE THING WE CAN DO...
...AND THAT'S RUN!
7

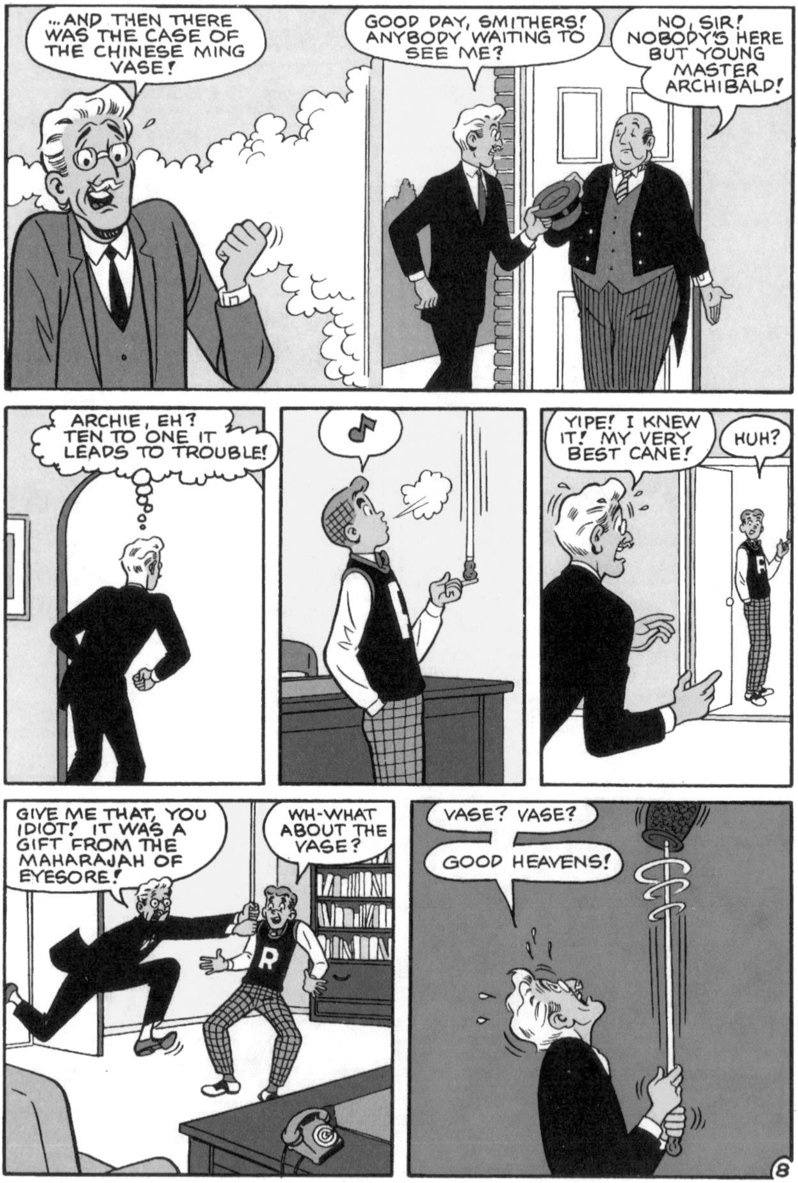
...AND THEN THERE WAS THE CASE OF THE CHINESE MING VASE!
GOOD DAY, SMITHERS! ANYBODY WAITING TO SEE ME?
NO, SIR! NOBODY'S HERE BUT YOUNG MASTER ARCHIBALD!
ARCHIE, EH? TEN TO ONE IT LEADS TO TROUBLE!
♪
YIPE! I KNEW IT! MY VERY BEST CANE!
HUH?
GIVE ME THAT, YOU IDIOT! IT WAS A GIFT FROM THE MAHARAJAH OF EYESORE!
WH-WHAT ABOUT THE VASE?
VASE? VASE?
GOOD HEAVENS!
8

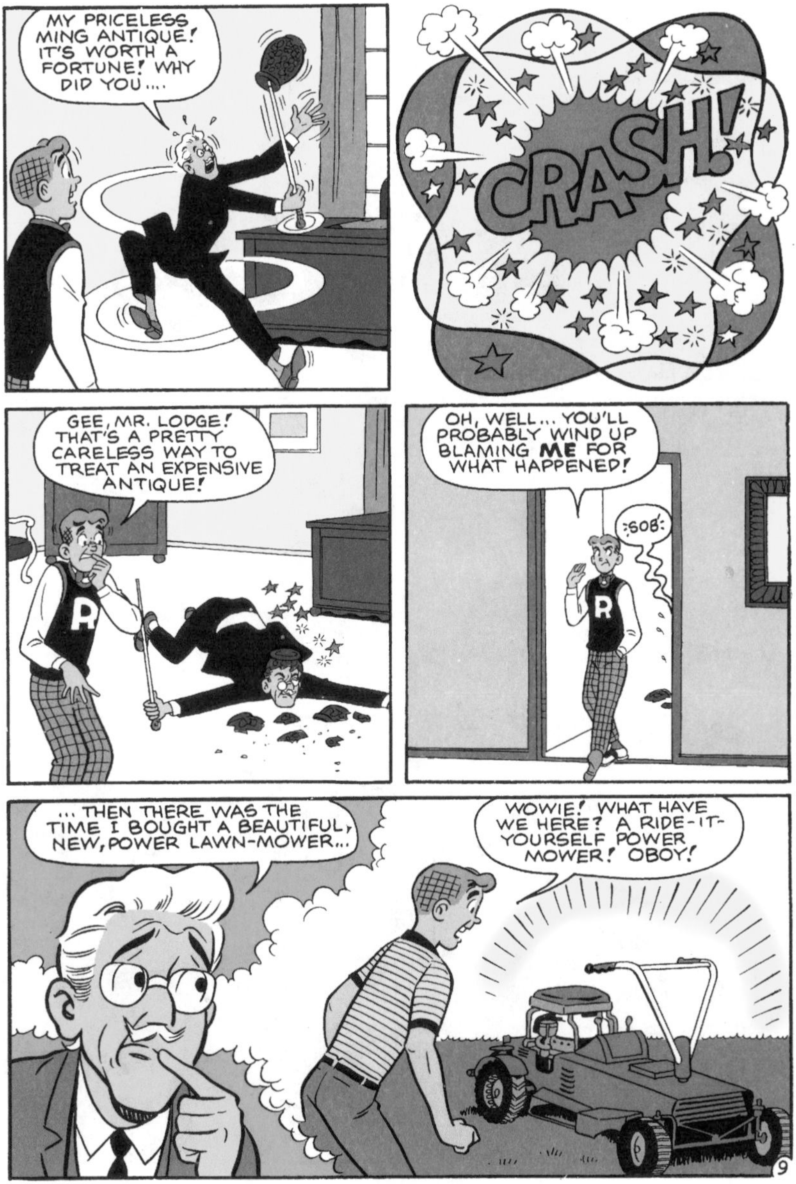
MY PRICELESS MING ANTIQUE! IT'S WORTH A FORTUNE! WHY DID YOU....
CRASH!
GEE, MR. LODGE! THAT'S A PRETTY CARELESS WAY TO TREAT AN EXPENSIVE ANTIQUE!
OH, WELL... YOU'LL PROBABLY WIND UP BLAMING ME FOR WHAT HAPPENED!
SOB
...THEN THERE WAS THE TIME I BOUGHT A BEAUTIFUL, NEW, POWER LAWN-MOWER...
WOWIE! WHAT HAVE WE HERE? A RIDE-IT-YOURSELF POWER MOWER! OBOY!
9

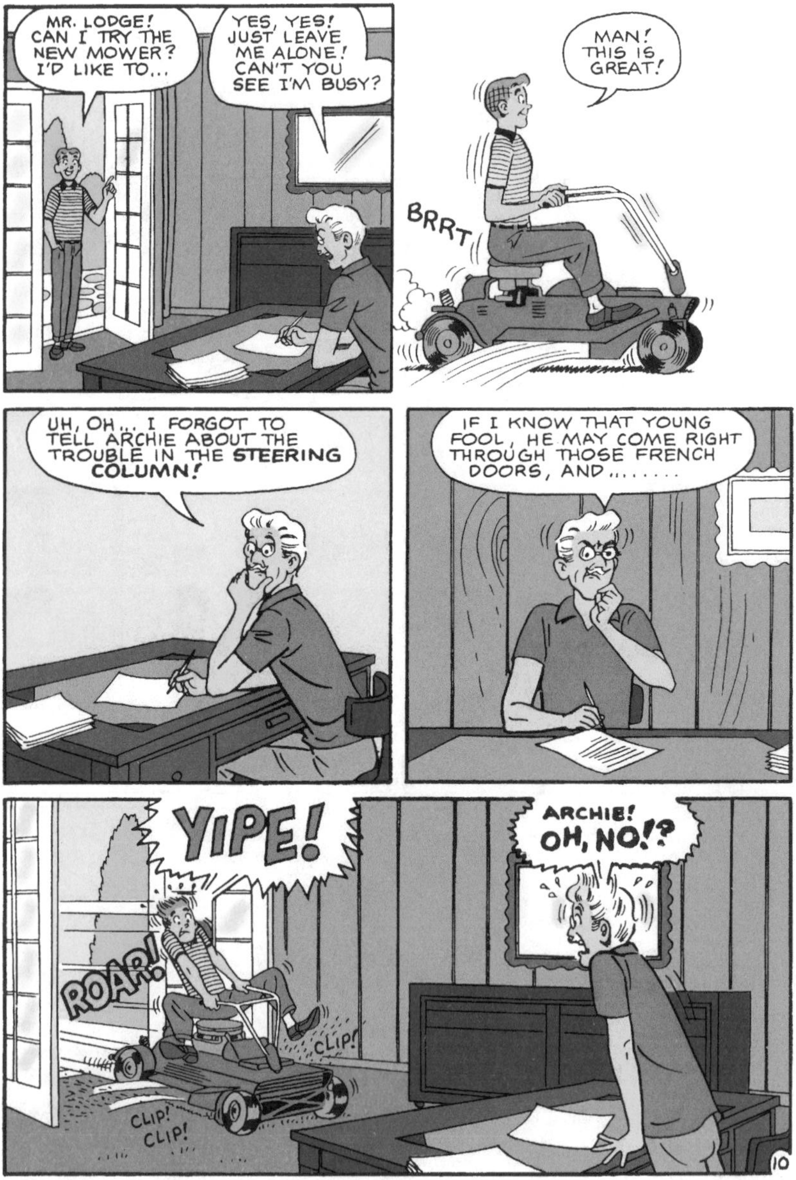
MR. LODGE! CAN I TRY THE NEW MOWER? I'D LIKE TO...
YES, YES! JUST LEAVE ME ALONE! CAN'T YOU SEE I'M BUSY?
MAN! THIS IS GREAT!
BRRT
UH, OH... I FORGOT TO TELL ARCHIE ABOUT THE TROUBLE IN THE STEERING COLUMN!
IF I KNOW THAT YOUNG FOOL, HE MAY COME RIGHT THROUGH THOSE FRENCH DOORS, AND.......
YIPE!
ARCHIE! OH, NO!?
ROAR!
CLIP!
CLIP! CLIP!
10

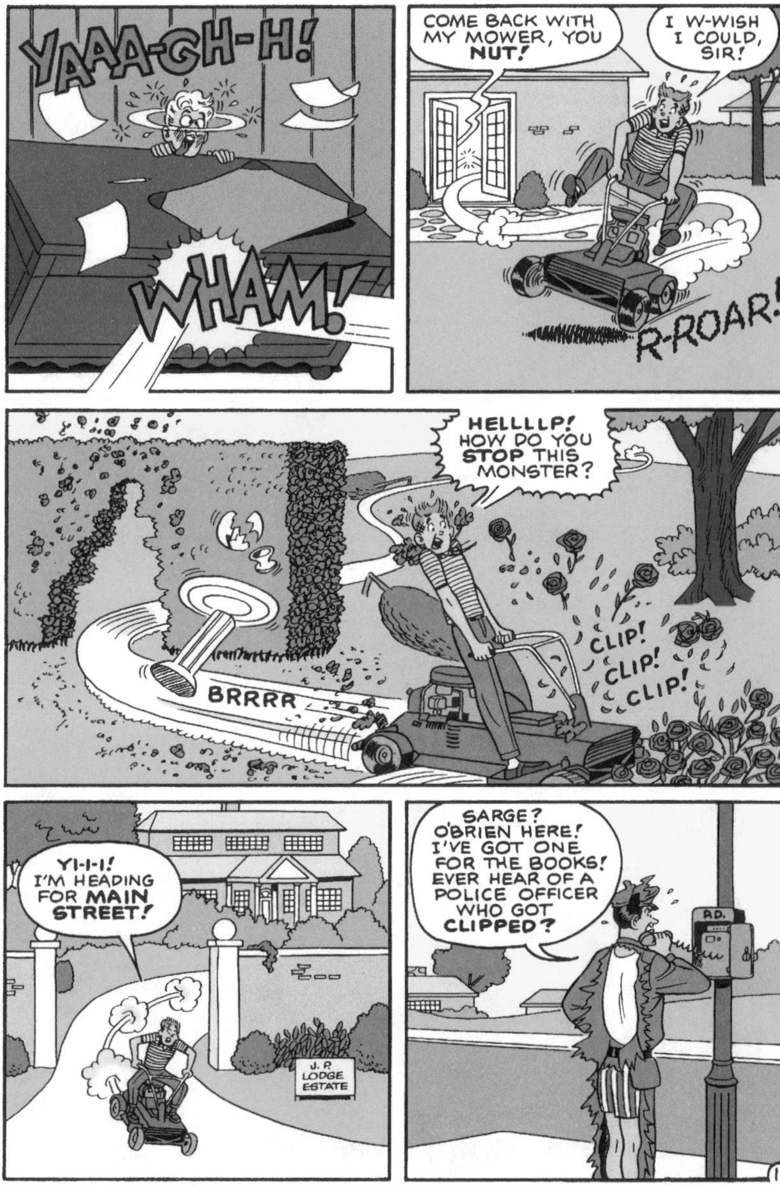
YAAA-GH-H!
WHAM!
COME BACK WITH MY MOWER, YOU NUT!
I W-WISH I COULD, SIR!
R-ROAR!
HELLLLP! HOW DO YOU STOP THIS MONSTER?
BRRRR
CLIP! CLIP! CLIP!
YI-I-I! I'M HEADING FOR MAIN STREET!
J. P. LODGE ESTATE
SARGE? O'BRIEN HERE! I'VE GOT ONE FOR THE BOOKS! EVER HEAR OF A POLICE OFFICER WHO GOT CLIPPED?
P.D.
11

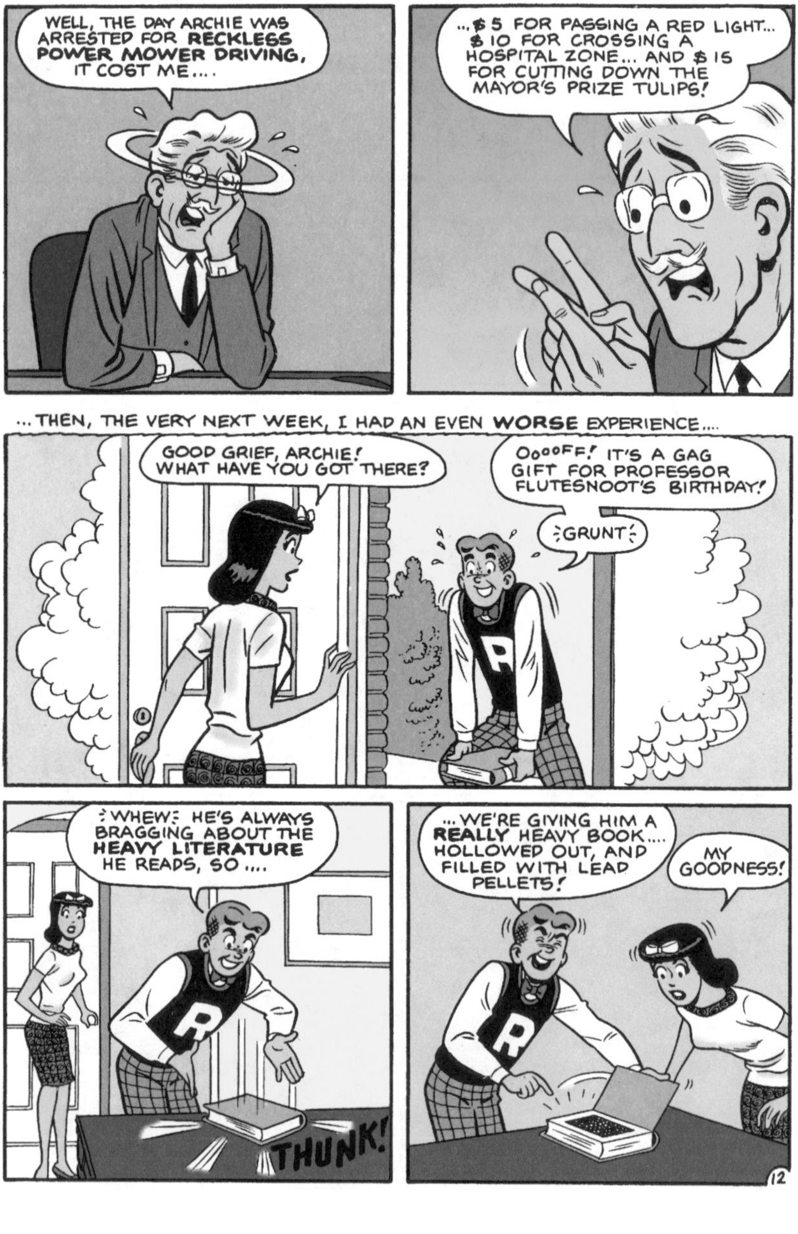
WELL, THE DAY ARCHIE WAS ARRESTED FOR RECKLESS POWER MOWER DRIVING, IT COST ME....
...$5 FOR PASSING A RED LIGHT... $10 FOR CROSSING A HOSPITAL ZONE... AND $15 FOR CUTTING DOWN THE MAYOR'S PRIZE TULIPS!
...THEN, THE VERY NEXT WEEK, I HAD AN EVEN WORSE EXPERIENCE....
GOOD GRIEF, ARCHIE! WHAT HAVE YOU GOT THERE?
OooFF! IT'S A GAG GIFT FOR PROFESSOR FLUTESNOOT'S BIRTHDAY!
GRUNT
WHEW! HE'S ALWAYS BRAGGING ABOUT THE HEAVY LITERATURE HE READS, SO....
THUNK!
...WE'RE GIVING HIM A REALLY HEAVY BOOK.... HOLLOWED OUT, AND FILLED WITH LEAD PELLETS!
MY GOODNESS!

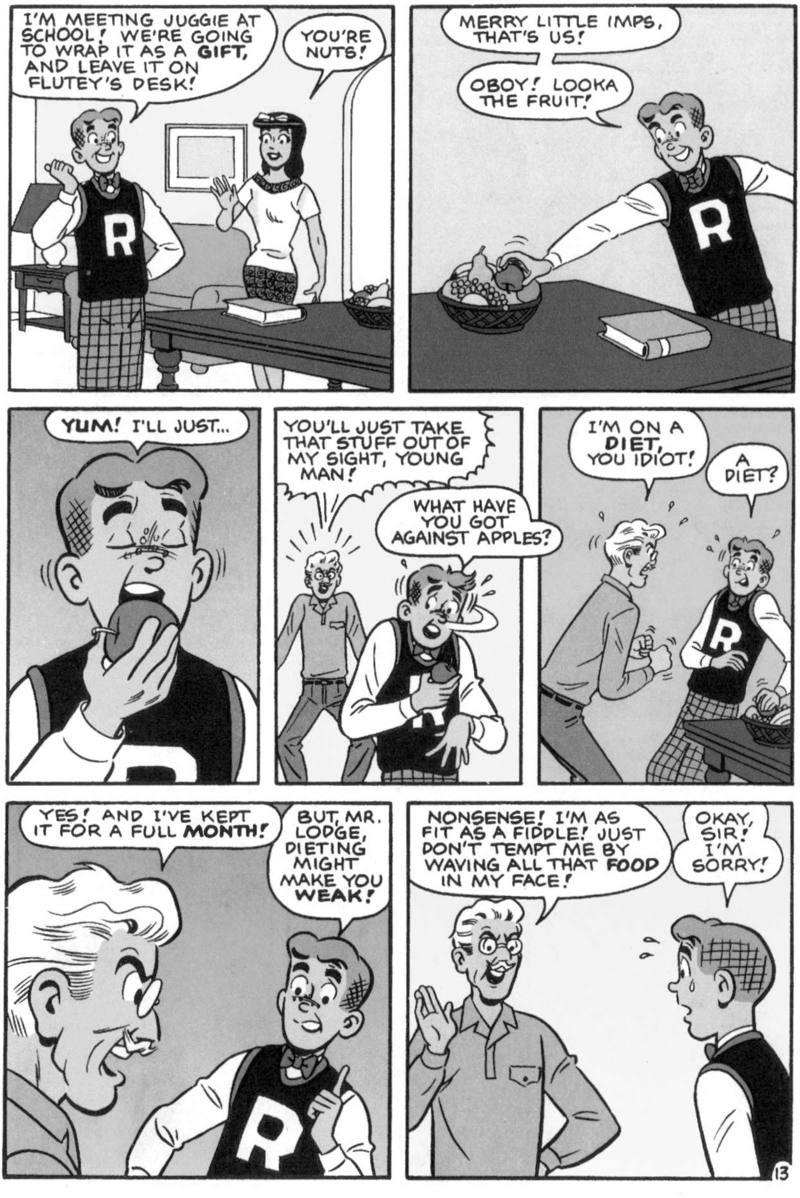
I'M MEETING JUGGIE AT SCHOOL! WE'RE GOING TO WRAP IT AS A GIFT, AND LEAVE IT ON FLUTEY'S DESK!
YOU'RE NUTS!
MERRY LITTLE IMPS, THAT'S US!
OBOY! LOOKA THE FRUIT!
YUM! I'LL JUST...
YOU'LL JUST TAKE THAT STUFF OUT OF MY SIGHT, YOUNG MAN!
WHAT HAVE YOU GOT AGAINST APPLES?
I'M ON A DIET, YOU IDIOT!
A DIET?
YES! AND I'VE KEPT IT FOR A FULL MONTH!
BUT, MR. LODGE, DIETING MIGHT MAKE YOU WEAK!
NONSENSE! I'M AS FIT AS A FIDDLE! JUST DON'T TEMPT ME BY WAVING ALL THAT FOOD IN MY FACE!
OKAY, SIR! I'M SORRY!
13

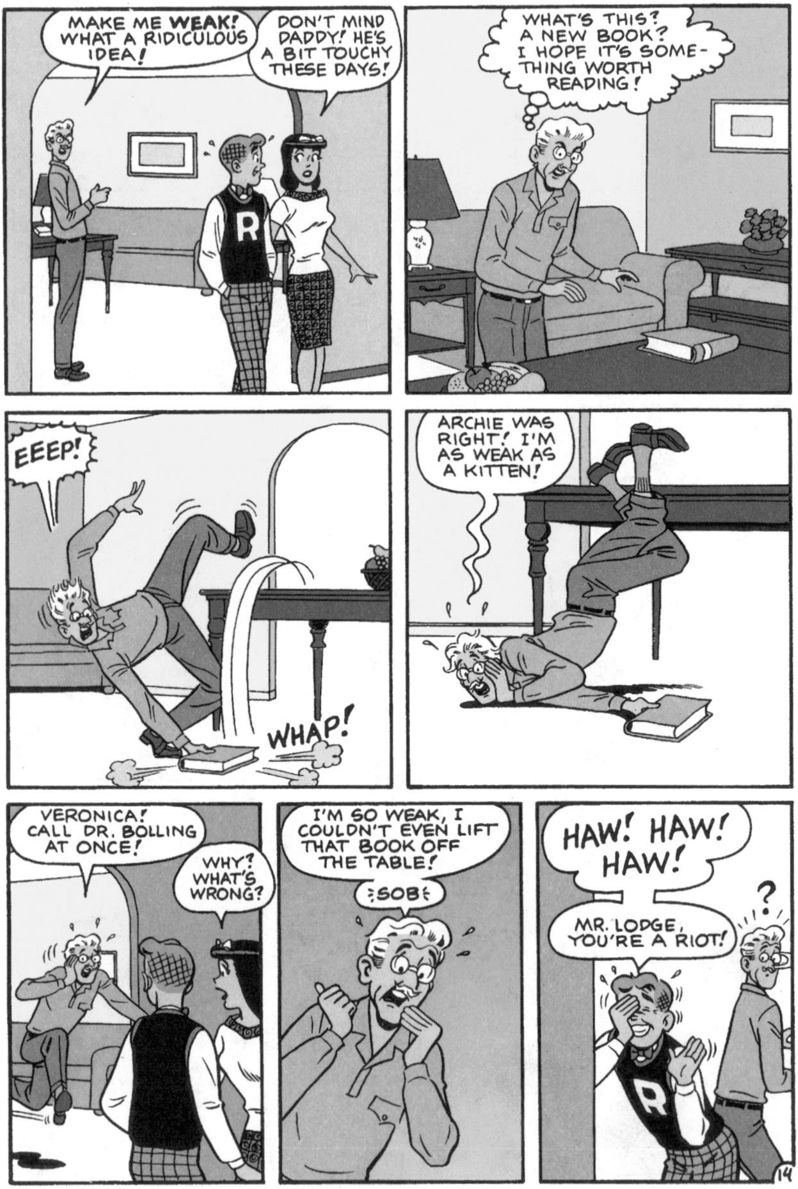
MAKE ME WEAK! WHAT A RIDICULOUS IDEA!
DON'T MIND DADDY! HE'S A BIT TOUCHY THESE DAYS!
WHAT'S THIS? A NEW BOOK? I HOPE IT'S SOME-THING WORTH READING!
EEEP!
WHAP!
ARCHIE WAS RIGHT! I'M AS WEAK AS A KITTEN!
VERONICA! CALL DR. BOLLING AT ONCE!
WHY? WHAT'S WRONG?
I'M SO WEAK, I COULDN'T EVEN LIFT THAT BOOK OFF THE TABLE!
SOB
HAW! HAW! HAW!
?
MR. LODGE, YOU'RE A RIOT!
14

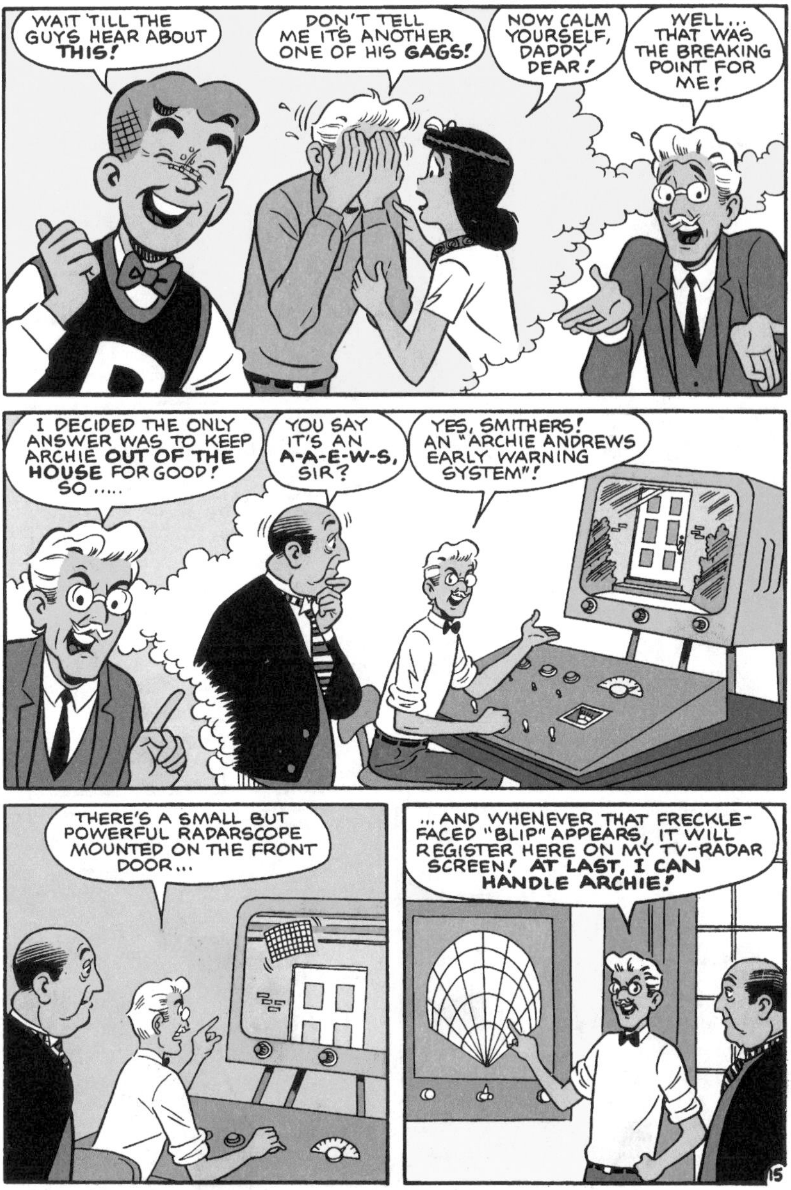
WAIT 'TILL THE GUYS HEAR ABOUT **THIS!**
DON'T TELL ME IT'S ANOTHER ONE OF HIS **GAGS!**
NOW CALM YOURSELF, DADDY DEAR!
WELL... THAT WAS THE BREAKING POINT FOR ME!
I DECIDED THE ONLY ANSWER WAS TO KEEP ARCHIE **OUT OF THE HOUSE** FOR GOOD! SO .....
YOU SAY IT'S AN **A-A-E-W-S,** SIR?
YES, SMITHERS! AN "ARCHIE ANDREWS EARLY WARNING SYSTEM"!
THERE'S A SMALL BUT POWERFUL RADARSCOPE MOUNTED ON THE FRONT DOOR...
...AND WHENEVER THAT FRECKLE-FACED "BLIP" APPEARS, IT WILL REGISTER HERE ON MY TV-RADAR SCREEN! **AT LAST, I CAN HANDLE ARCHIE!**
15

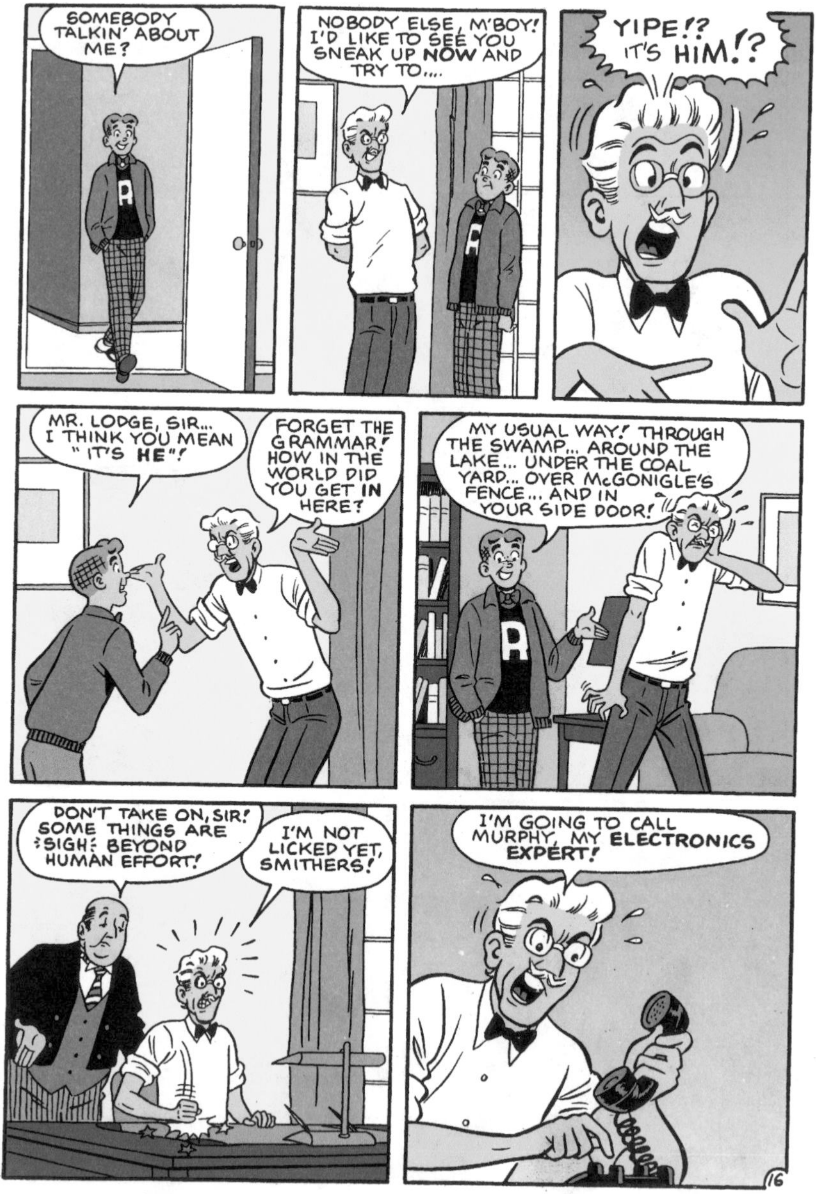
SOMEBODY TALKIN' ABOUT ME?
NOBODY ELSE, M'BOY! I'D LIKE TO SEE YOU SNEAK UP NOW AND TRY TO....
YIPE!? IT'S HIM!?
MR. LODGE, SIR... I THINK YOU MEAN "IT'S HE"!
FORGET THE GRAMMAR! HOW IN THE WORLD DID YOU GET IN HERE?
MY USUAL WAY! THROUGH THE SWAMP... AROUND THE LAKE... UNDER THE COAL YARD... OVER McGONIGLE'S FENCE... AND IN YOUR SIDE DOOR!
DON'T TAKE ON, SIR! SOME THINGS ARE :SIGH: BEYOND HUMAN EFFORT!
I'M NOT LICKED YET, SMITHERS!
I'M GOING TO CALL MURPHY, MY ELECTRONICS EXPERT!
16

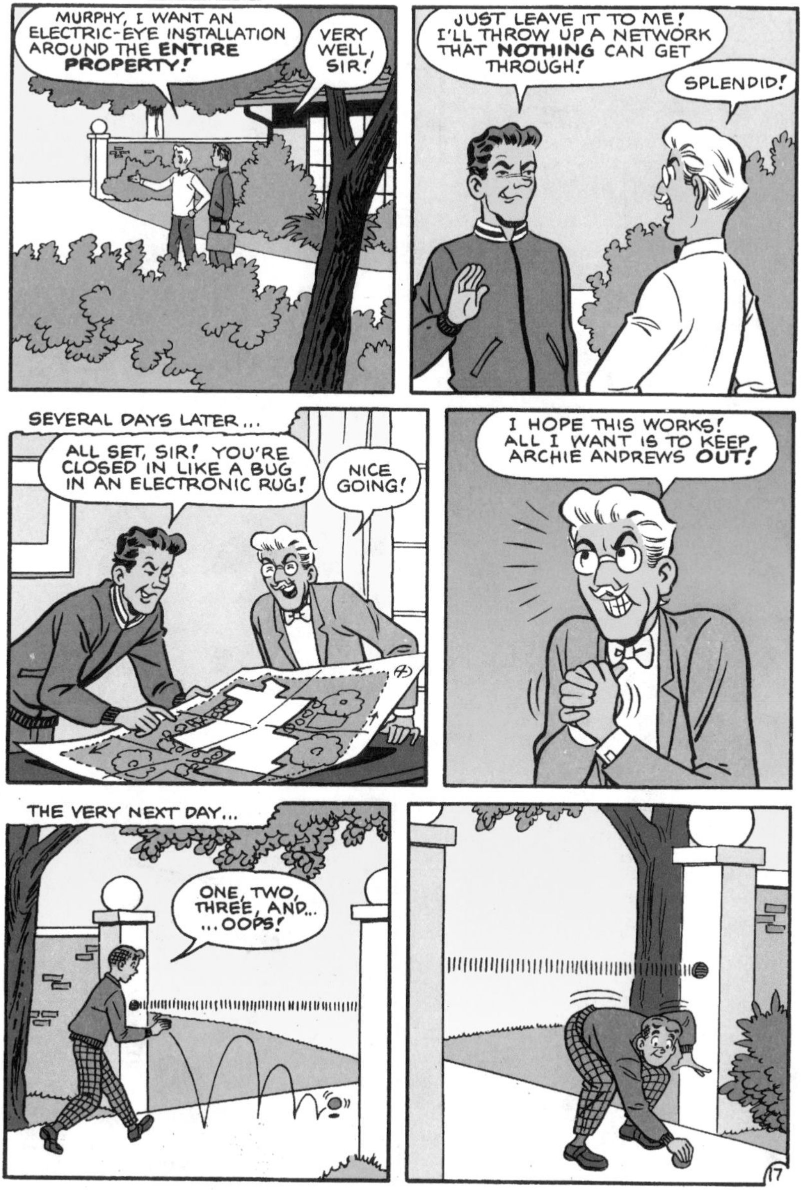
MURPHY, I WANT AN ELECTRIC-EYE INSTALLATION AROUND THE **ENTIRE PROPERTY!**
VERY WELL, SIR!
JUST LEAVE IT TO ME! I'LL THROW UP A NETWORK THAT **NOTHING** CAN GET THROUGH!
SPLENDID!
SEVERAL DAYS LATER...
ALL SET, SIR! YOU'RE CLOSED IN LIKE A BUG IN AN ELECTRONIC RUG!
NICE GOING!
I HOPE THIS WORKS! ALL I WANT IS TO KEEP ARCHIE ANDREWS **OUT!**
THE VERY NEXT DAY...
ONE, TWO, THREE, AND... ...OOPS!
17

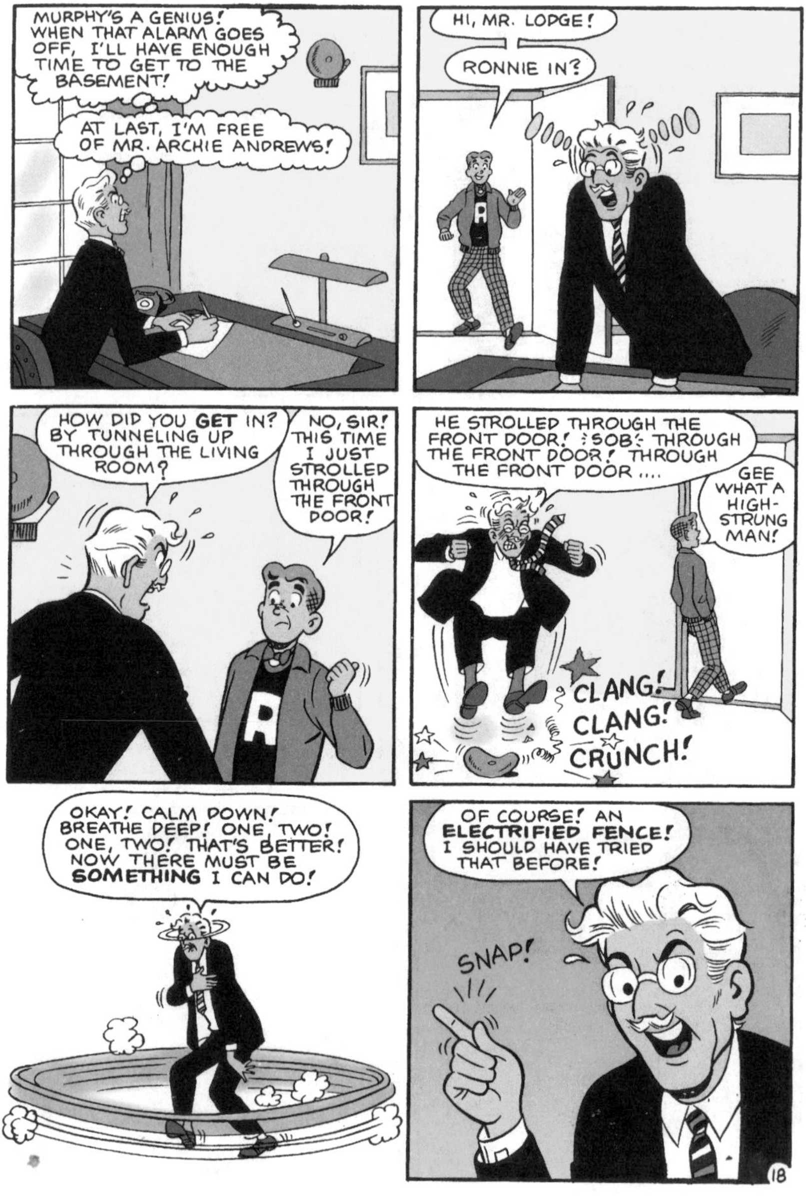
MURPHY'S A GENIUS! WHEN THAT ALARM GOES OFF, I'LL HAVE ENOUGH TIME TO GET TO THE BASEMENT!
AT LAST, I'M FREE OF MR. ARCHIE ANDREWS!
HI, MR. LODGE!
RONNIE IN?
HOW DID YOU GET IN? BY TUNNELING UP THROUGH THE LIVING ROOM?
NO, SIR! THIS TIME I JUST STROLLED THROUGH THE FRONT DOOR!
HE STROLLED THROUGH THE FRONT DOOR! :SOB: THROUGH THE FRONT DOOR! THROUGH THE FRONT DOOR....
GEE WHAT A HIGH-STRUNG MAN!
CLANG!
CLANG!
CRUNCH!
OKAY! CALM DOWN! BREATHE DEEP! ONE, TWO! ONE, TWO! THAT'S BETTER! NOW THERE MUST BE SOMETHING I CAN DO!
OF COURSE! AN ELECTRIFIED FENCE! I SHOULD HAVE TRIED THAT BEFORE!
SNAP!
18

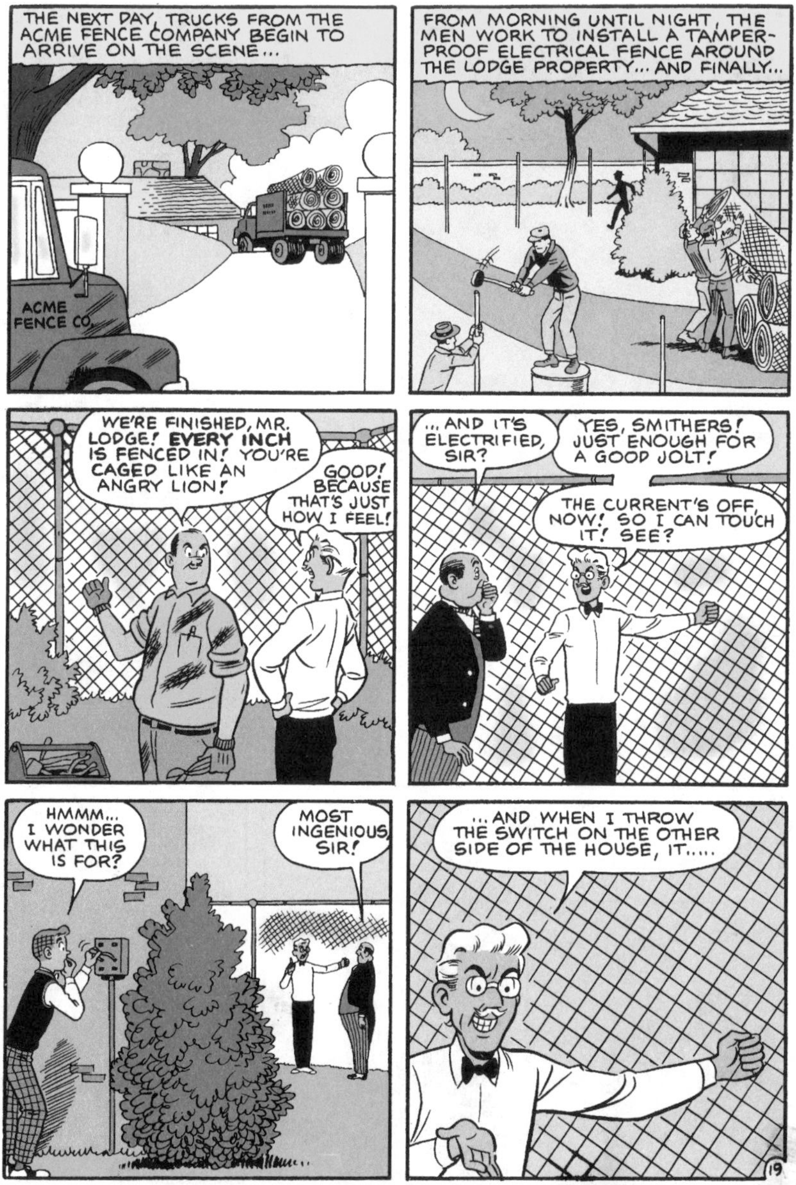

THE NEXT DAY, TRUCKS FROM THE ACME FENCE COMPANY BEGIN TO ARRIVE ON THE SCENE...
ACME FENCE CO.
FROM MORNING UNTIL NIGHT, THE MEN WORK TO INSTALL A TAMPER-PROOF ELECTRICAL FENCE AROUND THE LODGE PROPERTY... AND FINALLY...
WE'RE FINISHED, MR. LODGE! EVERY INCH IS FENCED IN! YOU'RE CAGED LIKE AN ANGRY LION!
GOOD! BECAUSE THAT'S JUST HOW I FEEL!
...AND IT'S ELECTRIFIED, SIR?
YES, SMITHERS! JUST ENOUGH FOR A GOOD JOLT!
THE CURRENT'S OFF, NOW! SO I CAN TOUCH IT! SEE?
HMMM... I WONDER WHAT THIS IS FOR?
MOST INGENIOUS, SIR!
...AND WHEN I THROW THE SWITCH ON THE OTHER SIDE OF THE HOUSE, IT.....
19

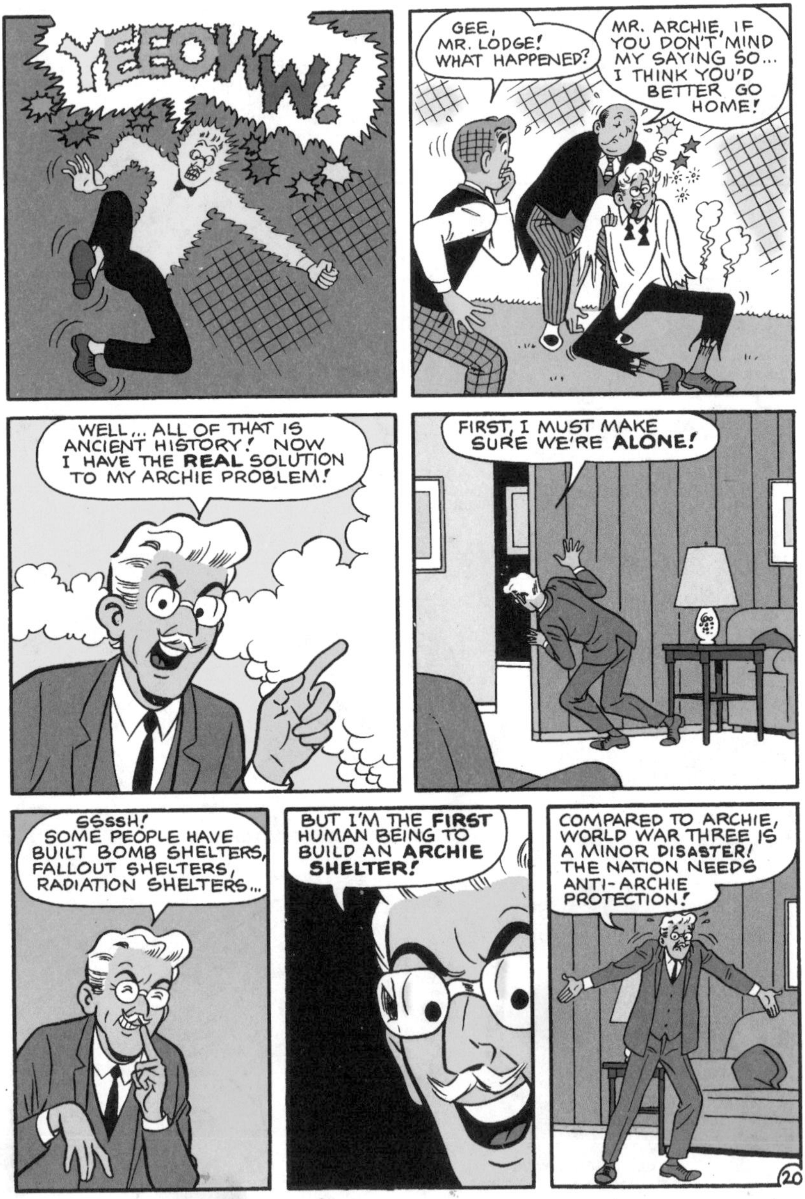
YEEOWW!
GEE, MR. LODGE! WHAT HAPPENED?
MR. ARCHIE, IF YOU DON'T MIND MY SAYING SO... I THINK YOU'D BETTER GO HOME!
WELL,.. ALL OF THAT IS ANCIENT HISTORY! NOW I HAVE THE REAL SOLUTION TO MY ARCHIE PROBLEM!
FIRST, I MUST MAKE SURE WE'RE ALONE!
SSssH! SOME PEOPLE HAVE BUILT BOMB SHELTERS, FALLOUT SHELTERS, RADIATION SHELTERS...
BUT I'M THE FIRST HUMAN BEING TO BUILD AN ARCHIE SHELTER!
COMPARED TO ARCHIE, WORLD WAR THREE IS A MINOR DISASTER! THE NATION NEEDS ANTI-ARCHIE PROTECTION!
20

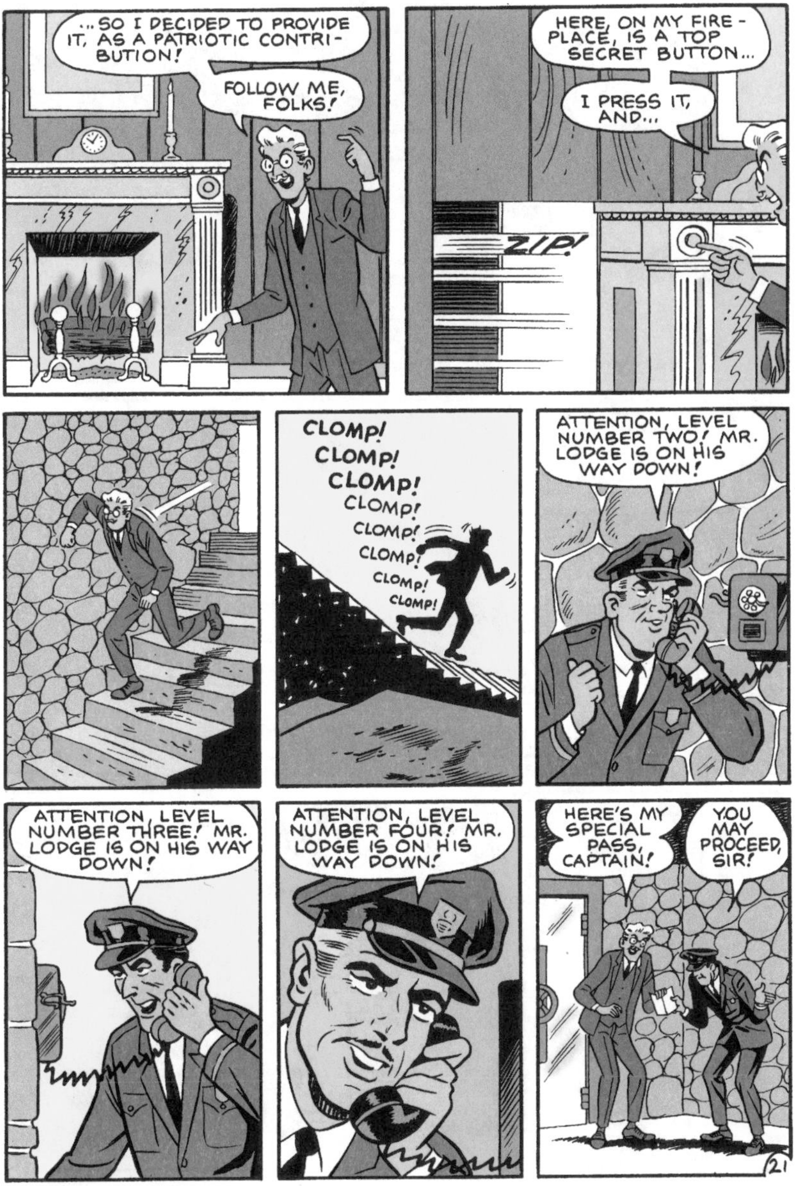
...SO I DECIDED TO PROVIDE IT, AS A PATRIOTIC CONTRIBUTION!
FOLLOW ME, FOLKS!
HERE, ON MY FIRE-PLACE, IS A TOP SECRET BUTTON...
I PRESS IT, AND...
ZIP!
CLOMP! CLOMP! CLOMP! CLOMP! CLOMP! CLOMP! CLOMP! CLOMP!
ATTENTION, LEVEL NUMBER TWO! MR. LODGE IS ON HIS WAY DOWN!
ATTENTION, LEVEL NUMBER THREE! MR. LODGE IS ON HIS WAY DOWN!
ATTENTION, LEVEL NUMBER FOUR! MR. LODGE IS ON HIS WAY DOWN!
HERE'S MY SPECIAL PASS, CAPTAIN!
YOU MAY PROCEED, SIR!
21

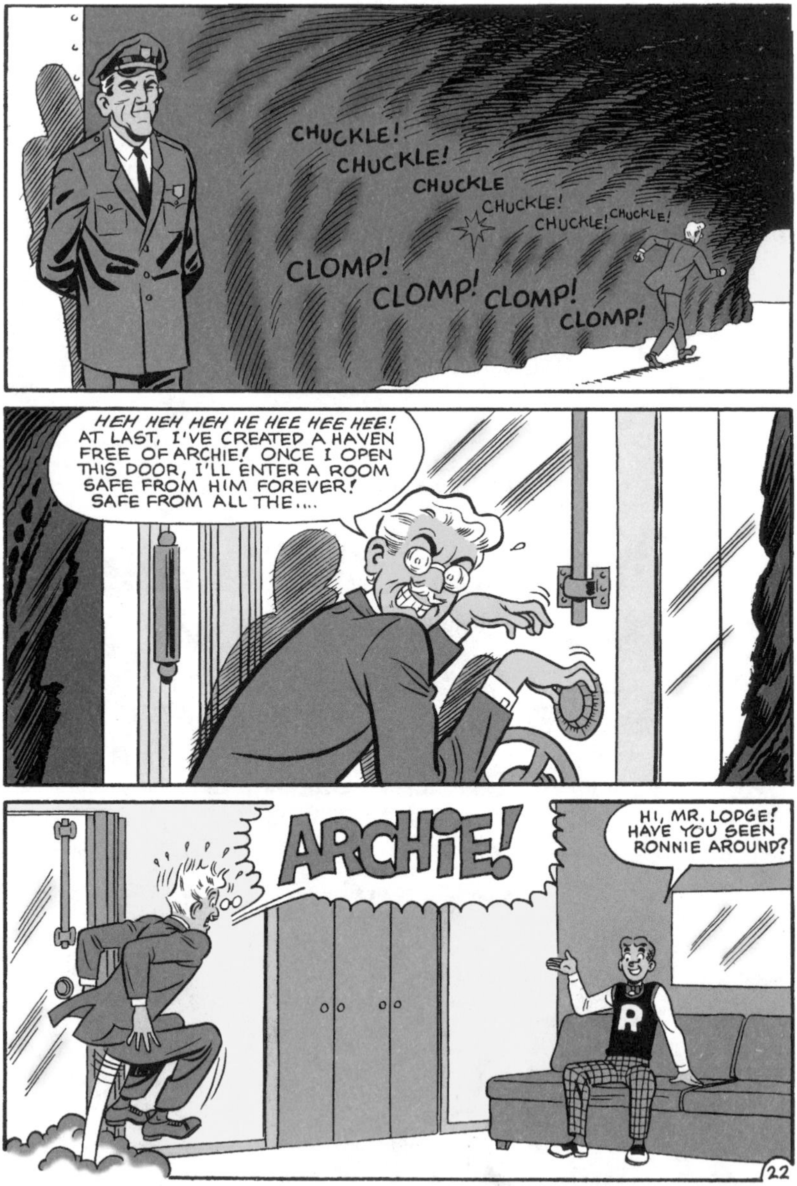
CHUCKLE!
CHUCKLE!
CHUCKLE
CHUCKLE!
CHUCKLE! CHUCKLE!
CLOMP!
CLOMP! CLOMP!
CLOMP!
HEH HEH HEH HE HEE HEE HEE! AT LAST, I'VE CREATED A HAVEN FREE OF ARCHIE! ONCE I OPEN THIS DOOR, I'LL ENTER A ROOM SAFE FROM HIM FOREVER! SAFE FROM ALL THE....
ARCHIE!
HI, MR. LODGE! HAVE YOU SEEN RONNIE AROUND?
22

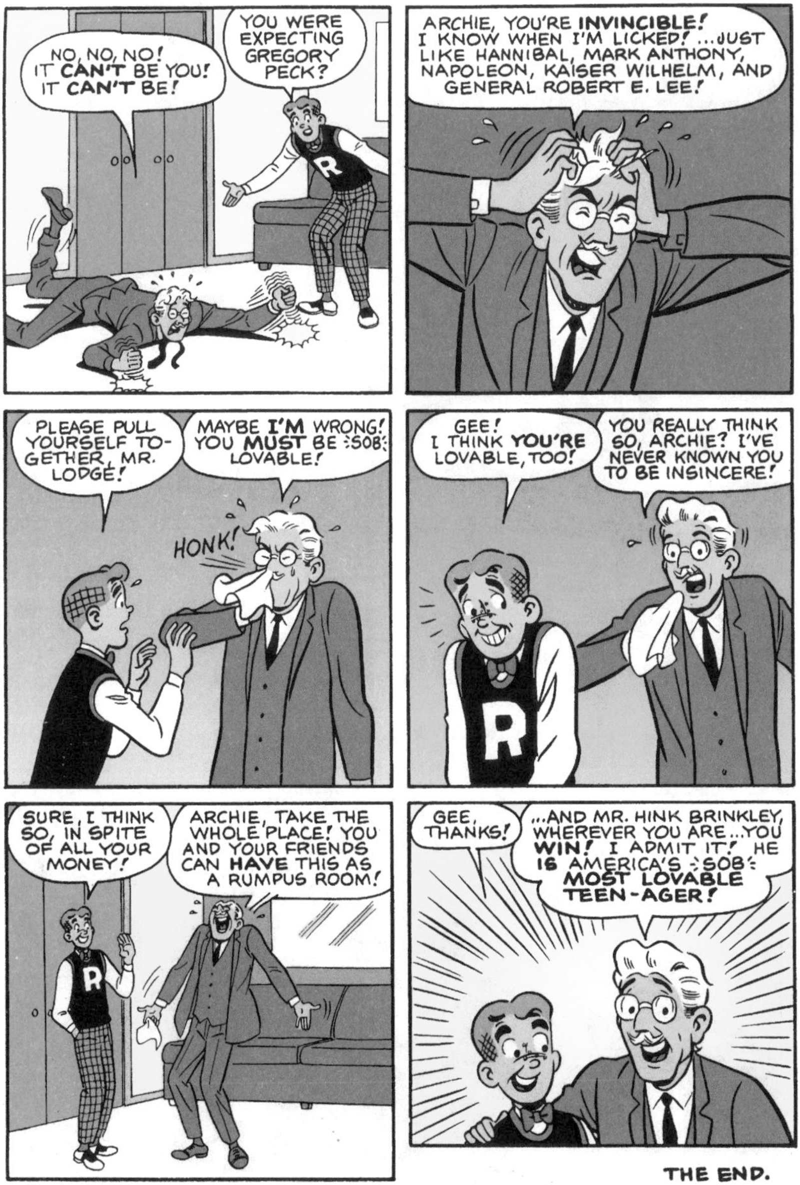
NO, NO, NO! IT CAN'T BE YOU! IT CAN'T BE!
YOU WERE EXPECTING GREGORY PECK?
ARCHIE, YOU'RE INVINCIBLE! I KNOW WHEN I'M LICKED! ...JUST LIKE HANNIBAL, MARK ANTHONY, NAPOLEON, KAISER WILHELM, AND GENERAL ROBERT E. LEE!
PLEASE PULL YOURSELF TO-GETHER, MR. LODGE!
MAYBE I'M WRONG! YOU MUST BE -SOB- LOVABLE!
HONK!
GEE! I THINK YOU'RE LOVABLE, TOO!
YOU REALLY THINK SO, ARCHIE? I'VE NEVER KNOWN YOU TO BE INSINCERE!
SURE, I THINK SO, IN SPITE OF ALL YOUR MONEY!
ARCHIE, TAKE THE WHOLE PLACE! YOU AND YOUR FRIENDS CAN HAVE THIS AS A RUMPUS ROOM!
GEE, THANKS!
...AND MR. HINK BRINKLEY, WHEREVER YOU ARE...YOU WIN! I ADMIT IT! HE IS AMERICA'S -SOB- MOST LOVABLE TEEN-AGER!

THE END.

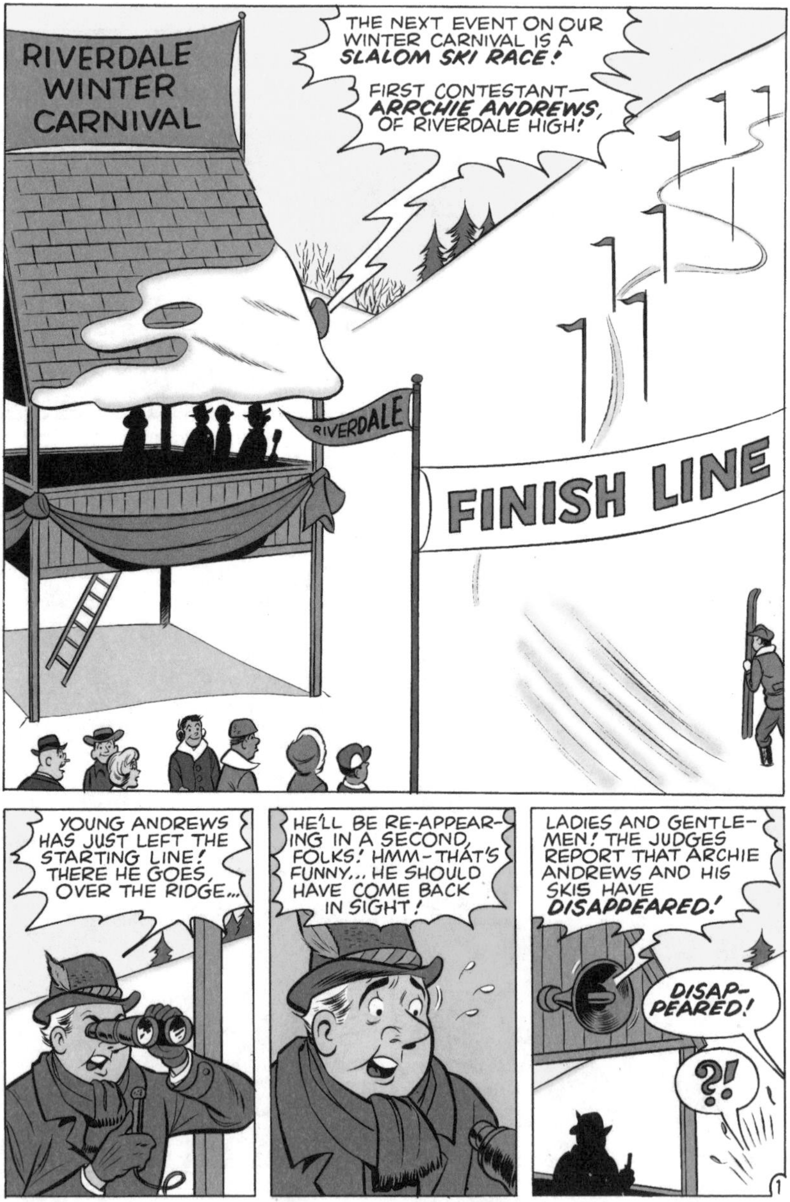
RIVERDALE WINTER CARNIVAL
THE NEXT EVENT ON OUR WINTER CARNIVAL IS A SLALOM SKI RACE!
FIRST CONTESTANT— ARRCHIE ANDREWS, OF RIVERDALE HIGH!
RIVERDALE
FINISH LINE
YOUNG ANDREWS HAS JUST LEFT THE STARTING LINE! THERE HE GOES, OVER THE RIDGE...
HE'LL BE RE-APPEARING IN A SECOND, FOLKS! HMM-THAT'S FUNNY... HE SHOULD HAVE COME BACK IN SIGHT!
LADIES AND GENTLEMEN! THE JUDGES REPORT THAT ARCHIE ANDREWS AND HIS SKIS HAVE DISAPPEARED!
DISAPPEARED!
?!
1

Story: Sy Reit Pencils: Bob White Inks & Letters: Marty Epp

Originally printed in LIFE WITH ARCHIE #26, March 1964

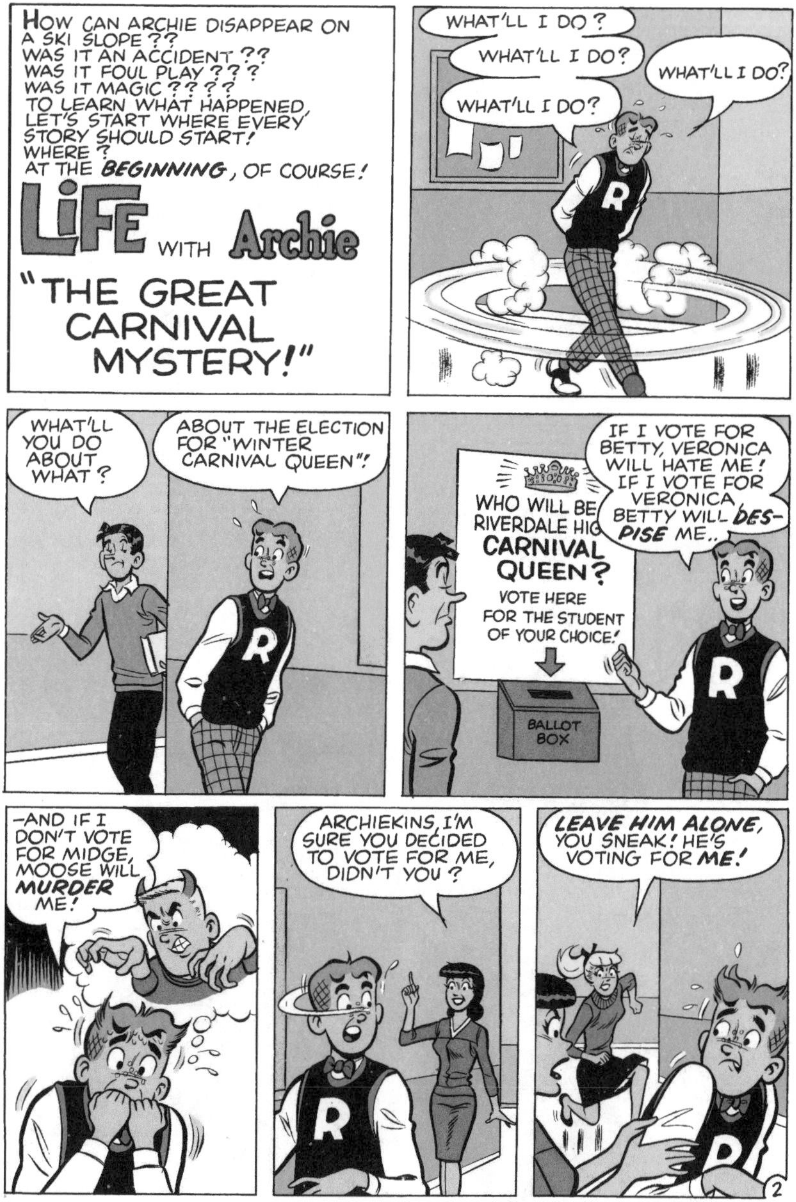
HOW CAN ARCHIE DISAPPEAR ON A SKI SLOPE ??
WAS IT AN ACCIDENT ??
WAS IT FOUL PLAY ???
WAS IT MAGIC ????
TO LEARN WHAT HAPPENED, LET'S START WHERE EVERY STORY SHOULD START!
WHERE ?
AT THE BEGINNING, OF COURSE!
LIFE WITH Archie
"THE GREAT CARNIVAL MYSTERY!"
WHAT'LL I DO ?
WHAT'LL I DO?
WHAT'LL I DO?
WHAT'LL I DO?
WHAT'LL YOU DO ABOUT WHAT ?
ABOUT THE ELECTION FOR "WINTER CARNIVAL QUEEN"!
WHO WILL BE RIVERDALE HIG CARNIVAL QUEEN? VOTE HERE FOR THE STUDENT OF YOUR CHOICE!
BALLOT BOX
IF I VOTE FOR BETTY, VERONICA WILL HATE ME! IF I VOTE FOR VERONICA, BETTY WILL DESPISE ME..
-AND IF I DON'T VOTE FOR MIDGE, MOOSE WILL MURDER ME!
ARCHIEKINS, I'M SURE YOU DECIDED TO VOTE FOR ME, DIDN'T YOU ?
LEAVE HIM ALONE, YOU SNEAK! HE'S VOTING FOR ME!
2

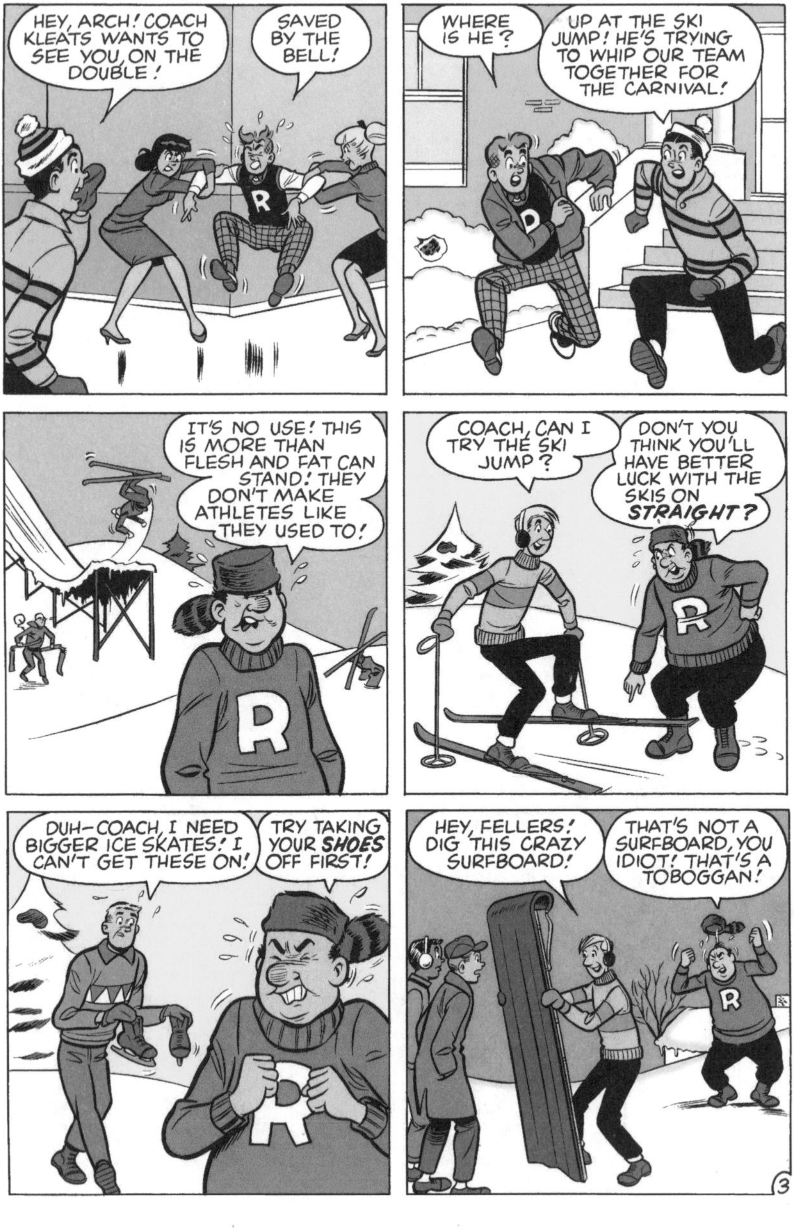
HEY, ARCH! COACH KLEATS WANTS TO SEE YOU, ON THE DOUBLE!
SAVED BY THE BELL!
WHERE IS HE?
UP AT THE SKI JUMP! HE'S TRYING TO WHIP OUR TEAM TOGETHER FOR THE CARNIVAL!
IT'S NO USE! THIS IS MORE THAN FLESH AND FAT CAN STAND! THEY DON'T MAKE ATHLETES LIKE THEY USED TO!
COACH, CAN I TRY THE SKI JUMP?
DON'T YOU THINK YOU'LL HAVE BETTER LUCK WITH THE SKIS ON STRAIGHT?
DUH—COACH, I NEED BIGGER ICE SKATES! I CAN'T GET THESE ON!
TRY TAKING YOUR SHOES OFF FIRST!
HEY, FELLERS! DIG THIS CRAZY SURFBOARD!
THAT'S NOT A SURFBOARD, YOU IDIOT! THAT'S A TOBOGGAN!
3

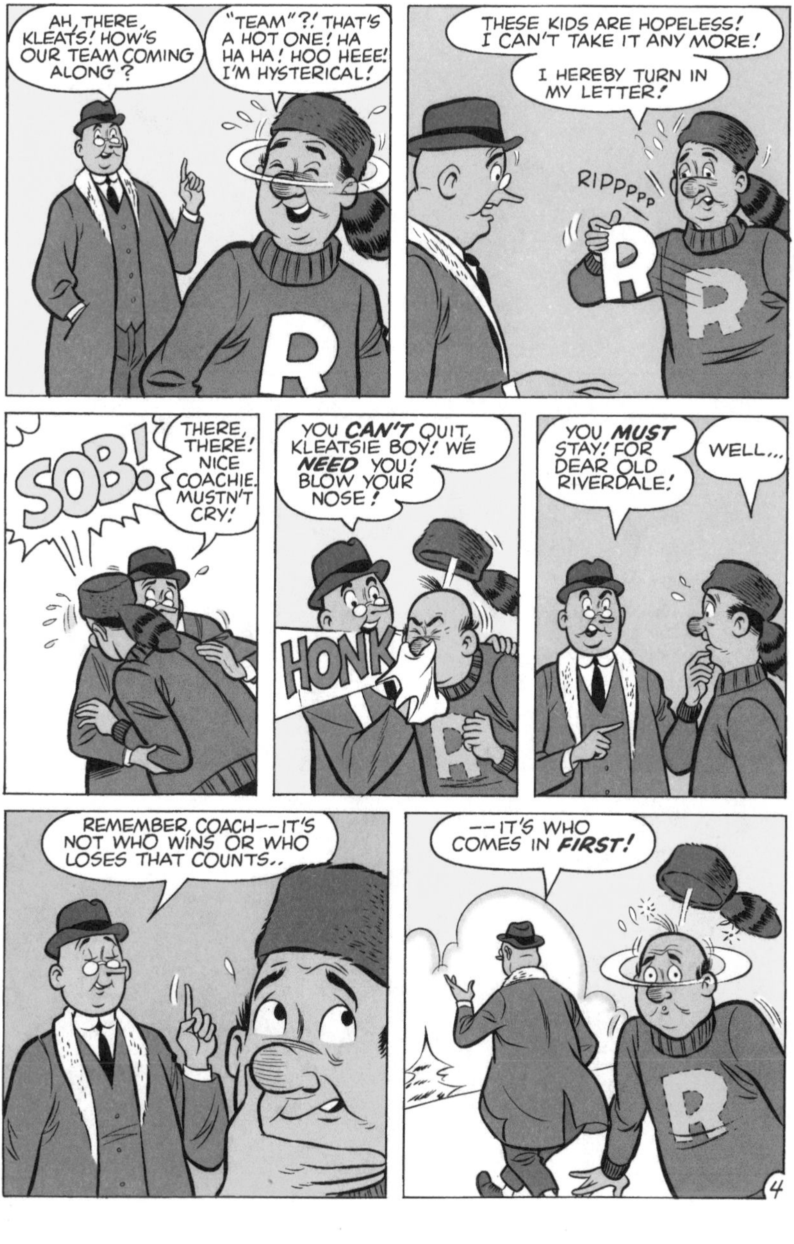
AH, THERE, KLEATS! HOW'S OUR TEAM COMING ALONG?
"TEAM"?! THAT'S A HOT ONE! HA HA HA! HOO HEEE! I'M HYSTERICAL!
THESE KIDS ARE HOPELESS! I CAN'T TAKE IT ANY MORE!
I HEREBY TURN IN MY LETTER!
RIPPPPPP
SOB!
THERE, THERE! NICE COACHIE. MUSTN'T CRY!
YOU CAN'T QUIT, KLEATSIE BOY! WE NEED YOU! BLOW YOUR NOSE!
HONK
YOU MUST STAY! FOR DEAR OLD RIVERDALE!
WELL...
REMEMBER, COACH--IT'S NOT WHO WINS OR WHO LOSES THAT COUNTS..
--IT'S WHO COMES IN FIRST!
4

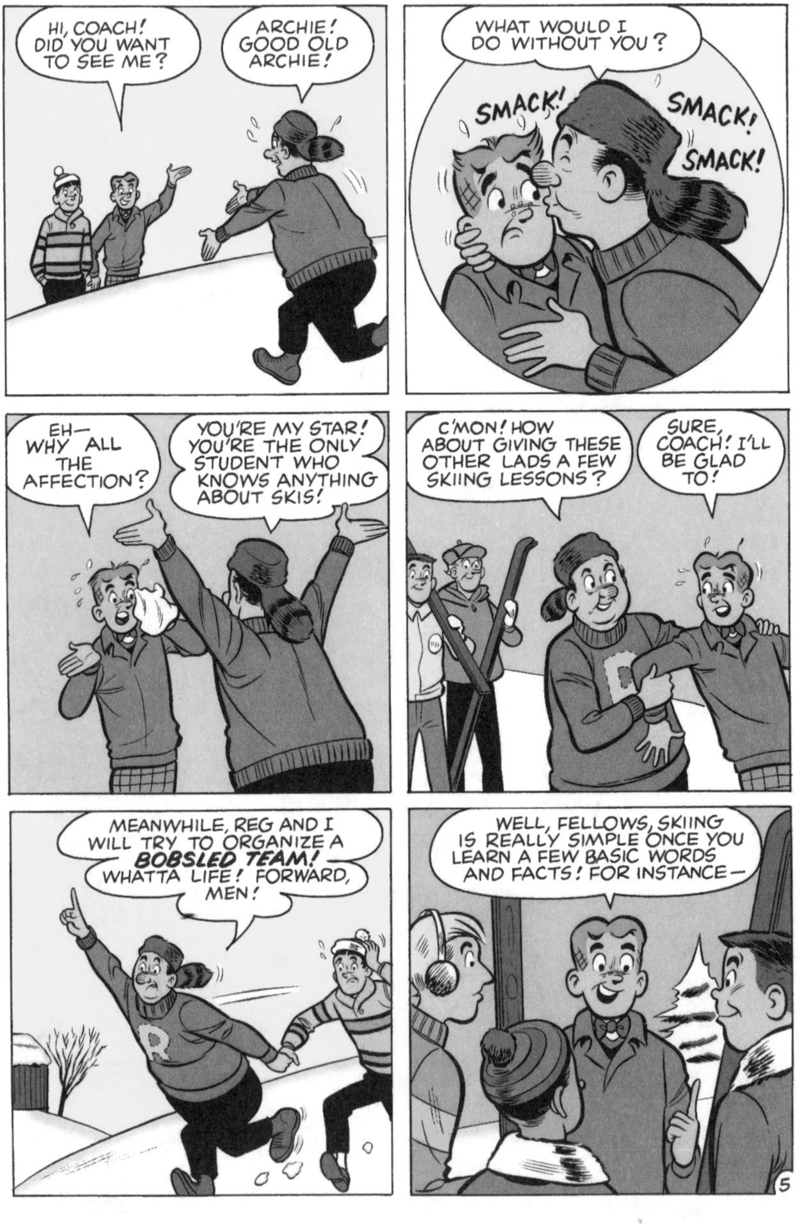
HI, COACH! DID YOU WANT TO SEE ME?
ARCHIE! GOOD OLD ARCHIE!
WHAT WOULD I DO WITHOUT YOU?
SMACK!
SMACK!
SMACK!
EH— WHY ALL THE AFFECTION?
YOU'RE MY STAR! YOU'RE THE ONLY STUDENT WHO KNOWS ANYTHING ABOUT SKIS!
C'MON! HOW ABOUT GIVING THESE OTHER LADS A FEW SKIING LESSONS?
SURE, COACH! I'LL BE GLAD TO!
MEANWHILE, REG AND I WILL TRY TO ORGANIZE A BOBSLED TEAM! WHATTA LIFE! FORWARD, MEN!
WELL, FELLOWS, SKIING IS REALLY SIMPLE ONCE YOU LEARN A FEW BASIC WORDS AND FACTS! FOR INSTANCE—
5

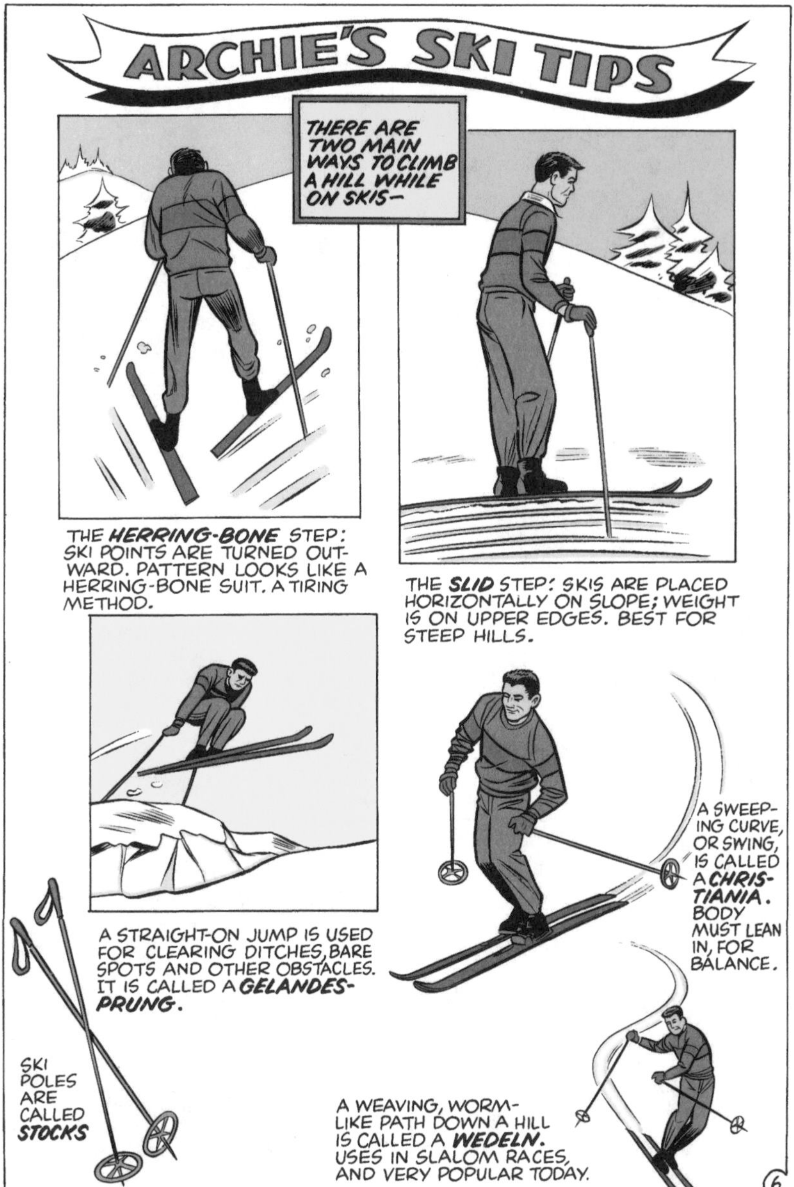
ARCHIE'S SKI TIPS
THERE ARE TWO MAIN WAYS TO CLIMB A HILL WHILE ON SKIS—
THE HERRING-BONE STEP: SKI POINTS ARE TURNED OUTWARD. PATTERN LOOKS LIKE A HERRING-BONE SUIT. A TIRING METHOD.
THE SLID STEP: SKIS ARE PLACED HORIZONTALLY ON SLOPE; WEIGHT IS ON UPPER EDGES. BEST FOR STEEP HILLS.
A STRAIGHT-ON JUMP IS USED FOR CLEARING DITCHES, BARE SPOTS AND OTHER OBSTACLES. IT IS CALLED A GELANDESPRUNG.
A SWEEPING CURVE, OR SWING, IS CALLED A CHRISTIANIA. BODY MUST LEAN IN, FOR BALANCE.
SKI POLES ARE CALLED STOCKS
A WEAVING, WORM-LIKE PATH DOWN A HILL IS CALLED A WEDELN. USES IN SLALOM RACES, AND VERY POPULAR TODAY.
6

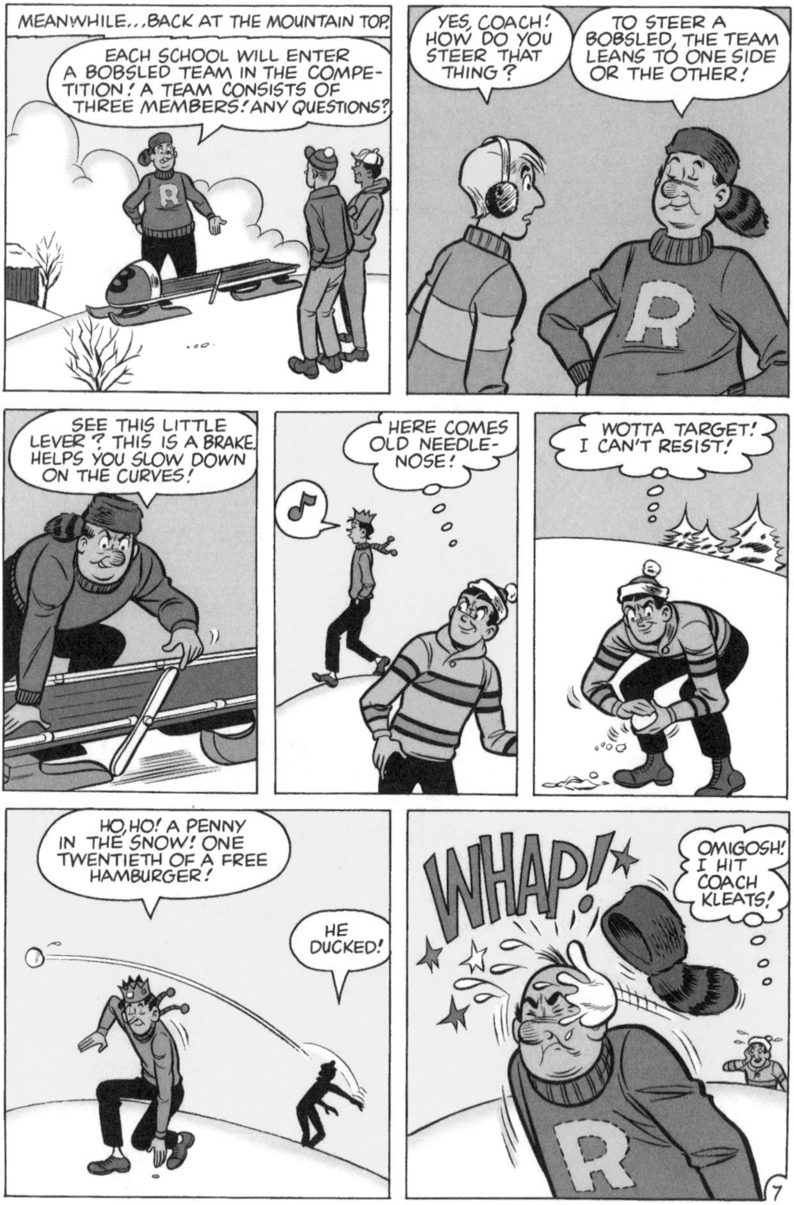
MEANWHILE...BACK AT THE MOUNTAIN TOP.
EACH SCHOOL WILL ENTER A BOBSLED TEAM IN THE COMPETITION! A TEAM CONSISTS OF THREE MEMBERS! ANY QUESTIONS?
YES, COACH! HOW DO YOU STEER THAT THING?
TO STEER A BOBSLED, THE TEAM LEANS TO ONE SIDE OR THE OTHER!
SEE THIS LITTLE LEVER? THIS IS A BRAKE. HELPS YOU SLOW DOWN ON THE CURVES!
HERE COMES OLD NEEDLE-NOSE!
WOTTA TARGET! I CAN'T RESIST!
HO, HO! A PENNY IN THE SNOW! ONE TWENTIETH OF A FREE HAMBURGER!
HE DUCKED!
WHAP!
OMIGOSH! I HIT COACH KLEATS!
7

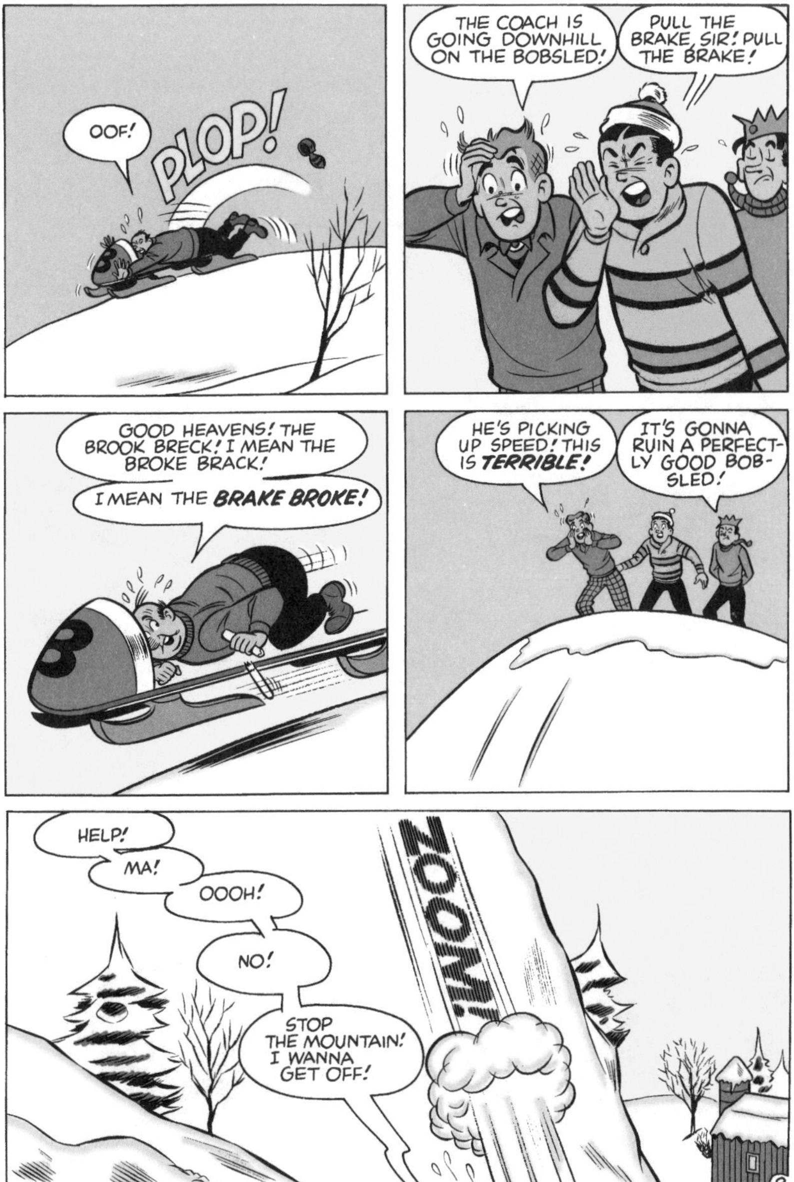
OOF!
PLOP!
THE COACH IS GOING DOWNHILL ON THE BOBSLED!
PULL THE BRAKE, SIR! PULL THE BRAKE!
GOOD HEAVENS! THE BROOK BRECK! I MEAN THE BROKE BRACK!
I MEAN THE **BRAKE BROKE!**
HE'S PICKING UP SPEED! THIS IS **TERRIBLE!**
IT'S GONNA RUIN A PERFECTLY GOOD BOBSLED!
HELP!
MA!
OOOH!
NO!
STOP THE MOUNTAIN! I WANNA GET OFF!
ZOOM!
8

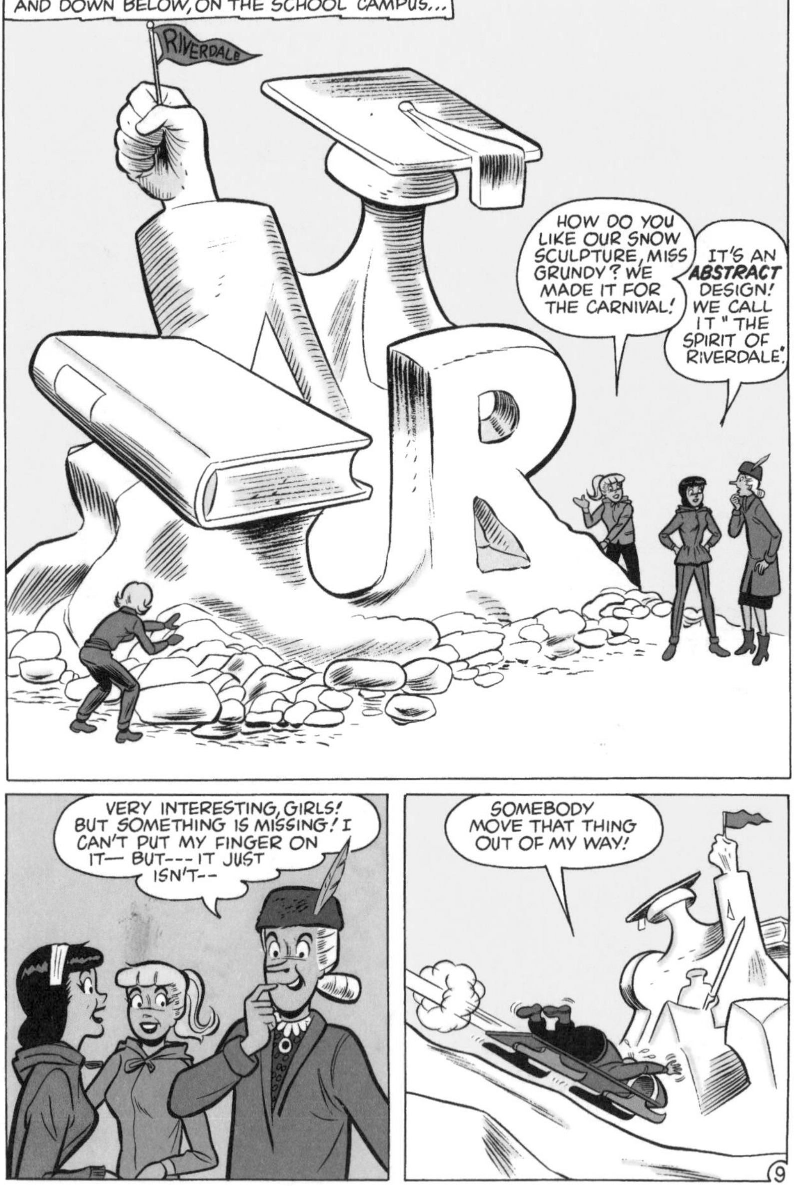
AND DOWN BELOW, ON THE SCHOOL CAMPUS...
RIVERDALE
HOW DO YOU LIKE OUR SNOW SCULPTURE, MISS GRUNDY? WE MADE IT FOR THE CARNIVAL!
IT'S AN **ABSTRACT** DESIGN! WE CALL IT "THE SPIRIT OF RIVERDALE".
VERY INTERESTING, GIRLS! BUT SOMETHING IS MISSING! I CAN'T PUT MY FINGER ON IT— BUT--- IT JUST ISN'T--
SOMEBODY MOVE THAT THING OUT OF MY WAY!
9

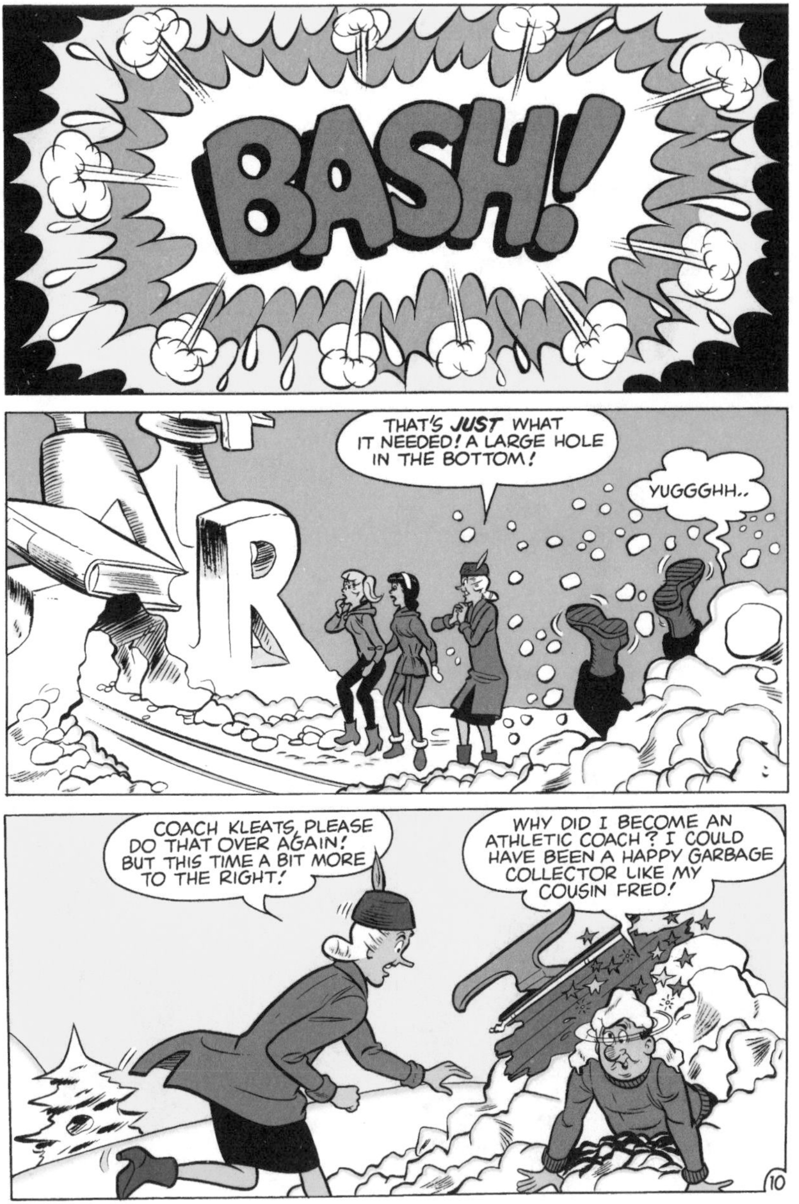
BASH!
THAT'S JUST WHAT IT NEEDED! A LARGE HOLE IN THE BOTTOM!
YUGGGHH..
COACH KLEATS, PLEASE DO THAT OVER AGAIN! BUT THIS TIME A BIT MORE TO THE RIGHT!
WHY DID I BECOME AN ATHLETIC COACH? I COULD HAVE BEEN A HAPPY GARBAGE COLLECTOR LIKE MY COUSIN FRED!
10

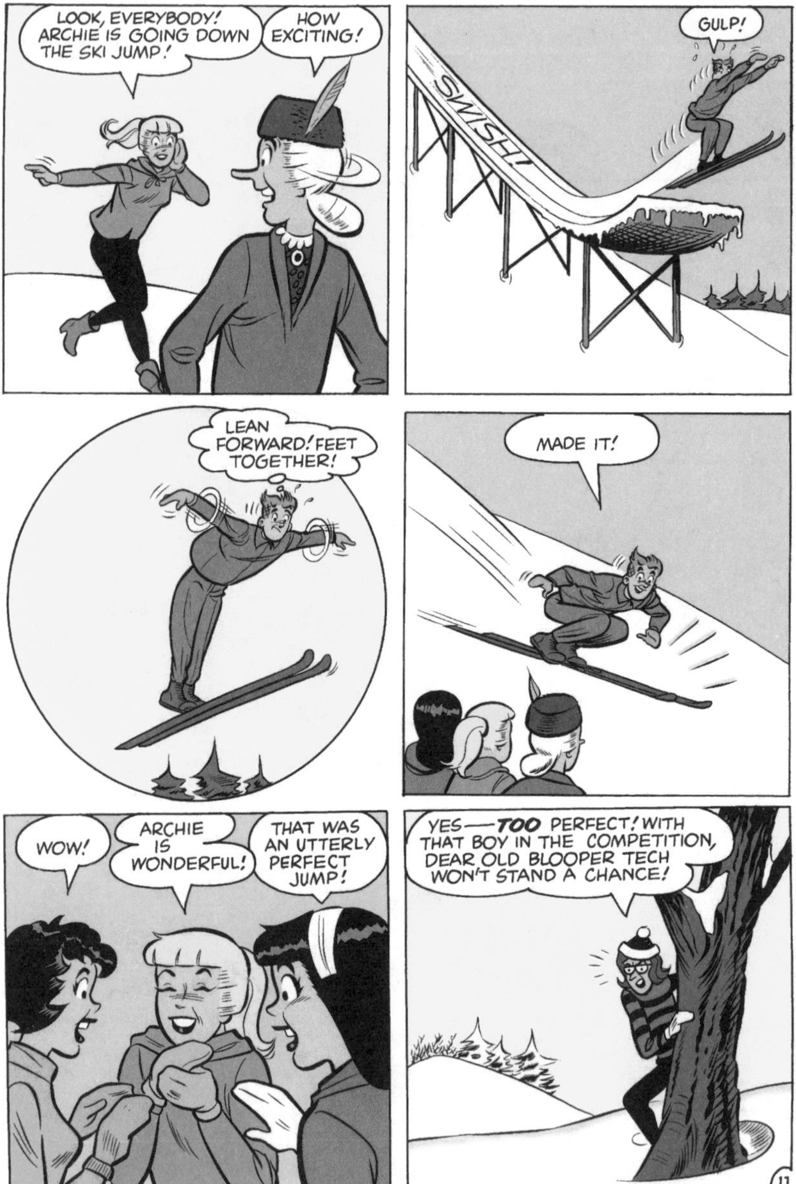
LOOK, EVERYBODY! ARCHIE IS GOING DOWN THE SKI JUMP!
HOW EXCITING!
GULP!
SWISH!
LEAN FORWARD! FEET TOGETHER!
MADE IT!
WOW!
ARCHIE IS WONDERFUL!
THAT WAS AN UTTERLY PERFECT JUMP!
YES—TOO PERFECT! WITH THAT BOY IN THE COMPETITION, DEAR OLD BLOOPER TECH WON'T STAND A CHANCE!
11

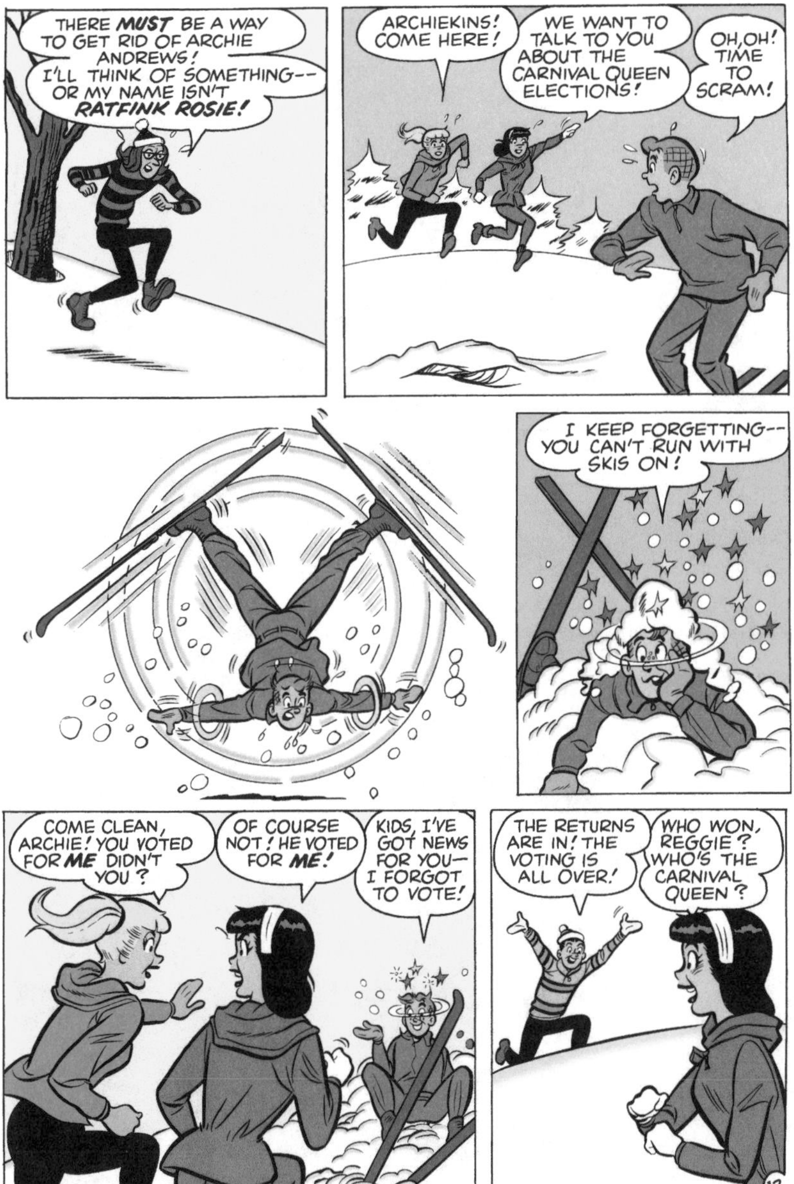
THERE MUST BE A WAY TO GET RID OF ARCHIE ANDREWS!
I'LL THINK OF SOMETHING-- OR MY NAME ISN'T RATFINK ROSIE!
ARCHIEKINS! COME HERE!
WE WANT TO TALK TO YOU ABOUT THE CARNIVAL QUEEN ELECTIONS!
OH,OH! TIME TO SCRAM!
I KEEP FORGETTING-- YOU CAN'T RUN WITH SKIS ON!
COME CLEAN, ARCHIE! YOU VOTED FOR ME DIDN'T YOU?
OF COURSE NOT! HE VOTED FOR ME!
KIDS, I'VE GOT NEWS FOR YOU— I FORGOT TO VOTE!
THE RETURNS ARE IN! THE VOTING IS ALL OVER!
WHO WON, REGGIE? WHO'S THE CARNIVAL QUEEN?
12

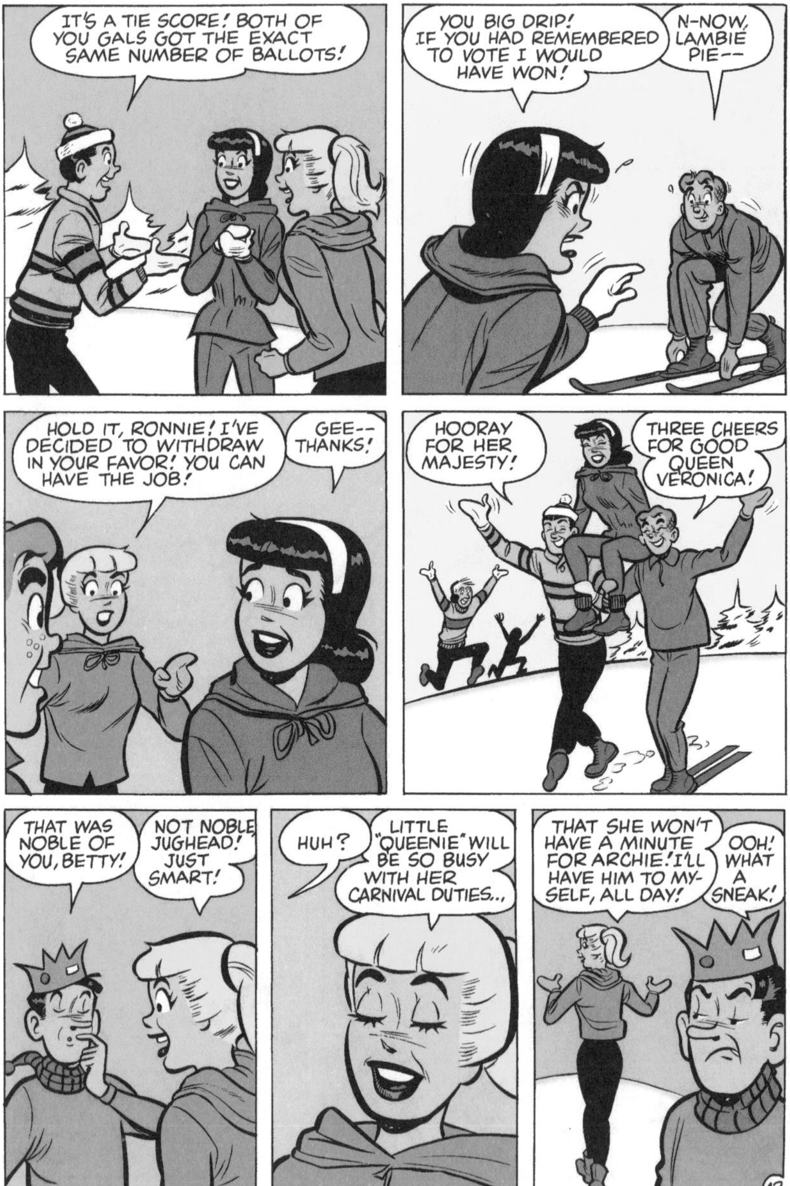
IT'S A TIE SCORE! BOTH OF YOU GALS GOT THE EXACT SAME NUMBER OF BALLOTS!
YOU BIG DRIP! IF YOU HAD REMEMBERED TO VOTE I WOULD HAVE WON!
N-NOW, LAMBIE PIE--
HOLD IT, RONNIE! I'VE DECIDED TO WITHDRAW IN YOUR FAVOR! YOU CAN HAVE THE JOB!
GEE--THANKS!
HOORAY FOR HER MAJESTY!
THREE CHEERS FOR GOOD QUEEN VERONICA!
THAT WAS NOBLE OF YOU, BETTY!
NOT NOBLE, JUGHEAD! JUST SMART!
HUH?
LITTLE "QUEENIE" WILL BE SO BUSY WITH HER CARNIVAL DUTIES..,
THAT SHE WON'T HAVE A MINUTE FOR ARCHIE! I'LL HAVE HIM TO MY-SELF, ALL DAY!
OOH! WHAT A SNEAK!
13

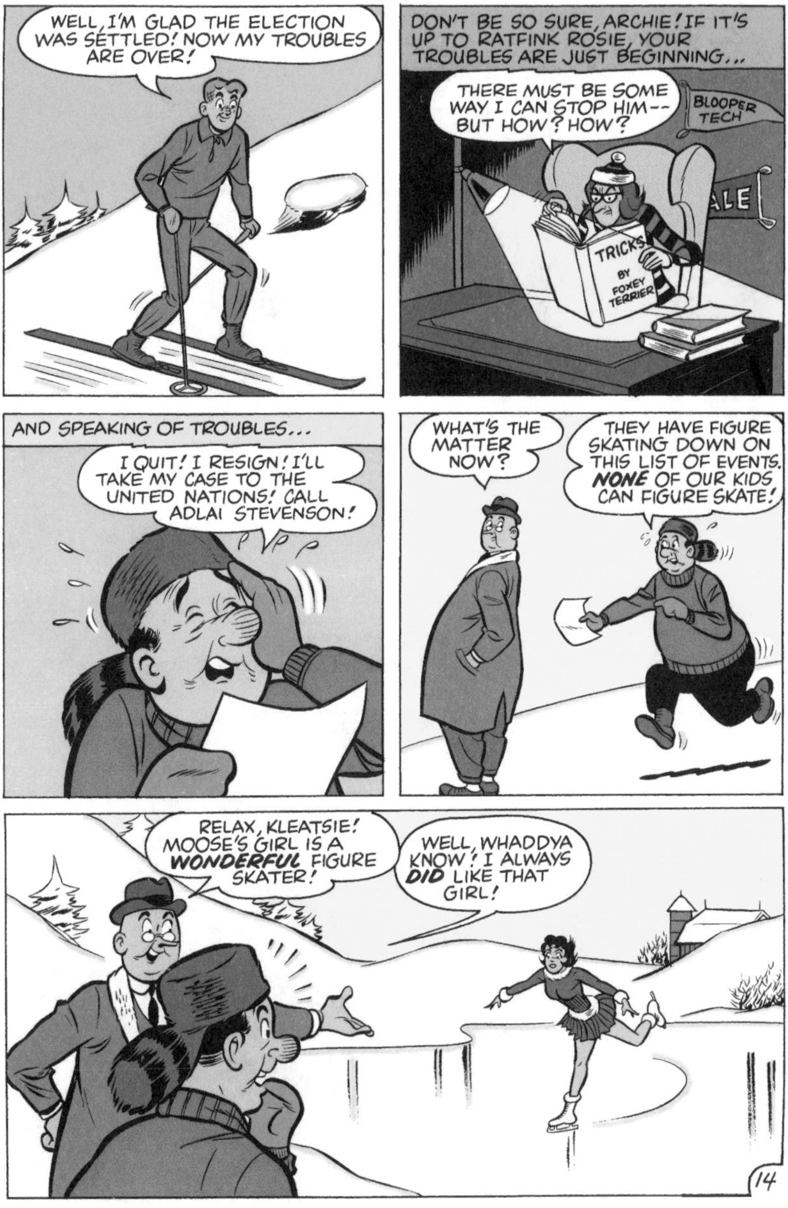
WELL, I'M GLAD THE ELECTION WAS SETTLED! NOW MY TROUBLES ARE OVER!
DON'T BE SO SURE, ARCHIE! IF IT'S UP TO RATFINK ROSIE, YOUR TROUBLES ARE JUST BEGINNING...
THERE MUST BE SOME WAY I CAN STOP HIM-- BUT HOW? HOW?
BLOOPER TECH
ALE
TRICKS BY FOXEY TERRIER
AND SPEAKING OF TROUBLES...
I QUIT! I RESIGN! I'LL TAKE MY CASE TO THE UNITED NATIONS! CALL ADLAI STEVENSON!
WHAT'S THE MATTER NOW?
THEY HAVE FIGURE SKATING DOWN ON THIS LIST OF EVENTS. NONE OF OUR KIDS CAN FIGURE SKATE!
RELAX, KLEATSIE! MOOSE'S GIRL IS A WONDERFUL FIGURE SKATER!
WELL, WHADDYA KNOW! I ALWAYS DID LIKE THAT GIRL!
14

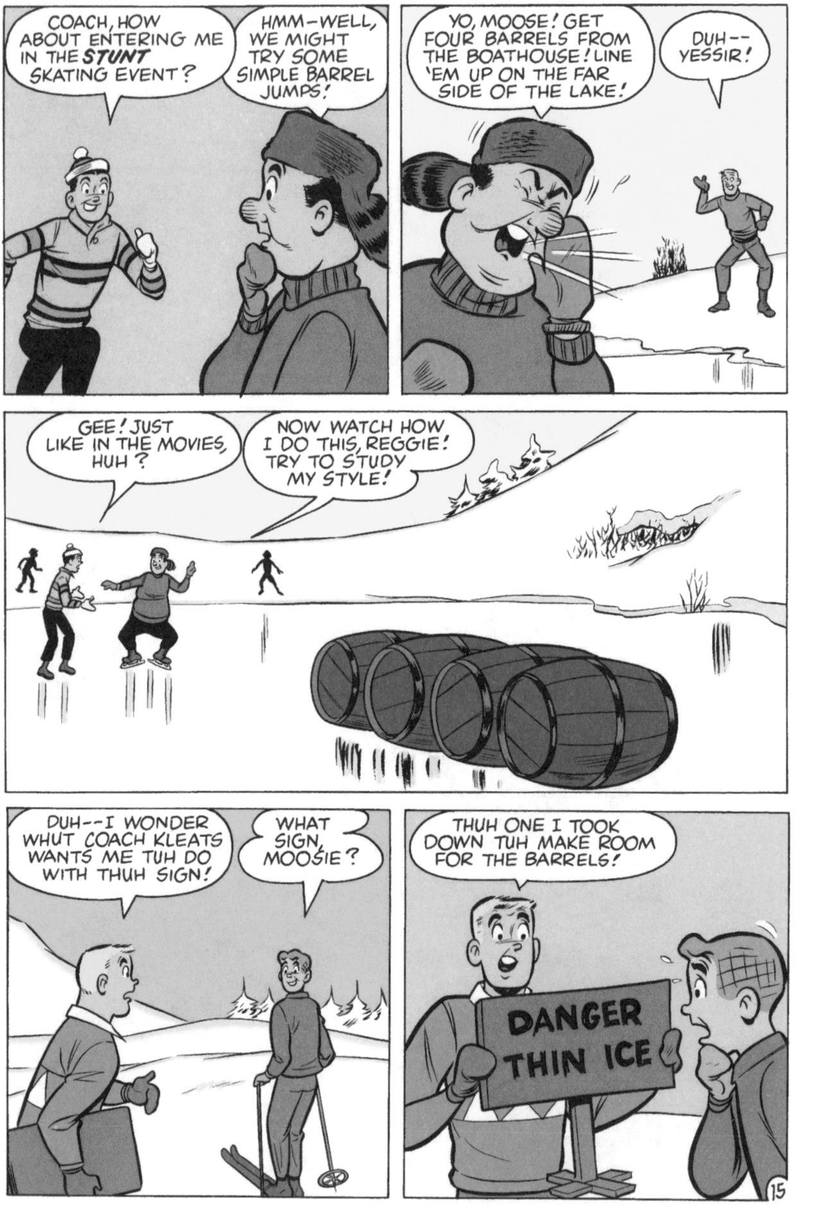
COACH, HOW ABOUT ENTERING ME IN THE STUNT SKATING EVENT?
HMM-WELL, WE MIGHT TRY SOME SIMPLE BARREL JUMPS!
YO, MOOSE! GET FOUR BARRELS FROM THE BOATHOUSE! LINE 'EM UP ON THE FAR SIDE OF THE LAKE!
DUH-- YESSIR!
GEE! JUST LIKE IN THE MOVIES, HUH?
NOW WATCH HOW I DO THIS, REGGIE! TRY TO STUDY MY STYLE!
DUH--I WONDER WHUT COACH KLEATS WANTS ME TUH DO WITH THUH SIGN!
WHAT SIGN, MOOSIE?
THUH ONE I TOOK DOWN TUH MAKE ROOM FOR THE BARRELS!
DANGER THIN ICE
15

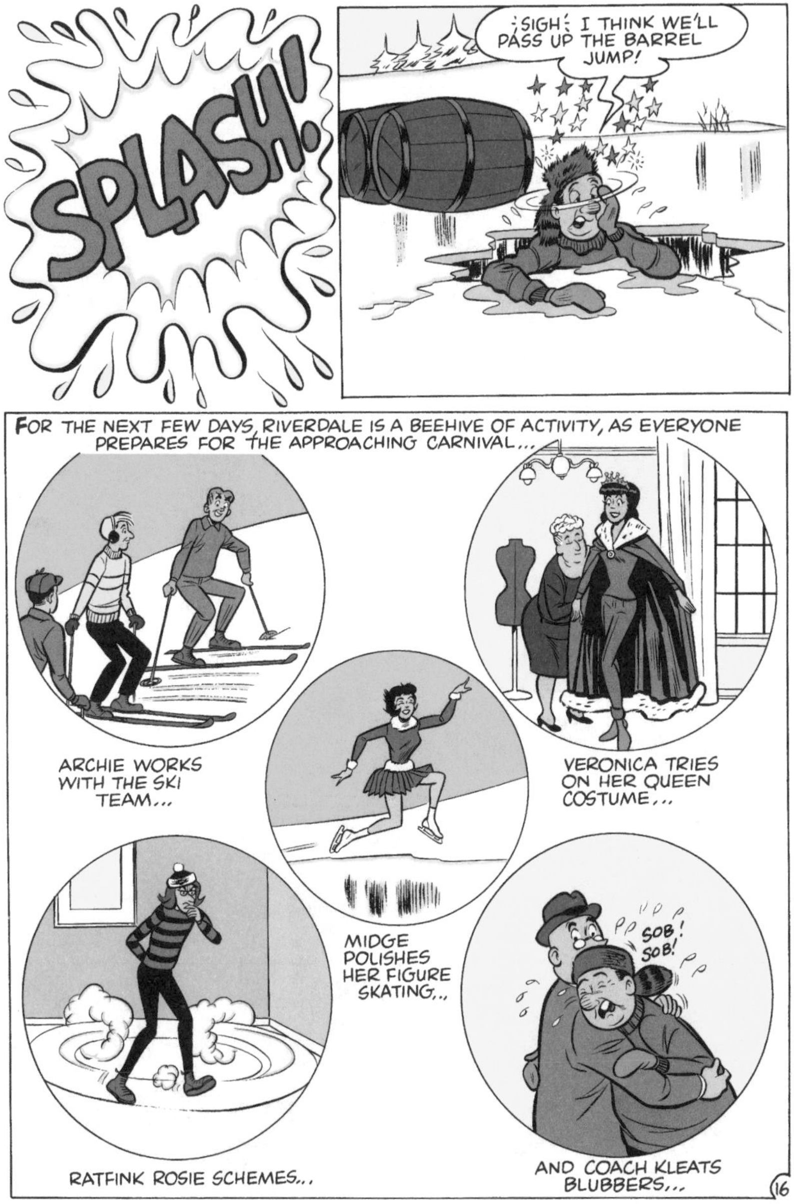
SPLASH!
:SIGH: I THINK WE'LL PASS UP THE BARREL JUMP!
FOR THE NEXT FEW DAYS, RIVERDALE IS A BEEHIVE OF ACTIVITY, AS EVERYONE PREPARES FOR THE APPROACHING CARNIVAL...
ARCHIE WORKS WITH THE SKI TEAM...
VERONICA TRIES ON HER QUEEN COSTUME...
MIDGE POLISHES HER FIGURE SKATING...
RATFINK ROSIE SCHEMES...
SOB! SOB!
AND COACH KLEATS BLUBBERS...
16

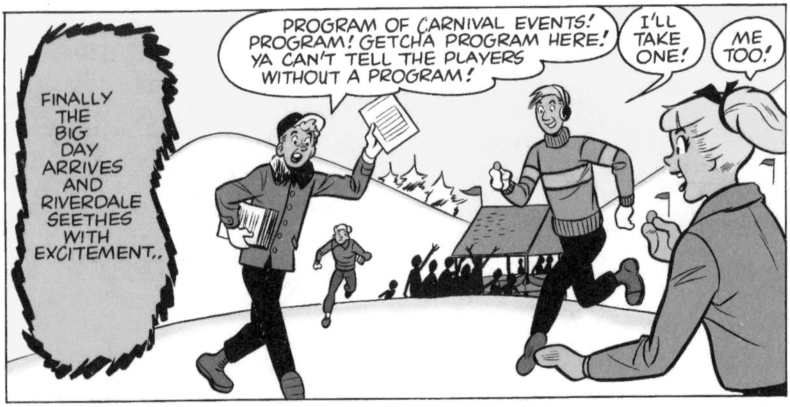
FINALLY THE BIG DAY ARRIVES AND RIVERDALE SEETHES WITH EXCITEMENT..
PROGRAM OF CARNIVAL EVENTS! PROGRAM! GETCHA PROGRAM HERE! YA CAN'T TELL THE PLAYERS WITHOUT A PROGRAM!
I'LL TAKE ONE!
ME TOO!

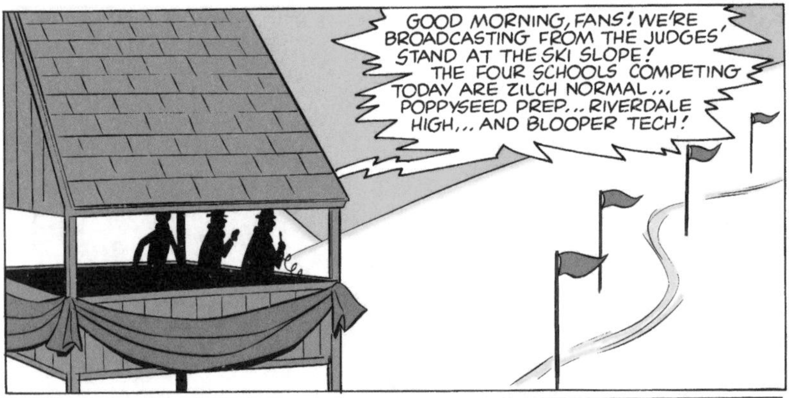
GOOD MORNING, FANS! WE'RE BROADCASTING FROM THE JUDGES' STAND AT THE SKI SLOPE! THE FOUR SCHOOLS COMPETING TODAY ARE ZILCH NORMAL... POPPYSEED PREP... RIVERDALE HIGH... AND BLOOPER TECH!

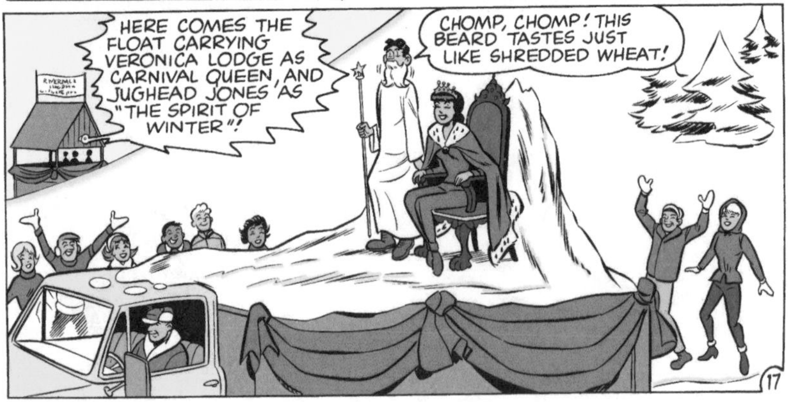
HERE COMES THE FLOAT CARRYING VERONICA LODGE AS CARNIVAL QUEEN, AND JUGHEAD JONES AS "THE SPIRIT OF WINTER"!
CHOMP, CHOMP! THIS BEARD TASTES JUST LIKE SHREDDED WHEAT!
17

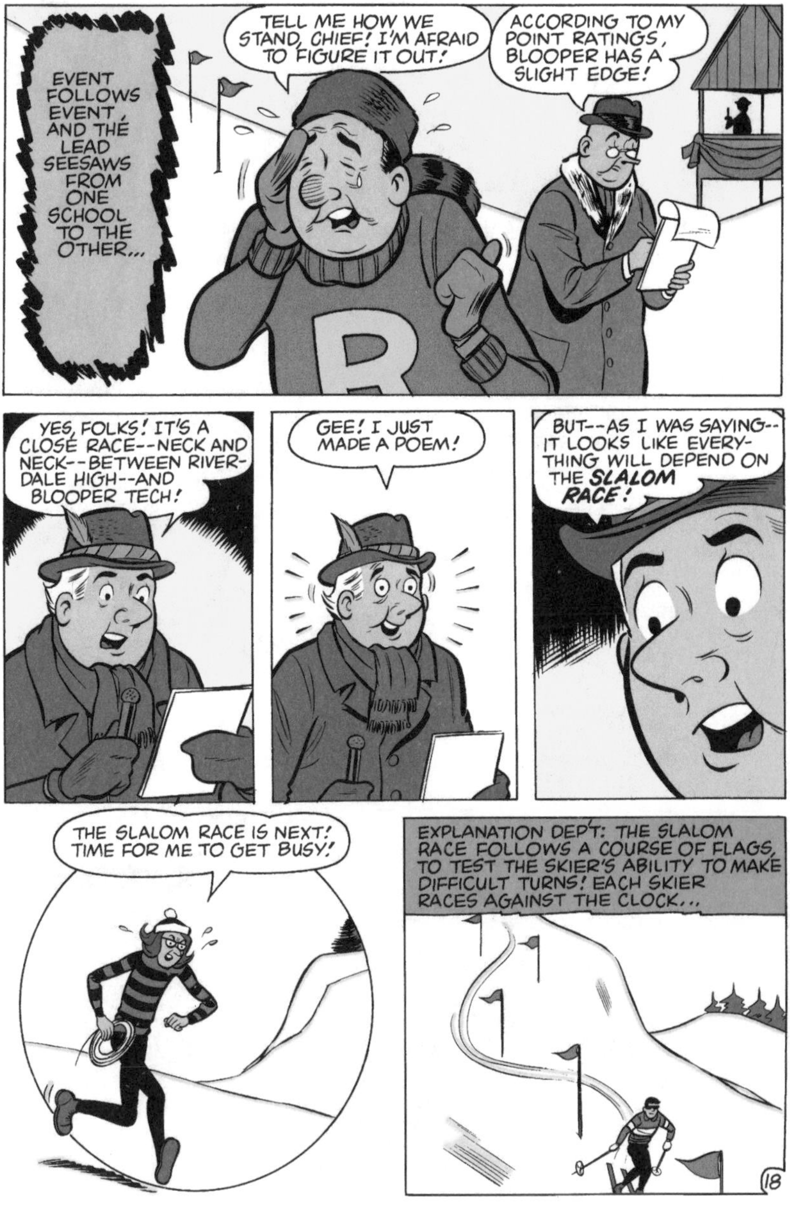
EVENT FOLLOWS EVENT, AND THE LEAD SEESAWS FROM ONE SCHOOL TO THE OTHER...
TELL ME HOW WE STAND, CHIEF! I'M AFRAID TO FIGURE IT OUT!
ACCORDING TO MY POINT RATINGS, BLOOPER HAS A SLIGHT EDGE!
YES, FOLKS! IT'S A CLOSE RACE--NECK AND NECK--BETWEEN RIVERDALE HIGH--AND BLOOPER TECH!
GEE! I JUST MADE A POEM!
BUT--AS I WAS SAYING--IT LOOKS LIKE EVERYTHING WILL DEPEND ON THE SLALOM RACE!
THE SLALOM RACE IS NEXT! TIME FOR ME TO GET BUSY!
EXPLANATION DEP'T: THE SLALOM RACE FOLLOWS A COURSE OF FLAGS, TO TEST THE SKIER'S ABILITY TO MAKE DIFFICULT TURNS! EACH SKIER RACES AGAINST THE CLOCK...
18

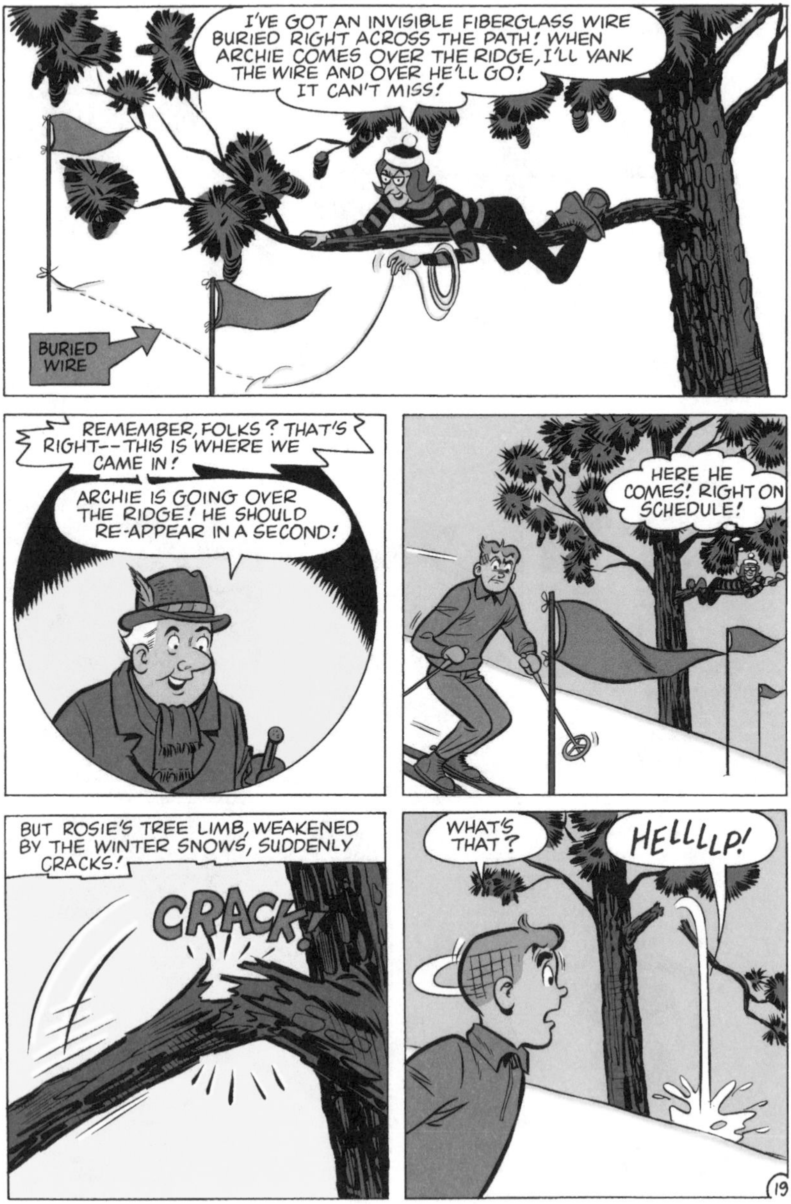
I'VE GOT AN INVISIBLE FIBERGLASS WIRE BURIED RIGHT ACROSS THE PATH! WHEN ARCHIE COMES OVER THE RIDGE, I'LL YANK THE WIRE AND OVER HE'LL GO! IT CAN'T MISS!
BURIED WIRE
REMEMBER, FOLKS? THAT'S RIGHT--THIS IS WHERE WE CAME IN!
ARCHIE IS GOING OVER THE RIDGE! HE SHOULD RE-APPEAR IN A SECOND!
HERE HE COMES! RIGHT ON SCHEDULE!
BUT ROSIE'S TREE LIMB, WEAKENED BY THE WINTER SNOWS, SUDDENLY CRACKS!
CRACK!
WHAT'S THAT?
HELLLLP!
19

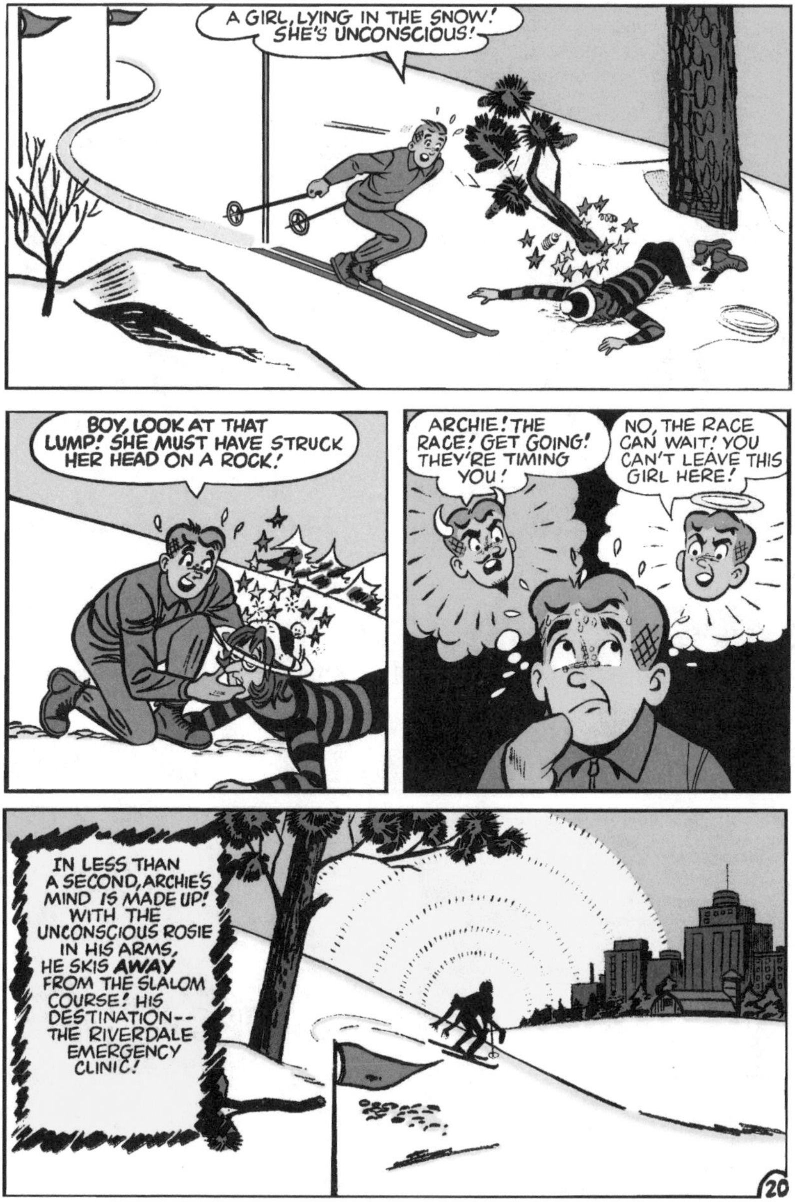
A GIRL, LYING IN THE SNOW! SHE'S UNCONSCIOUS!
BOY, LOOK AT THAT LUMP! SHE MUST HAVE STRUCK HER HEAD ON A ROCK!
ARCHIE! THE RACE! GET GOING! THEY'RE TIMING YOU!
NO, THE RACE CAN WAIT! YOU CAN'T LEAVE THIS GIRL HERE!
IN LESS THAN A SECOND, ARCHIE'S MIND IS MADE UP! WITH THE UNCONSCIOUS ROSIE IN HIS ARMS, HE SKIS AWAY FROM THE SLALOM COURSE! HIS DESTINATION-- THE RIVERDALE EMERGENCY CLINIC!
20

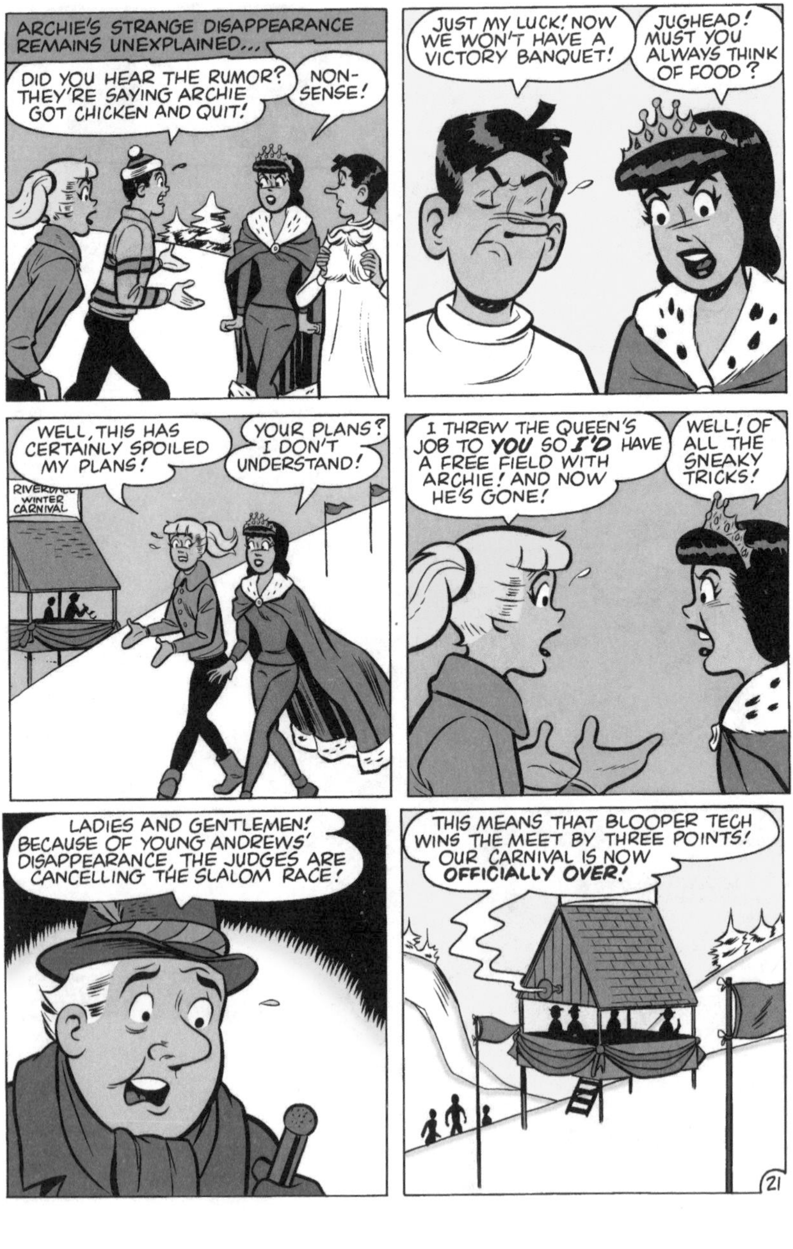

ARCHIE'S STRANGE DISAPPEARANCE REMAINS UNEXPLAINED...
DID YOU HEAR THE RUMOR? THEY'RE SAYING ARCHIE GOT CHICKEN AND QUIT!
NON-SENSE!
JUST MY LUCK! NOW WE WON'T HAVE A VICTORY BANQUET!
JUGHEAD! MUST YOU ALWAYS THINK OF FOOD?
WELL, THIS HAS CERTAINLY SPOILED MY PLANS!
YOUR PLANS? I DON'T UNDERSTAND!
RIVERDALE WINTER CARNIVAL
I THREW THE QUEEN'S JOB TO YOU SO I'D HAVE A FREE FIELD WITH ARCHIE! AND NOW HE'S GONE!
WELL! OF ALL THE SNEAKY TRICKS!
LADIES AND GENTLEMEN! BECAUSE OF YOUNG ANDREWS' DISAPPEARANCE, THE JUDGES ARE CANCELLING THE SLALOM RACE!
THIS MEANS THAT BLOOPER TECH WINS THE MEET BY THREE POINTS! OUR CARNIVAL IS NOW OFFICIALLY OVER!
21

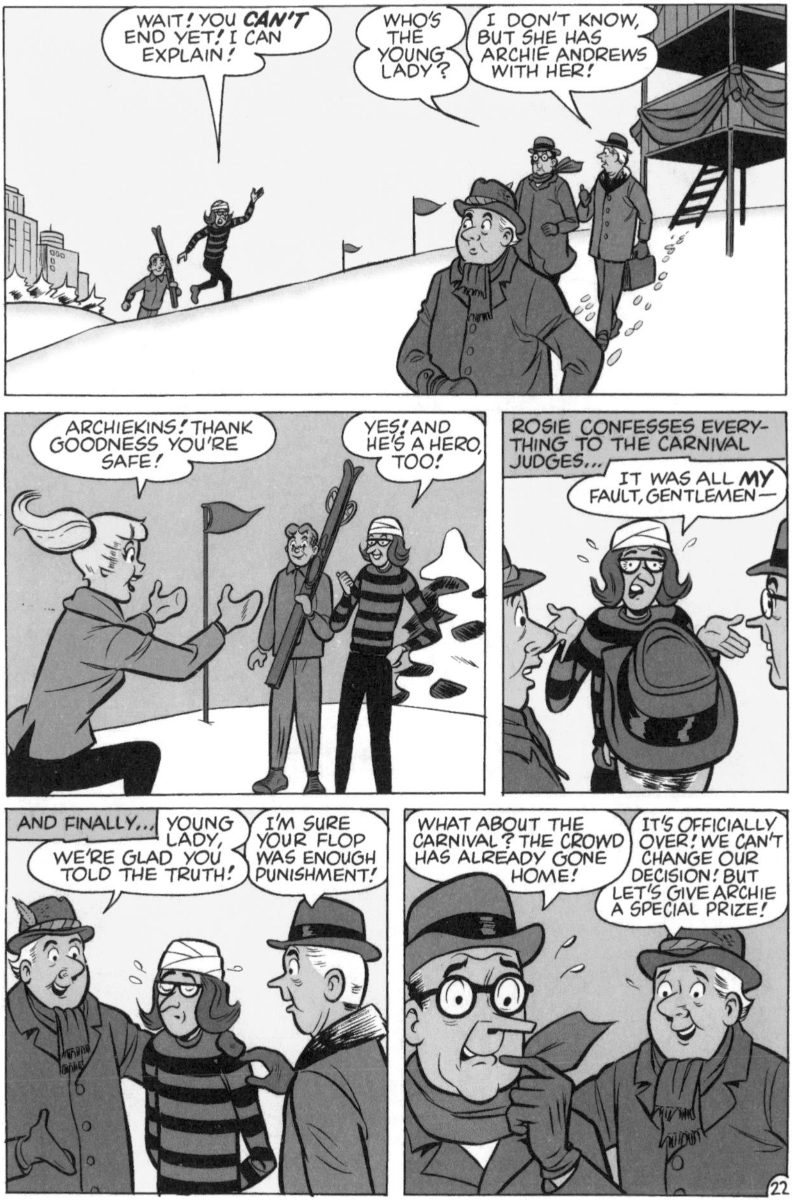
WAIT! YOU CAN'T END YET! I CAN EXPLAIN!
WHO'S THE YOUNG LADY?
I DON'T KNOW, BUT SHE HAS ARCHIE ANDREWS WITH HER!
ARCHIEKINS! THANK GOODNESS YOU'RE SAFE!
YES! AND HE'S A HERO, TOO!
ROSIE CONFESSES EVERYTHING TO THE CARNIVAL JUDGES...
IT WAS ALL MY FAULT, GENTLEMEN—
AND FINALLY...
YOUNG LADY, WE'RE GLAD YOU TOLD THE TRUTH!
I'M SURE YOUR FLOP WAS ENOUGH PUNISHMENT!
WHAT ABOUT THE CARNIVAL? THE CROWD HAS ALREADY GONE HOME!
IT'S OFFICIALLY OVER! WE CAN'T CHANGE OUR DECISION! BUT LET'S GIVE ARCHIE A SPECIAL PRIZE!
22

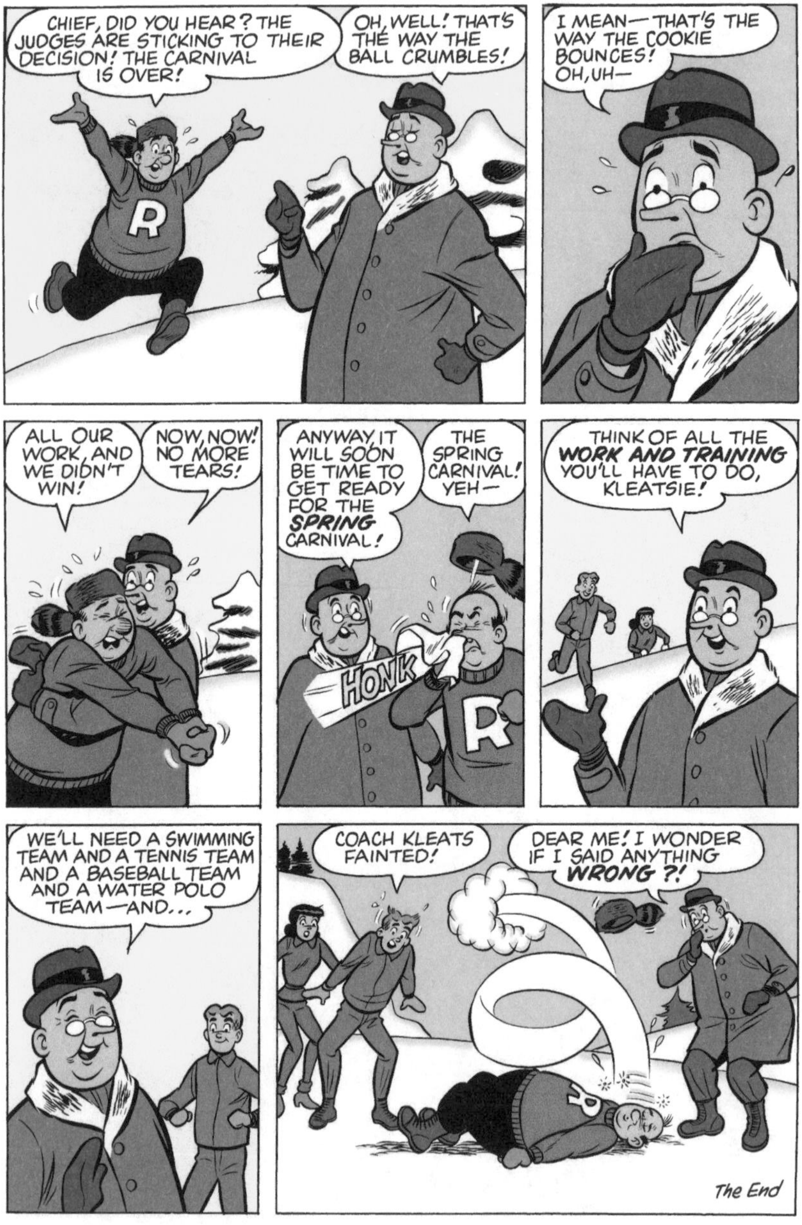
CHIEF, DID YOU HEAR? THE JUDGES ARE STICKING TO THEIR DECISION! THE CARNIVAL IS OVER!
OH, WELL! THAT'S THE WAY THE BALL CRUMBLES!
I MEAN— THAT'S THE WAY THE COOKIE BOUNCES! OH, UH—
ALL OUR WORK, AND WE DIDN'T WIN!
NOW, NOW! NO MORE TEARS!
ANYWAY, IT WILL SOON BE TIME TO GET READY FOR THE SPRING CARNIVAL!
HONK
THE SPRING CARNIVAL! YEH—
THINK OF ALL THE WORK AND TRAINING YOU'LL HAVE TO DO, KLEATSIE!
WE'LL NEED A SWIMMING TEAM AND A TENNIS TEAM AND A BASEBALL TEAM AND A WATER POLO TEAM—AND...
COACH KLEATS FAINTED!
DEAR ME! I WONDER IF I SAID ANYTHING WRONG ?!
The End

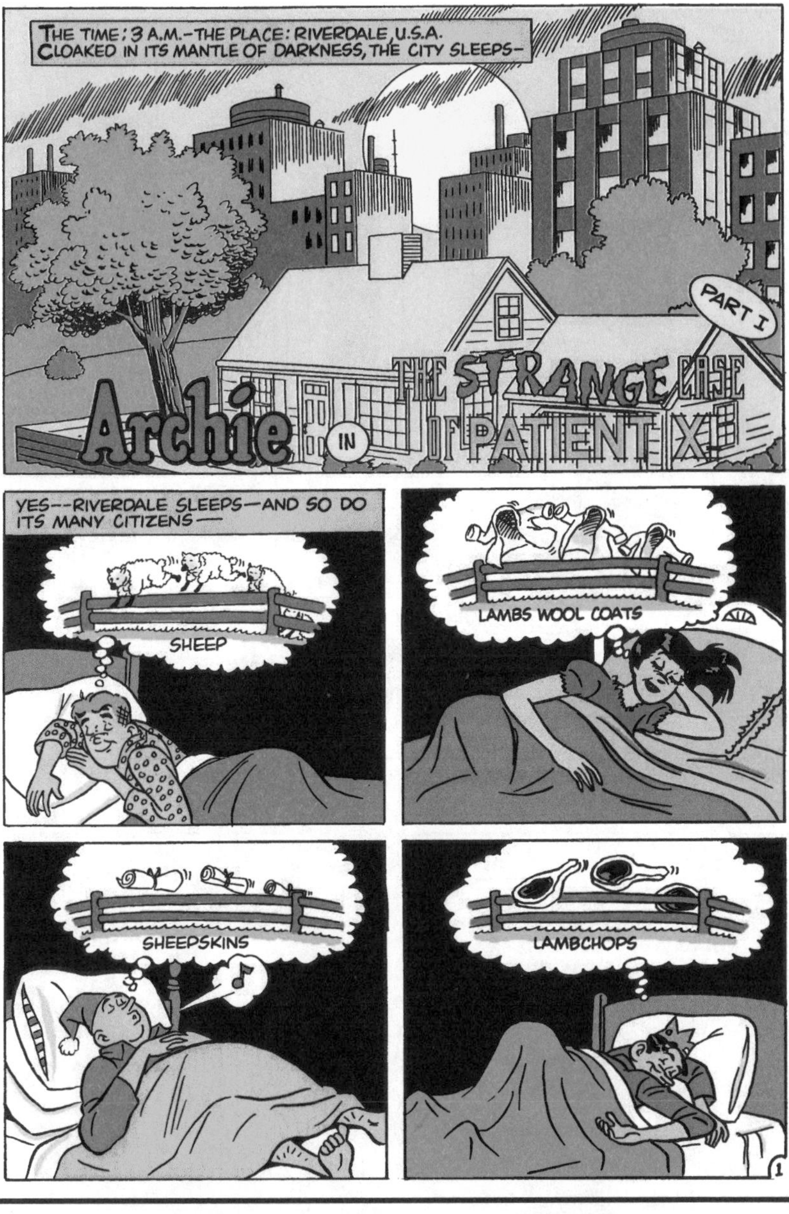
THE TIME: 3 A.M.-THE PLACE: RIVERDALE, U.S.A.
CLOAKED IN ITS MANTLE OF DARKNESS, THE CITY SLEEPS-
PART I
Archie IN THE STRANGE CASE OF PATIENT X!
YES--RIVERDALE SLEEPS—AND SO DO ITS MANY CITIZENS—
SHEEP
LAMBS WOOL COATS
SHEEPSKINS
LAMBCHOPS
1

Story: George Gladir Pencils: Bob White
Inks & Letters: Marty Epp Colors: Barry Grossman

Originally printed in LIFE WITH ARCHIE #27, May 1964

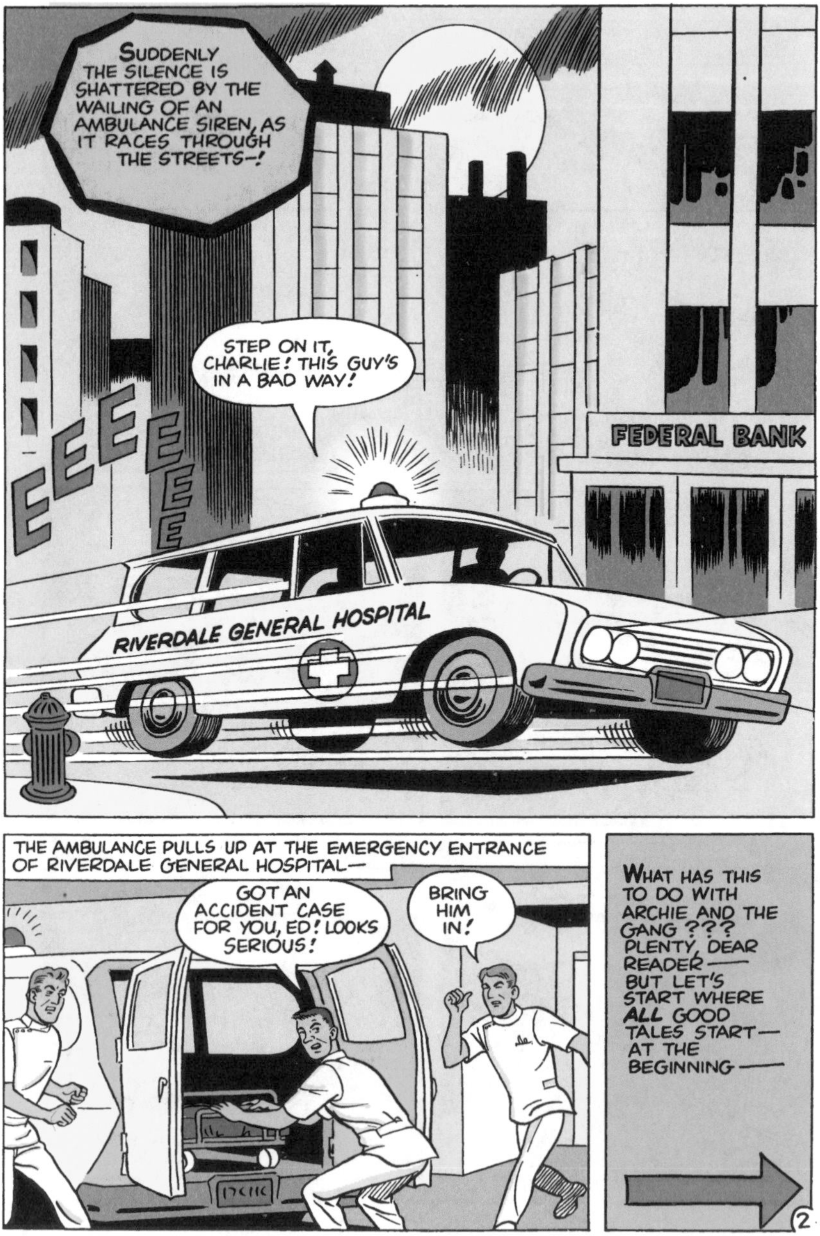
SUDDENLY THE SILENCE IS SHATTERED BY THE WAILING OF AN AMBULANCE SIREN, AS IT RACES THROUGH THE STREETS—!
EEEEEEE
STEP ON IT, CHARLIE! THIS GUY'S IN A BAD WAY!
FEDERAL BANK
RIVERDALE GENERAL HOSPITAL
THE AMBULANCE PULLS UP AT THE EMERGENCY ENTRANCE OF RIVERDALE GENERAL HOSPITAL—
GOT AN ACCIDENT CASE FOR YOU, ED! LOOKS SERIOUS!
BRING HIM IN!
WHAT HAS THIS TO DO WITH ARCHIE AND THE GANG ??? PLENTY, DEAR READER— BUT LET'S START WHERE ***ALL*** GOOD TALES START— AT THE BEGINNING——
2

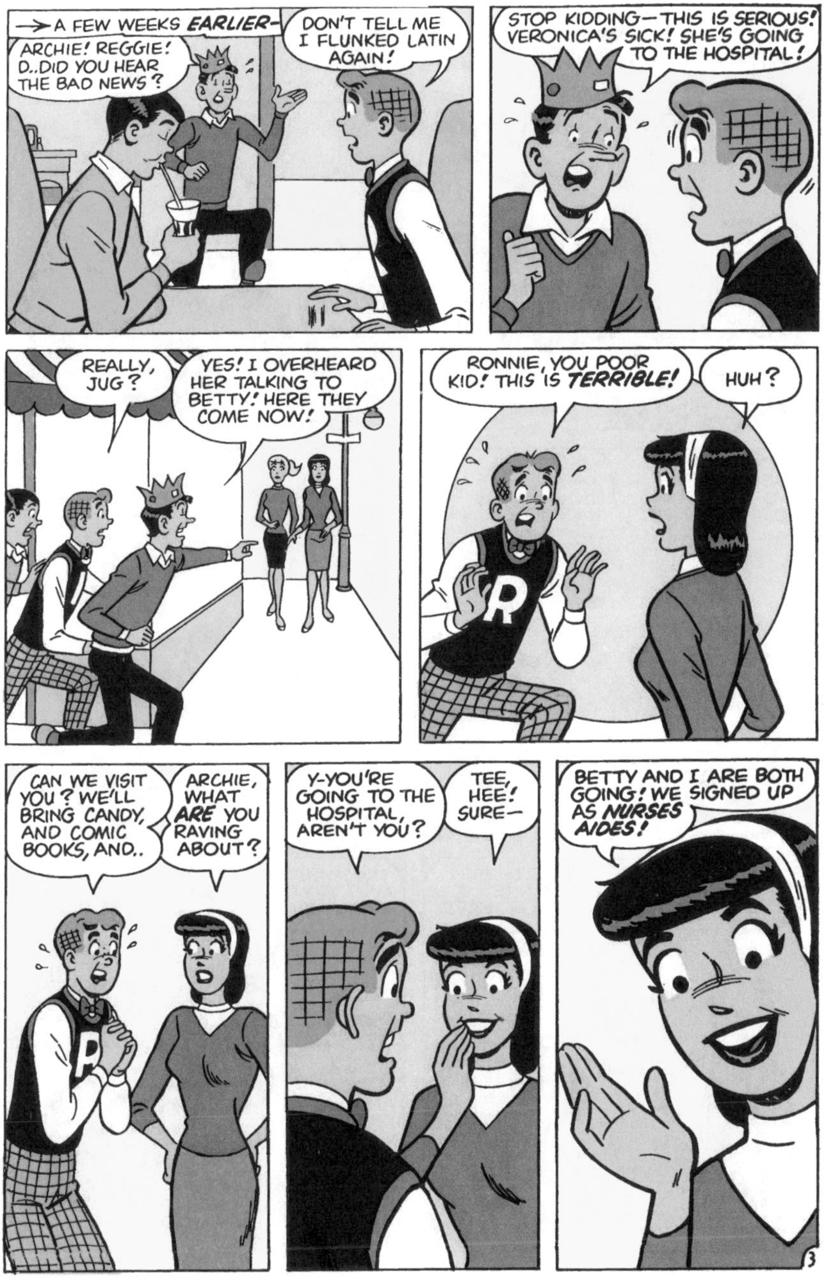
→ A FEW WEEKS EARLIER-
ARCHIE! REGGIE! D..DID YOU HEAR THE BAD NEWS?
DON'T TELL ME I FLUNKED LATIN AGAIN!
STOP KIDDING—THIS IS SERIOUS! VERONICA'S SICK! SHE'S GOING TO THE HOSPITAL!
REALLY, JUG?
YES! I OVERHEARD HER TALKING TO BETTY! HERE THEY COME NOW!
RONNIE, YOU POOR KID! THIS IS TERRIBLE!
HUH?
CAN WE VISIT YOU? WE'LL BRING CANDY, AND COMIC BOOKS, AND..
ARCHIE, WHAT ARE YOU RAVING ABOUT?
Y-YOU'RE GOING TO THE HOSPITAL, AREN'T YOU?
TEE, HEE! SURE—
BETTY AND I ARE BOTH GOING! WE SIGNED UP AS NURSES AIDES!
3

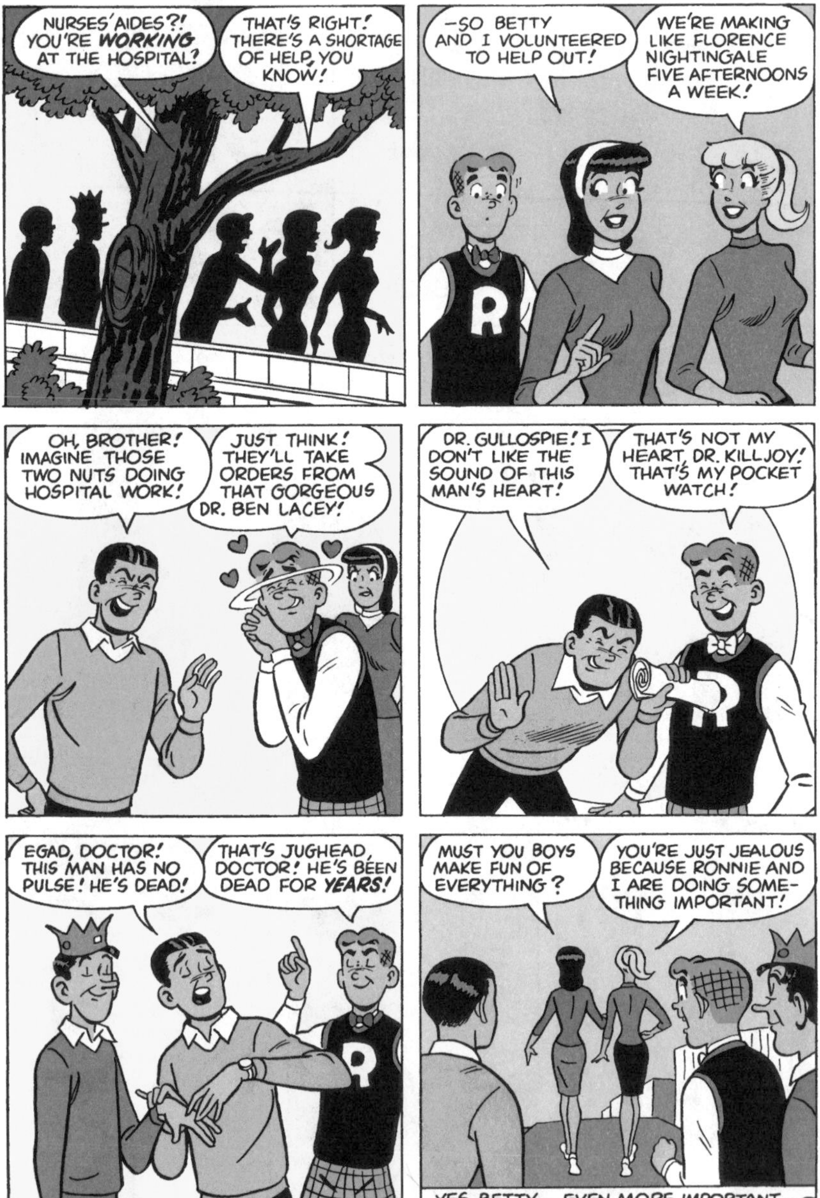
NURSES' AIDES?! YOU'RE WORKING AT THE HOSPITAL?
THAT'S RIGHT! THERE'S A SHORTAGE OF HELP, YOU KNOW!
—SO BETTY AND I VOLUNTEERED TO HELP OUT!
WE'RE MAKING LIKE FLORENCE NIGHTINGALE FIVE AFTERNOONS A WEEK!
OH, BROTHER! IMAGINE THOSE TWO NUTS DOING HOSPITAL WORK!
JUST THINK! THEY'LL TAKE ORDERS FROM THAT GORGEOUS DR. BEN LACEY!
DR. GULLOSPIE! I DON'T LIKE THE SOUND OF THIS MAN'S HEART!
THAT'S NOT MY HEART, DR. KILLJOY! THAT'S MY POCKET WATCH!
EGAD, DOCTOR! THIS MAN HAS NO PULSE! HE'S DEAD!
THAT'S JUGHEAD, DOCTOR! HE'S BEEN DEAD FOR YEARS!
MUST YOU BOYS MAKE FUN OF EVERYTHING?
YOU'RE JUST JEALOUS BECAUSE RONNIE AND I ARE DOING SOMETHING IMPORTANT!
YES, BETTY... EVEN MORE IMPORTANT THAN YOU THINK!
4

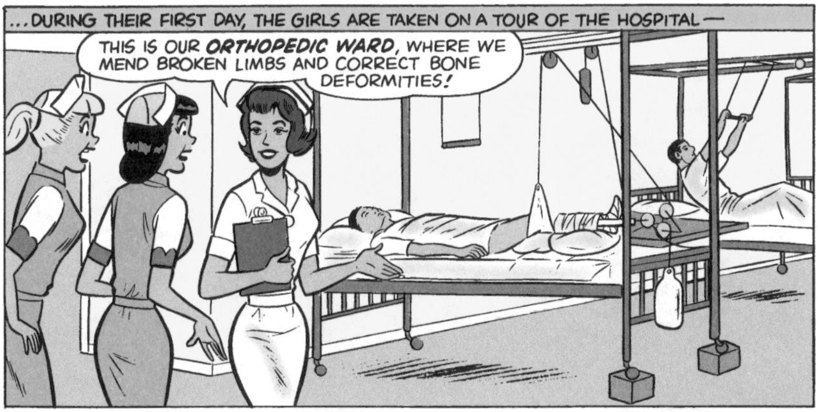
...DURING THEIR FIRST DAY, THE GIRLS ARE TAKEN ON A TOUR OF THE HOSPITAL—
THIS IS OUR ORTHOPEDIC WARD, WHERE WE MEND BROKEN LIMBS AND CORRECT BONE DEFORMITIES!

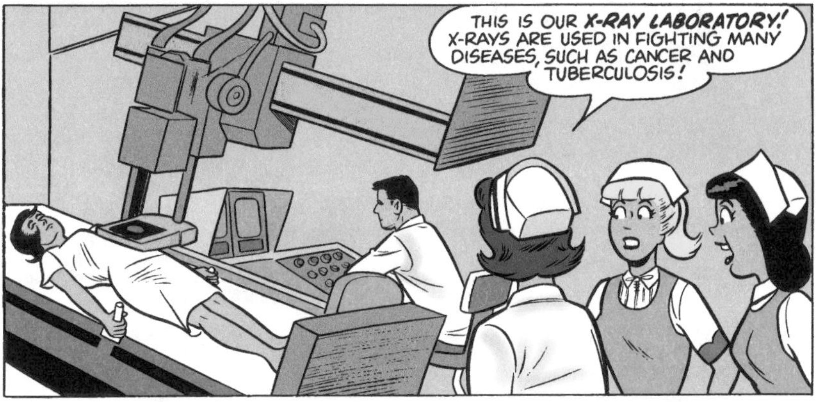
THIS IS OUR X-RAY LABORATORY! X-RAYS ARE USED IN FIGHTING MANY DISEASES, SUCH AS CANCER AND TUBERCULOSIS!

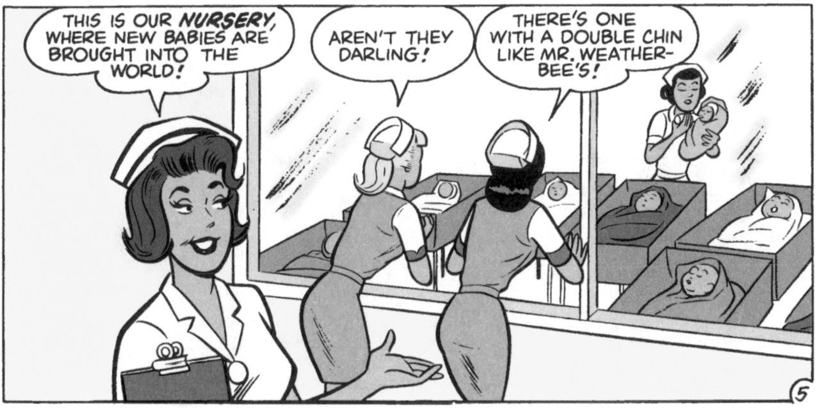
THIS IS OUR NURSERY, WHERE NEW BABIES ARE BROUGHT INTO THE WORLD!
AREN'T THEY DARLING!
THERE'S ONE WITH A DOUBLE CHIN LIKE MR. WEATHER-BEE'S!
5

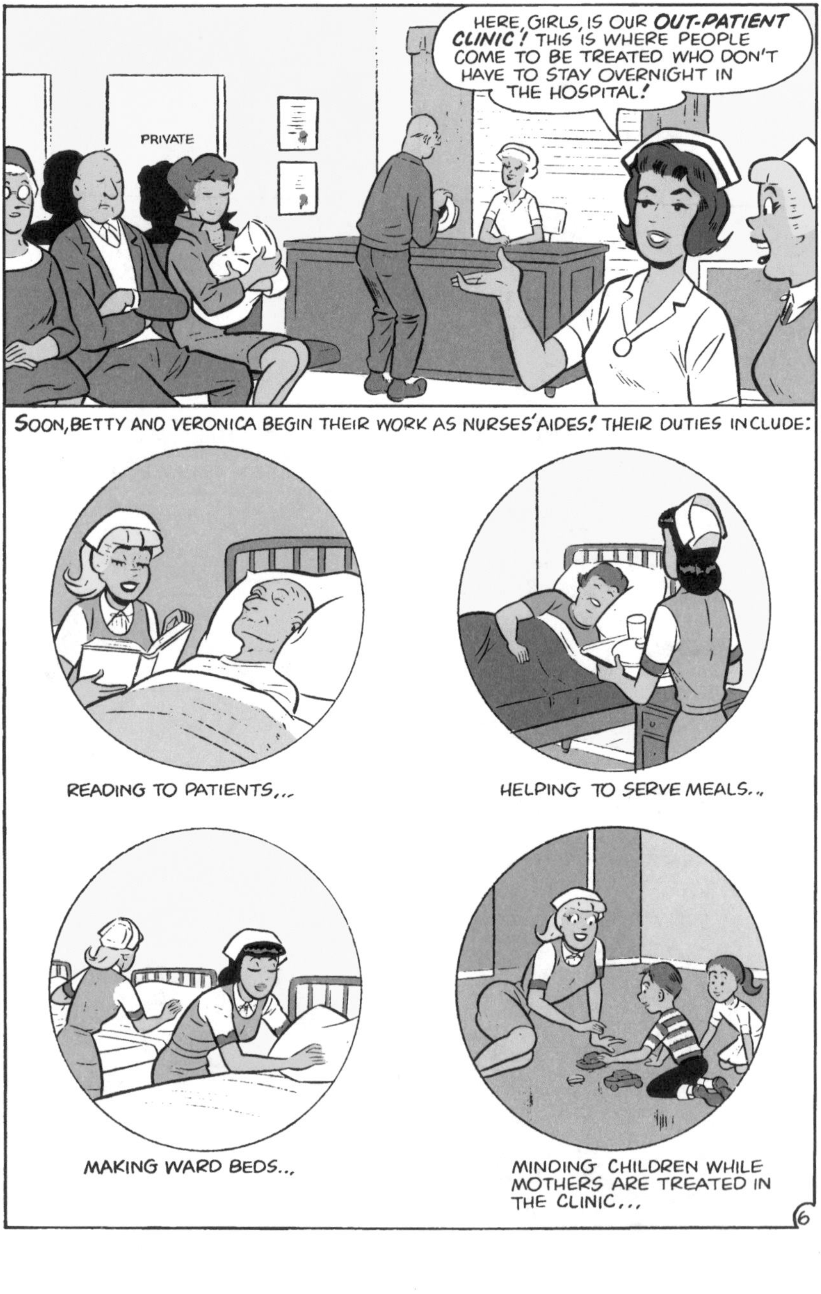
PRIVATE
HERE, GIRLS, IS OUR OUT-PATIENT CLINIC! THIS IS WHERE PEOPLE COME TO BE TREATED WHO DON'T HAVE TO STAY OVERNIGHT IN THE HOSPITAL!
SOON, BETTY AND VERONICA BEGIN THEIR WORK AS NURSES' AIDES! THEIR DUTIES INCLUDE:
READING TO PATIENTS,...
HELPING TO SERVE MEALS...
MAKING WARD BEDS...
MINDING CHILDREN WHILE MOTHERS ARE TREATED IN THE CLINIC...
6

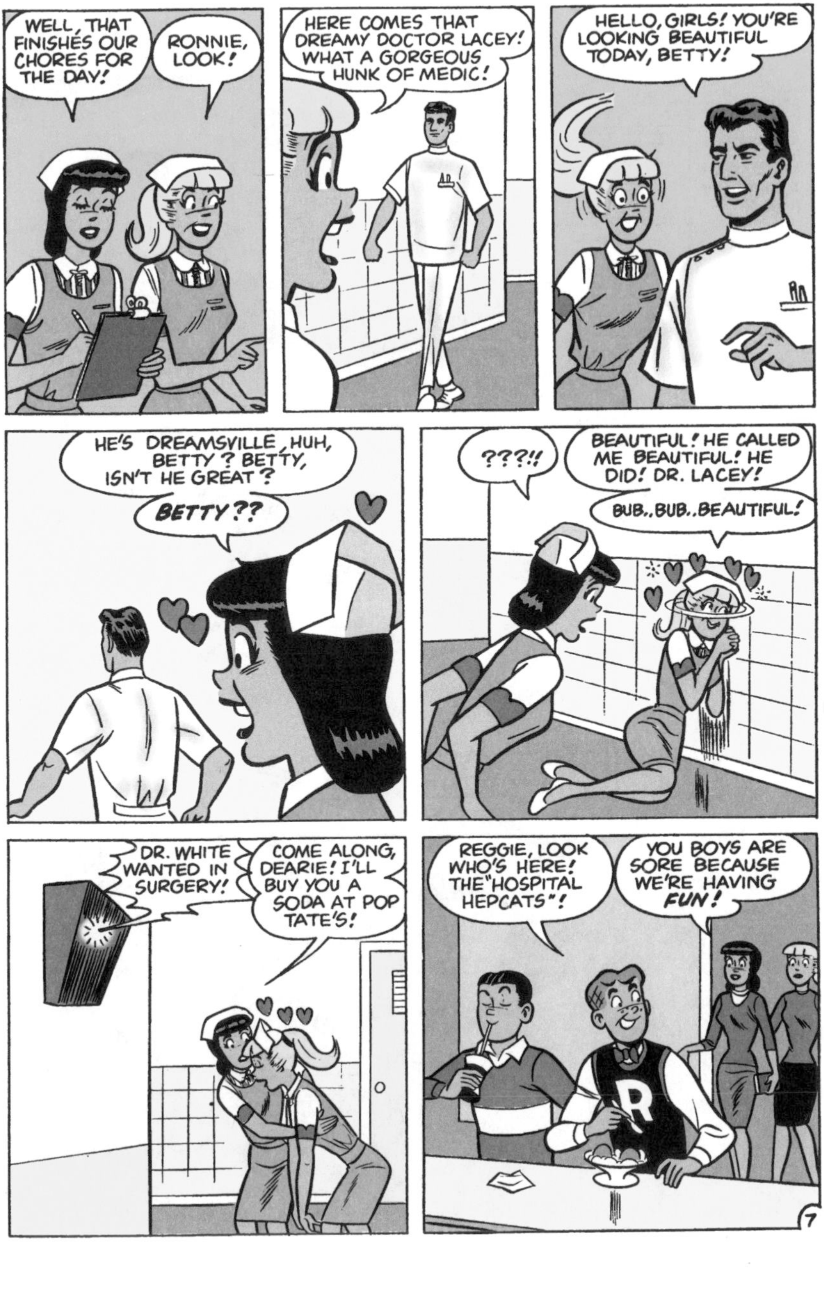
WELL, THAT FINISHES OUR CHORES FOR THE DAY!
RONNIE, LOOK!
HERE COMES THAT DREAMY DOCTOR LACEY! WHAT A GORGEOUS HUNK OF MEDIC!
HELLO, GIRLS! YOU'RE LOOKING BEAUTIFUL TODAY, BETTY!
HE'S DREAMSVILLE, HUH, BETTY? BETTY, ISN'T HE GREAT?
BETTY??
???!!
BEAUTIFUL! HE CALLED ME BEAUTIFUL! HE DID! DR. LACEY!
BUB..BUB..BEAUTIFUL!
DR. WHITE WANTED IN SURGERY!
COME ALONG, DEARIE! I'LL BUY YOU A SODA AT POP TATE'S!
REGGIE, LOOK WHO'S HERE! THE "HOSPITAL HEPCATS"!
YOU BOYS ARE SORE BECAUSE WE'RE HAVING FUN!
7

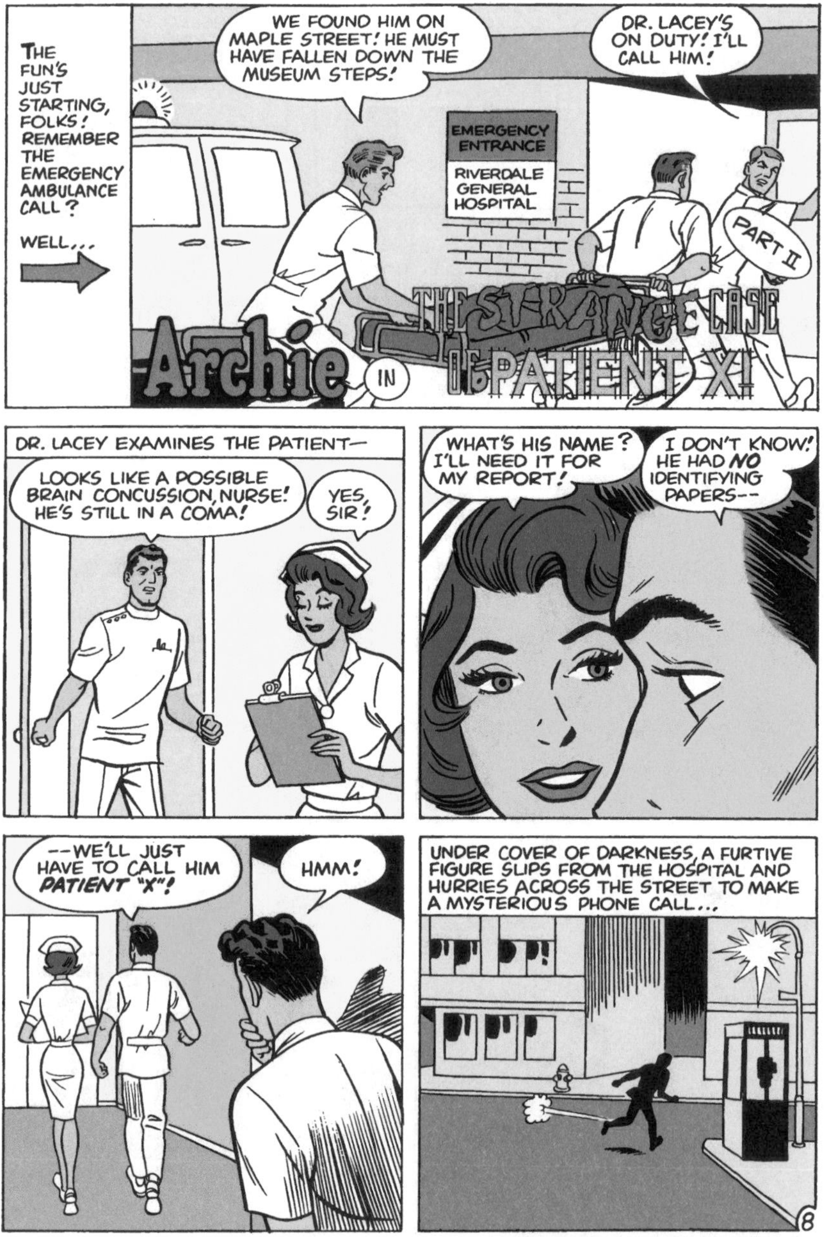
THE FUN'S JUST STARTING, FOLKS! REMEMBER THE EMERGENCY AMBULANCE CALL? WELL...
WE FOUND HIM ON MAPLE STREET! HE MUST HAVE FALLEN DOWN THE MUSEUM STEPS!
DR. LACEY'S ON DUTY! I'LL CALL HIM!
EMERGENCY ENTRANCE
RIVERDALE GENERAL HOSPITAL
PART II
Archie IN THE STRANGE CASE OF PATIENT X!
DR. LACEY EXAMINES THE PATIENT—
LOOKS LIKE A POSSIBLE BRAIN CONCUSSION, NURSE! HE'S STILL IN A COMA!
YES, SIR!
WHAT'S HIS NAME? I'LL NEED IT FOR MY REPORT!
I DON'T KNOW! HE HAD NO IDENTIFYING PAPERS--
--WE'LL JUST HAVE TO CALL HIM PATIENT "X"!
HMM!
UNDER COVER OF DARKNESS, A FURTIVE FIGURE SLIPS FROM THE HOSPITAL AND HURRIES ACROSS THE STREET TO MAKE A MYSTERIOUS PHONE CALL...
8

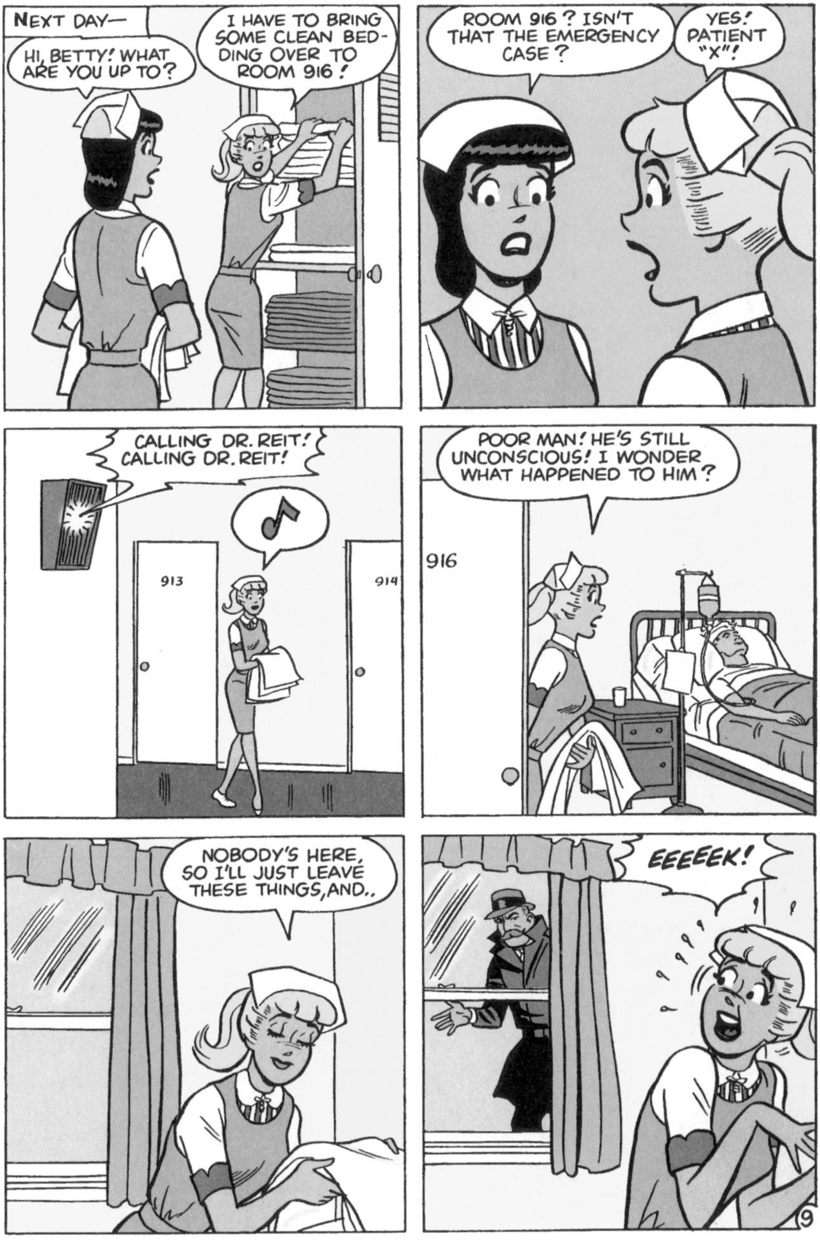
NEXT DAY—
HI, BETTY! WHAT ARE YOU UP TO?
I HAVE TO BRING SOME CLEAN BED-DING OVER TO ROOM 916!
ROOM 916? ISN'T THAT THE EMERGENCY CASE?
YES! PATIENT "X"!
CALLING DR. REIT! CALLING DR. REIT!
913
914
POOR MAN! HE'S STILL UNCONSCIOUS! I WONDER WHAT HAPPENED TO HIM?
916
NOBODY'S HERE, SO I'LL JUST LEAVE THESE THINGS, AND..
EEEEEK!
9

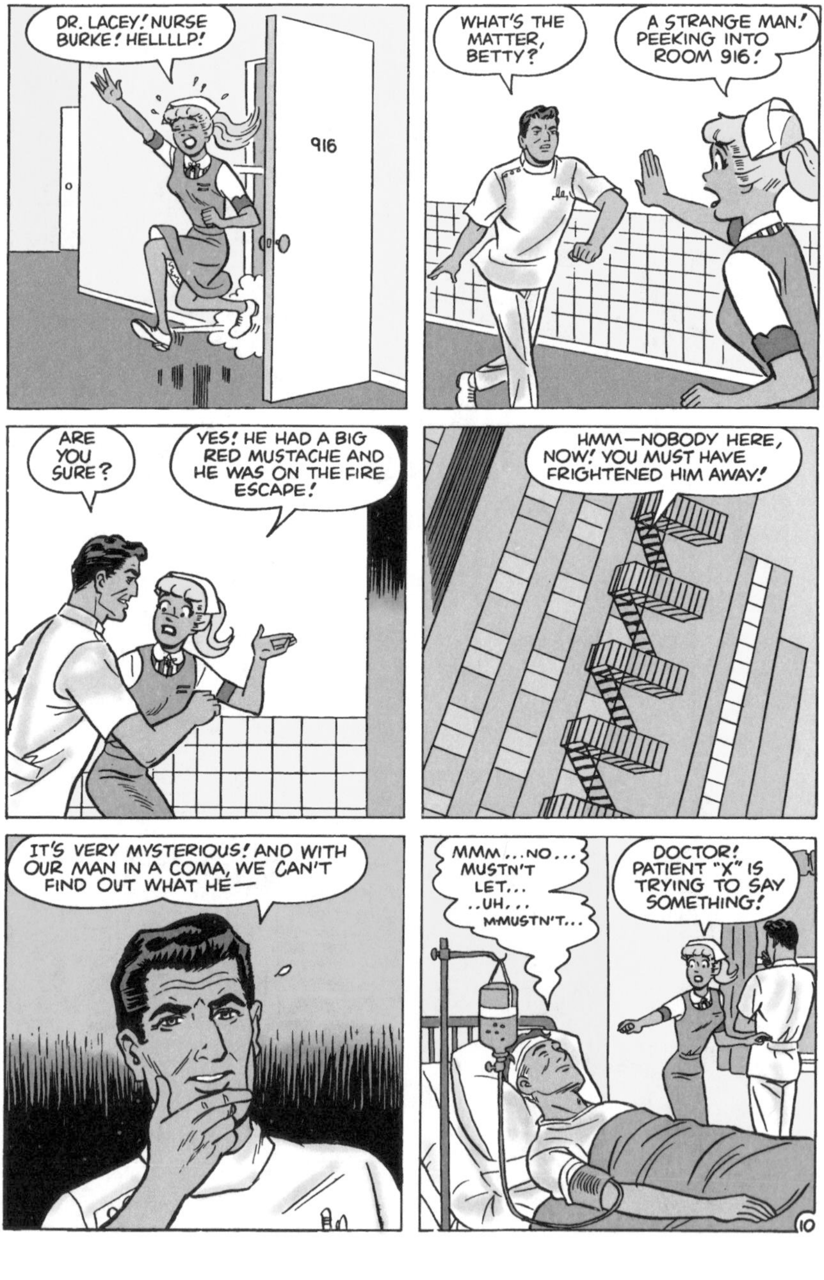
DR. LACEY! NURSE BURKE! HELLLLP!
916
WHAT'S THE MATTER, BETTY?
A STRANGE MAN! PEEKING INTO ROOM 916!
ARE YOU SURE?
YES! HE HAD A BIG RED MUSTACHE AND HE WAS ON THE FIRE ESCAPE!
HMM—NOBODY HERE, NOW! YOU MUST HAVE FRIGHTENED HIM AWAY!
IT'S VERY MYSTERIOUS! AND WITH OUR MAN IN A COMA, WE CAN'T FIND OUT WHAT HE—
MMM... NO... MUSTN'T LET... ..UH... M-MUSTN'T...
DOCTOR! PATIENT "X" IS TRYING TO SAY SOMETHING!
10

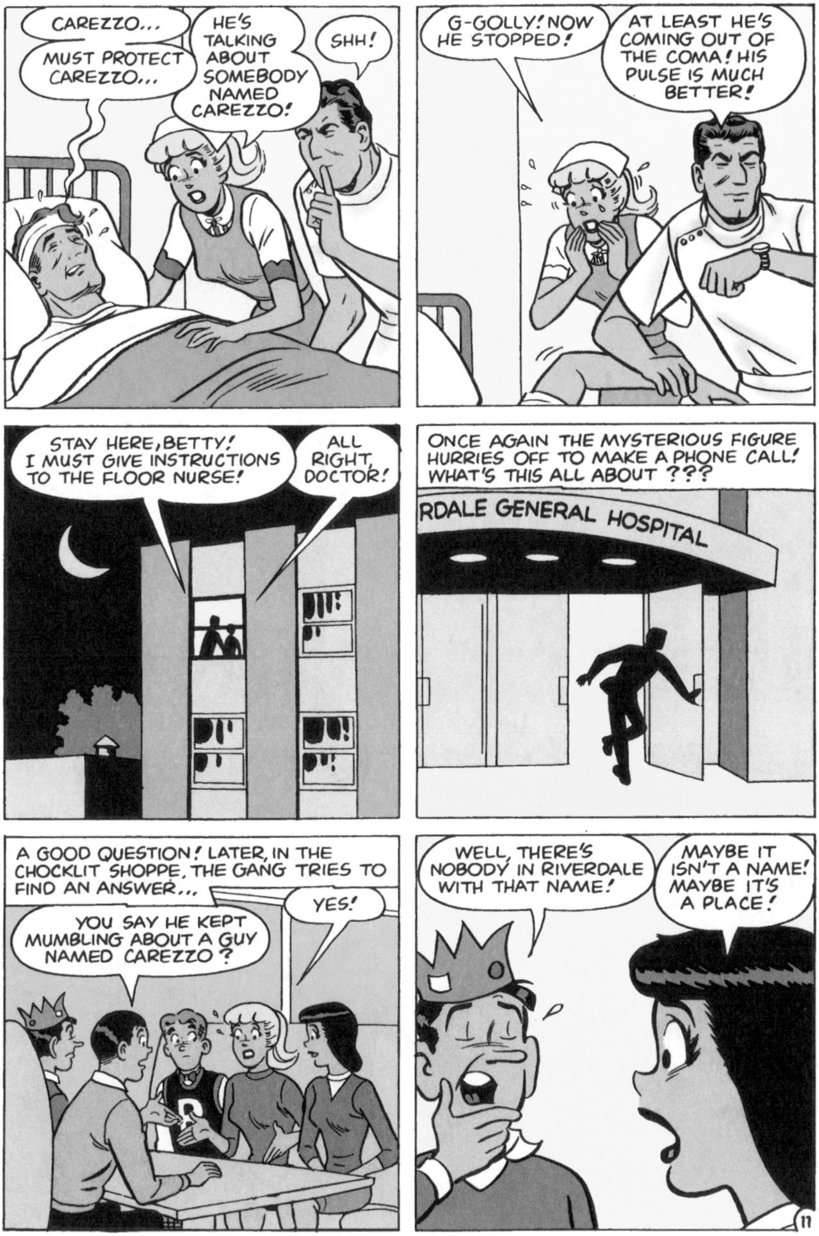
CAREZZO...
MUST PROTECT CAREZZO...
HE'S TALKING ABOUT SOMEBODY NAMED CAREZZO!
SHH!
G-GOLLY! NOW HE STOPPED!
AT LEAST HE'S COMING OUT OF THE COMA! HIS PULSE IS MUCH BETTER!
STAY HERE, BETTY! I MUST GIVE INSTRUCTIONS TO THE FLOOR NURSE!
ALL RIGHT, DOCTOR!
ONCE AGAIN THE MYSTERIOUS FIGURE HURRIES OFF TO MAKE A PHONE CALL! WHAT'S THIS ALL ABOUT ???
RDALE GENERAL HOSPITAL
A GOOD QUESTION! LATER, IN THE CHOCKLIT SHOPPE, THE GANG TRIES TO FIND AN ANSWER...
YOU SAY HE KEPT MUMBLING ABOUT A GUY NAMED CAREZZO?
YES!
WELL, THERE'S NOBODY IN RIVERDALE WITH THAT NAME!
MAYBE IT ISN'T A NAME! MAYBE IT'S A PLACE!
11

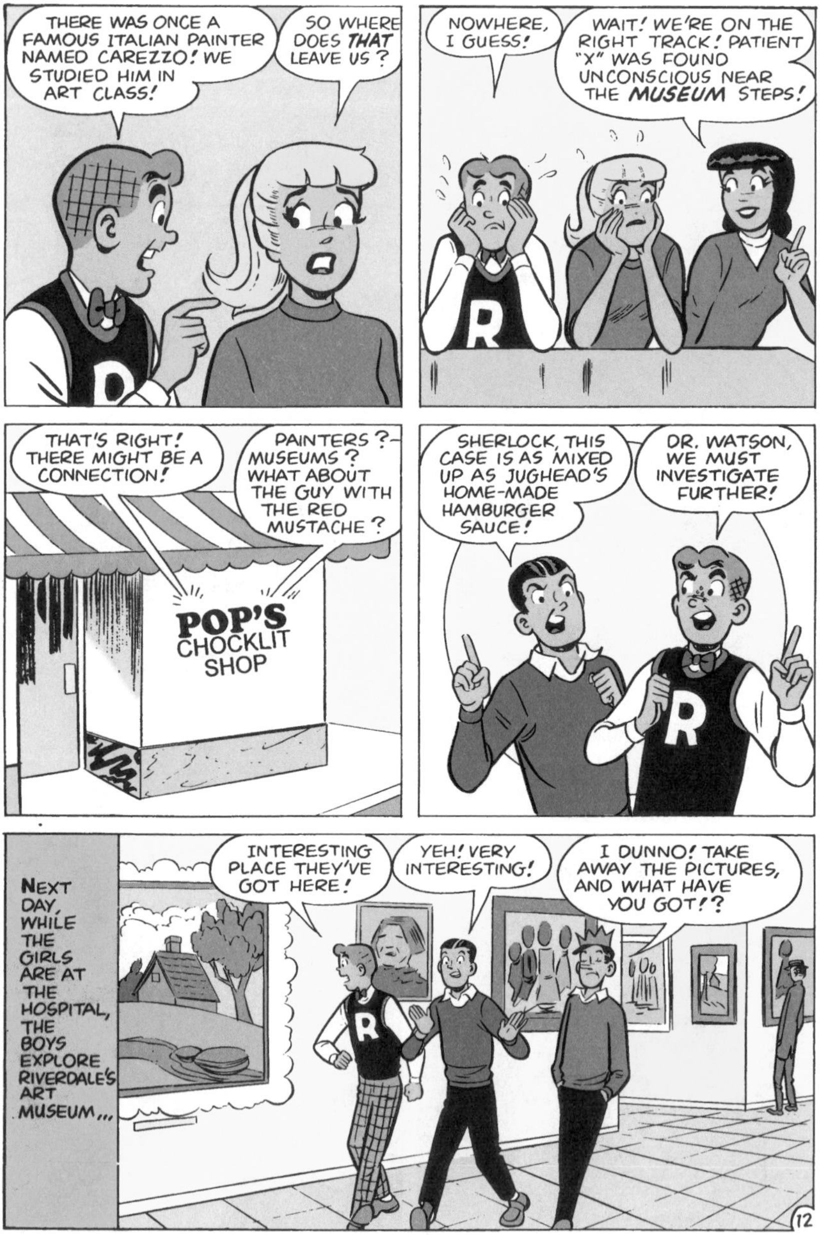
THERE WAS ONCE A FAMOUS ITALIAN PAINTER NAMED CAREZZO! WE STUDIED HIM IN ART CLASS!
SO WHERE DOES THAT LEAVE US?
NOWHERE, I GUESS!
WAIT! WE'RE ON THE RIGHT TRACK! PATIENT "X" WAS FOUND UNCONSCIOUS NEAR THE MUSEUM STEPS!
THAT'S RIGHT! THERE MIGHT BE A CONNECTION!
PAINTERS?— MUSEUMS? WHAT ABOUT THE GUY WITH THE RED MUSTACHE?
POP'S CHOCKLIT SHOP
SHERLOCK, THIS CASE IS AS MIXED UP AS JUGHEAD'S HOME-MADE HAMBURGER SAUCE!
DR. WATSON, WE MUST INVESTIGATE FURTHER!
NEXT DAY, WHILE THE GIRLS ARE AT THE HOSPITAL, THE BOYS EXPLORE RIVERDALE'S ART MUSEUM...
INTERESTING PLACE THEY'VE GOT HERE!
YEH! VERY INTERESTING!
I DUNNO! TAKE AWAY THE PICTURES, AND WHAT HAVE YOU GOT!?
12

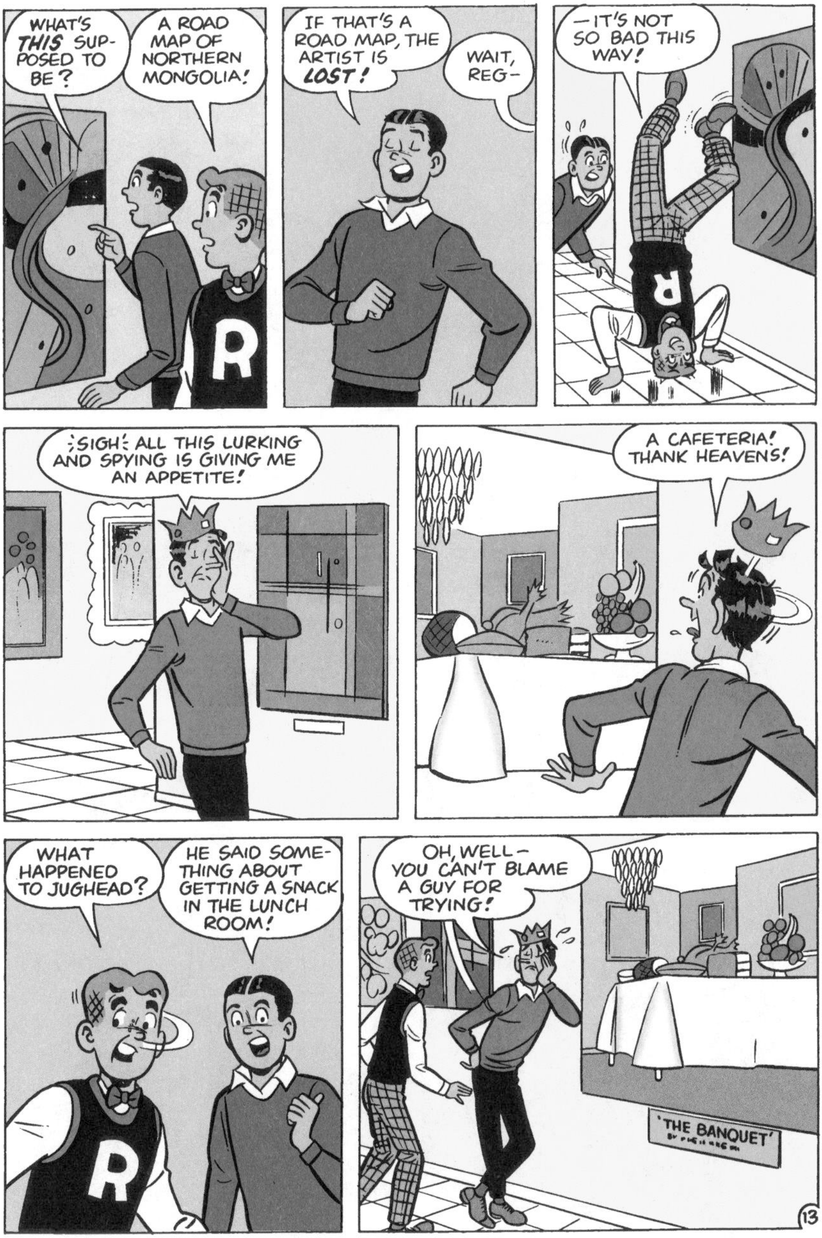
WHAT'S THIS SUP-POSED TO BE?
A ROAD MAP OF NORTHERN MONGOLIA!
IF THAT'S A ROAD MAP, THE ARTIST IS LOST!
WAIT, REG-
—IT'S NOT SO BAD THIS WAY!
;SIGH; ALL THIS LURKING AND SPYING IS GIVING ME AN APPETITE!
A CAFETERIA! THANK HEAVENS!
WHAT HAPPENED TO JUGHEAD?
HE SAID SOME-THING ABOUT GETTING A SNACK IN THE LUNCH ROOM!
OH, WELL- YOU CAN'T BLAME A GUY FOR TRYING!
'THE BANQUET'
13

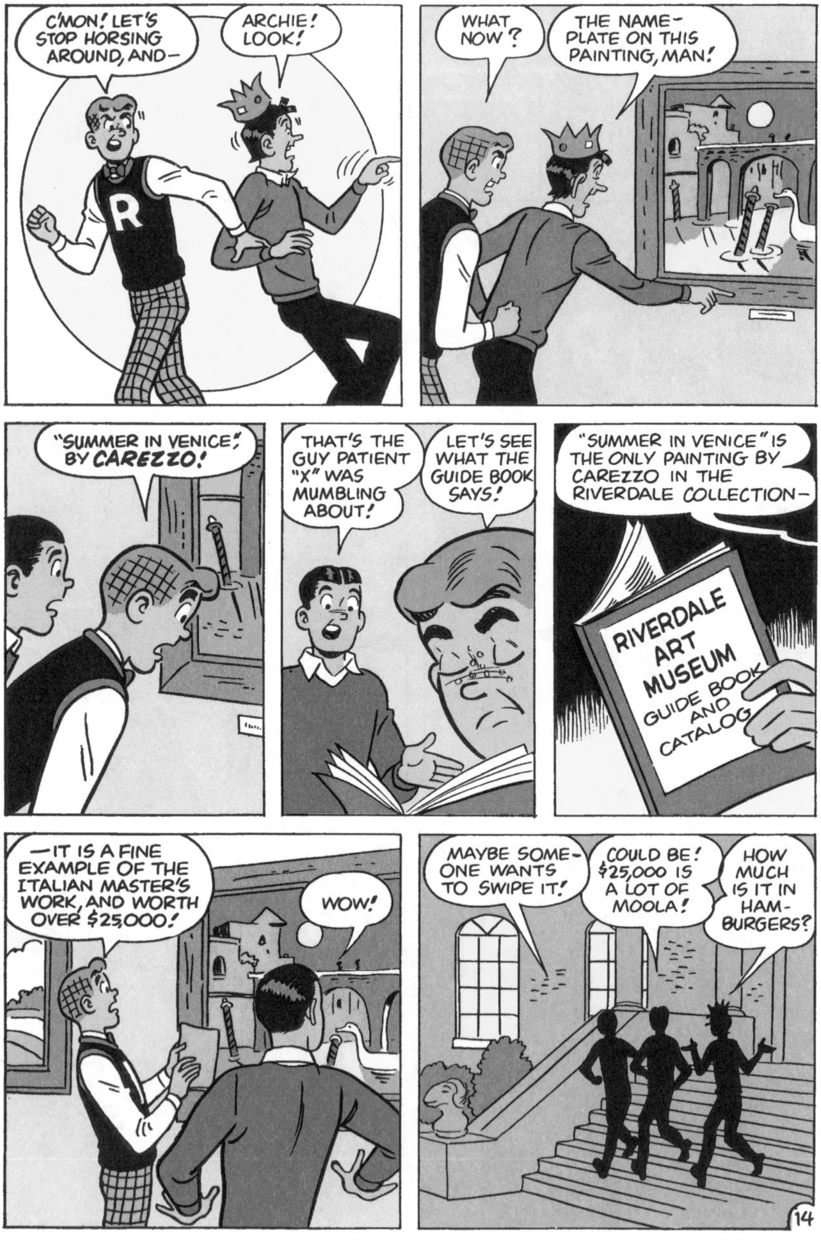
C'MON! LET'S STOP HORSING AROUND, AND—
ARCHIE! LOOK!
WHAT NOW?
THE NAME-PLATE ON THIS PAINTING, MAN!
"SUMMER IN VENICE," BY CAREZZO!
THAT'S THE GUY PATIENT "X" WAS MUMBLING ABOUT!
LET'S SEE WHAT THE GUIDE BOOK SAYS!
"SUMMER IN VENICE" IS THE ONLY PAINTING BY CAREZZO IN THE RIVERDALE COLLECTION—
RIVERDALE ART MUSEUM GUIDE BOOK AND CATALOG
—IT IS A FINE EXAMPLE OF THE ITALIAN MASTER'S WORK, AND WORTH OVER $25,000!
WOW!
MAYBE SOME-ONE WANTS TO SWIPE IT!
COULD BE! $25,000 IS A LOT OF MOOLA!
HOW MUCH IS IT IN HAM-BURGERS?
14

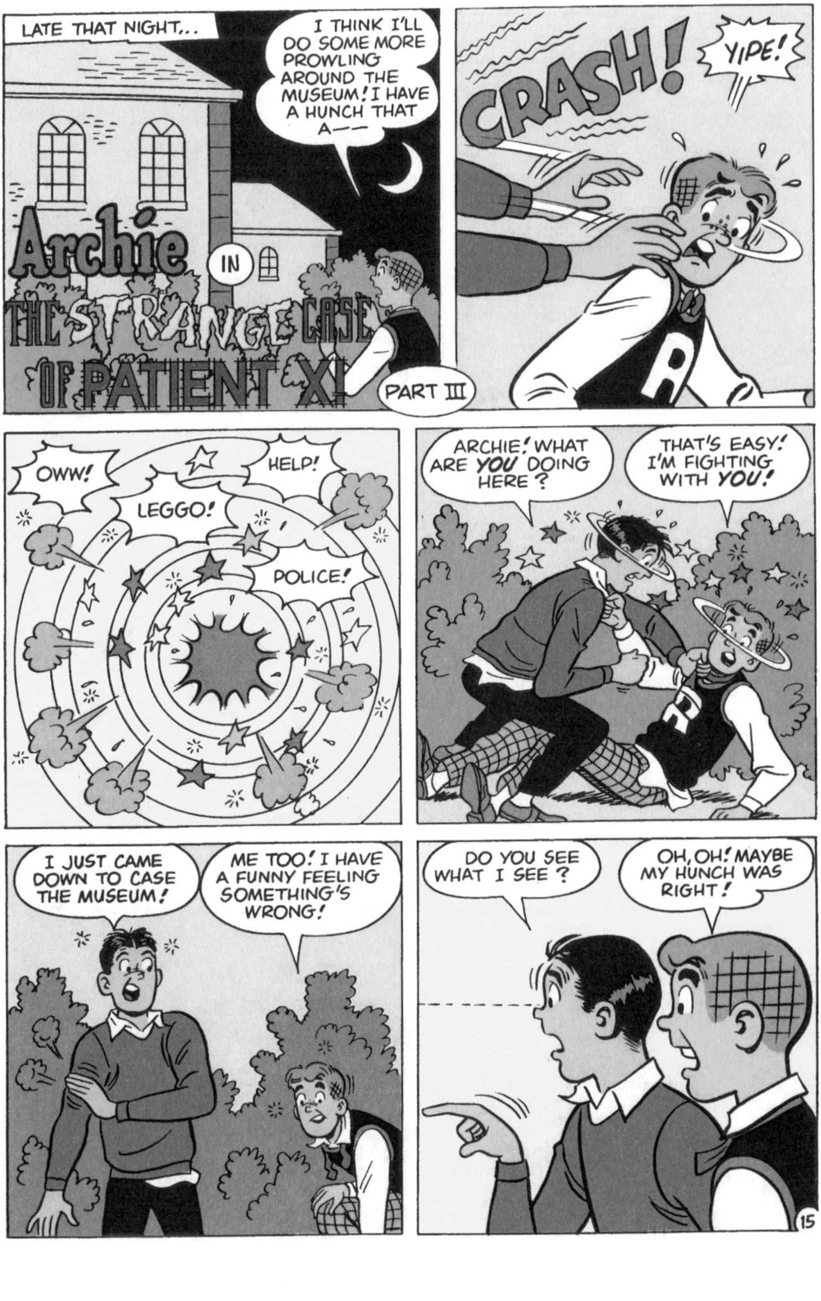
LATE THAT NIGHT...
I THINK I'LL DO SOME MORE PROWLING AROUND THE MUSEUM! I HAVE A HUNCH THAT A——
Archie IN THE STRANGE CASE OF PATIENT X!
PART III
CRASH!
YIPE!
OWW!
HELP!
LEGGO!
POLICE!
ARCHIE! WHAT ARE YOU DOING HERE?
THAT'S EASY! I'M FIGHTING WITH YOU!
I JUST CAME DOWN TO CASE THE MUSEUM!
ME TOO! I HAVE A FUNNY FEELING SOMETHING'S WRONG!
DO YOU SEE WHAT I SEE?
OH, OH! MAYBE MY HUNCH WAS RIGHT!
15

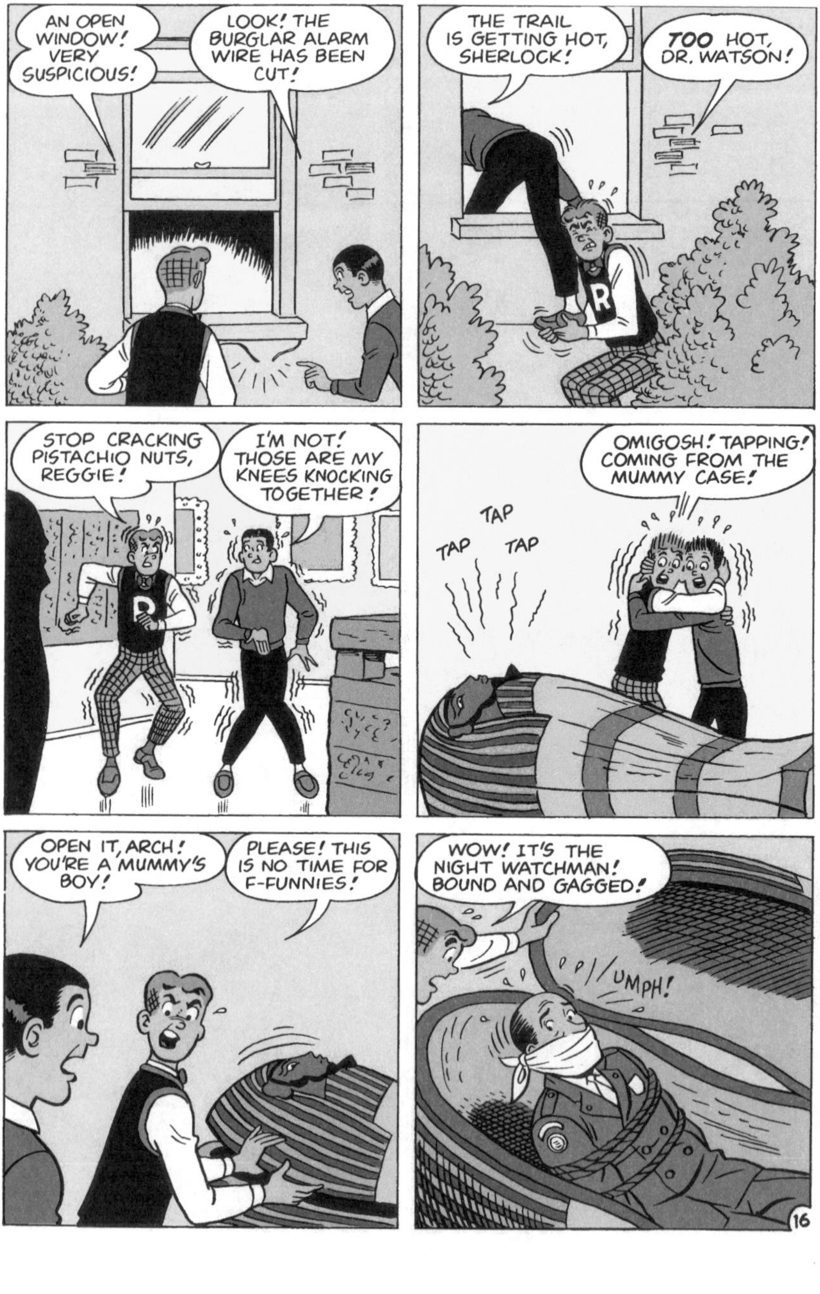
AN OPEN WINDOW! VERY SUSPICIOUS!
LOOK! THE BURGLAR ALARM WIRE HAS BEEN CUT!
THE TRAIL IS GETTING HOT, SHERLOCK!
TOO HOT, DR. WATSON!
STOP CRACKING PISTACHIO NUTS, REGGIE!
I'M NOT! THOSE ARE MY KNEES KNOCKING TOGETHER!
OMIGOSH! TAPPING! COMING FROM THE MUMMY CASE!
TAP
TAP
TAP
OPEN IT, ARCH! YOU'RE A MUMMY'S BOY!
PLEASE! THIS IS NO TIME FOR F-FUNNIES!
WOW! IT'S THE NIGHT WATCHMAN! BOUND AND GAGGED!
UMPH!
16

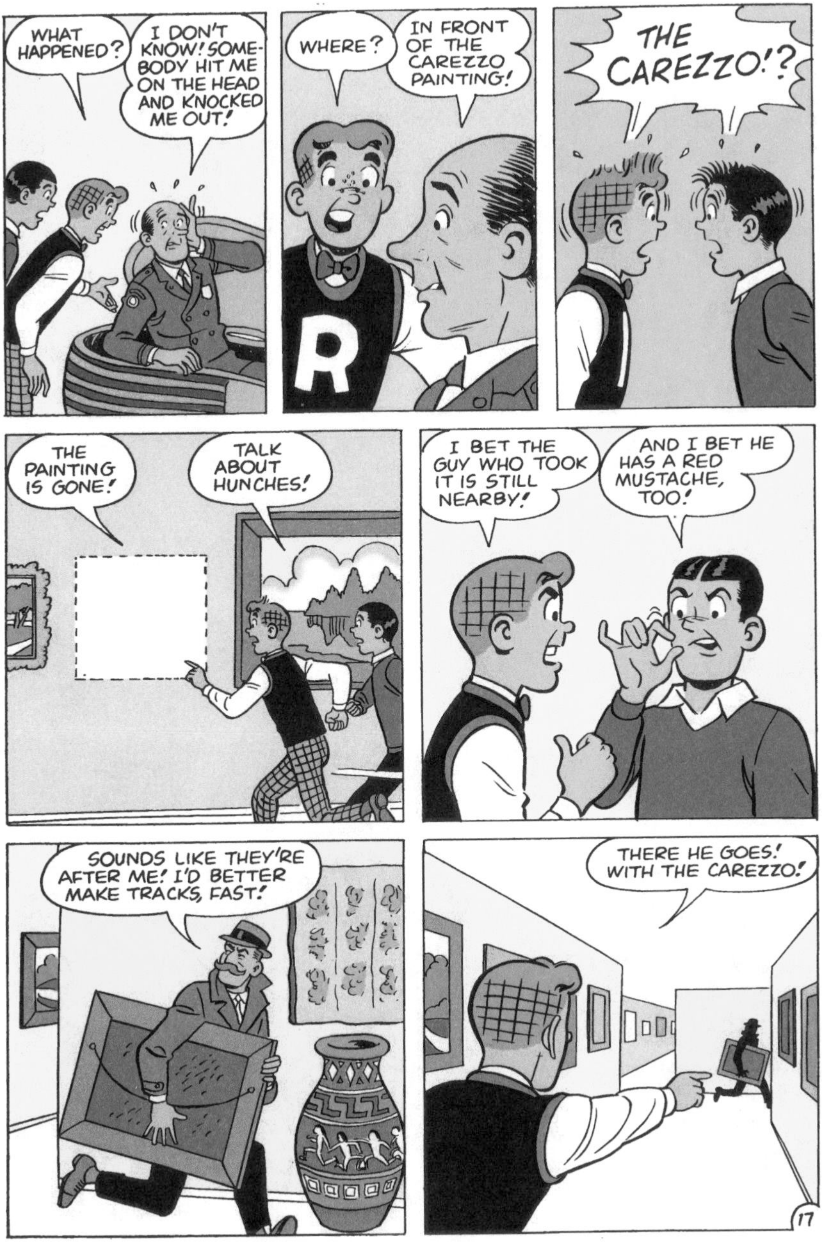
WHAT HAPPENED?
I DON'T KNOW! SOMEBODY HIT ME ON THE HEAD AND KNOCKED ME OUT!
WHERE?
IN FRONT OF THE CAREZZO PAINTING!
THE CAREZZO!?
THE PAINTING IS GONE!
TALK ABOUT HUNCHES!
I BET THE GUY WHO TOOK IT IS STILL NEARBY!
AND I BET HE HAS A RED MUSTACHE, TOO!
SOUNDS LIKE THEY'RE AFTER ME! I'D BETTER MAKE TRACKS, FAST!
THERE HE GOES! WITH THE CAREZZO!
17

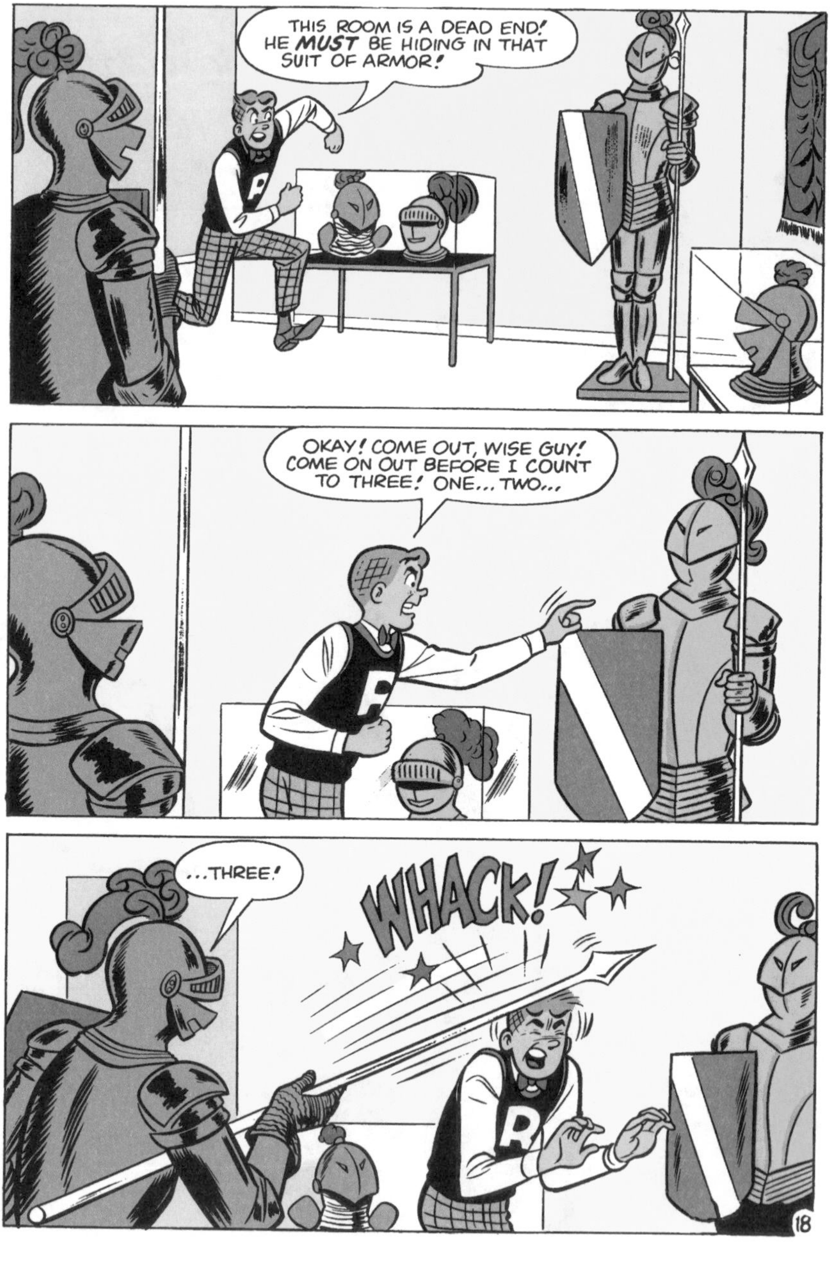
THIS ROOM IS A DEAD END! HE MUST BE HIDING IN THAT SUIT OF ARMOR!
OKAY! COME OUT, WISE GUY! COME ON OUT BEFORE I COUNT TO THREE! ONE... TWO...
...THREE!
WHACK!
18

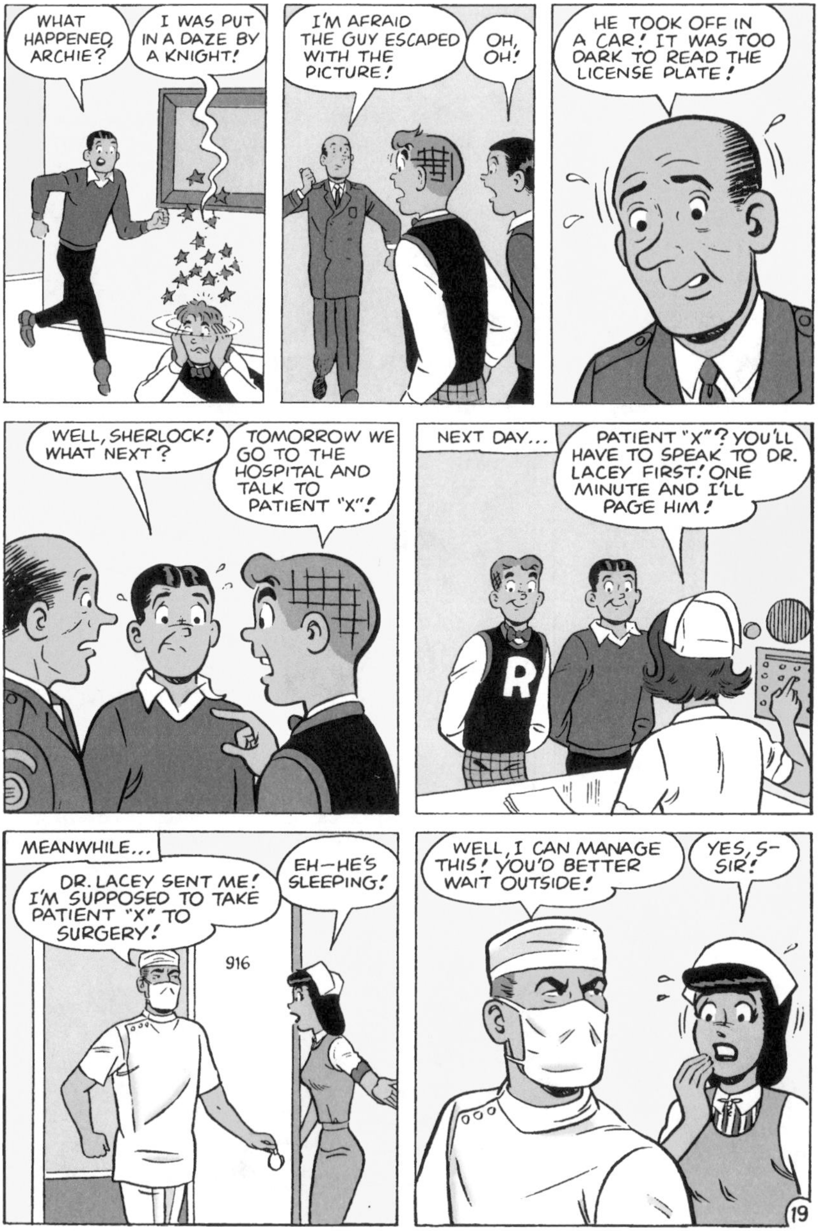
WHAT HAPPENED, ARCHIE?
I WAS PUT IN A DAZE BY A KNIGHT!
I'M AFRAID THE GUY ESCAPED WITH THE PICTURE!
OH, OH!
HE TOOK OFF IN A CAR! IT WAS TOO DARK TO READ THE LICENSE PLATE!
WELL, SHERLOCK! WHAT NEXT?
TOMORROW WE GO TO THE HOSPITAL AND TALK TO PATIENT "X"!
NEXT DAY...
PATIENT "X"? YOU'LL HAVE TO SPEAK TO DR. LACEY FIRST! ONE MINUTE AND I'LL PAGE HIM!
MEANWHILE...
DR. LACEY SENT ME! I'M SUPPOSED TO TAKE PATIENT "X" TO SURGERY!
EH—HE'S SLEEPING!
916
WELL, I CAN MANAGE THIS! YOU'D BETTER WAIT OUTSIDE!
YES, S-SIR!
19

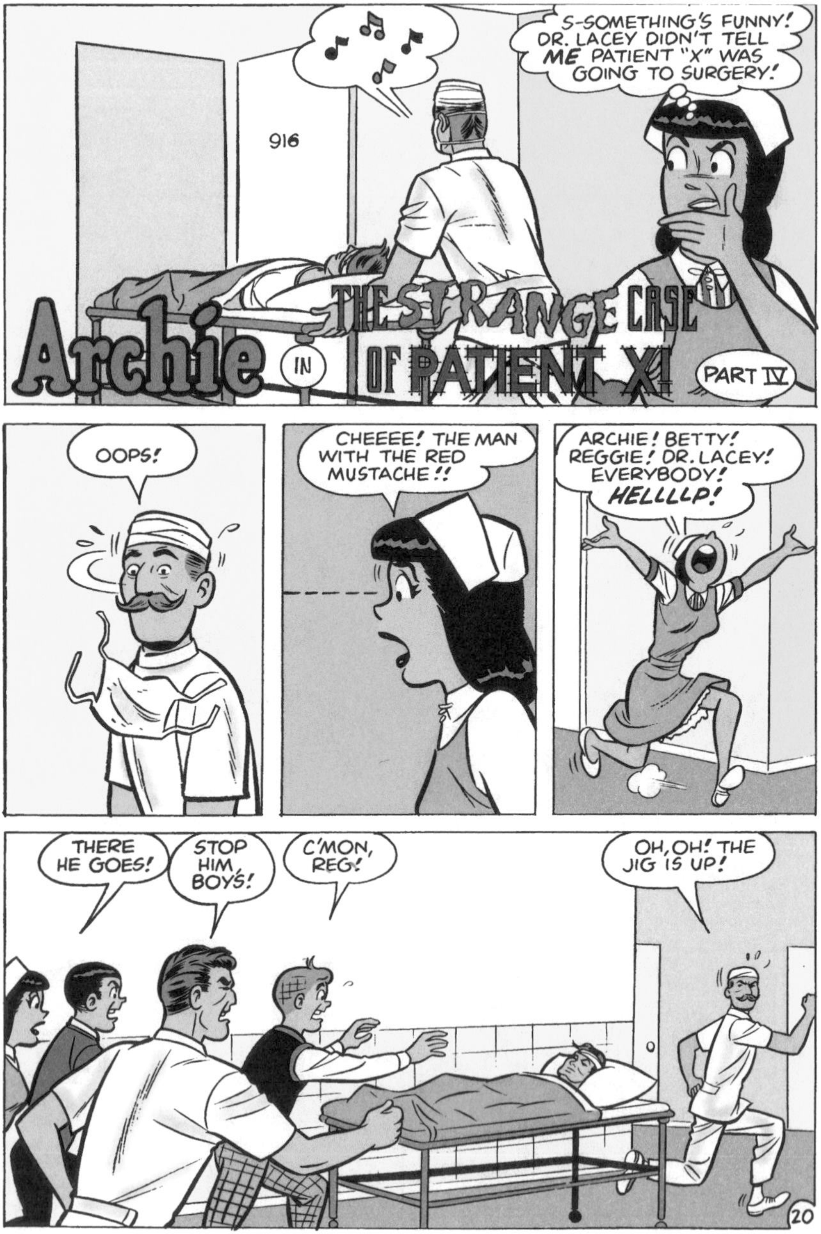
S-SOMETHING'S FUNNY! DR. LACEY DIDN'T TELL ME PATIENT "X" WAS GOING TO SURGERY!
916
Archie IN THE STRANGE CASE OF PATIENT X!
PART IV
OOPS!
CHEEEE! THE MAN WITH THE RED MUSTACHE!!
ARCHIE! BETTY! REGGIE! DR. LACEY! EVERYBODY! HELLLLP!
THERE HE GOES!
STOP HIM, BOYS!
C'MON, REG!
OH, OH! THE JIG IS UP!
20

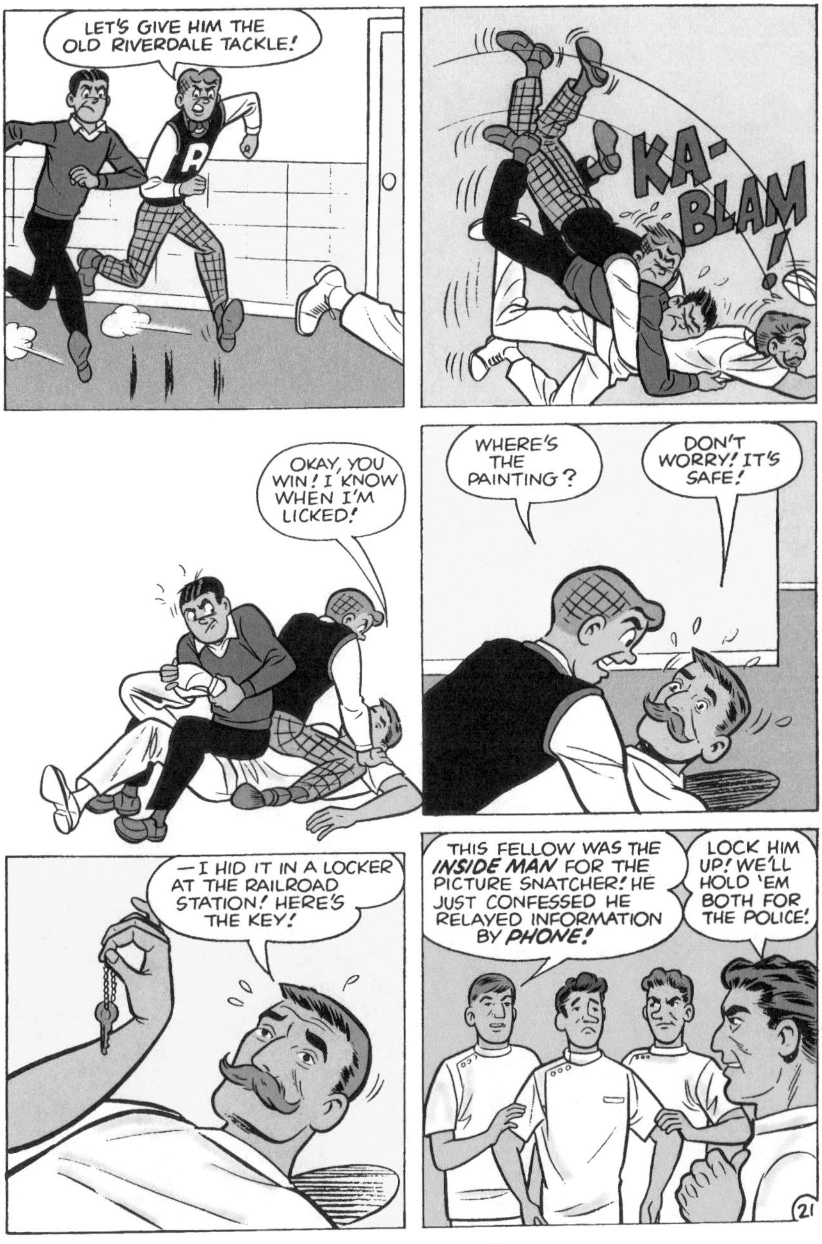
LET'S GIVE HIM THE OLD RIVERDALE TACKLE!
KA-BLAM!
OKAY, YOU WIN! I KNOW WHEN I'M LICKED!
WHERE'S THE PAINTING?
DON'T WORRY! IT'S SAFE!
—I HID IT IN A LOCKER AT THE RAILROAD STATION! HERE'S THE KEY!
THIS FELLOW WAS THE INSIDE MAN FOR THE PICTURE SNATCHER! HE JUST CONFESSED HE RELAYED INFORMATION BY PHONE!
LOCK HIM UP! WE'LL HOLD 'EM BOTH FOR THE POLICE!
21

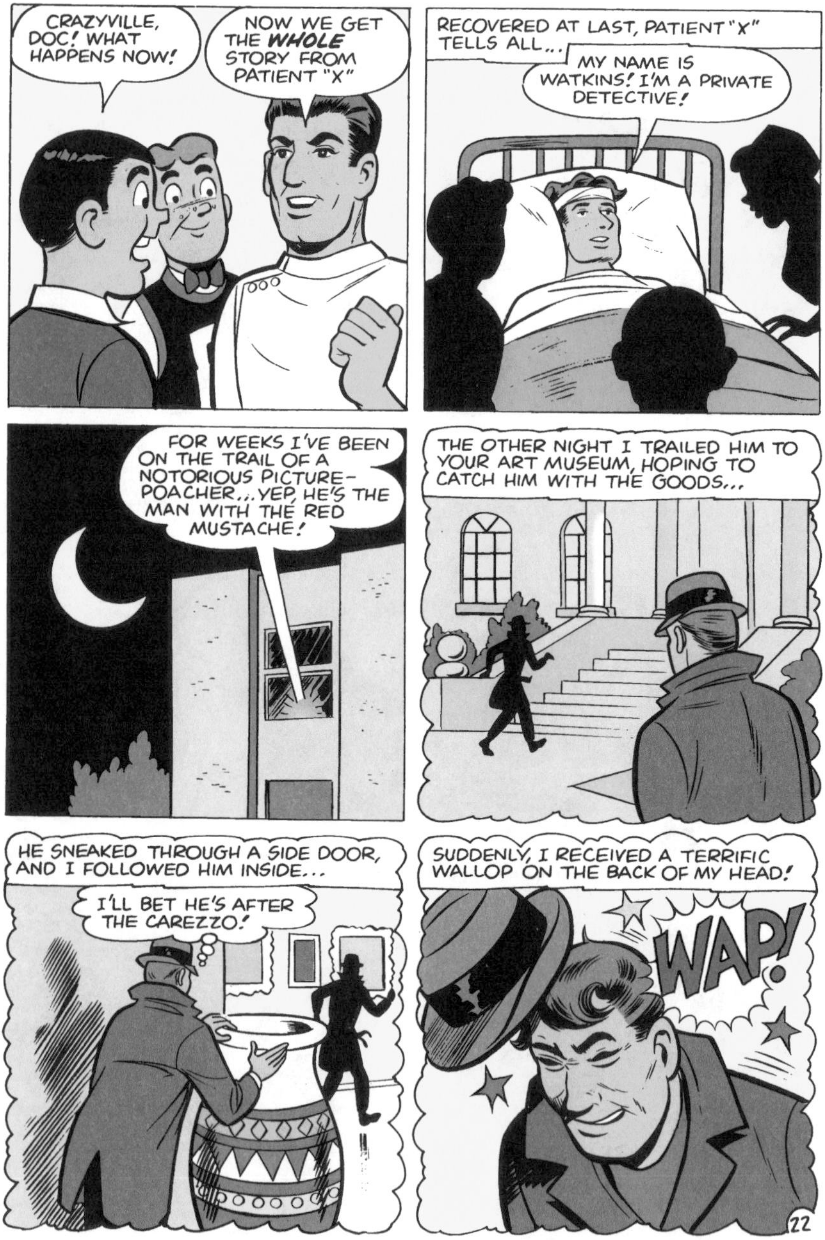
CRAZYVILLE, DOC! WHAT HAPPENS NOW!
NOW WE GET THE **WHOLE** STORY FROM PATIENT "X"
RECOVERED AT LAST, PATIENT "X" TELLS ALL...
MY NAME IS WATKINS! I'M A PRIVATE DETECTIVE!
FOR WEEKS I'VE BEEN ON THE TRAIL OF A NOTORIOUS PICTURE-POACHER...YEP, HE'S THE MAN WITH THE RED MUSTACHE!
THE OTHER NIGHT I TRAILED HIM TO YOUR ART MUSEUM, HOPING TO CATCH HIM WITH THE GOODS...
HE SNEAKED THROUGH A SIDE DOOR, AND I FOLLOWED HIM INSIDE...
I'LL BET HE'S AFTER THE CAREZZO!
SUDDENLY, I RECEIVED A TERRIFIC WALLOP ON THE BACK OF MY HEAD!
WAP!
22

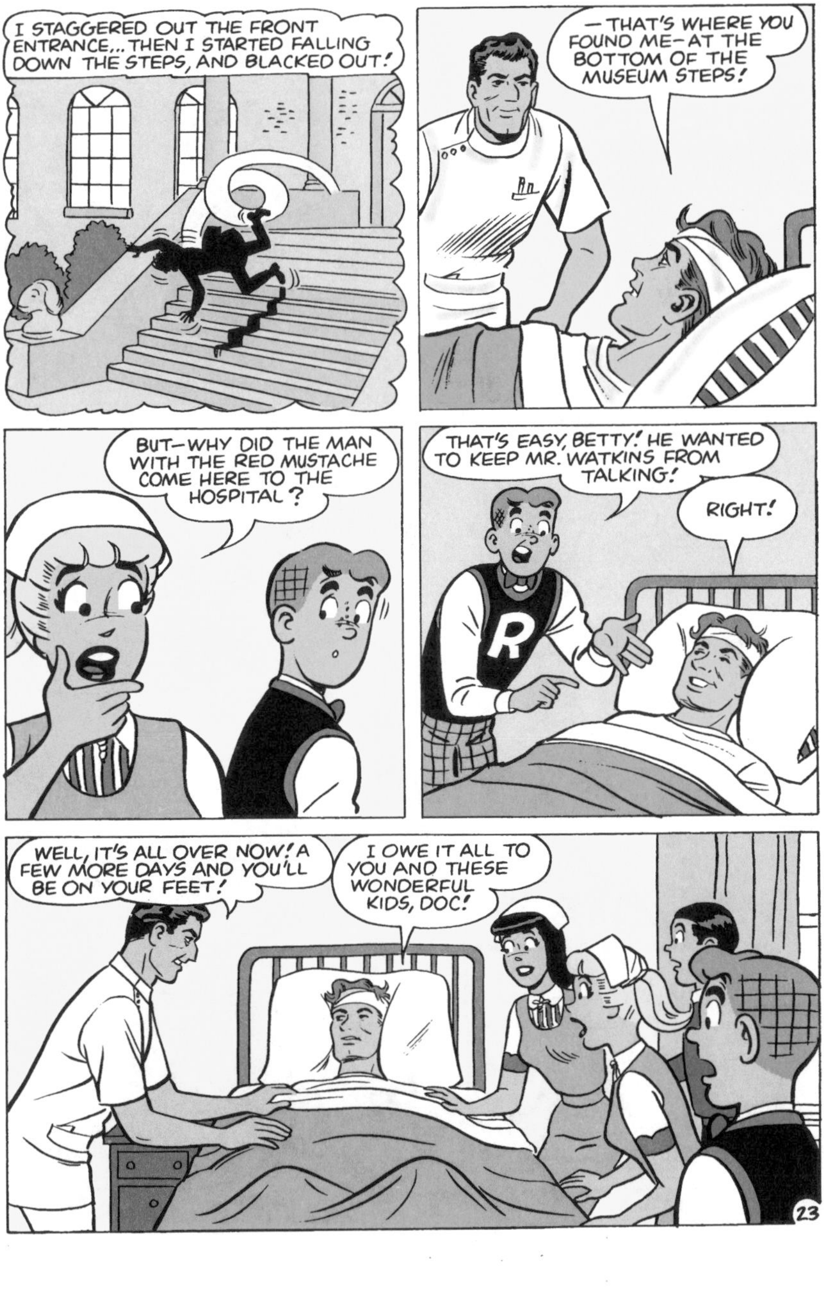
I STAGGERED OUT THE FRONT ENTRANCE,.. THEN I STARTED FALLING DOWN THE STEPS, AND BLACKED OUT!
—THAT'S WHERE YOU FOUND ME—AT THE BOTTOM OF THE MUSEUM STEPS!
BUT—WHY DID THE MAN WITH THE RED MUSTACHE COME HERE TO THE HOSPITAL?
THAT'S EASY, BETTY! HE WANTED TO KEEP MR. WATKINS FROM TALKING!
RIGHT!
WELL, IT'S ALL OVER NOW! A FEW MORE DAYS AND YOU'LL BE ON YOUR FEET!
I OWE IT ALL TO YOU AND THESE WONDERFUL KIDS, DOC!
23

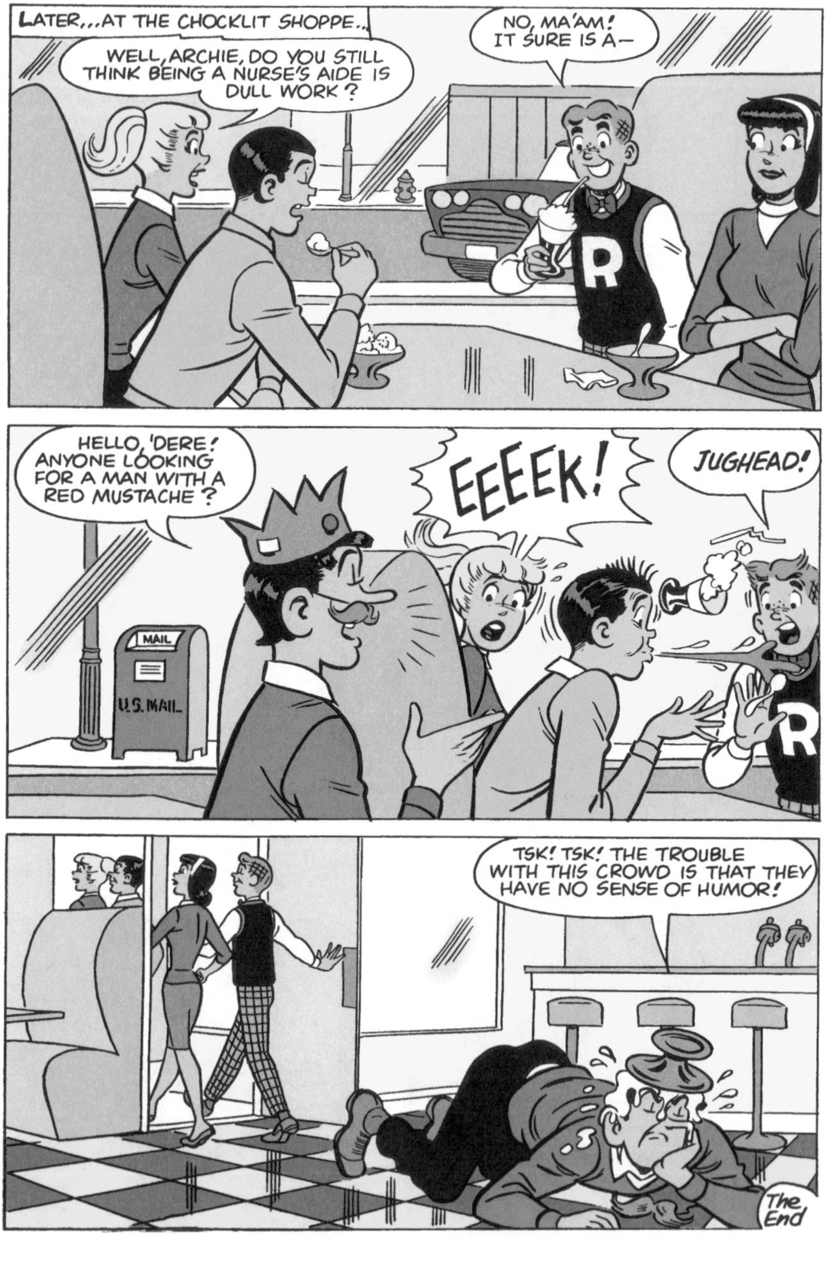
LATER,..AT THE CHOCKLIT SHOPPE..
WELL, ARCHIE, DO YOU STILL THINK BEING A NURSE'S AIDE IS DULL WORK ?
NO, MA'AM! IT SURE IS A—
HELLO, 'DERE! ANYONE LOOKING FOR A MAN WITH A RED MUSTACHE ?
EEEEK!
JUGHEAD!
MAIL
U.S. MAIL
TSK! TSK! THE TROUBLE WITH THIS CROWD IS THAT THEY HAVE NO SENSE OF HUMOR!
The End

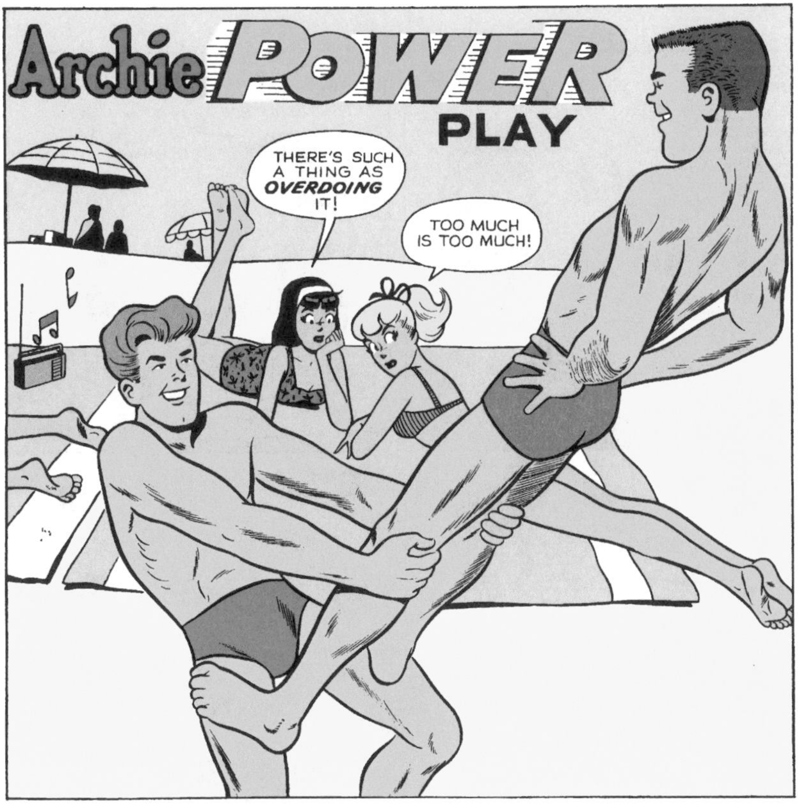
Archie POWER PLAY
THERE'S SUCH A THING AS OVERDOING IT!
TOO MUCH IS TOO MUCH!

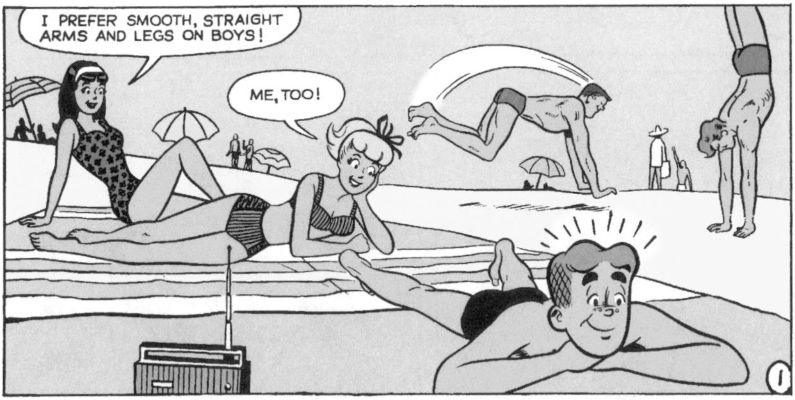
I PREFER SMOOTH, STRAIGHT ARMS AND LEGS ON BOYS!
ME, TOO!
1

Story: Frank Doyle — Pencils: Harry Lucey
Inks & Letters: Mario Acquaviva — Colors: Barry Grossman

Originally printed in LIFE WITH ARCHIE #30, October 1964

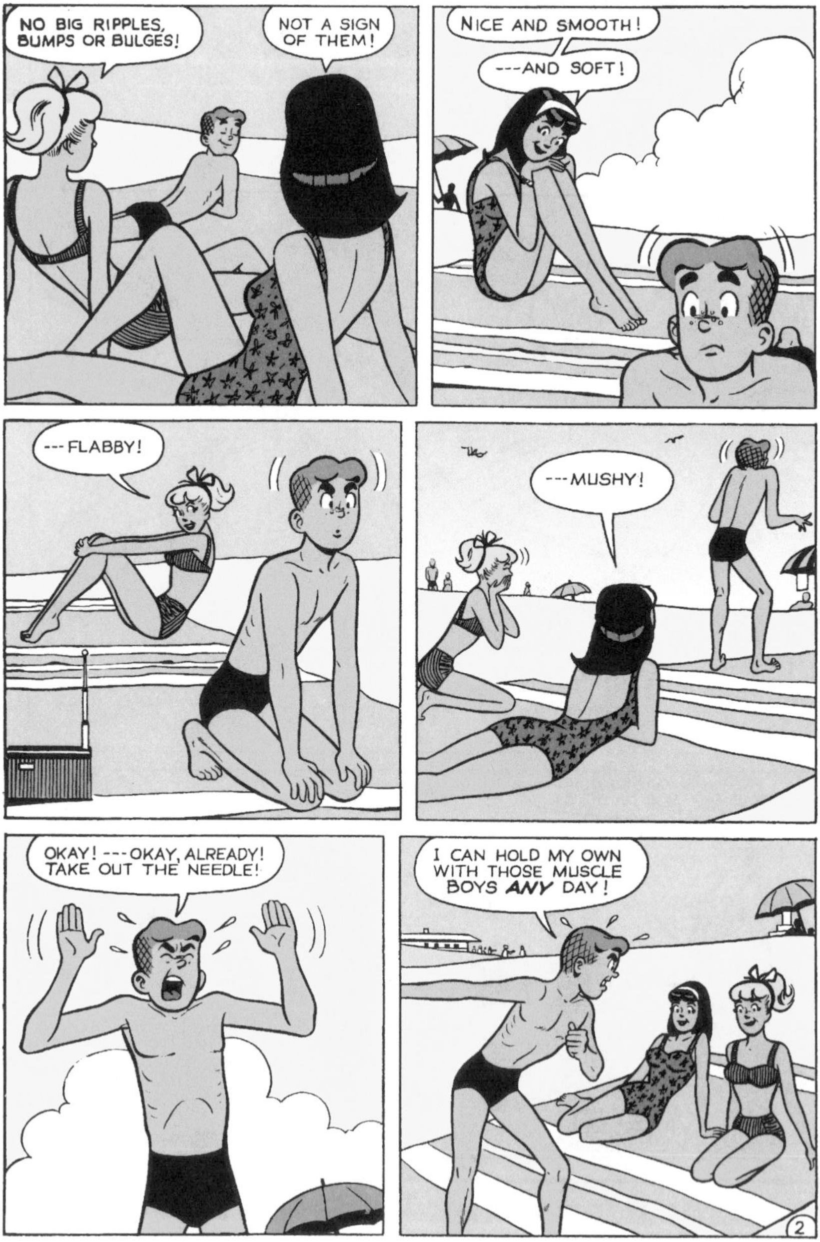
NO BIG RIPPLES, BUMPS OR BULGES!
NOT A SIGN OF THEM!
NICE AND SMOOTH!
---AND SOFT!
---FLABBY!
---MUSHY!
OKAY! ---OKAY, ALREADY! TAKE OUT THE NEEDLE!
I CAN HOLD MY OWN WITH THOSE MUSCLE BOYS ANY DAY!
2

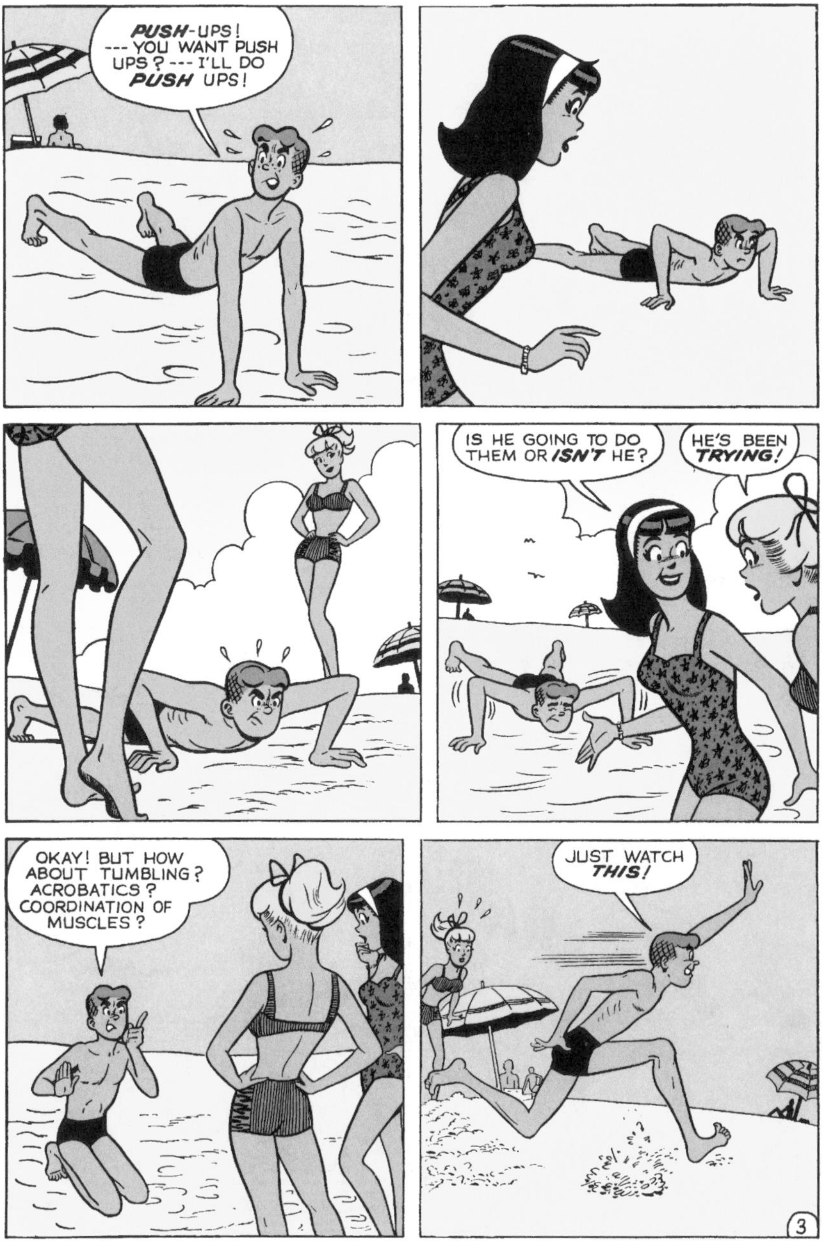

PUSH-UPS! --- YOU WANT PUSH UPS? --- I'LL DO PUSH UPS!
IS HE GOING TO DO THEM OR ISN'T HE?
HE'S BEEN TRYING!
OKAY! BUT HOW ABOUT TUMBLING? ACROBATICS? COORDINATION OF MUSCLES?
JUST WATCH THIS!
3

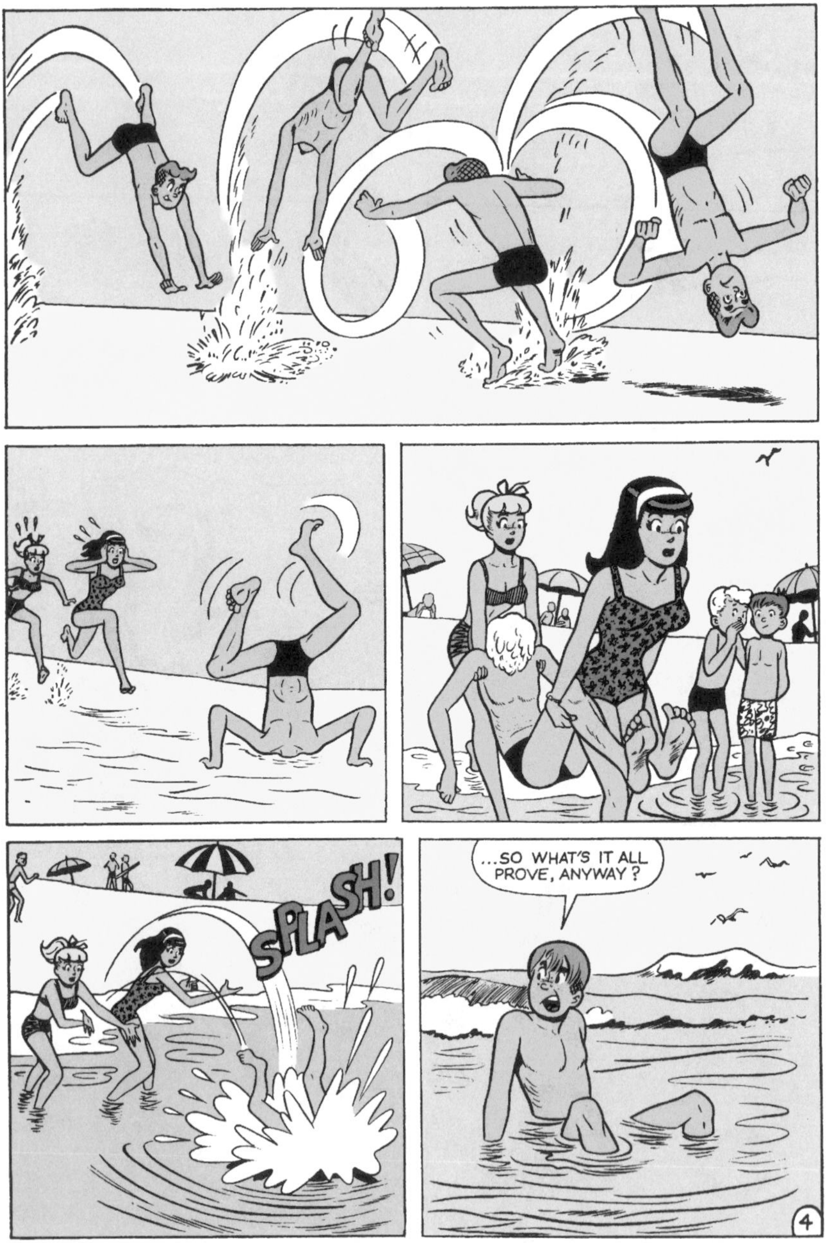
SPLASH!
...SO WHAT'S IT ALL PROVE, ANYWAY?
4

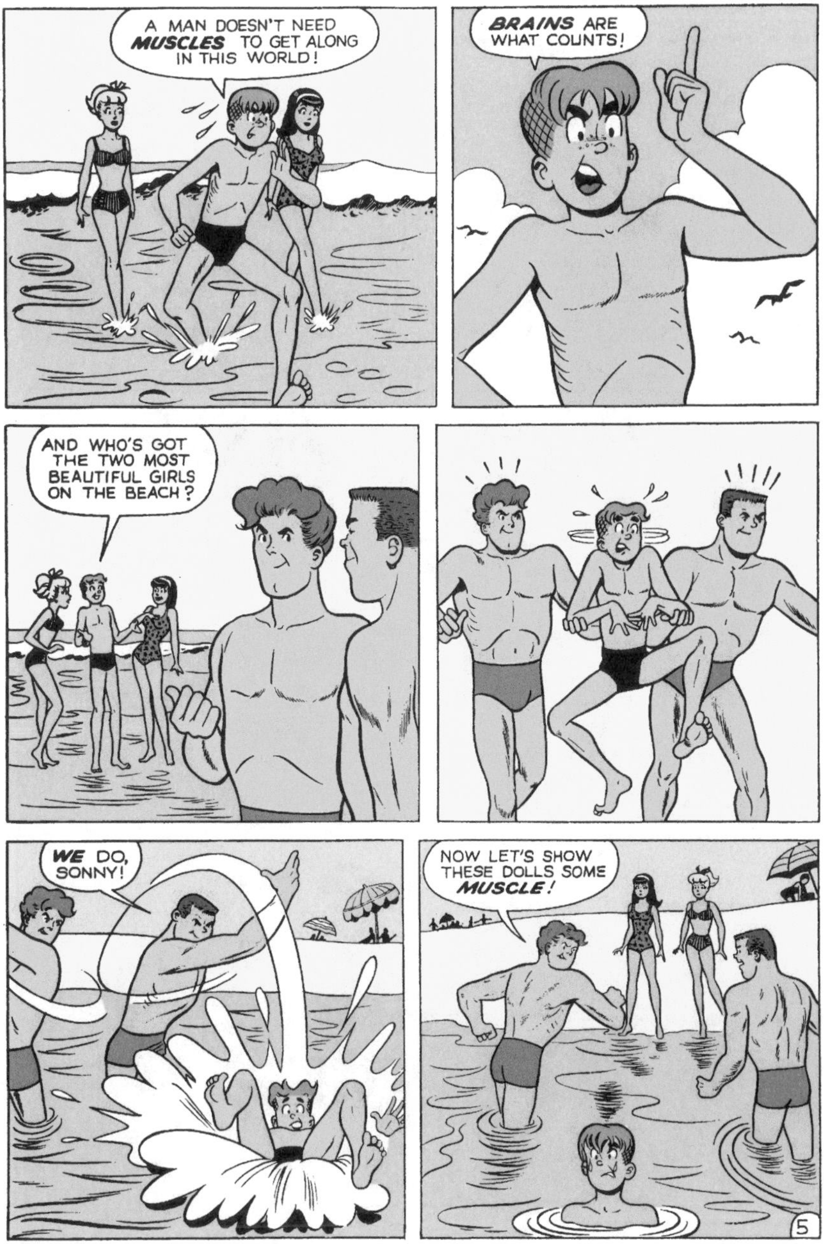
A MAN DOESN'T NEED MUSCLES TO GET ALONG IN THIS WORLD!
BRAINS ARE WHAT COUNTS!
AND WHO'S GOT THE TWO MOST BEAUTIFUL GIRLS ON THE BEACH?
WE DO, SONNY!
NOW LET'S SHOW THESE DOLLS SOME MUSCLE!
5

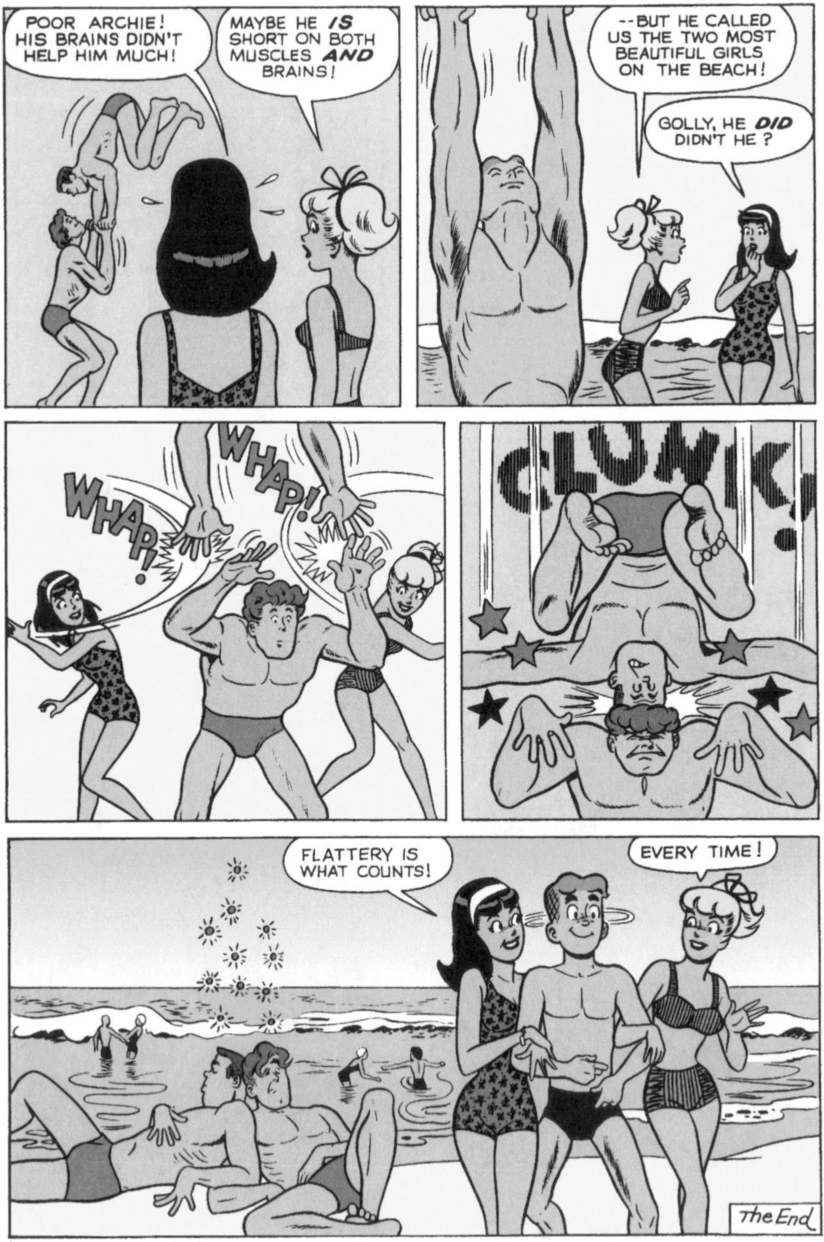
POOR ARCHIE! HIS BRAINS DIDN'T HELP HIM MUCH!
MAYBE HE IS SHORT ON BOTH MUSCLES AND BRAINS!
--BUT HE CALLED US THE TWO MOST BEAUTIFUL GIRLS ON THE BEACH!
GOLLY, HE DID DIDN'T HE ?
WHAP!
WHAP!
CLUNK!
FLATTERY IS WHAT COUNTS!
EVERY TIME!
The End

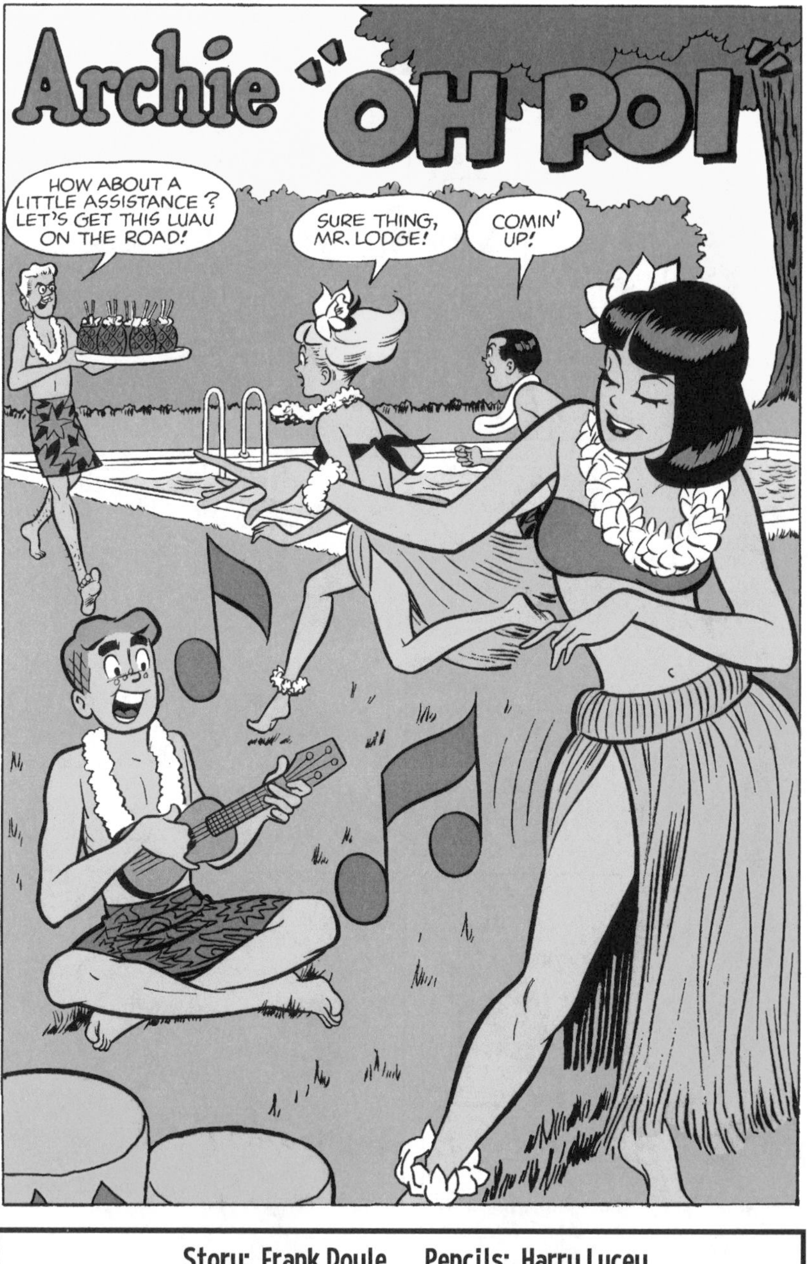
Archie "OH POI"
HOW ABOUT A LITTLE ASSISTANCE ? LET'S GET THIS LUAU ON THE ROAD!
SURE THING, MR. LODGE!
COMIN' UP!

Story: Frank Doyle Pencils: Harry Lucey
Inks & Letters: Marty Epp Colors: Barry Grossman

Originally printed in LIFE WITH ARCHIE #30, October 1964

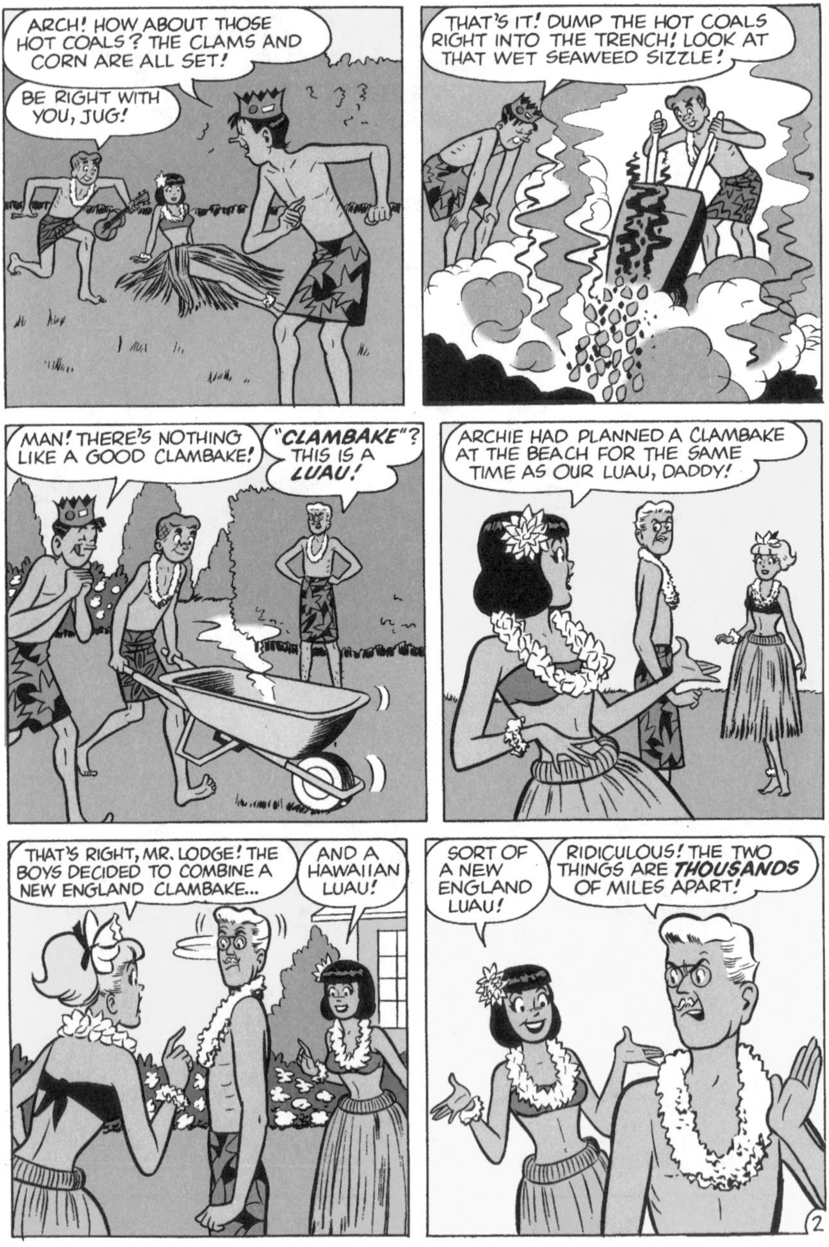
ARCH! HOW ABOUT THOSE HOT COALS? THE CLAMS AND CORN ARE ALL SET!
BE RIGHT WITH YOU, JUG!
THAT'S IT! DUMP THE HOT COALS RIGHT INTO THE TRENCH! LOOK AT THAT WET SEAWEED SIZZLE!
MAN! THERE'S NOTHING LIKE A GOOD CLAMBAKE!
"CLAMBAKE"? THIS IS A LUAU!
ARCHIE HAD PLANNED A CLAMBAKE AT THE BEACH FOR THE SAME TIME AS OUR LUAU, DADDY!
THAT'S RIGHT, MR. LODGE! THE BOYS DECIDED TO COMBINE A NEW ENGLAND CLAMBAKE...
AND A HAWAIIAN LUAU!
SORT OF A NEW ENGLAND LUAU!
RIDICULOUS! THE TWO THINGS ARE THOUSANDS OF MILES APART!
2

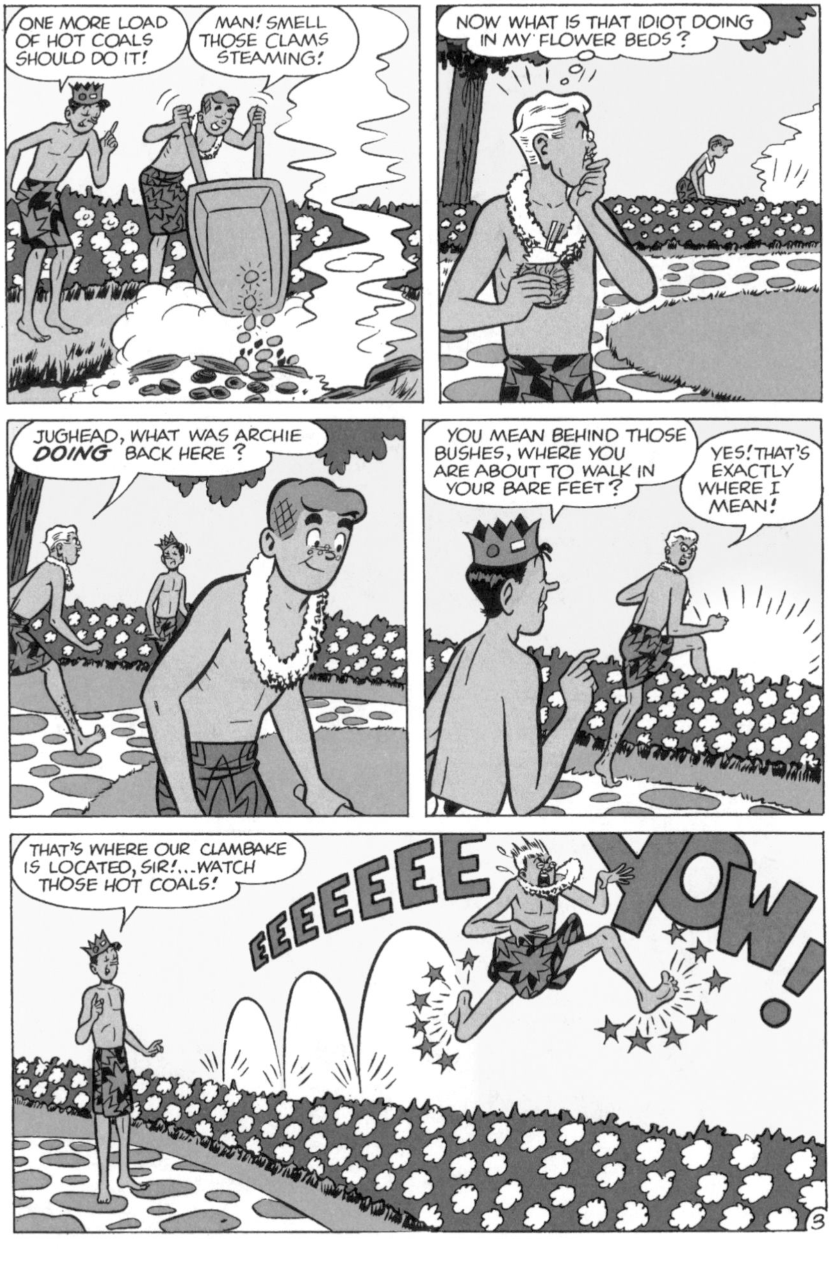
ONE MORE LOAD OF HOT COALS SHOULD DO IT!
MAN! SMELL THOSE CLAMS STEAMING!
NOW WHAT IS THAT IDIOT DOING IN MY FLOWER BEDS?
JUGHEAD, WHAT WAS ARCHIE DOING BACK HERE?
YOU MEAN BEHIND THOSE BUSHES, WHERE YOU ARE ABOUT TO WALK IN YOUR BARE FEET?
YES! THAT'S EXACTLY WHERE I MEAN!
THAT'S WHERE OUR CLAMBAKE IS LOCATED, SIR!...WATCH THOSE HOT COALS!
EEEEEEE
YOW!
3

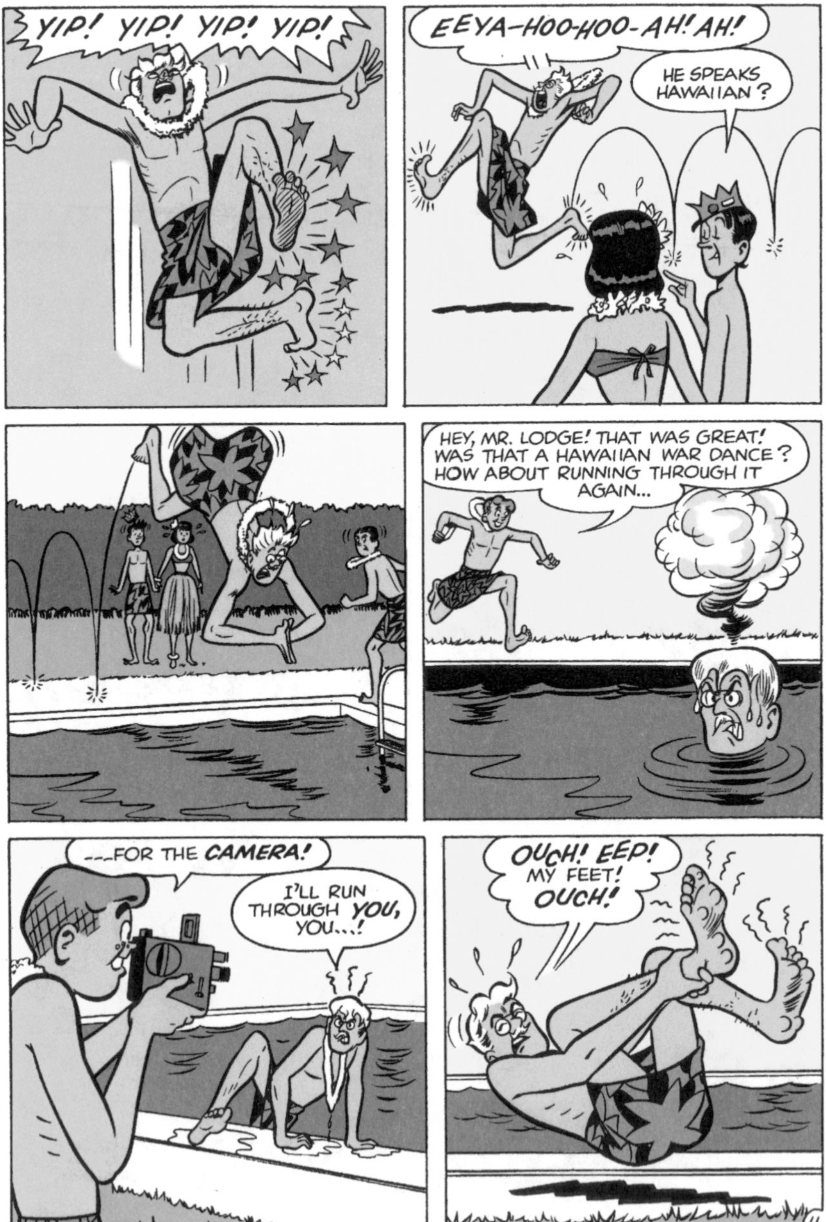
YIP! YIP! YIP! YIP!
EEYA-HOO-HOO-AH! AH!
HE SPEAKS HAWAIIAN?
HEY, MR. LODGE! THAT WAS GREAT! WAS THAT A HAWAIIAN WAR DANCE? HOW ABOUT RUNNING THROUGH IT AGAIN...
---FOR THE CAMERA!
I'LL RUN THROUGH YOU, YOU...!
OUCH! EEP! MY FEET! OUCH!
4

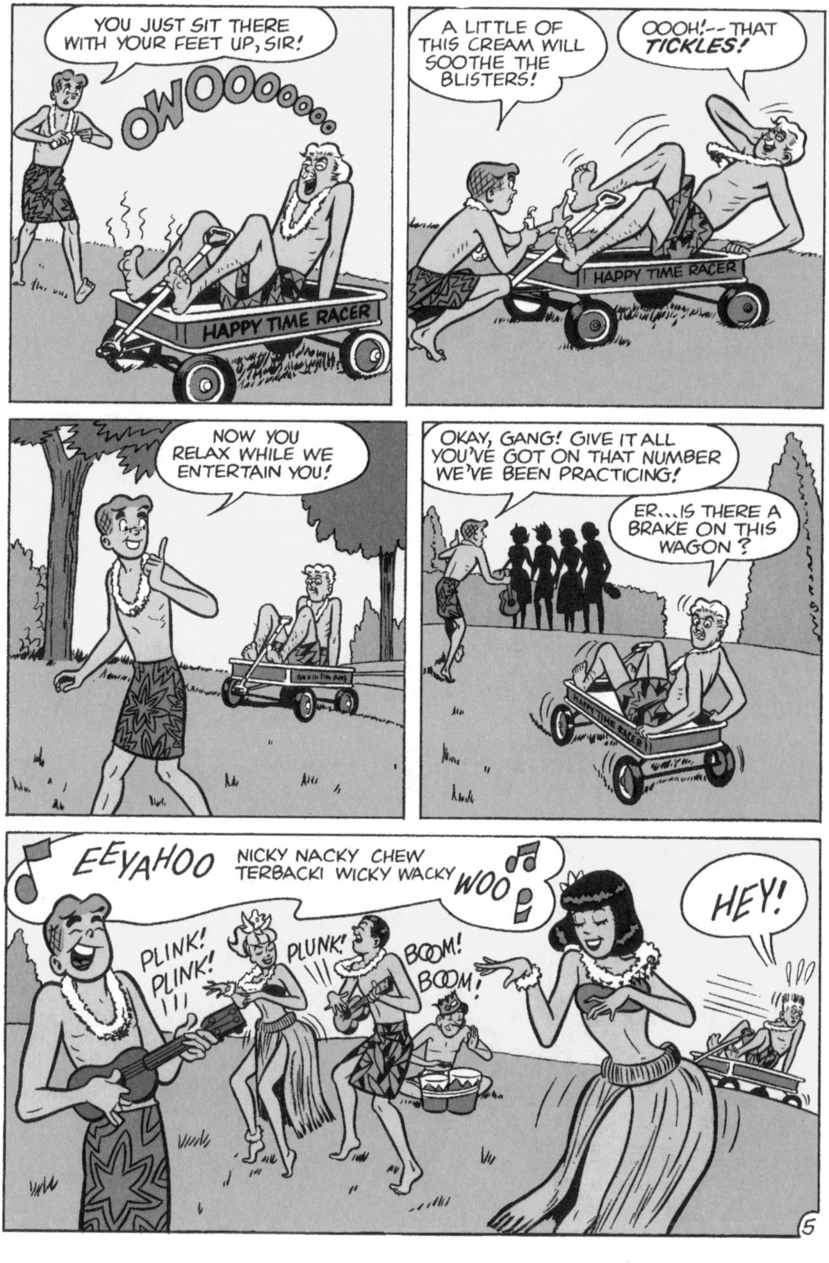
YOU JUST SIT THERE WITH YOUR FEET UP, SIR!
OWOOOoooo
HAPPY TIME RACER
A LITTLE OF THIS CREAM WILL SOOTHE THE BLISTERS!
OOOH!-- THAT TICKLES!
HAPPY TIME RACER
NOW YOU RELAX WHILE WE ENTERTAIN YOU!
OKAY, GANG! GIVE IT ALL YOU'VE GOT ON THAT NUMBER WE'VE BEEN PRACTICING!
ER...IS THERE A BRAKE ON THIS WAGON?
HAPPY TIME RACER
EEYAHOO NICKY NACKY CHEW TERBACKI WICKY WACKY WOO
HEY!
PLINK! PLINK!
PLUNK!
BOOM! BOOM!
5

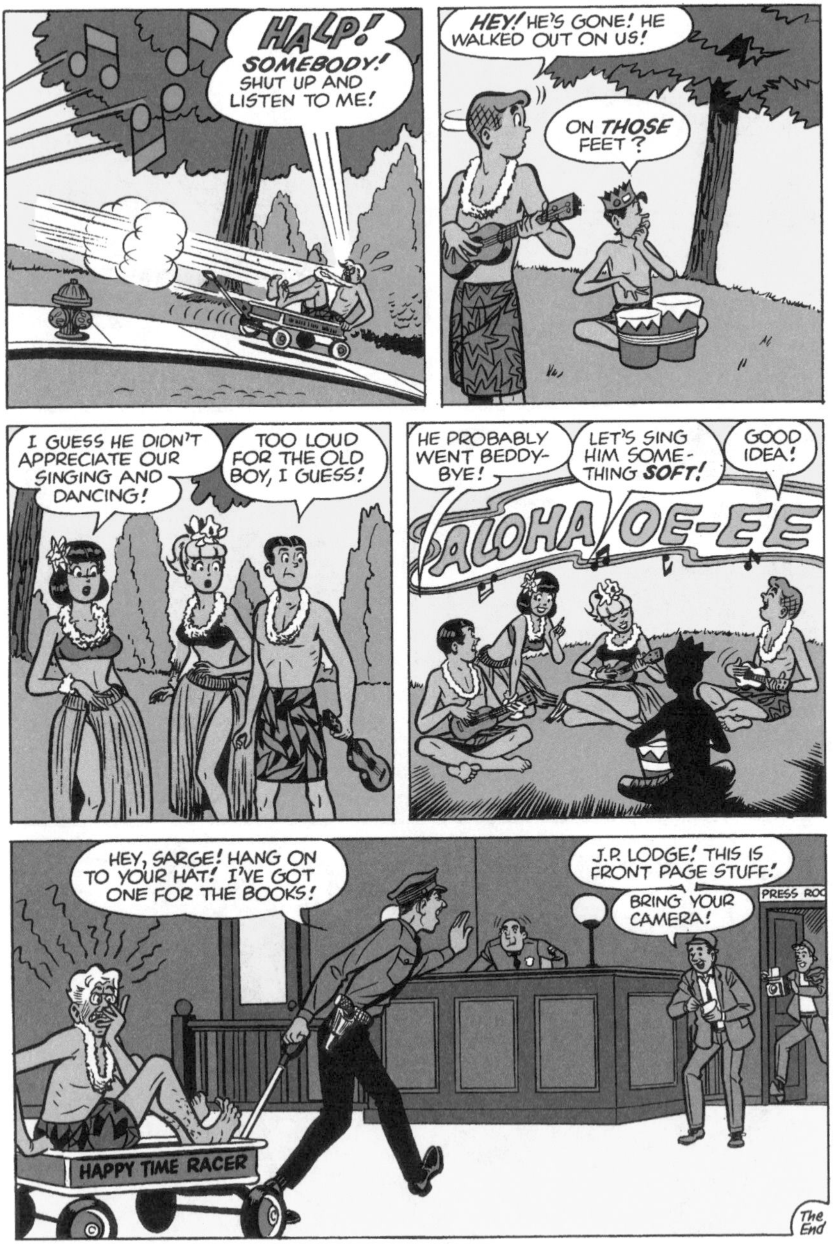
HALP!
SOMEBODY! SHUT UP AND LISTEN TO ME!
HEY! HE'S GONE! HE WALKED OUT ON US!
ON THOSE FEET?
I GUESS HE DIDN'T APPRECIATE OUR SINGING AND DANCING!
TOO LOUD FOR THE OLD BOY, I GUESS!
HE PROBABLY WENT BEDDY-BYE!
LET'S SING HIM SOME-THING SOFT!
GOOD IDEA!
ALOHA OE-EE
HEY, SARGE! HANG ON TO YOUR HAT! I'VE GOT ONE FOR THE BOOKS!
J.P. LODGE! THIS IS FRONT PAGE STUFF!
BRING YOUR CAMERA!
PRESS ROO
HAPPY TIME RACER
The End

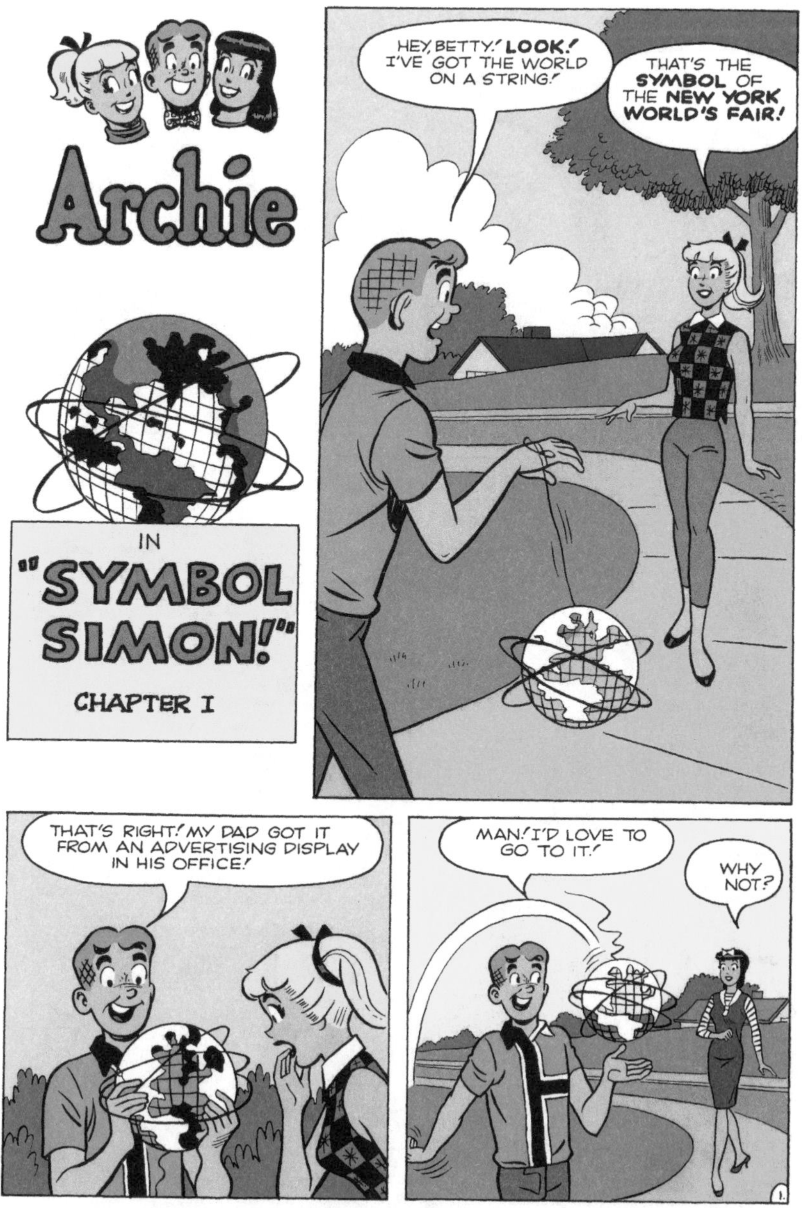
Archie
IN
"SYMBOL SIMON!"
CHAPTER I
HEY, BETTY! LOOK! I'VE GOT THE WORLD ON A STRING!
THAT'S THE SYMBOL OF THE NEW YORK WORLD'S FAIR!
THAT'S RIGHT! MY DAD GOT IT FROM AN ADVERTISING DISPLAY IN HIS OFFICE!
MAN! I'D LOVE TO GO TO IT!
WHY NOT?
1.

Story: George Gladir Art: Bob White Letters: Victor Gorelick

Originally printed in LIFE WITH ARCHIE #31, November 1964

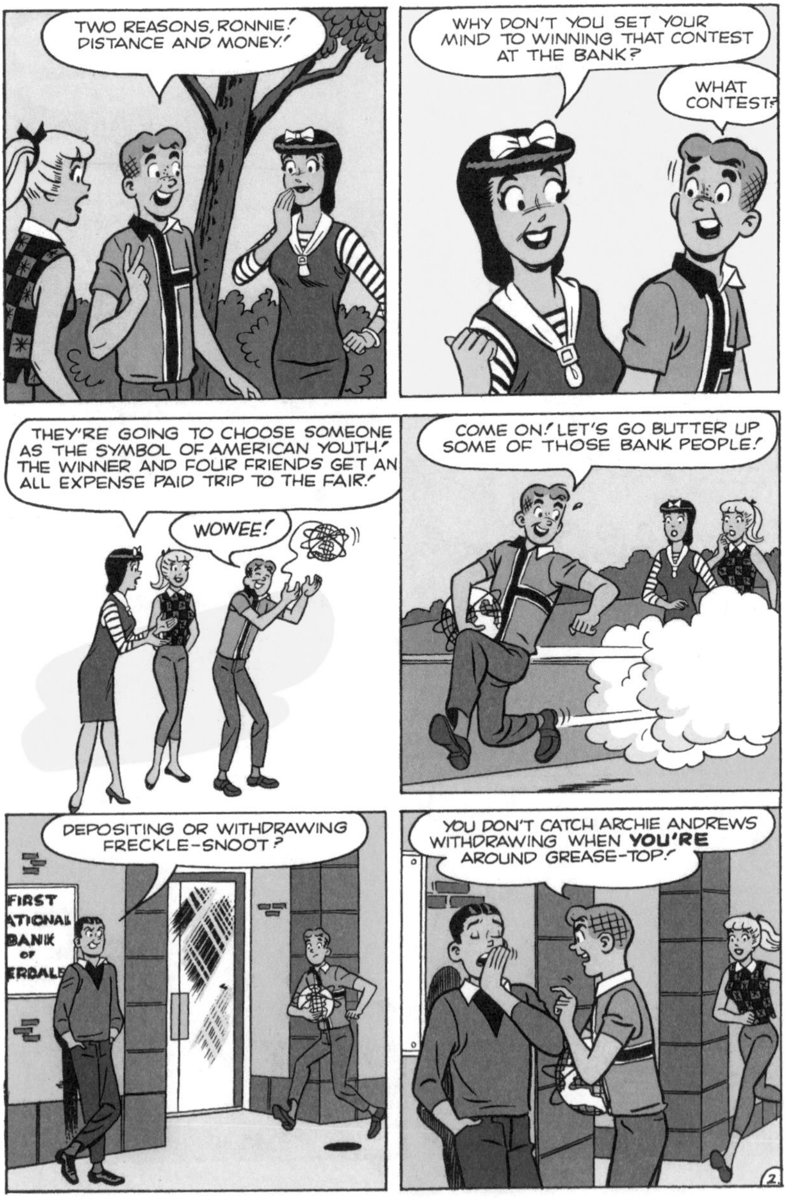
TWO REASONS, RONNIE! DISTANCE AND MONEY!
WHY DON'T YOU SET YOUR MIND TO WINNING THAT CONTEST AT THE BANK?
WHAT CONTEST?
THEY'RE GOING TO CHOOSE SOMEONE AS THE SYMBOL OF AMERICAN YOUTH! THE WINNER AND FOUR FRIENDS GET AN ALL EXPENSE PAID TRIP TO THE FAIR!
WOWEE!
COME ON! LET'S GO BUTTER UP SOME OF THOSE BANK PEOPLE!
DEPOSITING OR WITHDRAWING FRECKLE-SNOOT?
FIRST
ATIONAL
BANK
OF
ERDALE
YOU DON'T CATCH ARCHIE ANDREWS WITHDRAWING WHEN **YOU'RE** AROUND GREASE-TOP!
2.

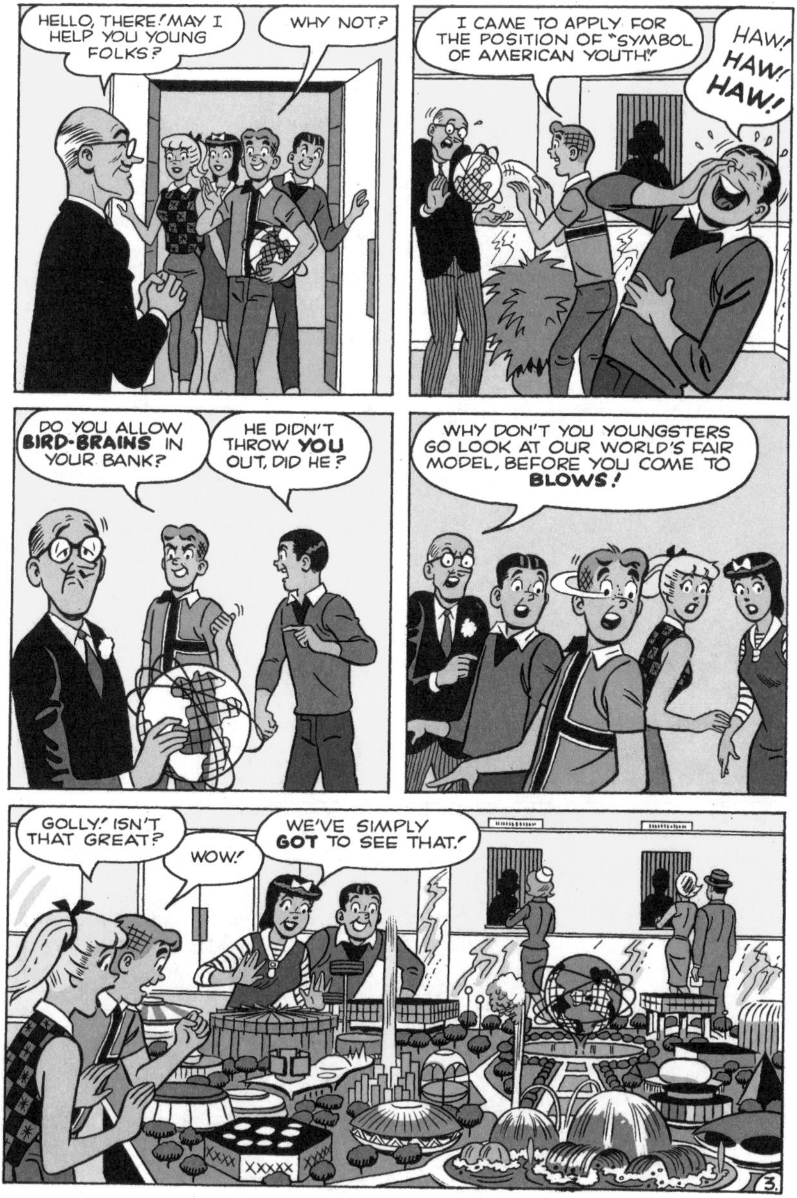
HELLO, THERE! MAY I HELP YOU YOUNG FOLKS?
WHY NOT?
I CAME TO APPLY FOR THE POSITION OF "SYMBOL OF AMERICAN YOUTH!"
HAW! HAW! HAW!
DO YOU ALLOW BIRD-BRAINS IN YOUR BANK?
HE DIDN'T THROW YOU OUT, DID HE?
WHY DON'T YOU YOUNGSTERS GO LOOK AT OUR WORLD'S FAIR MODEL, BEFORE YOU COME TO BLOWS!
GOLLY! ISN'T THAT GREAT?
WOW!
WE'VE SIMPLY GOT TO SEE THAT!
3.

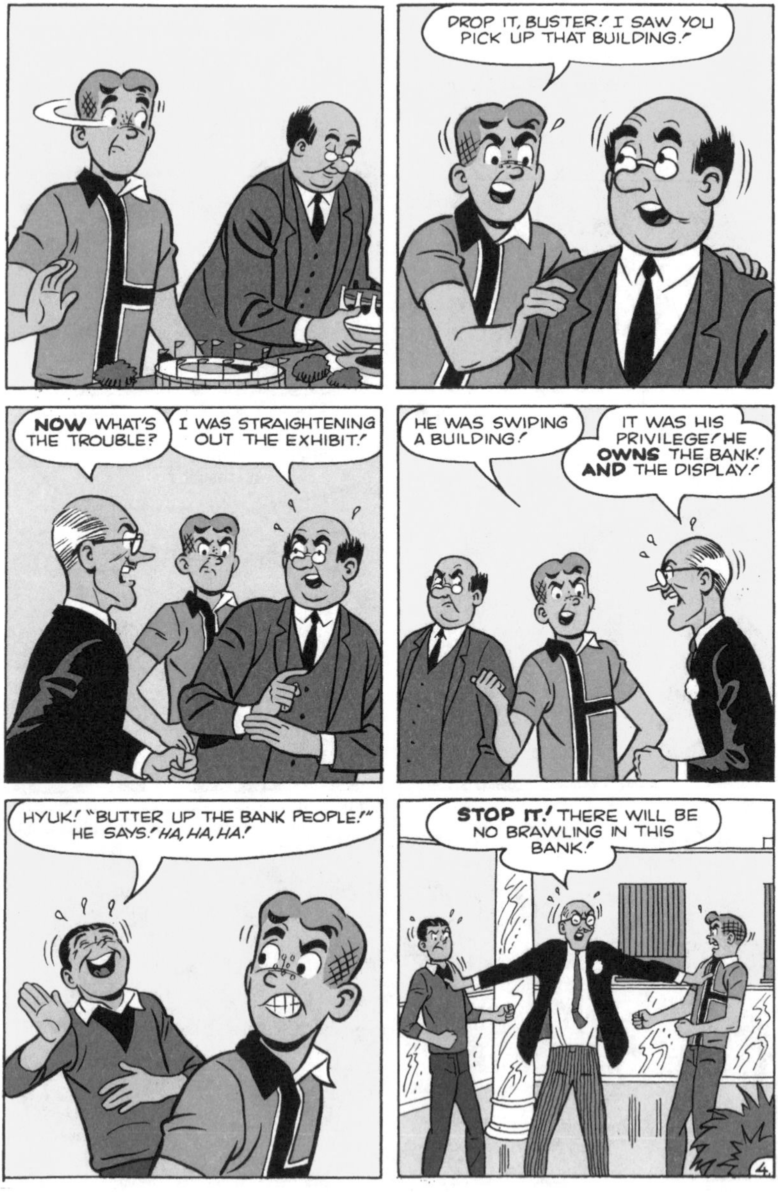
DROP IT, BUSTER! I SAW YOU PICK UP THAT BUILDING!
NOW WHAT'S THE TROUBLE?
I WAS STRAIGHTENING OUT THE EXHIBIT!
HE WAS SWIPING A BUILDING!
IT WAS HIS PRIVILEGE! HE OWNS THE BANK! AND THE DISPLAY!
HYUK! "BUTTER UP THE BANK PEOPLE!" HE SAYS! HA, HA, HA!
STOP IT! THERE WILL BE NO BRAWLING IN THIS BANK!
4.

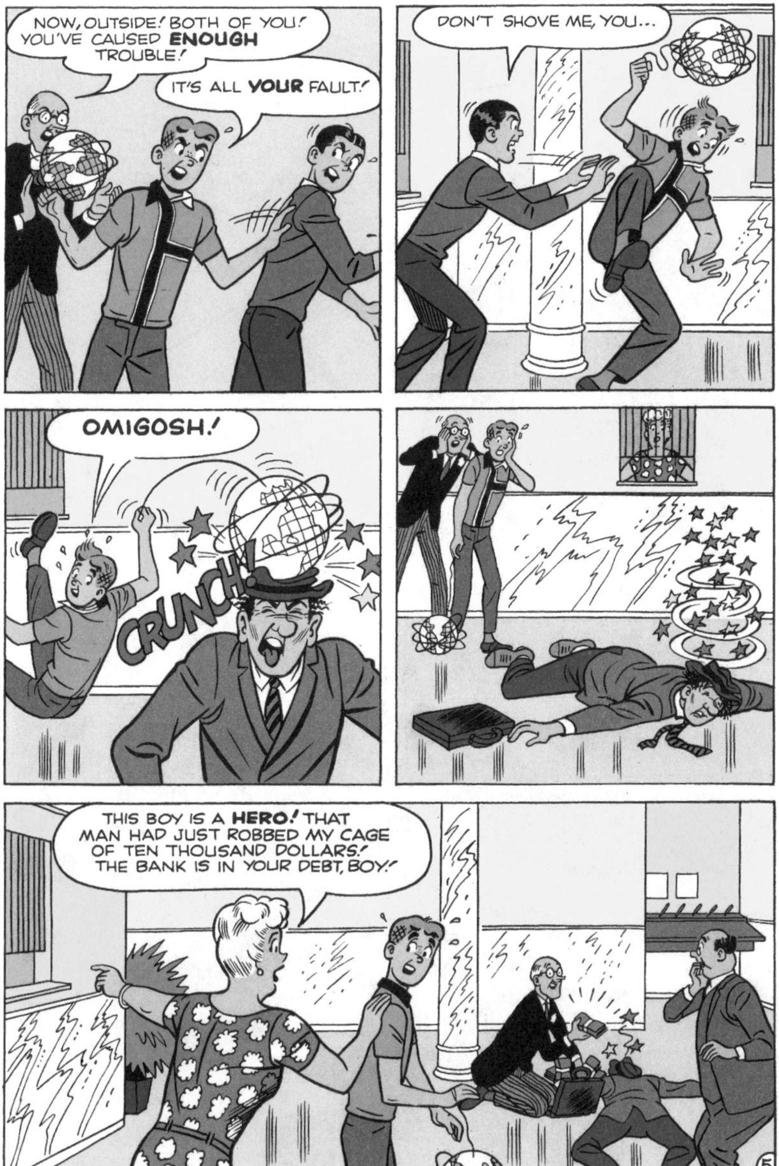
NOW, OUTSIDE! BOTH OF YOU! YOU'VE CAUSED ENOUGH TROUBLE!
IT'S ALL YOUR FAULT!
DON'T SHOVE ME, YOU...
OMIGOSH!
CRUNCH!
THIS BOY IS A HERO! THAT MAN HAD JUST ROBBED MY CAGE OF TEN THOUSAND DOLLARS! THE BANK IS IN YOUR DEBT, BOY!
5

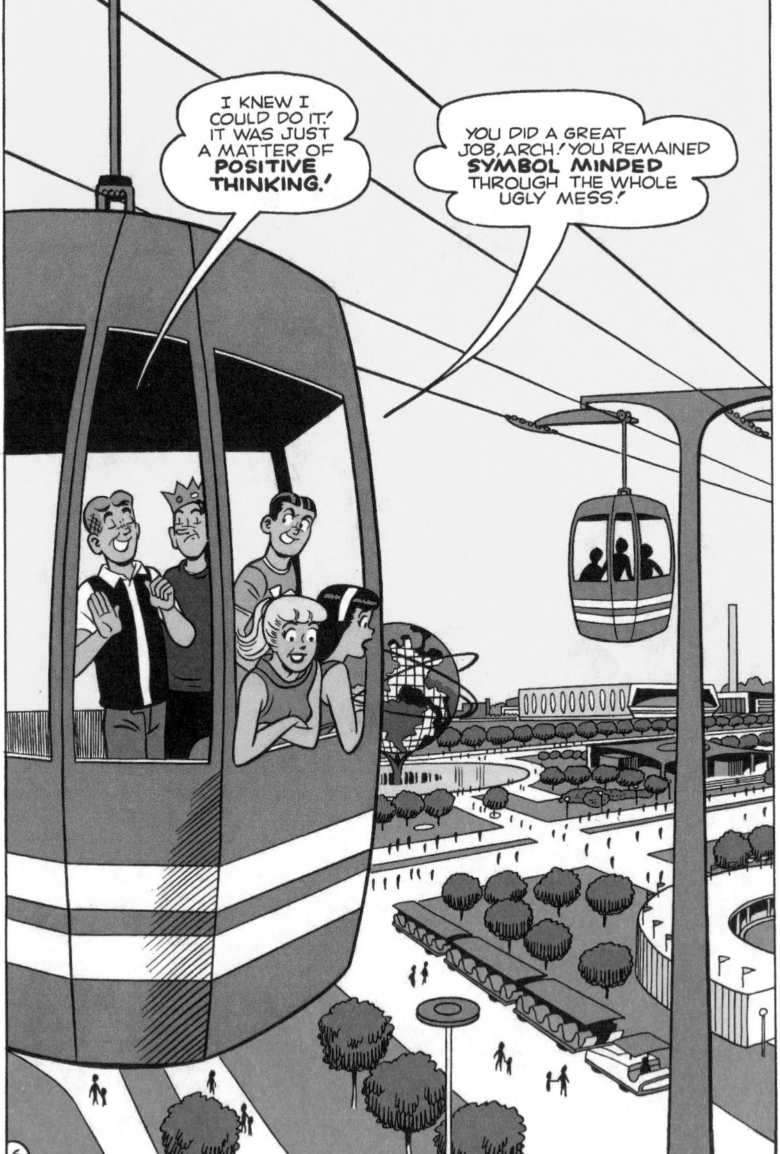
I KNEW I COULD DO IT! IT WAS JUST A MATTER OF POSITIVE THINKING!
YOU DID A GREAT JOB, ARCH! YOU REMAINED SYMBOL MINDED THROUGH THE WHOLE UGLY MESS!
6.

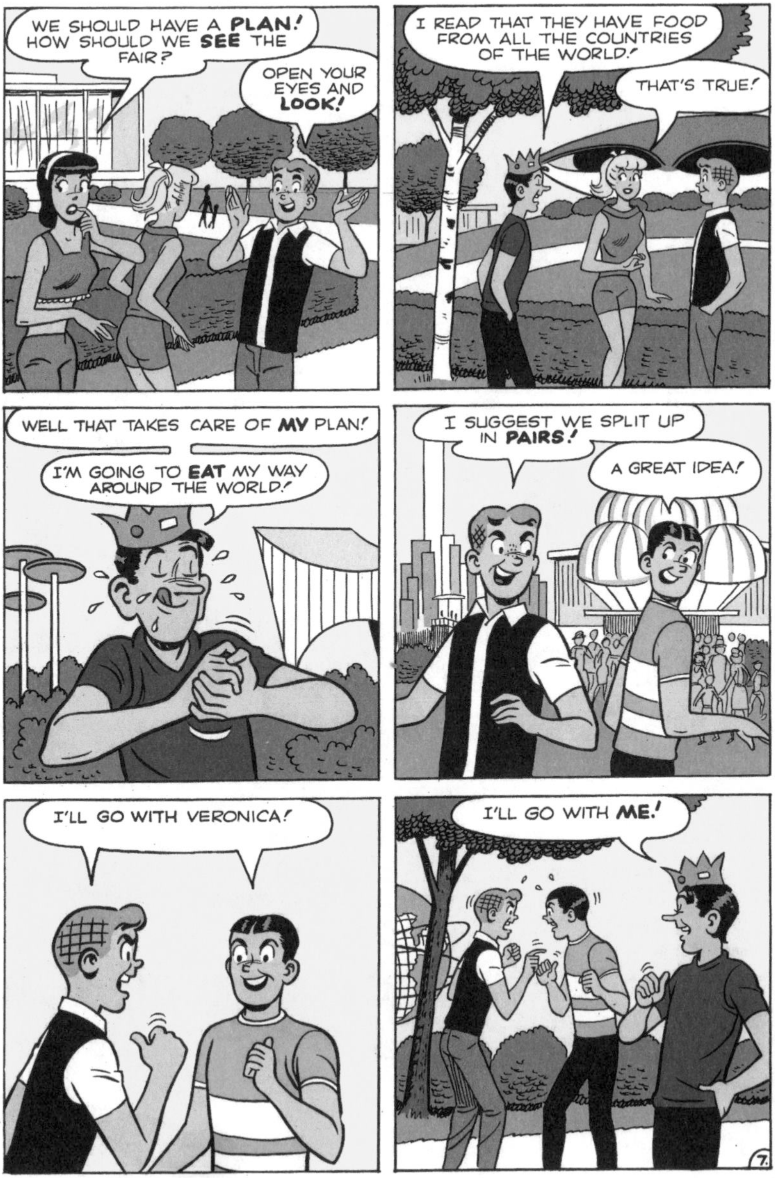
WE SHOULD HAVE A PLAN! HOW SHOULD WE SEE THE FAIR?
OPEN YOUR EYES AND LOOK!
I READ THAT THEY HAVE FOOD FROM ALL THE COUNTRIES OF THE WORLD!
THAT'S TRUE!
WELL THAT TAKES CARE OF MY PLAN!
I'M GOING TO EAT MY WAY AROUND THE WORLD!
I SUGGEST WE SPLIT UP IN PAIRS!
A GREAT IDEA!
I'LL GO WITH VERONICA!
I'LL GO WITH ME!
7

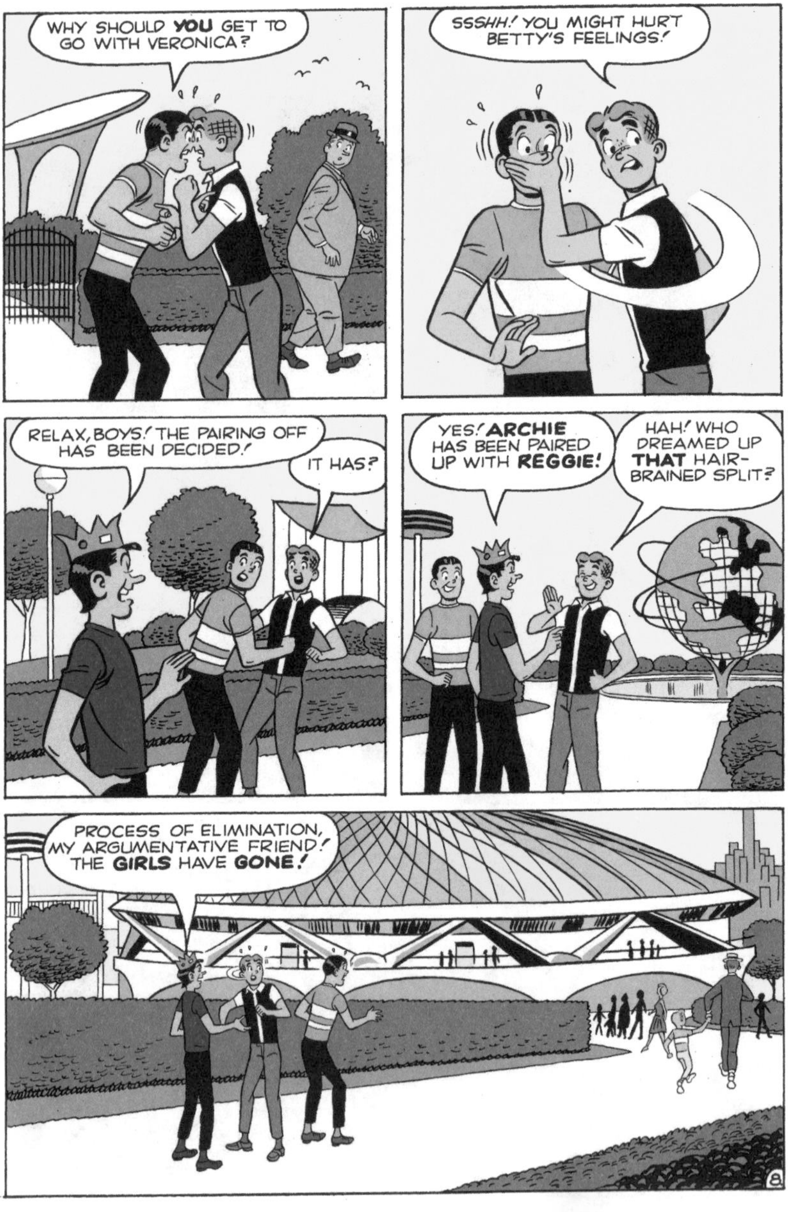
WHY SHOULD **YOU** GET TO GO WITH VERONICA?
SSSHH! YOU MIGHT HURT BETTY'S FEELINGS!
RELAX, BOYS! THE PAIRING OFF HAS BEEN DECIDED!
IT HAS?
YES! **ARCHIE** HAS BEEN PAIRED UP WITH **REGGIE**!
HAH! WHO DREAMED UP **THAT** HAIR-BRAINED SPLIT?
PROCESS OF ELIMINATION, MY ARGUMENTATIVE FRIEND! THE **GIRLS** HAVE **GONE**!
8

Archie *in* 'FAIR ENOUGH'

CHAPTER II

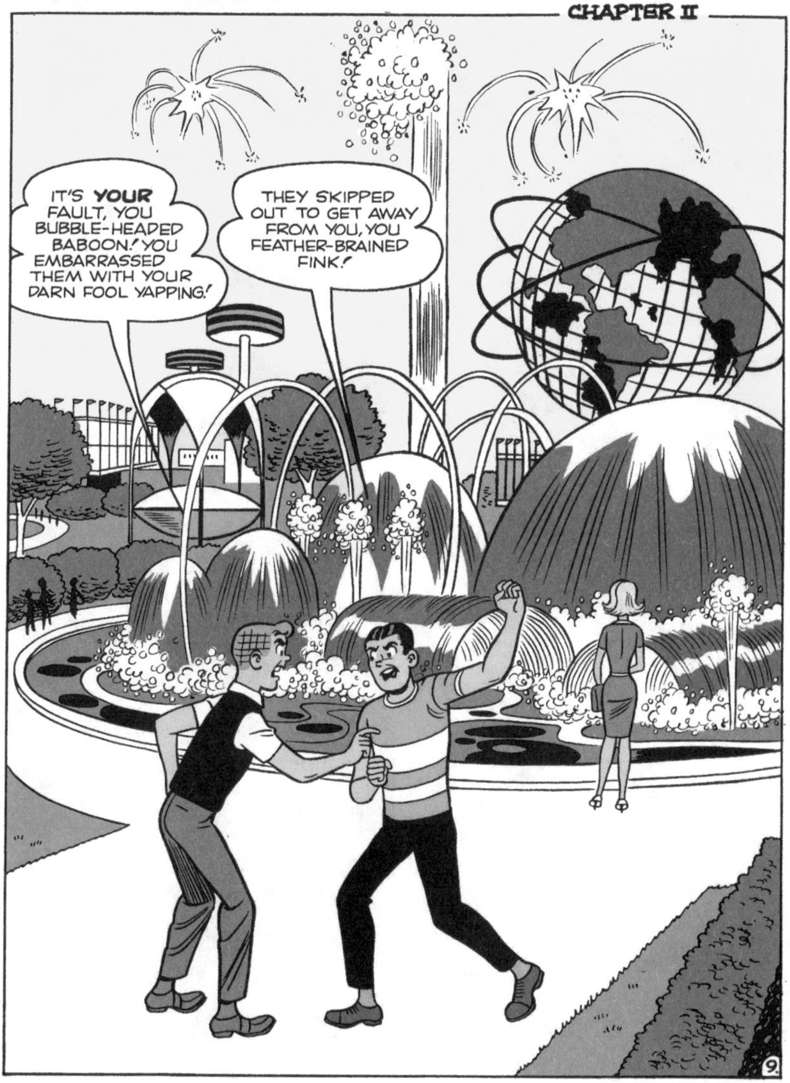
IT'S YOUR FAULT, YOU BUBBLE-HEADED BABOON! YOU EMBARRASSED THEM WITH YOUR DARN FOOL YAPPING!
THEY SKIPPED OUT TO GET AWAY FROM YOU, YOU FEATHER-BRAINED FINK!
9.

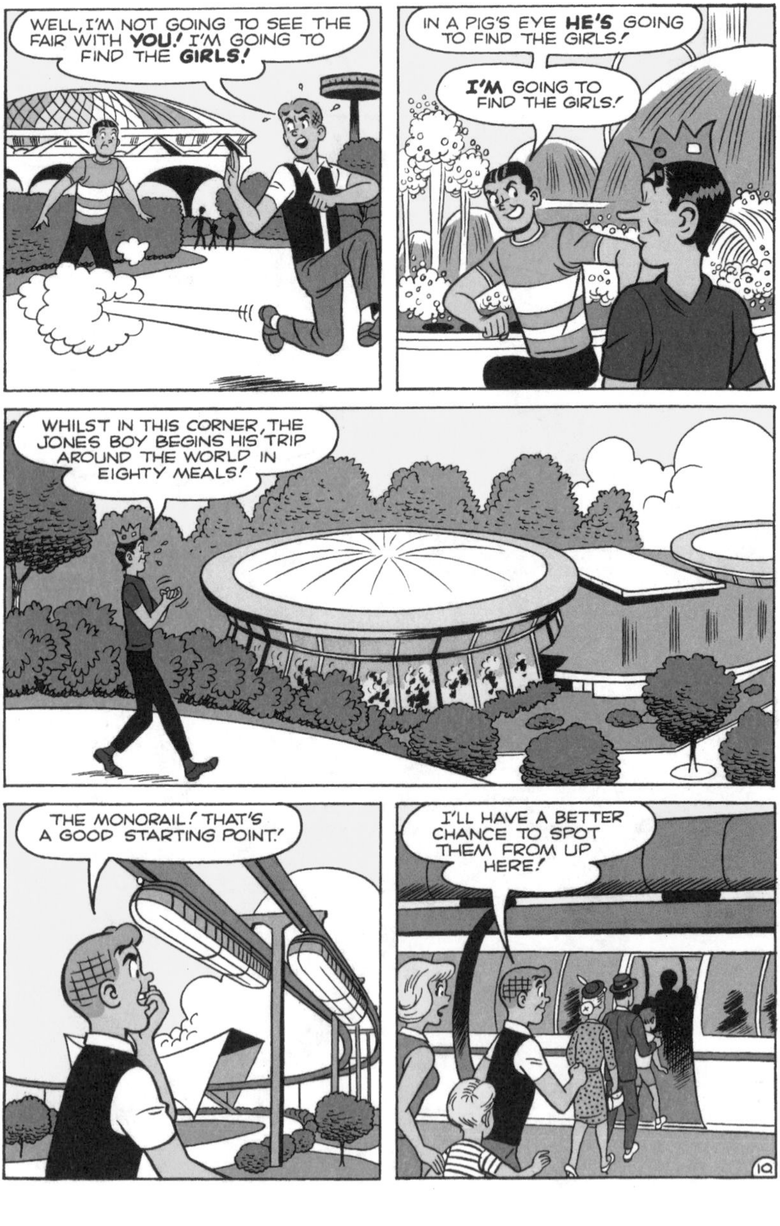
WELL, I'M NOT GOING TO SEE THE FAIR WITH YOU! I'M GOING TO FIND THE GIRLS!
IN A PIG'S EYE HE'S GOING TO FIND THE GIRLS!
I'M GOING TO FIND THE GIRLS!
WHILST IN THIS CORNER, THE JONES BOY BEGINS HIS TRIP AROUND THE WORLD IN EIGHTY MEALS!
THE MONORAIL! THAT'S A GOOD STARTING POINT!
I'LL HAVE A BETTER CHANCE TO SPOT THEM FROM UP HERE!
10

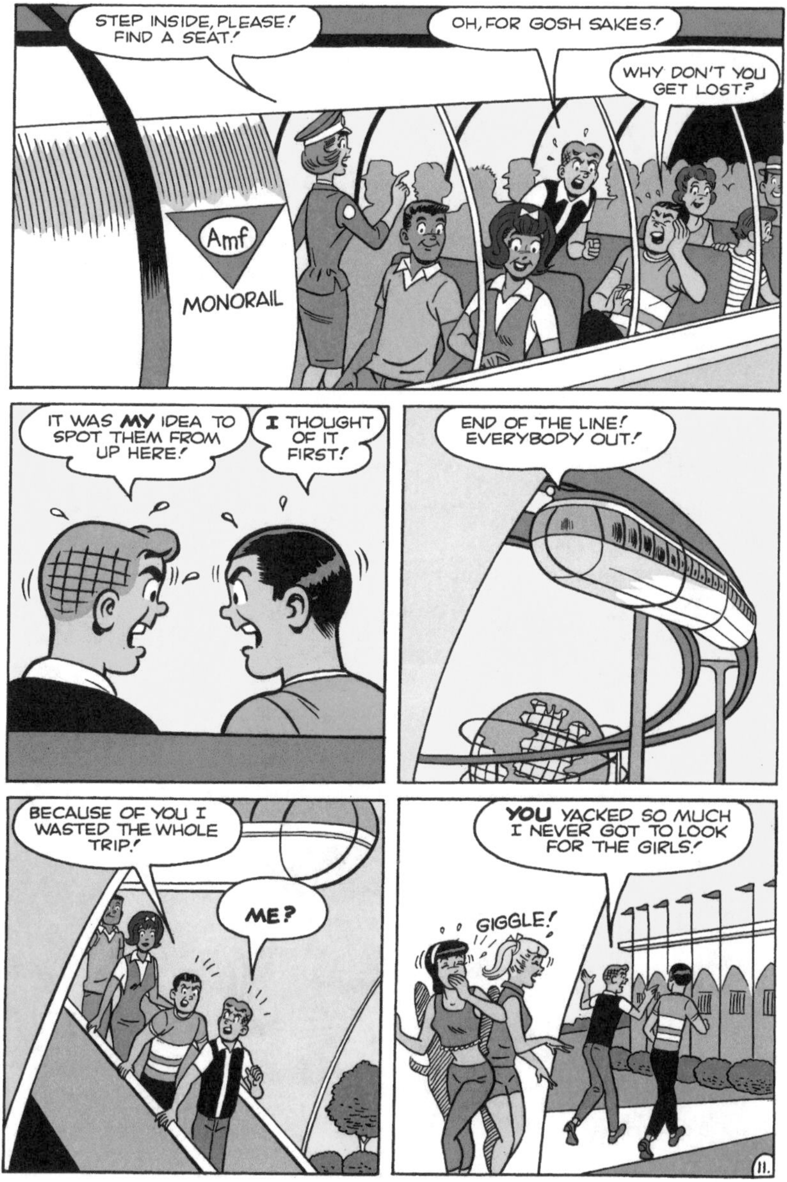
STEP INSIDE, PLEASE! FIND A SEAT!
OH, FOR GOSH SAKES!
WHY DON'T YOU GET LOST?
Amf
MONORAIL
IT WAS MY IDEA TO SPOT THEM FROM UP HERE!
I THOUGHT OF IT FIRST!
END OF THE LINE! EVERYBODY OUT!
BECAUSE OF YOU I WASTED THE WHOLE TRIP!
ME?
YOU YACKED SO MUCH I NEVER GOT TO LOOK FOR THE GIRLS!
GIGGLE!
11.

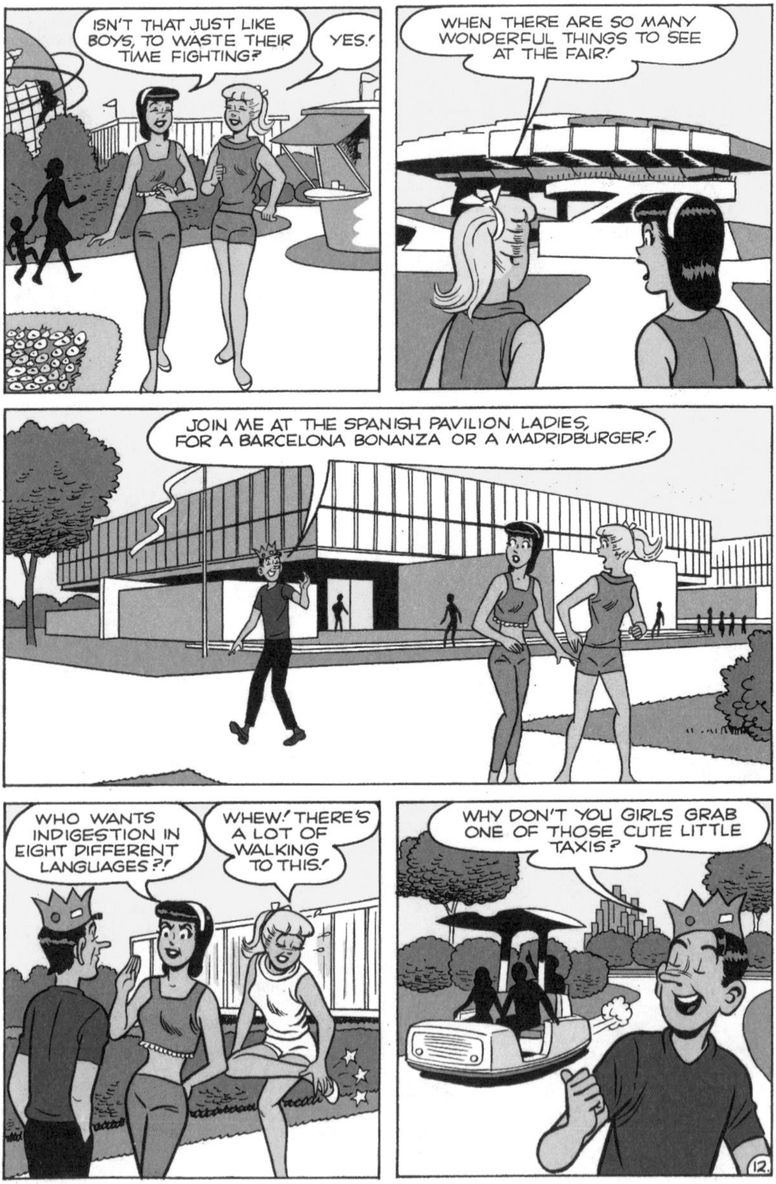
ISN'T THAT JUST LIKE BOYS, TO WASTE THEIR TIME FIGHTING?
YES!
WHEN THERE ARE SO MANY WONDERFUL THINGS TO SEE AT THE FAIR!
JOIN ME AT THE SPANISH PAVILION LADIES, FOR A BARCELONA BONANZA OR A MADRIDBURGER!
WHO WANTS INDIGESTION IN EIGHT DIFFERENT LANGUAGES?!
WHEW! THERE'S A LOT OF WALKING TO THIS!
WHY DON'T YOU GIRLS GRAB ONE OF THOSE CUTE LITTLE TAXIS?
12.

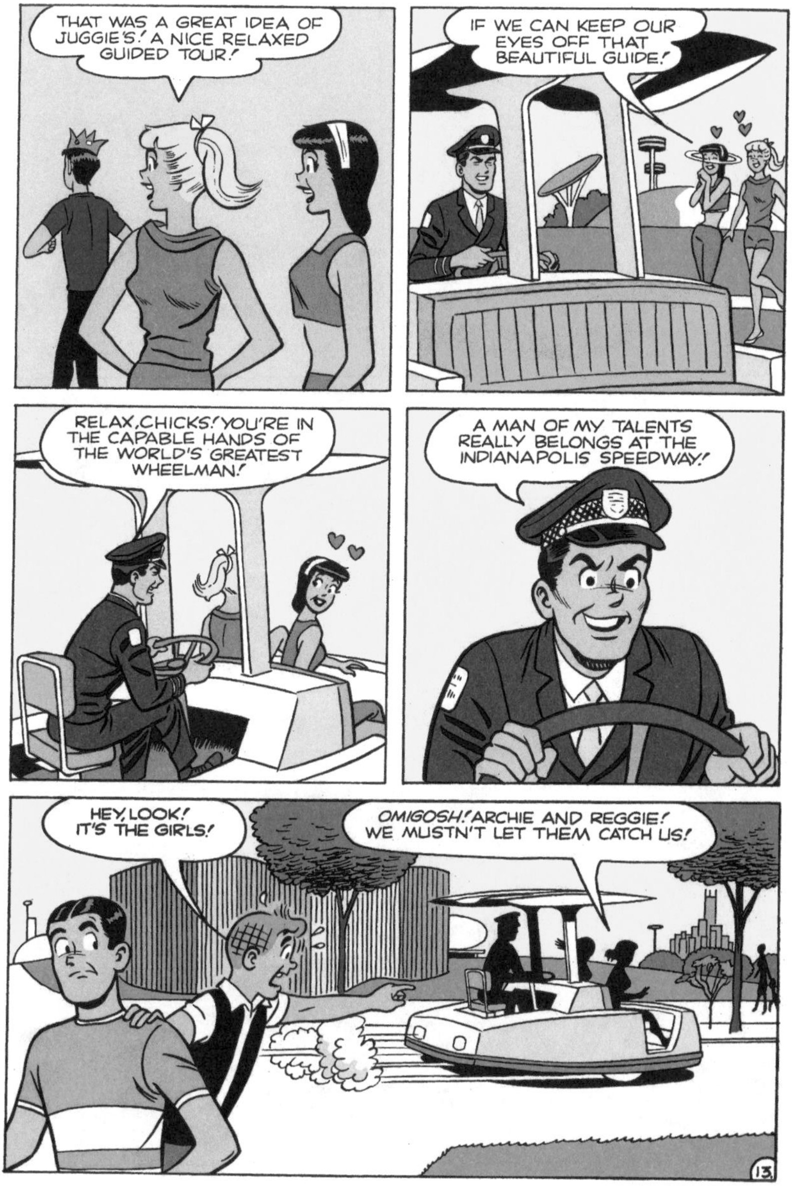
THAT WAS A GREAT IDEA OF JUGGIE'S! A NICE RELAXED GUIDED TOUR!
IF WE CAN KEEP OUR EYES OFF THAT BEAUTIFUL GUIDE!
RELAX, CHICKS! YOU'RE IN THE CAPABLE HANDS OF THE WORLD'S GREATEST WHEELMAN!
A MAN OF MY TALENTS REALLY BELONGS AT THE INDIANAPOLIS SPEEDWAY!
HEY, LOOK! IT'S THE GIRLS!
OMIGOSH! ARCHIE AND REGGIE! WE MUSTN'T LET THEM CATCH US!
13

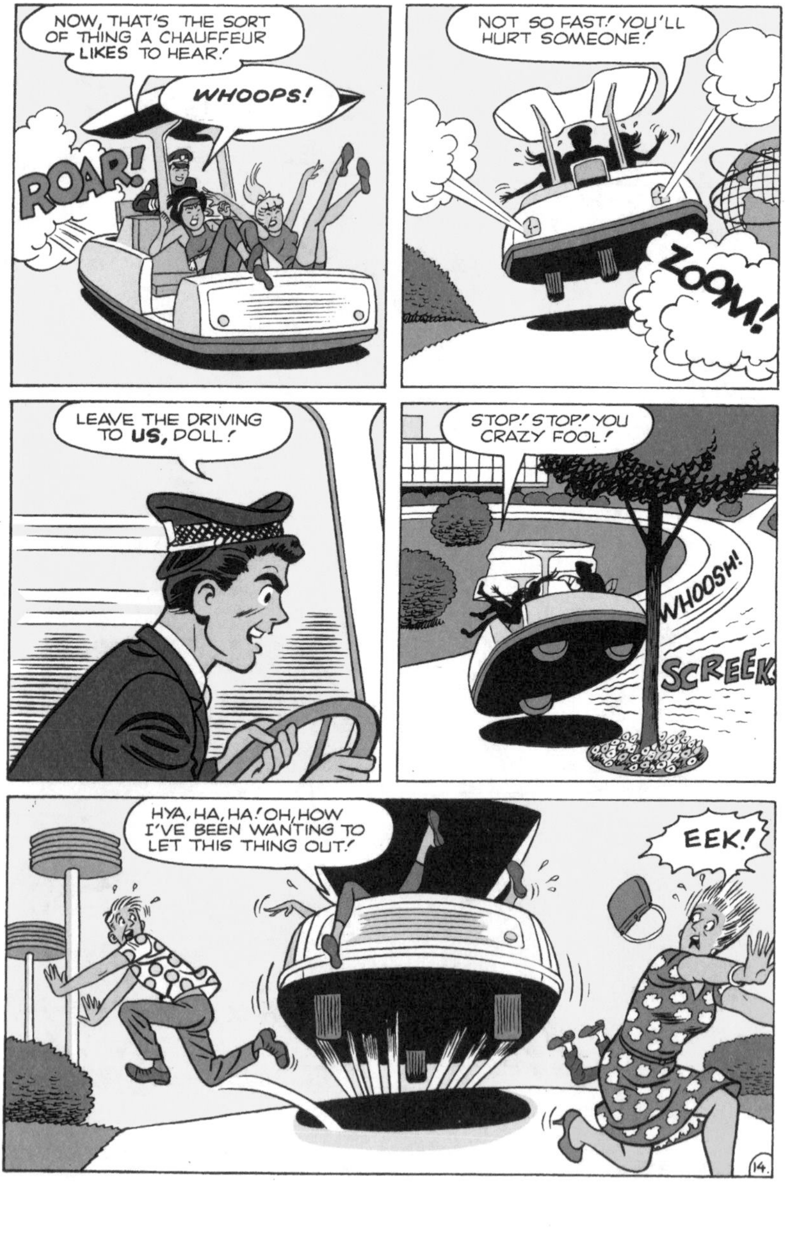
NOW, THAT'S THE SORT OF THING A CHAUFFEUR LIKES TO HEAR!
WHOOPS!
ROAR!
NOT SO FAST! YOU'LL HURT SOMEONE!
ZOOM!
LEAVE THE DRIVING TO US, DOLL!
STOP! STOP! YOU CRAZY FOOL!
WHOOSH!
SCREEK!
HYA, HA, HA! OH, HOW I'VE BEEN WANTING TO LET THIS THING OUT!
EEK!
14.

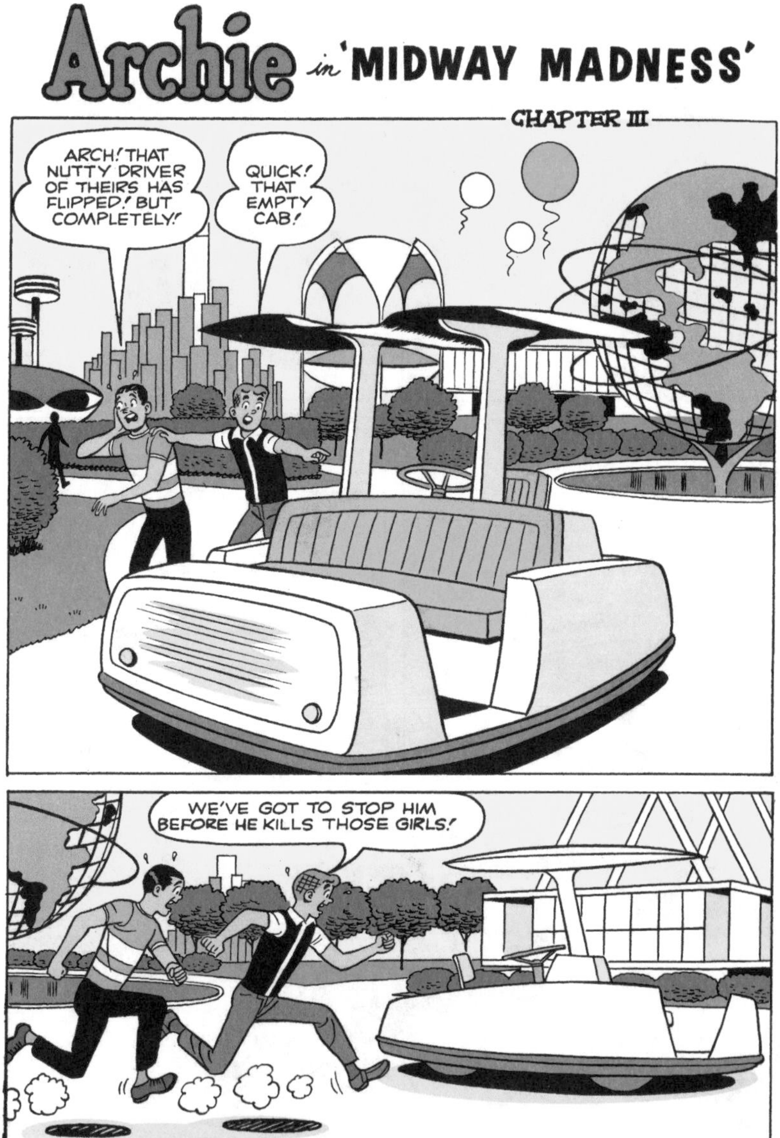
Archie in 'MIDWAY MADNESS'
CHAPTER III
ARCH! THAT NUTTY DRIVER OF THEIRS HAS FLIPPED! BUT COMPLETELY!
QUICK! THAT EMPTY CAB!
WE'VE GOT TO STOP HIM BEFORE HE KILLS THOSE GIRLS!
15

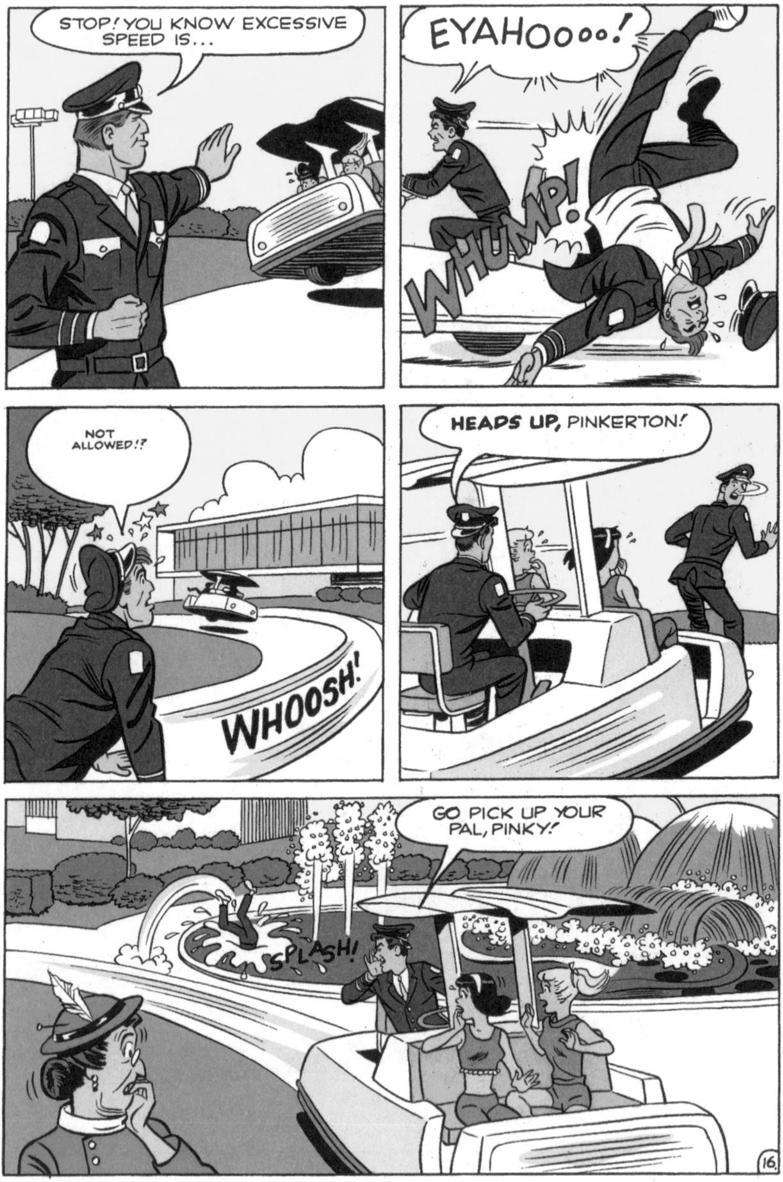
STOP! YOU KNOW EXCESSIVE SPEED IS...
EYAHOooo!
WHUMP!
NOT ALLOWED!?
WHOOSH!
HEADS UP, PINKERTON!
GO PICK UP YOUR PAL, PINKY!
SPLASH!
16

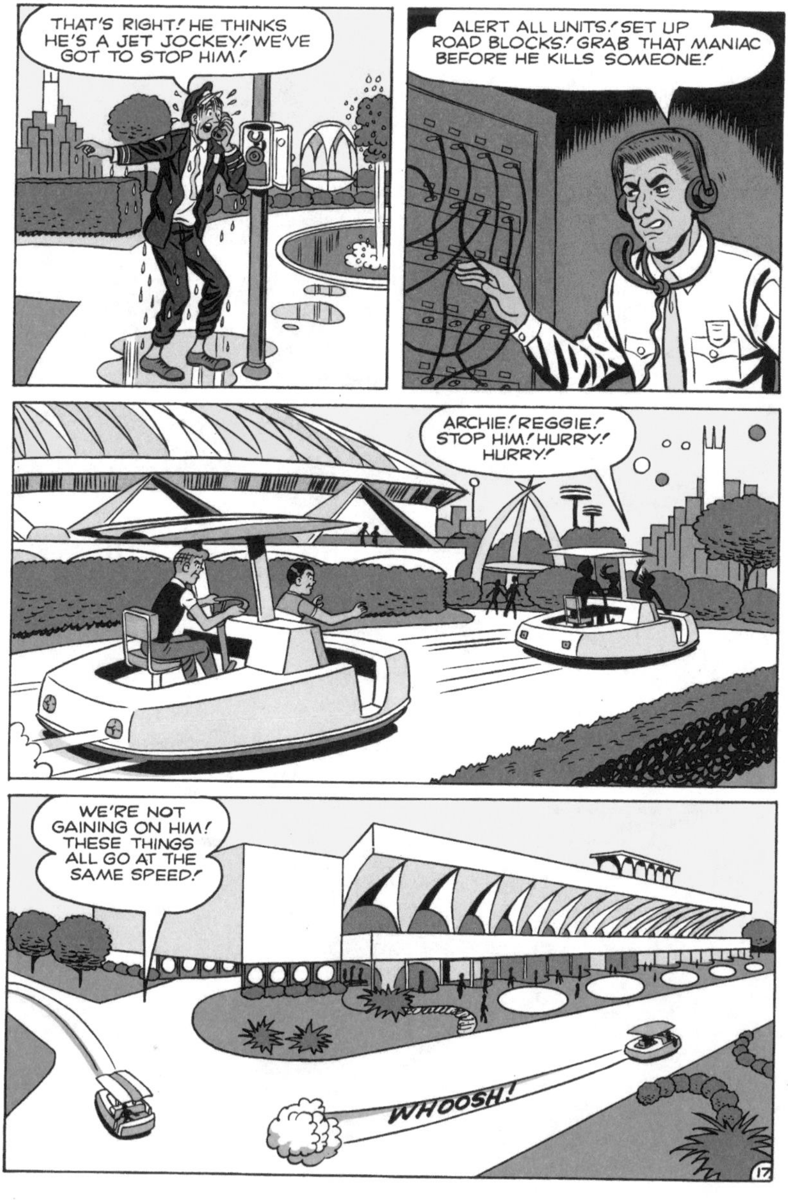
THAT'S RIGHT! HE THINKS HE'S A JET JOCKEY! WE'VE GOT TO STOP HIM!
ALERT ALL UNITS! SET UP ROAD BLOCKS! GRAB THAT MANIAC BEFORE HE KILLS SOMEONE!
ARCHIE! REGGIE! STOP HIM! HURRY! HURRY!
WE'RE NOT GAINING ON HIM! THESE THINGS ALL GO AT THE SAME SPEED!
WHOOSH!
17

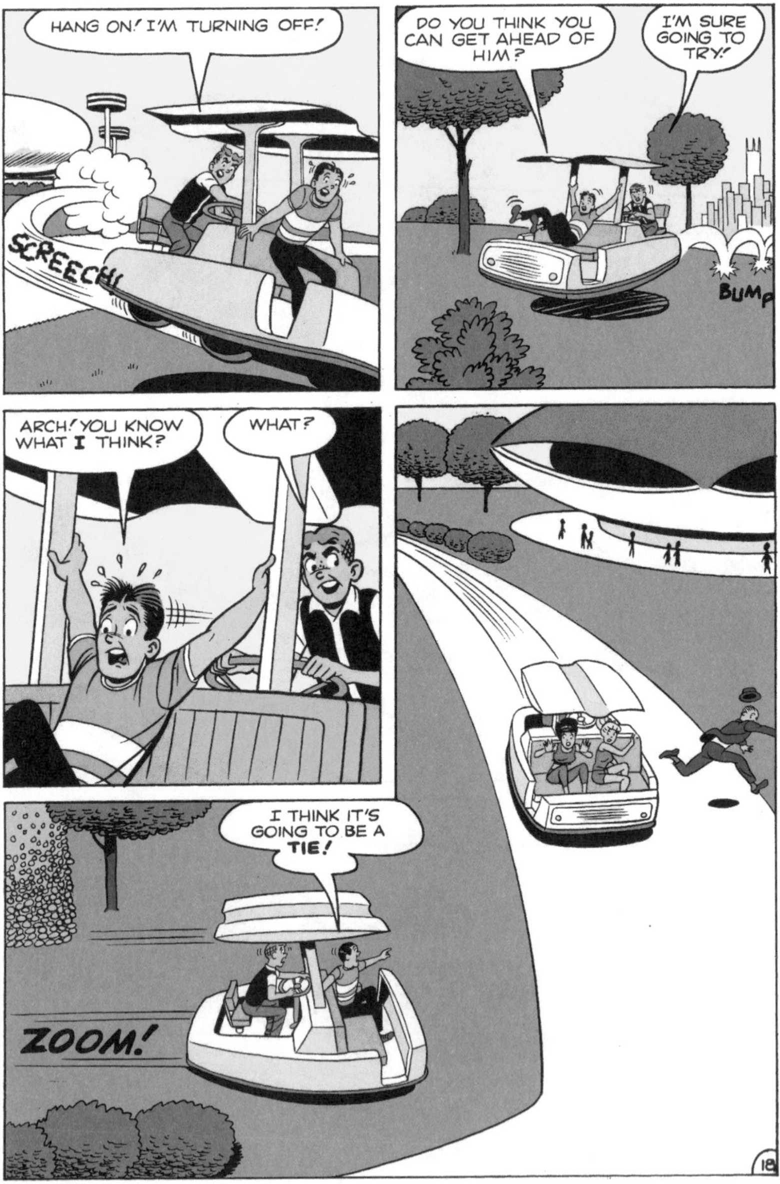
HANG ON! I'M TURNING OFF!
SCREECH!
DO YOU THINK YOU CAN GET AHEAD OF HIM?
I'M SURE GOING TO TRY!
BUMP
ARCH! YOU KNOW WHAT I THINK?
WHAT?
I THINK IT'S GOING TO BE A TIE!
ZOOM!
18

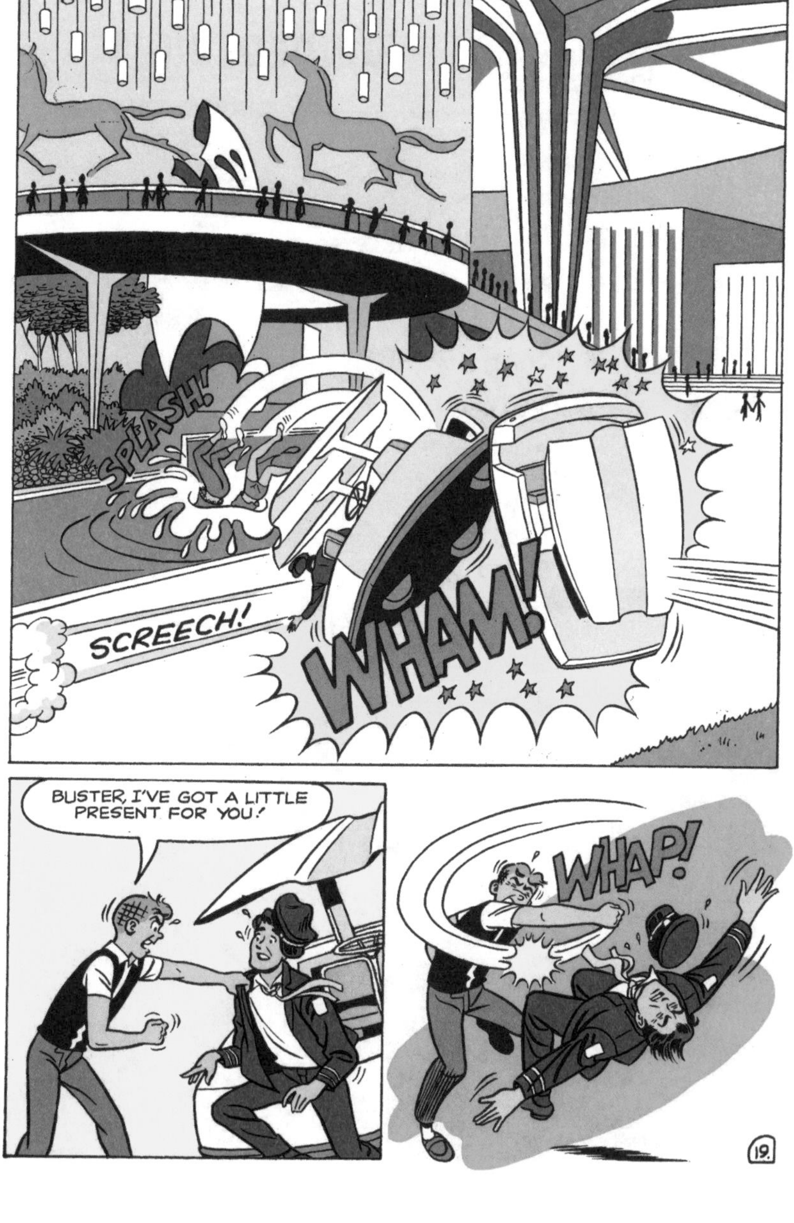
SPLASH!
SCREECH!
WHAM!
BUSTER, I'VE GOT A LITTLE PRESENT FOR YOU!
WHAP!
19.

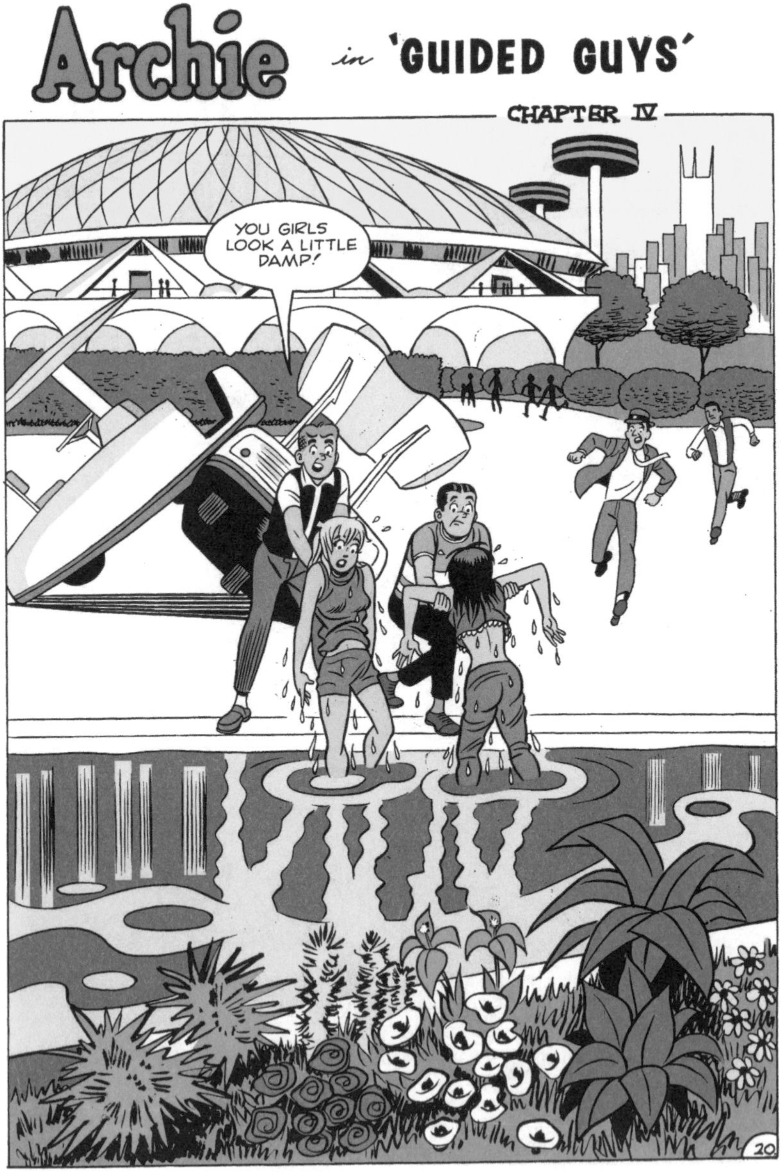
Archie in 'GUIDED GUYS'
CHAPTER IV
YOU GIRLS LOOK A LITTLE DAMP!
20

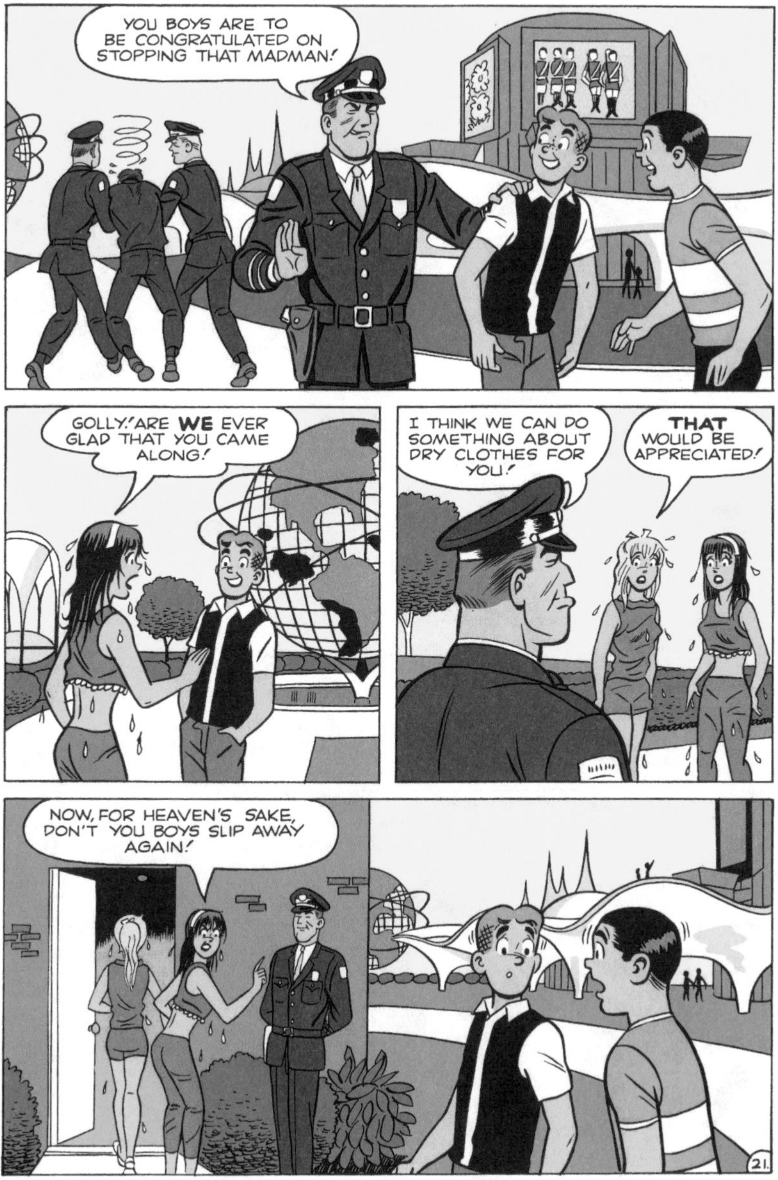
YOU BOYS ARE TO BE CONGRATULATED ON STOPPING THAT MADMAN!
GOLLY! ARE WE EVER GLAD THAT YOU CAME ALONG!
I THINK WE CAN DO SOMETHING ABOUT DRY CLOTHES FOR YOU!
THAT WOULD BE APPRECIATED!
NOW, FOR HEAVEN'S SAKE, DON'T YOU BOYS SLIP AWAY AGAIN!
21.

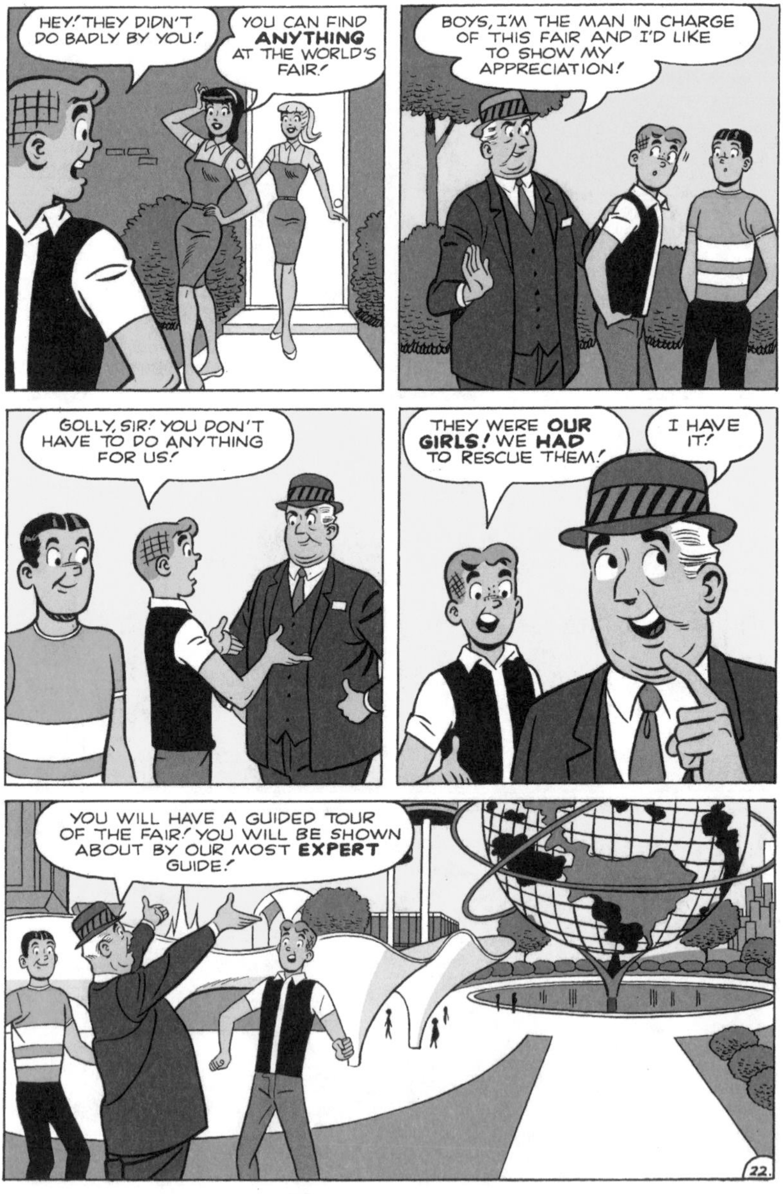
HEY! THEY DIDN'T DO BADLY BY YOU!
YOU CAN FIND ANYTHING AT THE WORLD'S FAIR!
BOYS, I'M THE MAN IN CHARGE OF THIS FAIR AND I'D LIKE TO SHOW MY APPRECIATION!
GOLLY, SIR! YOU DON'T HAVE TO DO ANYTHING FOR US!
THEY WERE OUR GIRLS! WE HAD TO RESCUE THEM!
I HAVE IT!
YOU WILL HAVE A GUIDED TOUR OF THE FAIR! YOU WILL BE SHOWN ABOUT BY OUR MOST EXPERT GUIDE!
22.

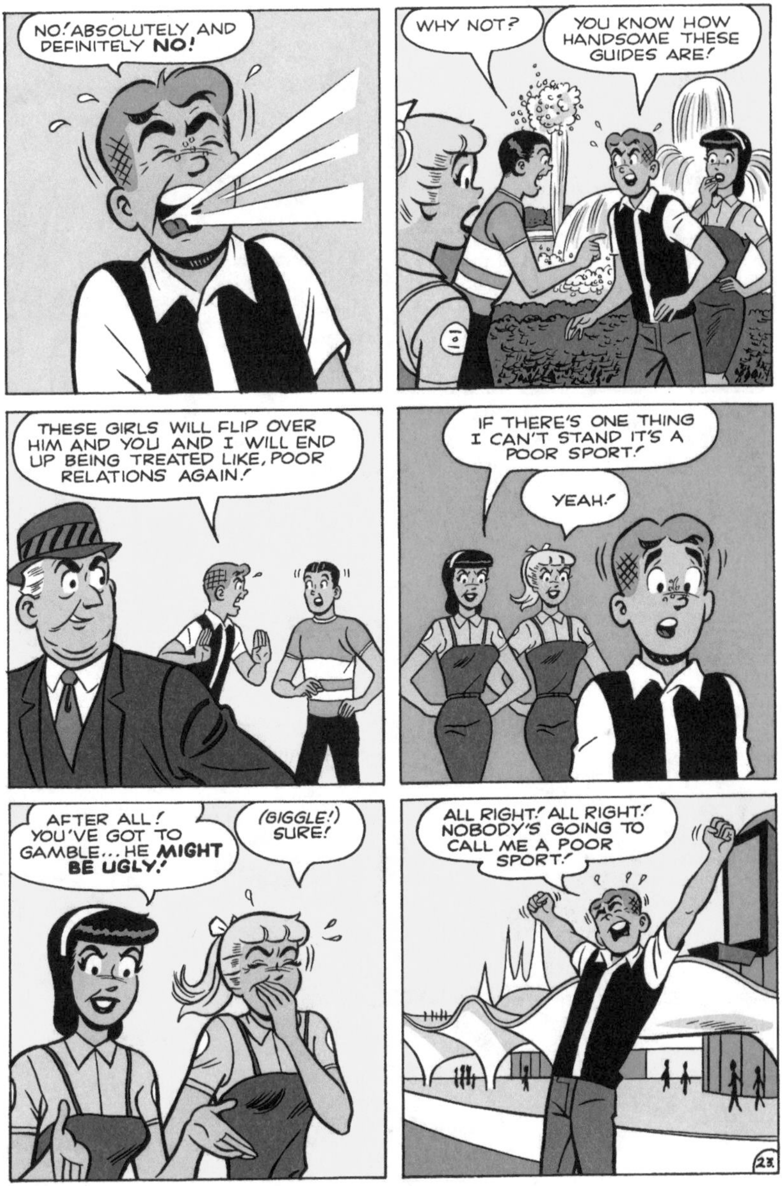
NO! ABSOLUTELY AND DEFINITELY **NO!**
WHY NOT?
YOU KNOW HOW HANDSOME THESE GUIDES ARE!
THESE GIRLS WILL FLIP OVER HIM AND YOU AND I WILL END UP BEING TREATED LIKE, POOR RELATIONS AGAIN!
IF THERE'S ONE THING I CAN'T STAND IT'S A POOR SPORT!
YEAH!
AFTER ALL! YOU'VE GOT TO GAMBLE... HE **MIGHT BE UGLY!**
(GIGGLE!) SURE!
ALL RIGHT! ALL RIGHT! NOBODY'S GOING TO CALL ME A POOR SPORT!
23

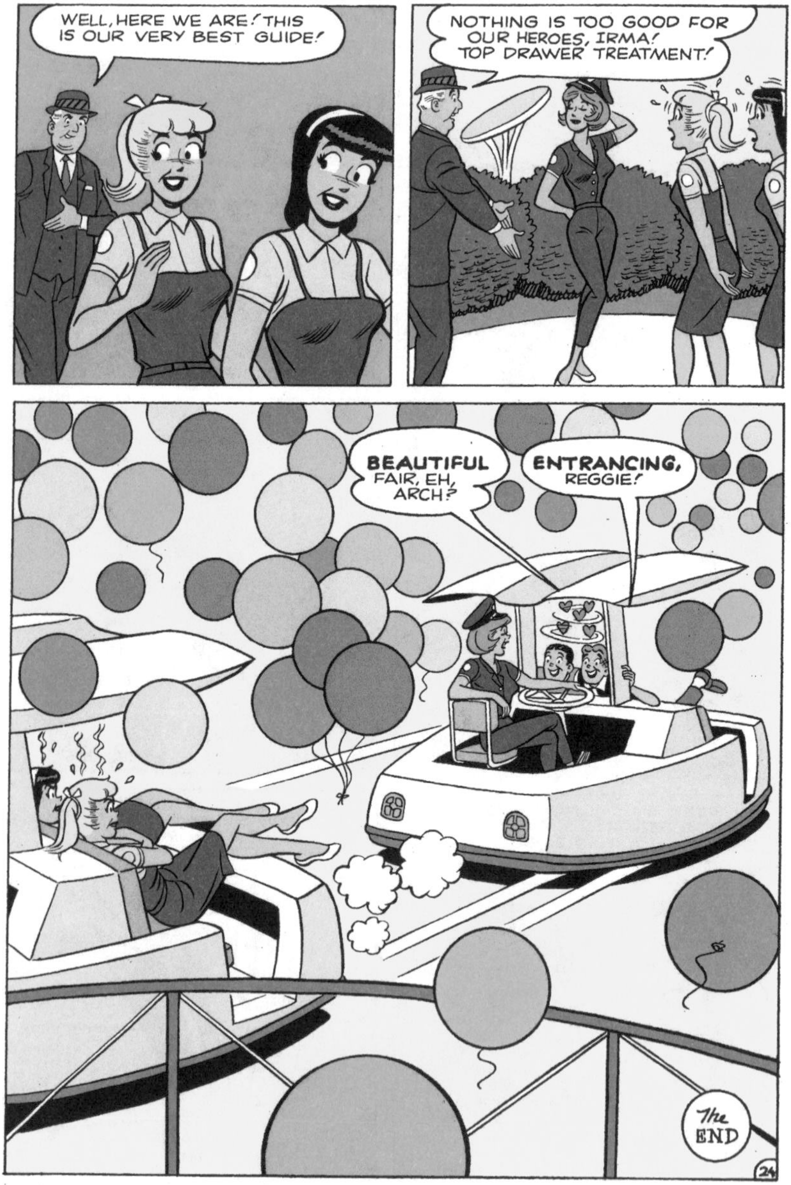
WELL, HERE WE ARE! THIS IS OUR VERY BEST GUIDE!
NOTHING IS TOO GOOD FOR OUR HEROES, IRMA! TOP DRAWER TREATMENT!
BEAUTIFUL FAIR, EH, ARCH?
ENTRANCING, REGGIE!
The END
24

LIFE with Archie "A Christmas Tale"
OH, YES I WILL, BETTY!
OH, NO YOU WON'T, RONNIE!
RIVERDALE HIGH GAZETTE ARCHIE ANDREWS-EDITOR
GIRLS, STOP IT! I'M GOING TO DO IT ANYWAY!
OH, NO YOU DON'T, ARCH!
OH, YES I WILL, REG!
1

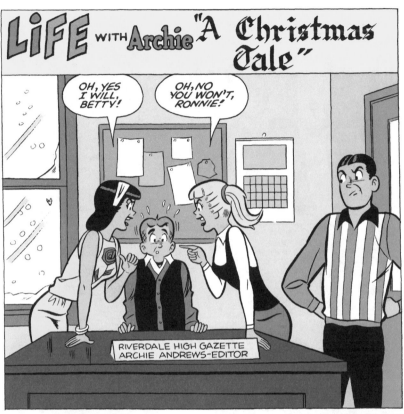

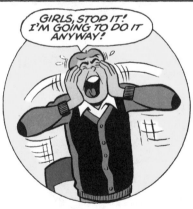

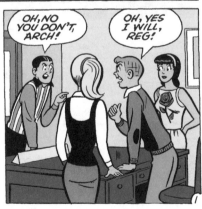

Story: Frank Doyle Pencils: Bob White Inks & Letters: Marty Epp

Originally printed in LIFE WITH ARCHIE #33, January 1965

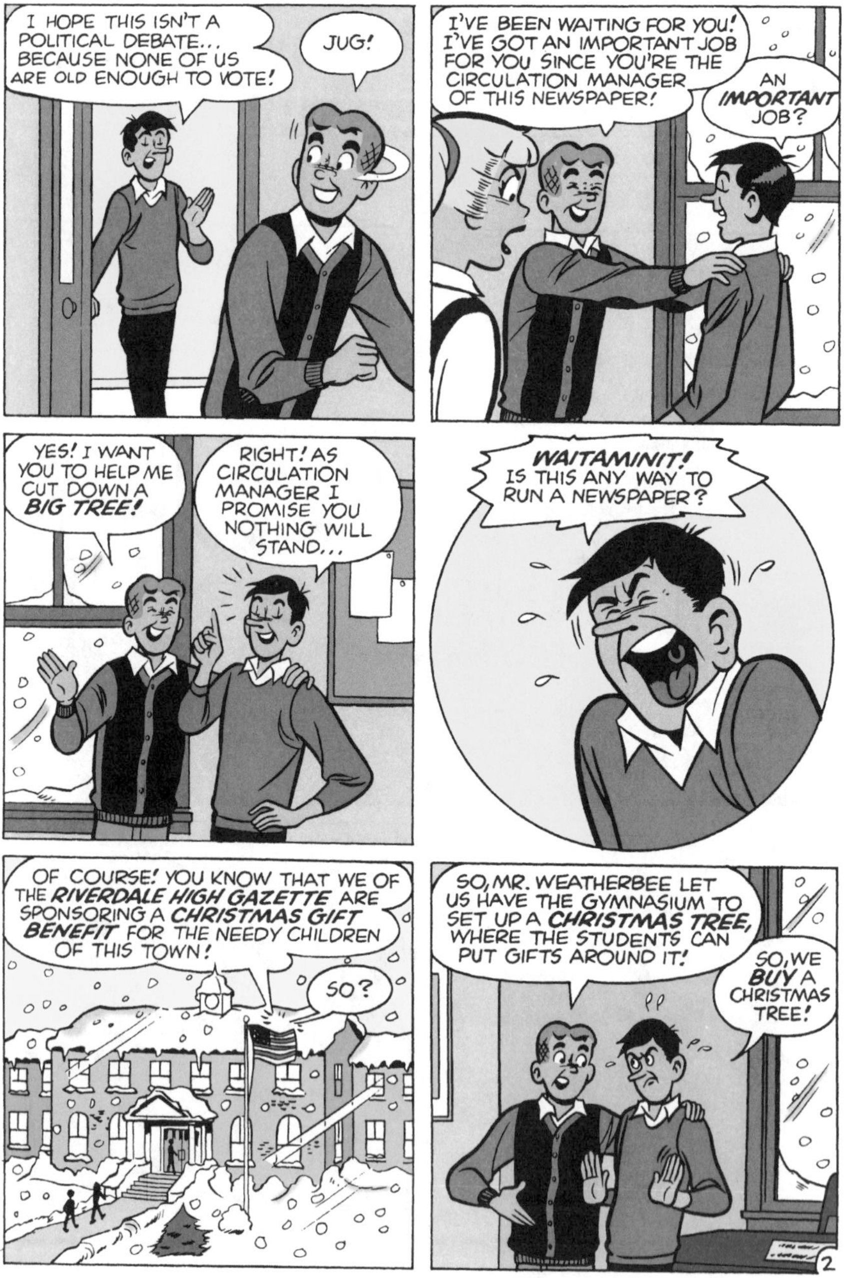
I HOPE THIS ISN'T A POLITICAL DEBATE... BECAUSE NONE OF US ARE OLD ENOUGH TO VOTE!
JUG!
I'VE BEEN WAITING FOR YOU! I'VE GOT AN IMPORTANT JOB FOR YOU SINCE YOU'RE THE CIRCULATION MANAGER OF THIS NEWSPAPER!
AN *IMPORTANT* JOB?
YES! I WANT YOU TO HELP ME CUT DOWN A *BIG TREE!*
RIGHT! AS CIRCULATION MANAGER I PROMISE YOU NOTHING WILL STAND...
WAITAMINIT! IS THIS ANY WAY TO RUN A NEWSPAPER?
OF COURSE! YOU KNOW THAT WE OF THE *RIVERDALE HIGH GAZETTE* ARE SPONSORING A *CHRISTMAS GIFT BENEFIT* FOR THE NEEDY CHILDREN OF THIS TOWN!
SO?
SO, MR. WEATHERBEE LET US HAVE THE GYMNASIUM TO SET UP A *CHRISTMAS TREE,* WHERE THE STUDENTS CAN PUT GIFTS AROUND IT!
SO, WE *BUY* A CHRISTMAS TREE!
2

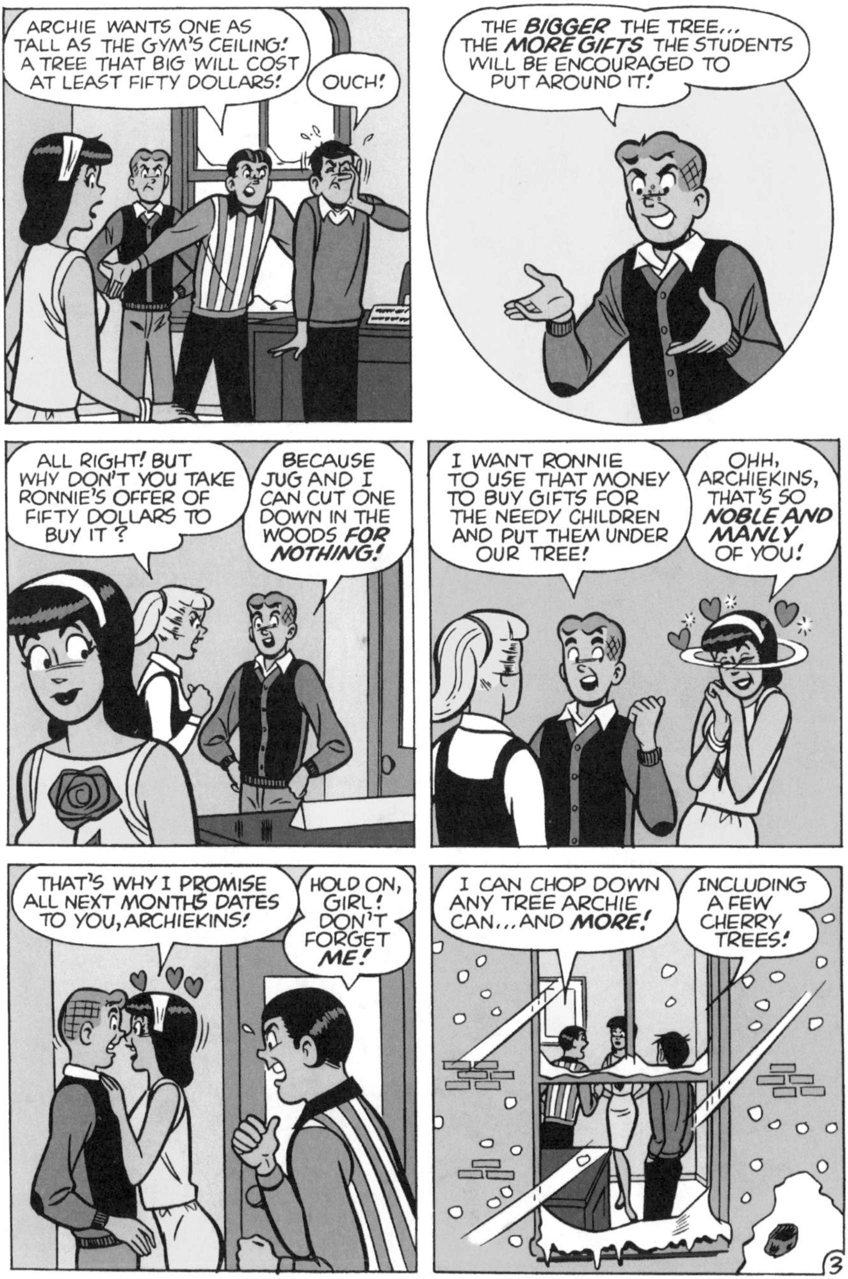
ARCHIE WANTS ONE AS TALL AS THE GYM'S CEILING! A TREE THAT BIG WILL COST AT LEAST FIFTY DOLLARS!
OUCH!
THE BIGGER THE TREE... THE MORE GIFTS THE STUDENTS WILL BE ENCOURAGED TO PUT AROUND IT!
ALL RIGHT! BUT WHY DON'T YOU TAKE RONNIE'S OFFER OF FIFTY DOLLARS TO BUY IT ?
BECAUSE JUG AND I CAN CUT ONE DOWN IN THE WOODS FOR NOTHING!
I WANT RONNIE TO USE THAT MONEY TO BUY GIFTS FOR THE NEEDY CHILDREN AND PUT THEM UNDER OUR TREE!
OHH, ARCHIEKINS, THAT'S SO NOBLE AND MANLY OF YOU!
THAT'S WHY I PROMISE ALL NEXT MONTH'S DATES TO YOU, ARCHIEKINS!
HOLD ON, GIRL! DON'T FORGET ME!
I CAN CHOP DOWN ANY TREE ARCHIE CAN...AND MORE!
INCLUDING A FEW CHERRY TREES!
3

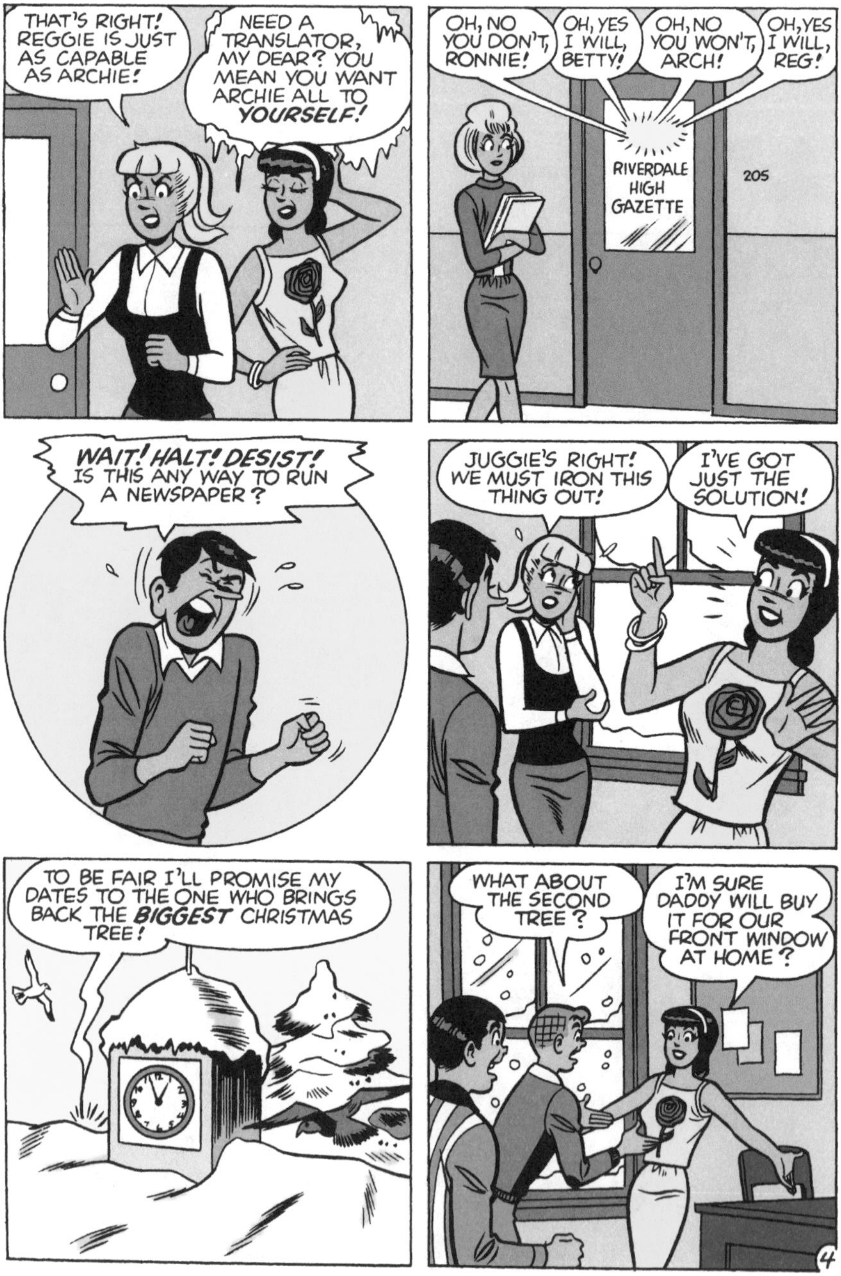
THAT'S RIGHT! REGGIE IS JUST AS CAPABLE AS ARCHIE!
NEED A TRANSLATOR, MY DEAR? YOU MEAN YOU WANT ARCHIE ALL TO YOURSELF!
OH, NO YOU DON'T, RONNIE!
OH, YES I WILL, BETTY!
OH, NO YOU WON'T, ARCH!
OH, YES I WILL, REG!
RIVERDALE HIGH GAZETTE
205
WAIT! HALT! DESIST! IS THIS ANY WAY TO RUN A NEWSPAPER?
JUGGIE'S RIGHT! WE MUST IRON THIS THING OUT!
I'VE GOT JUST THE SOLUTION!
TO BE FAIR I'LL PROMISE MY DATES TO THE ONE WHO BRINGS BACK THE BIGGEST CHRISTMAS TREE!
WHAT ABOUT THE SECOND TREE?
I'M SURE DADDY WILL BUY IT FOR OUR FRONT WINDOW AT HOME?
4

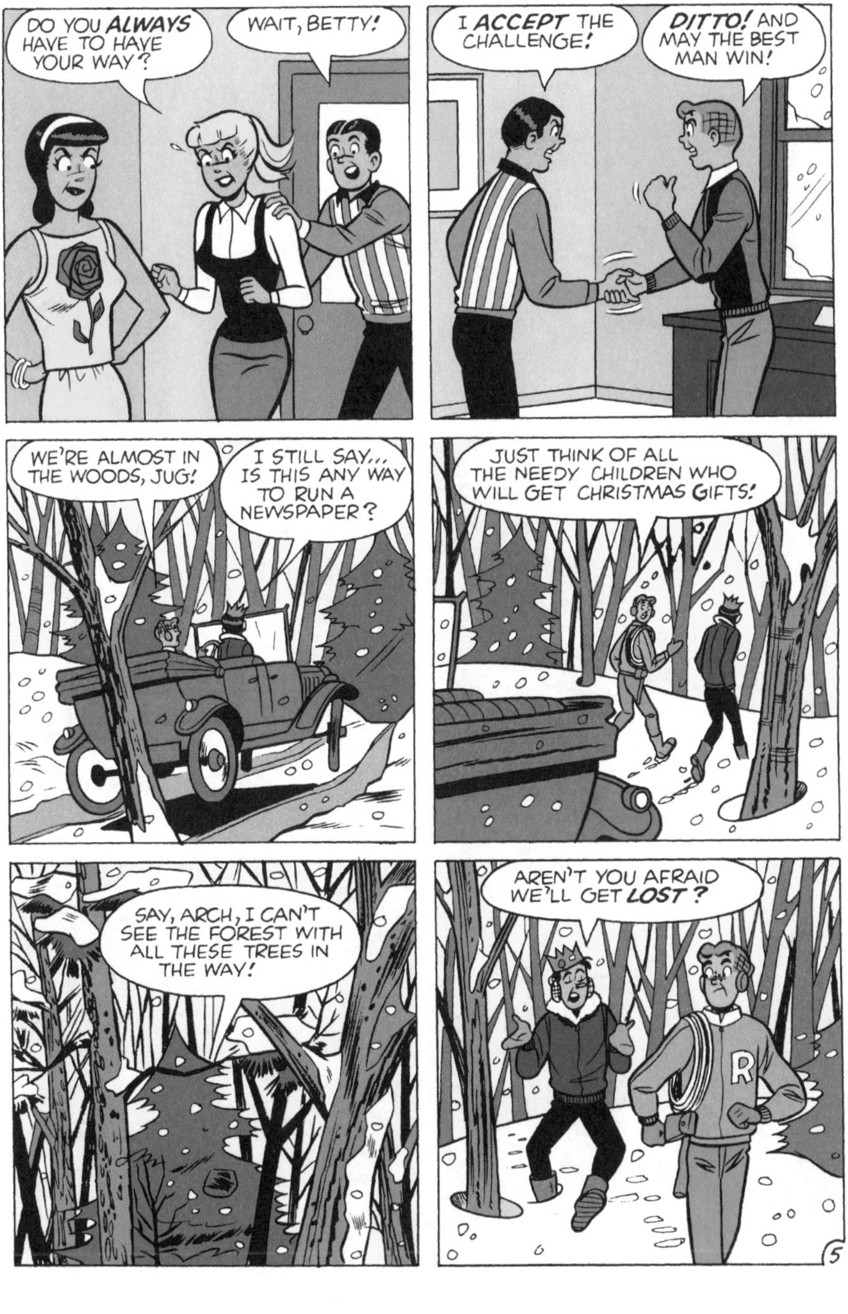
DO YOU ALWAYS HAVE TO HAVE YOUR WAY?
WAIT, BETTY!
I ACCEPT THE CHALLENGE!
DITTO! AND MAY THE BEST MAN WIN!
WE'RE ALMOST IN THE WOODS, JUG!
I STILL SAY... IS THIS ANY WAY TO RUN A NEWSPAPER?
JUST THINK OF ALL THE NEEDY CHILDREN WHO WILL GET CHRISTMAS GIFTS!
SAY, ARCH, I CAN'T SEE THE FOREST WITH ALL THESE TREES IN THE WAY!
AREN'T YOU AFRAID WE'LL GET LOST?
5

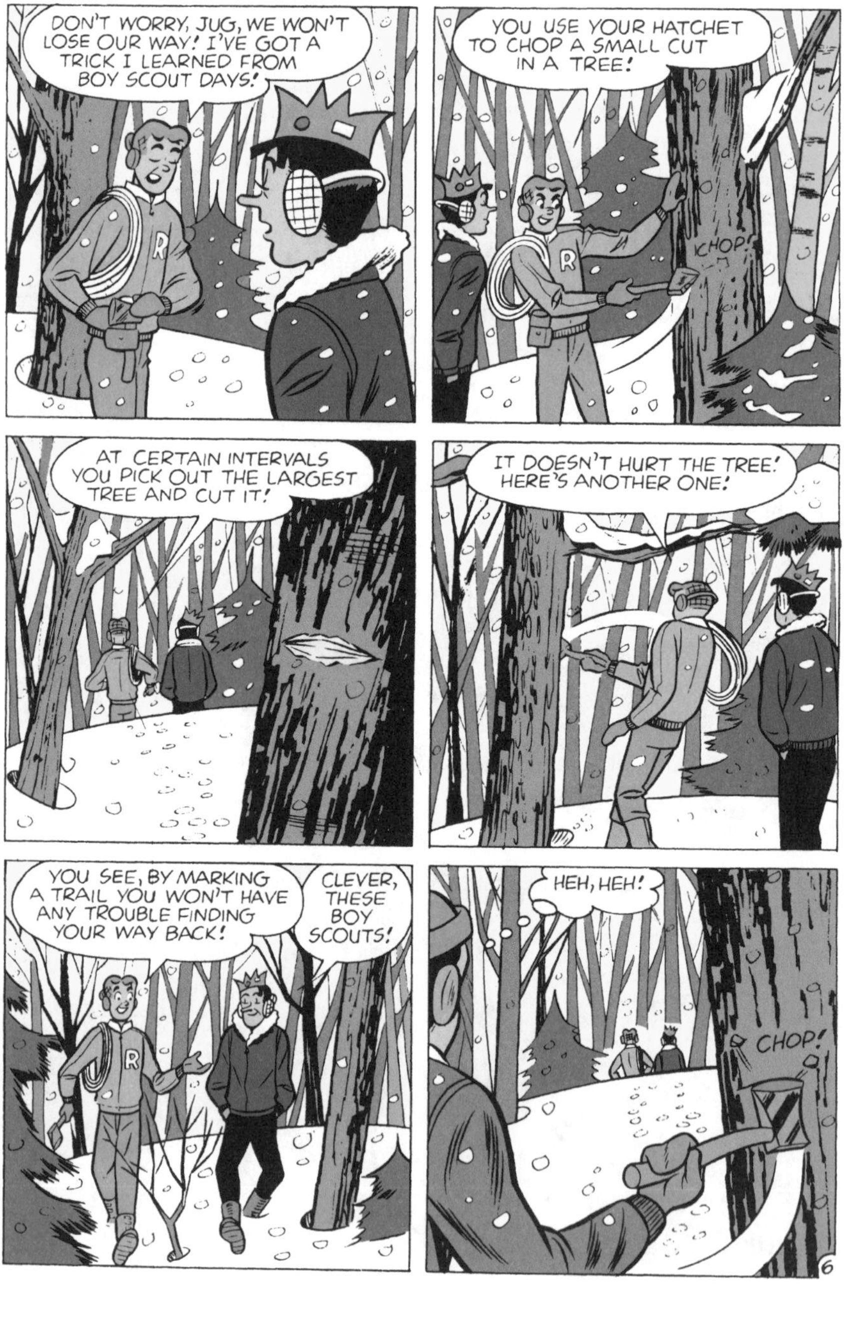
DON'T WORRY, JUG, WE WON'T LOSE OUR WAY! I'VE GOT A TRICK I LEARNED FROM BOY SCOUT DAYS!
YOU USE YOUR HATCHET TO CHOP A SMALL CUT IN A TREE!
CHOP!
AT CERTAIN INTERVALS YOU PICK OUT THE LARGEST TREE AND CUT IT!
IT DOESN'T HURT THE TREE! HERE'S ANOTHER ONE!
YOU SEE, BY MARKING A TRAIL YOU WON'T HAVE ANY TROUBLE FINDING YOUR WAY BACK!
CLEVER, THESE BOY SCOUTS!
HEH, HEH!
CHOP!
6

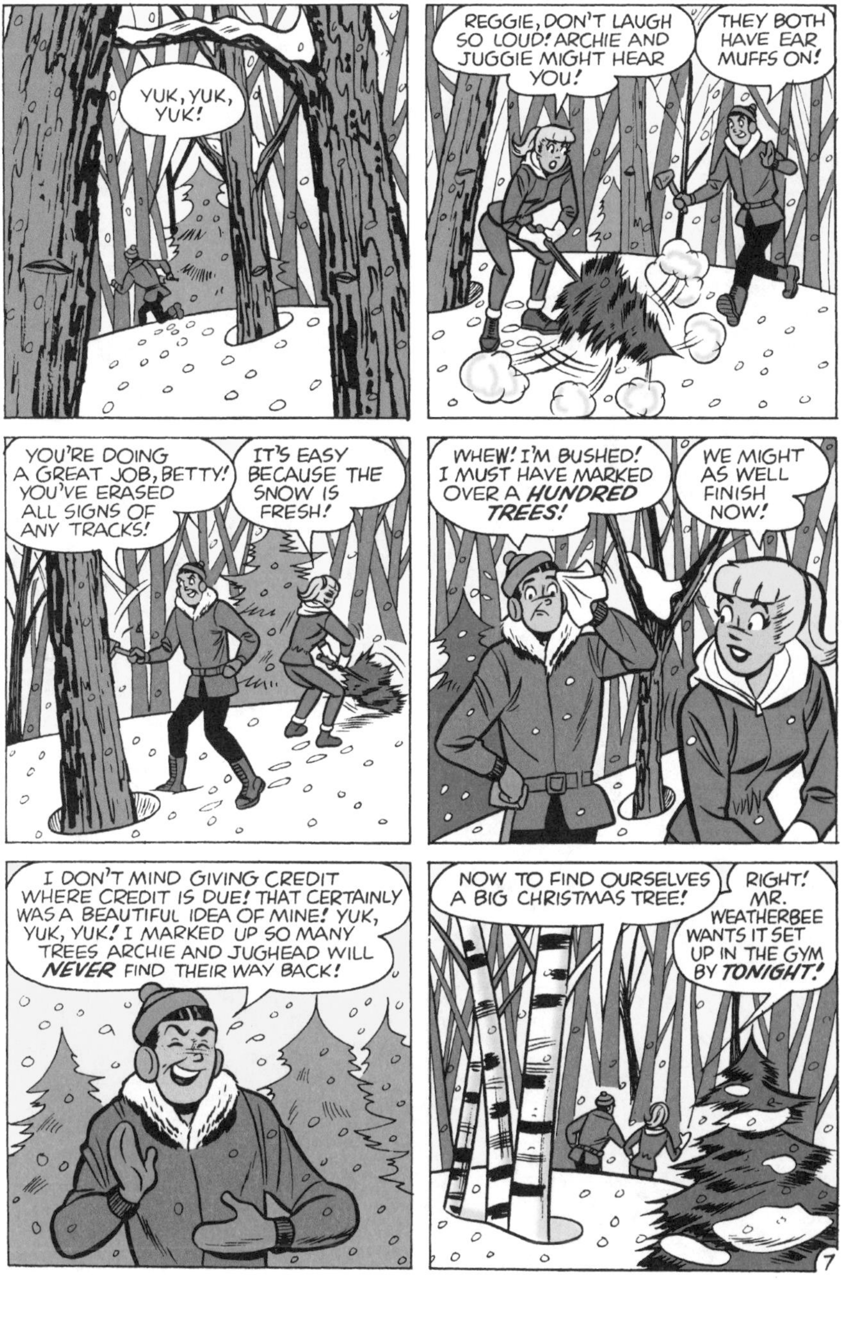

YUK, YUK, YUK!
REGGIE, DON'T LAUGH SO LOUD! ARCHIE AND JUGGIE MIGHT HEAR YOU!
THEY BOTH HAVE EAR MUFFS ON!
YOU'RE DOING A GREAT JOB, BETTY! YOU'VE ERASED ALL SIGNS OF ANY TRACKS!
IT'S EASY BECAUSE THE SNOW IS FRESH!
WHEW! I'M BUSHED! I MUST HAVE MARKED OVER A HUNDRED TREES!
WE MIGHT AS WELL FINISH NOW!
I DON'T MIND GIVING CREDIT WHERE CREDIT IS DUE! THAT CERTAINLY WAS A BEAUTIFUL IDEA OF MINE! YUK, YUK, YUK! I MARKED UP SO MANY TREES ARCHIE AND JUGHEAD WILL NEVER FIND THEIR WAY BACK!
NOW TO FIND OURSELVES A BIG CHRISTMAS TREE!
RIGHT! MR. WEATHERBEE WANTS IT SET UP IN THE GYM BY TONIGHT!
7

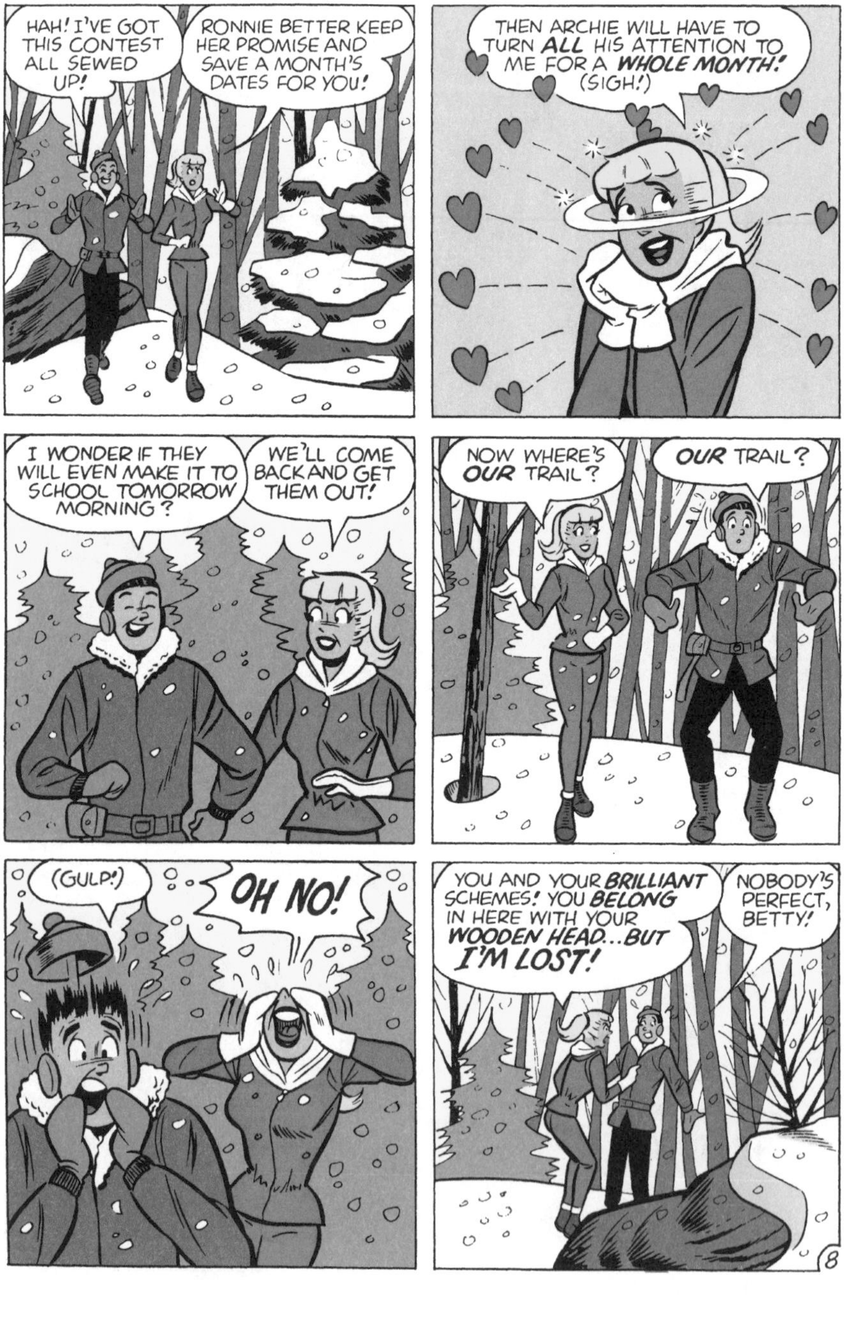
HAH! I'VE GOT THIS CONTEST ALL SEWED UP!
RONNIE BETTER KEEP HER PROMISE AND SAVE A MONTH'S DATES FOR YOU!
THEN ARCHIE WILL HAVE TO TURN ALL HIS ATTENTION TO ME FOR A WHOLE MONTH! (SIGH!)
I WONDER IF THEY WILL EVEN MAKE IT TO SCHOOL TOMORROW MORNING?
WE'LL COME BACK AND GET THEM OUT!
NOW WHERE'S OUR TRAIL?
OUR TRAIL?
(GULP!)
OH NO!
YOU AND YOUR BRILLIANT SCHEMES! YOU BELONG IN HERE WITH YOUR WOODEN HEAD...BUT I'M LOST!
NOBODY'S PERFECT, BETTY!
8

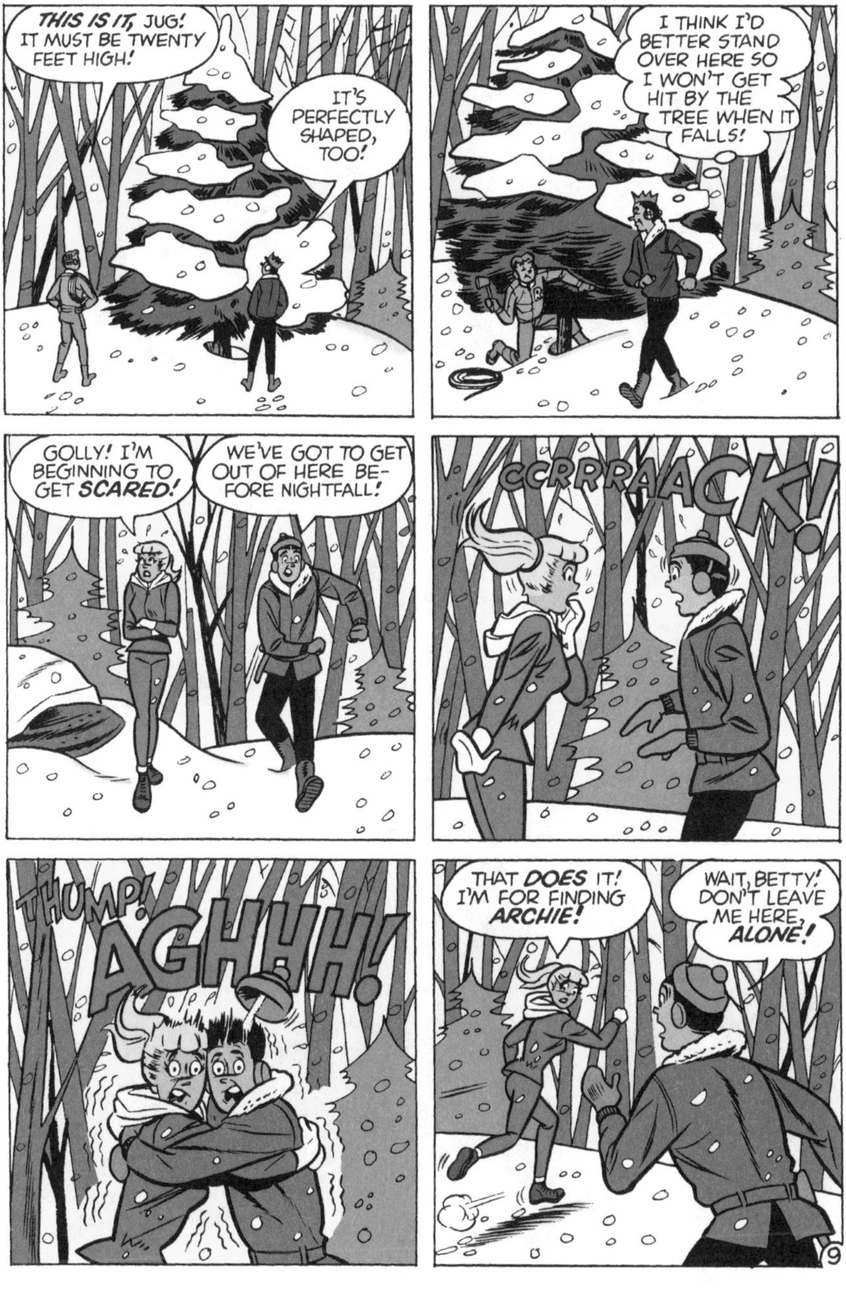
THIS IS IT, JUG! IT MUST BE TWENTY FEET HIGH!
IT'S PERFECTLY SHAPED, TOO!
I THINK I'D BETTER STAND OVER HERE SO I WON'T GET HIT BY THE TREE WHEN IT FALLS!
GOLLY! I'M BEGINNING TO GET SCARED!
WE'VE GOT TO GET OUT OF HERE BEFORE NIGHTFALL!
CCRRRRAACK!
THUMP!
AGHHH!
THAT DOES IT! I'M FOR FINDING ARCHIE!
WAIT, BETTY! DON'T LEAVE ME HERE, ALONE!
9

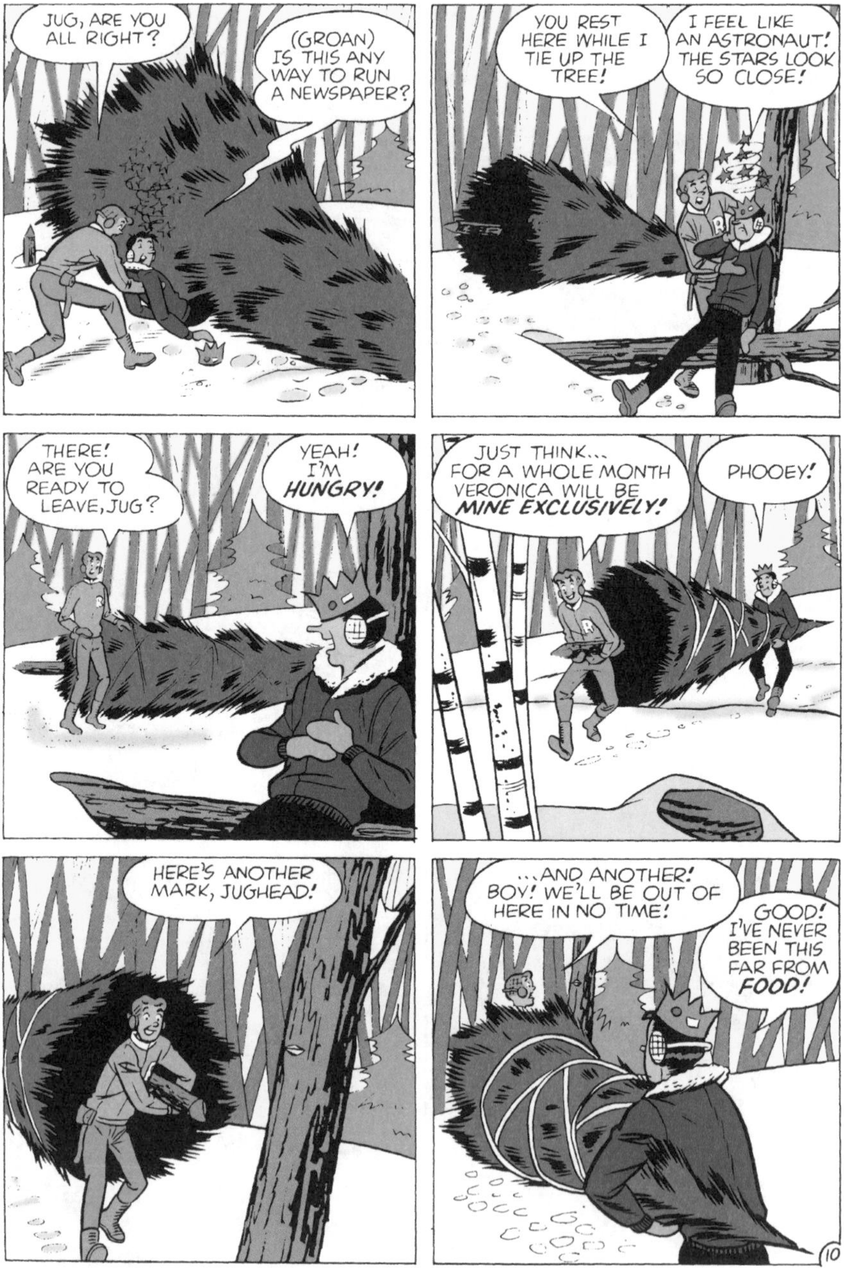
JUG, ARE YOU ALL RIGHT?
(GROAN) IS THIS ANY WAY TO RUN A NEWSPAPER?
YOU REST HERE WHILE I TIE UP THE TREE!
I FEEL LIKE AN ASTRONAUT! THE STARS LOOK SO CLOSE!
THERE! ARE YOU READY TO LEAVE, JUG?
YEAH! I'M HUNGRY!
JUST THINK... FOR A WHOLE MONTH VERONICA WILL BE MINE EXCLUSIVELY!
PHOOEY!
HERE'S ANOTHER MARK, JUGHEAD!
...AND ANOTHER! BOY! WE'LL BE OUT OF HERE IN NO TIME!
GOOD! I'VE NEVER BEEN THIS FAR FROM FOOD!
10

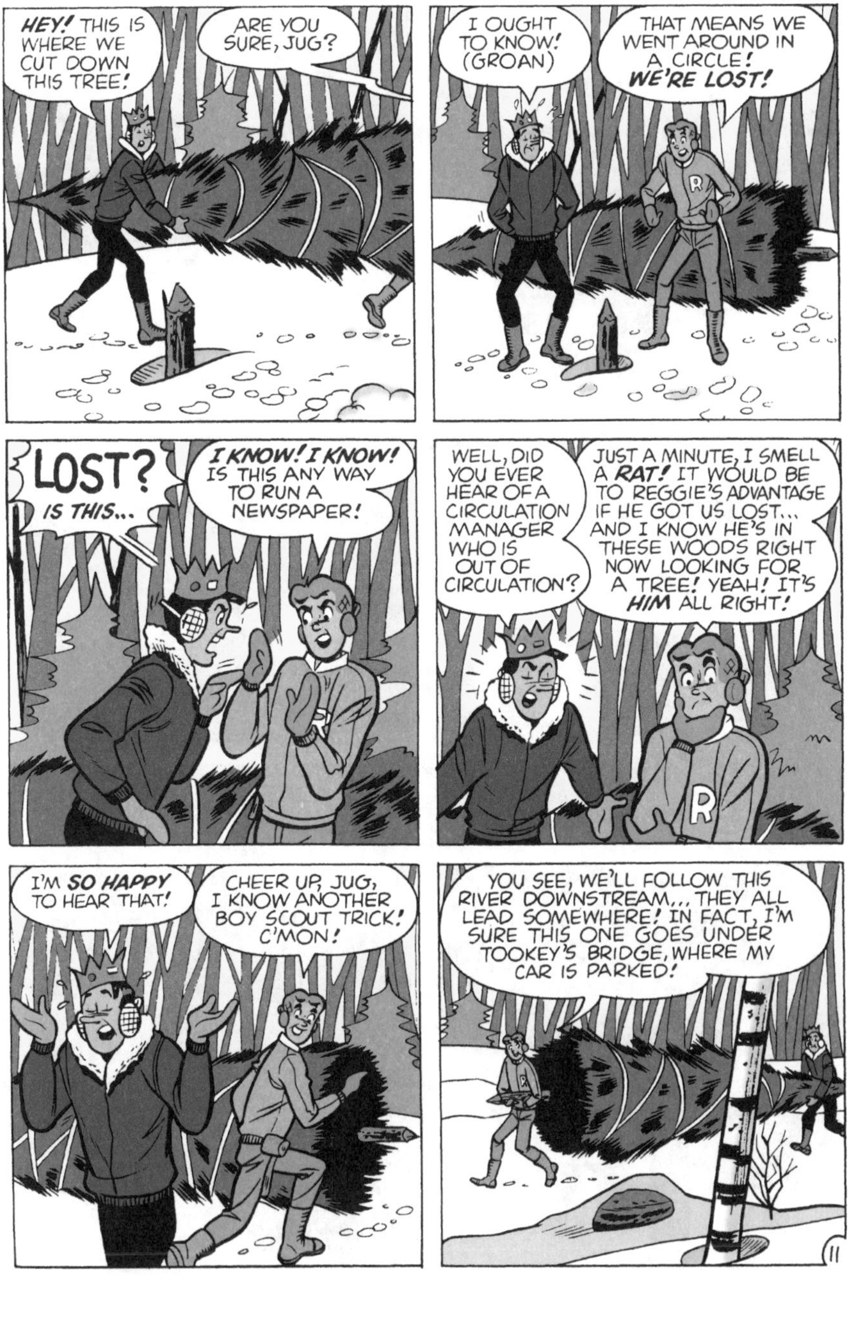
HEY! THIS IS WHERE WE CUT DOWN THIS TREE!
ARE YOU SURE, JUG?
I OUGHT TO KNOW! (GROAN)
THAT MEANS WE WENT AROUND IN A CIRCLE! WE'RE LOST!
LOST? IS THIS...
I KNOW! I KNOW! IS THIS ANY WAY TO RUN A NEWSPAPER!
WELL, DID YOU EVER HEAR OF A CIRCULATION MANAGER WHO IS OUT OF CIRCULATION?
JUST A MINUTE, I SMELL A RAT! IT WOULD BE TO REGGIE'S ADVANTAGE IF HE GOT US LOST... AND I KNOW HE'S IN THESE WOODS RIGHT NOW LOOKING FOR A TREE! YEAH! IT'S HIM ALL RIGHT!
I'M SO HAPPY TO HEAR THAT!
CHEER UP, JUG, I KNOW ANOTHER BOY SCOUT TRICK! C'MON!
YOU SEE, WE'LL FOLLOW THIS RIVER DOWNSTREAM,.. THEY ALL LEAD SOMEWHERE! IN FACT, I'M SURE THIS ONE GOES UNDER TOOKEY'S BRIDGE, WHERE MY CAR IS PARKED!
11

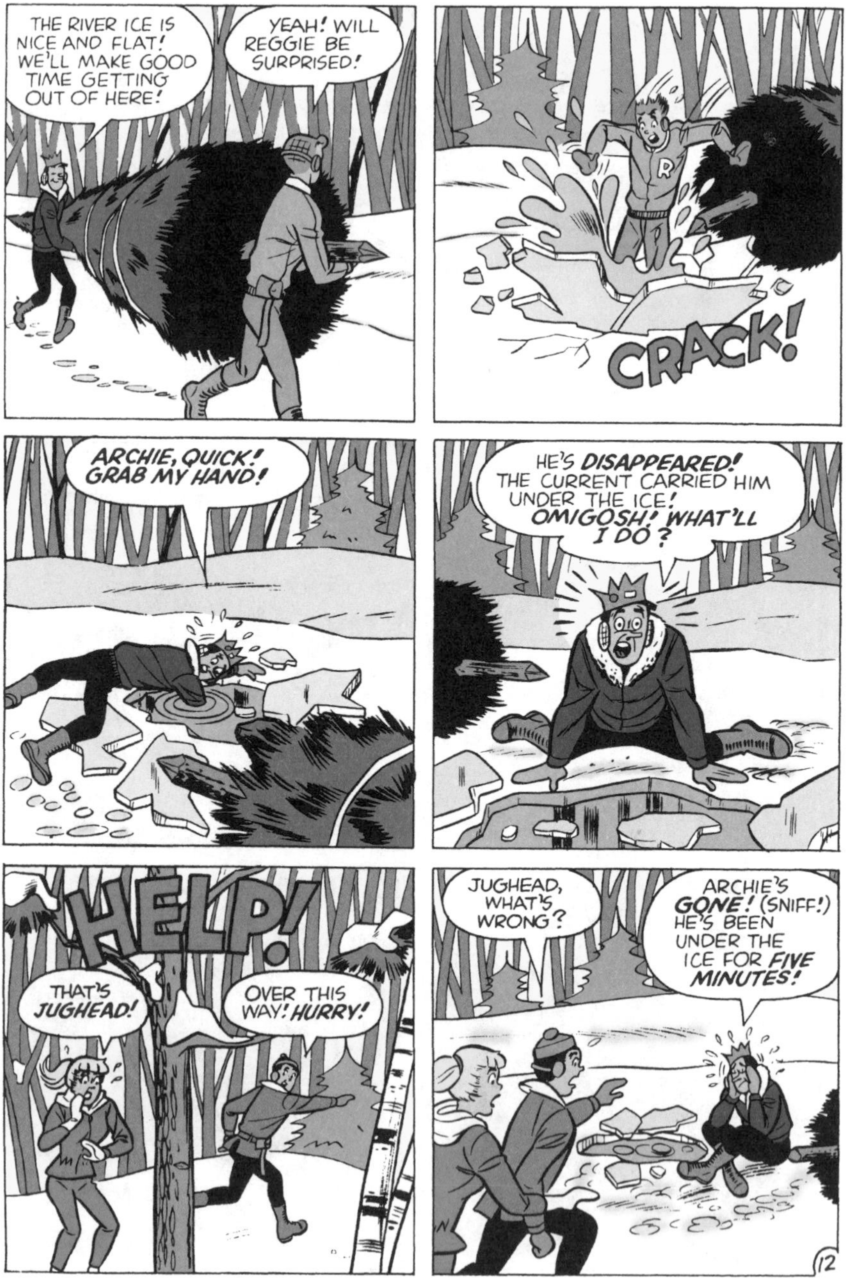
THE RIVER ICE IS NICE AND FLAT! WE'LL MAKE GOOD TIME GETTING OUT OF HERE!
YEAH! WILL REGGIE BE SURPRISED!
R
CRACK!
ARCHIE, QUICK! GRAB MY HAND!
HE'S DISAPPEARED! THE CURRENT CARRIED HIM UNDER THE ICE! OMIGOSH! WHAT'LL I DO?
HELP!
THAT'S JUGHEAD!
OVER THIS WAY! HURRY!
JUGHEAD, WHAT'S WRONG?
ARCHIE'S GONE! (SNIFF!) HE'S BEEN UNDER THE ICE FOR FIVE MINUTES!
12

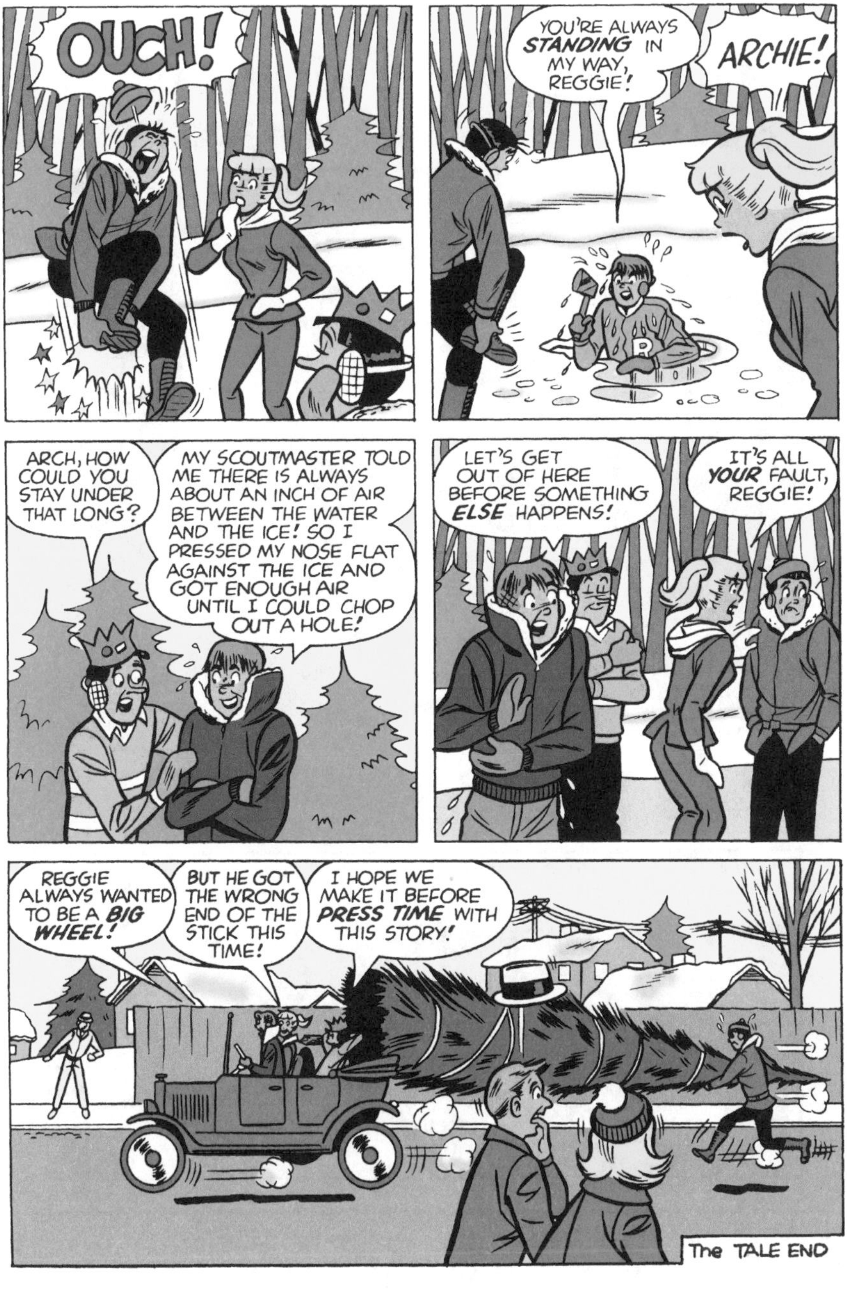
OUCH!
YOU'RE ALWAYS STANDING IN MY WAY, REGGIE!
ARCHIE!
ARCH, HOW COULD YOU STAY UNDER THAT LONG?
MY SCOUTMASTER TOLD ME THERE IS ALWAYS ABOUT AN INCH OF AIR BETWEEN THE WATER AND THE ICE! SO I PRESSED MY NOSE FLAT AGAINST THE ICE AND GOT ENOUGH AIR UNTIL I COULD CHOP OUT A HOLE!
LET'S GET OUT OF HERE BEFORE SOMETHING ELSE HAPPENS!
IT'S ALL YOUR FAULT, REGGIE!
REGGIE ALWAYS WANTED TO BE A BIG WHEEL!
BUT HE GOT THE WRONG END OF THE STICK THIS TIME!
I HOPE WE MAKE IT BEFORE PRESS TIME WITH THIS STORY!
The TALE END

Archie - IN - "ME TARPAN, YOU JANE!"

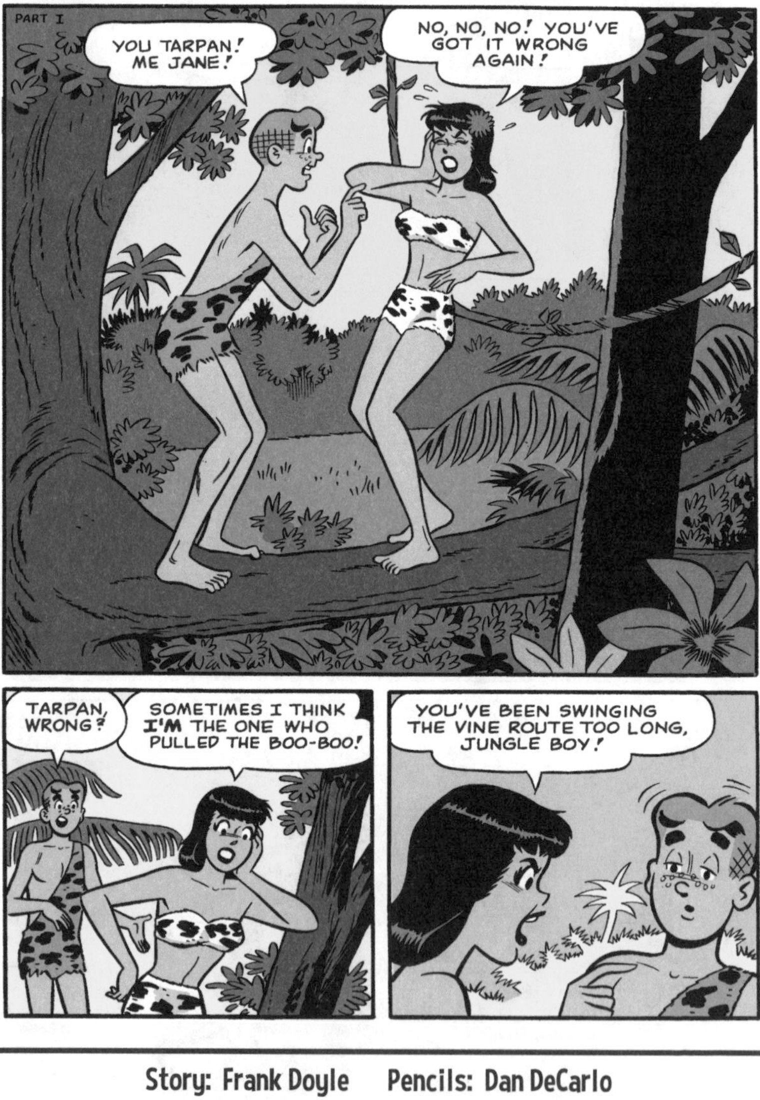
PART I
YOU TARPAN! ME JANE!
NO, NO, NO! YOU'VE GOT IT WRONG AGAIN!
TARPAN, WRONG?
SOMETIMES I THINK I'M THE ONE WHO PULLED THE BOO-BOO!
YOU'VE BEEN SWINGING THE VINE ROUTE TOO LONG, JUNGLE BOY!

Story: Frank Doyle Pencils: Dan DeCarlo
Inks: Rudy Lapick Letters: Vince DeCarlo

Originally printed in LIFE WITH ARCHIE #33, January 1965

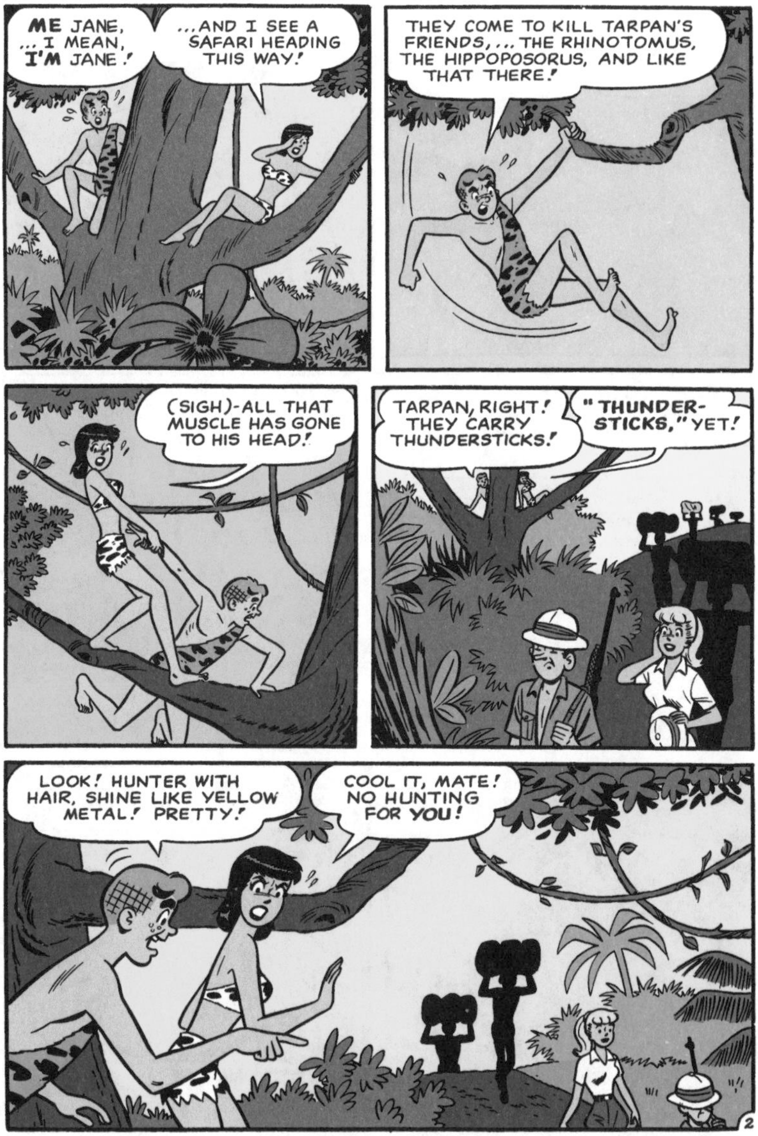
ME JANE, ... I MEAN, I'M JANE!
...AND I SEE A SAFARI HEADING THIS WAY!
THEY COME TO KILL TARPAN'S FRIENDS, ... THE RHINOTOMUS, THE HIPPOPOSORUS, AND LIKE THAT THERE!
(SIGH)-ALL THAT MUSCLE HAS GONE TO HIS HEAD!
TARPAN, RIGHT! THEY CARRY THUNDERSTICKS!
"THUNDER-STICKS," YET!
LOOK! HUNTER WITH HAIR, SHINE LIKE YELLOW METAL! PRETTY!
COOL IT, MATE! NO HUNTING FOR YOU!
2

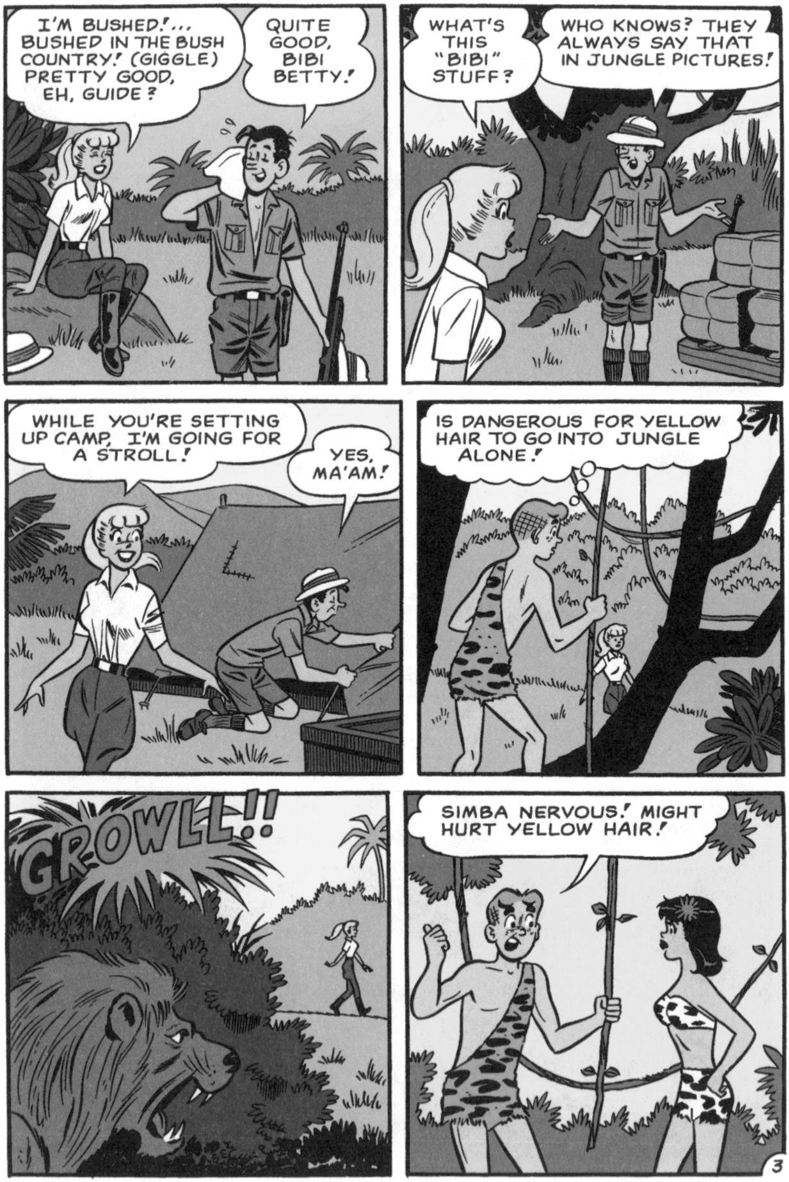
I'M BUSHED!... BUSHED IN THE BUSH COUNTRY! (GIGGLE) PRETTY GOOD, EH, GUIDE?
QUITE GOOD, BIBI BETTY!
WHAT'S THIS "BIBI" STUFF?
WHO KNOWS? THEY ALWAYS SAY THAT IN JUNGLE PICTURES!
WHILE YOU'RE SETTING UP CAMP, I'M GOING FOR A STROLL!
YES, MA'AM!
IS DANGEROUS FOR YELLOW HAIR TO GO INTO JUNGLE ALONE!
GROWLL!!
SIMBA NERVOUS! MIGHT HURT YELLOW HAIR!
3

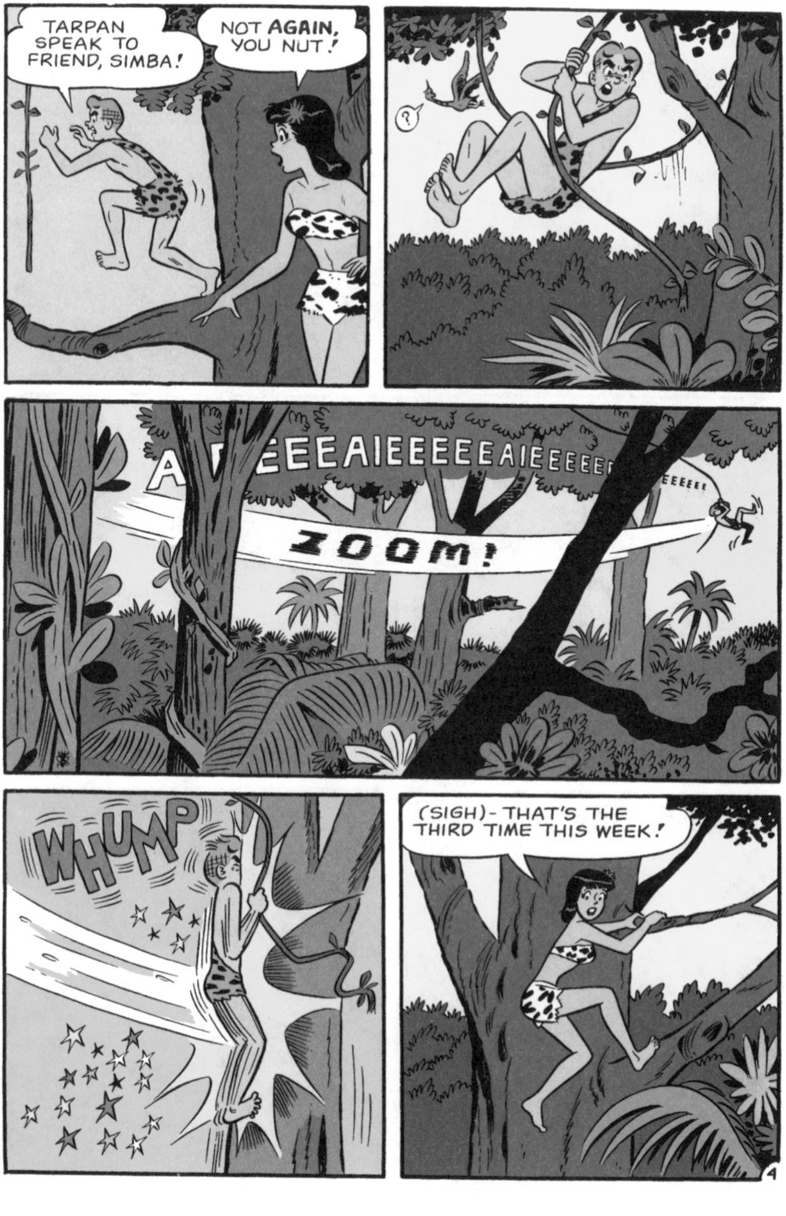
TARPAN SPEAK TO FRIEND, SIMBA!
NOT AGAIN, YOU NUT!
?
AIEEEEAIEEEEEEEAIEEEEEE
ZOOM!
WHUMP
(SIGH)- THAT'S THE THIRD TIME THIS WEEK!
4

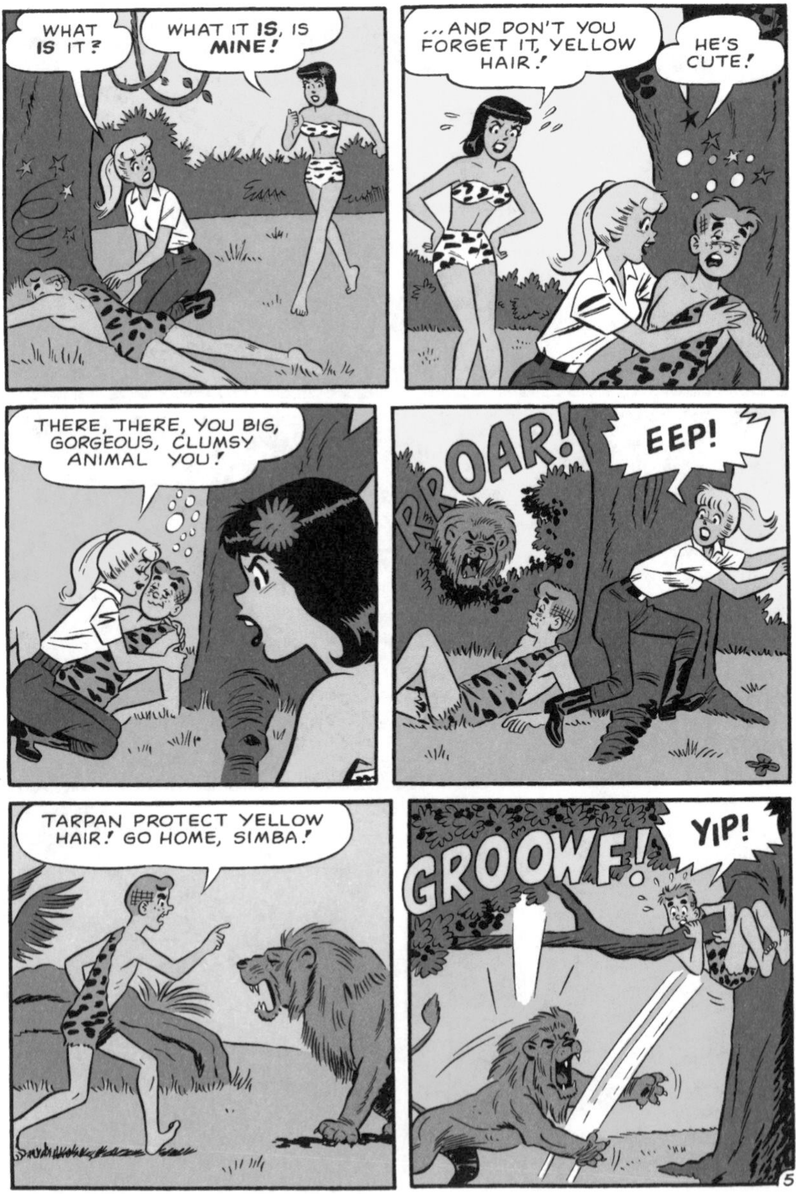
WHAT IS IT?
WHAT IT IS, IS MINE!
...AND DON'T YOU FORGET IT, YELLOW HAIR!
HE'S CUTE!
THERE, THERE, YOU BIG, GORGEOUS, CLUMSY ANIMAL YOU!
RROAR!
EEP!
TARPAN PROTECT YELLOW HAIR! GO HOME, SIMBA!
GROOWF!
YIP!
5

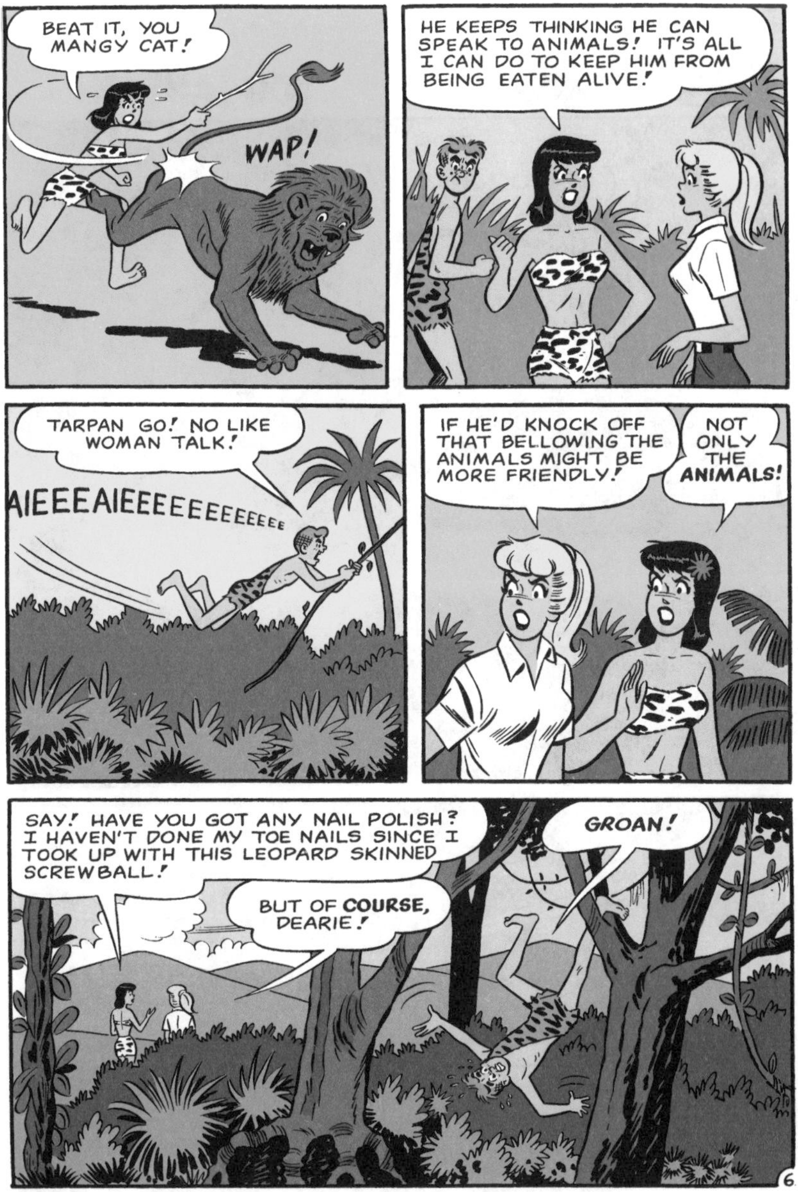
BEAT IT, YOU MANGY CAT!
WAP!
HE KEEPS THINKING HE CAN SPEAK TO ANIMALS! IT'S ALL I CAN DO TO KEEP HIM FROM BEING EATEN ALIVE!
TARPAN GO! NO LIKE WOMAN TALK!
AIEEEAIEEEEEEEEEEEE
IF HE'D KNOCK OFF THAT BELLOWING THE ANIMALS MIGHT BE MORE FRIENDLY!
NOT ONLY THE **ANIMALS**!
SAY! HAVE YOU GOT ANY NAIL POLISH? I HAVEN'T DONE MY TOE NAILS SINCE I TOOK UP WITH THIS LEOPARD SKINNED SCREWBALL!
BUT OF **COURSE**, DEARIE!
GROAN!
6

Archie -IN- "ME TARPAN, YOU JANE!"

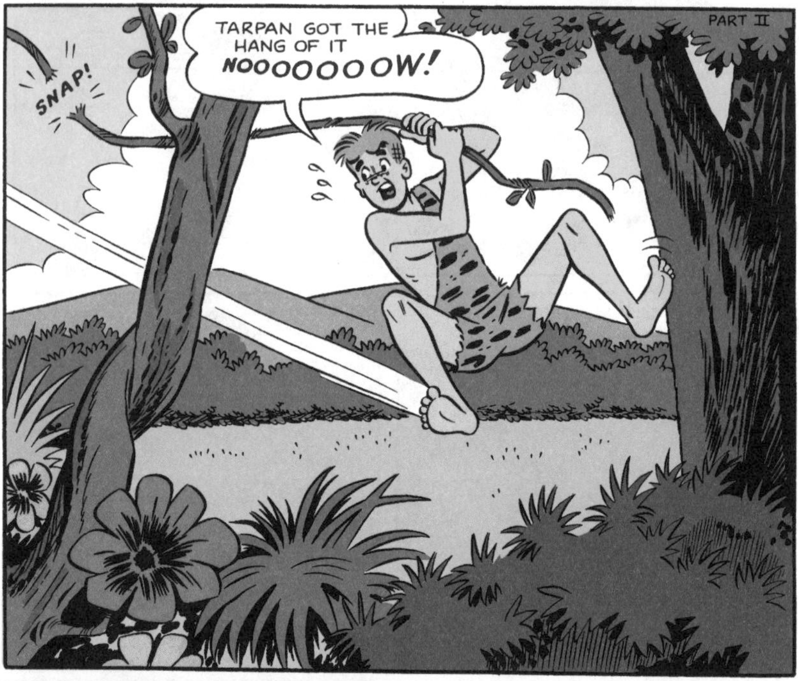
PART II
TARPAN GOT THE HANG OF IT NOOOOOOOOW!
SNAP!

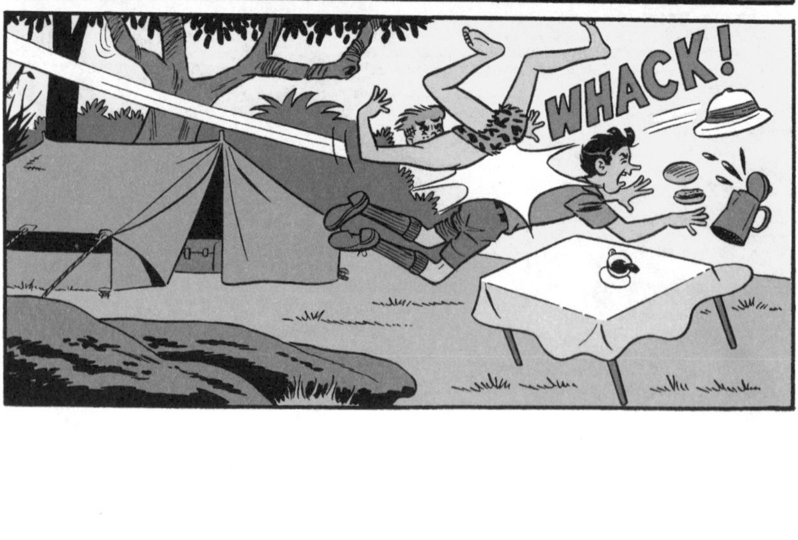
WHACK!

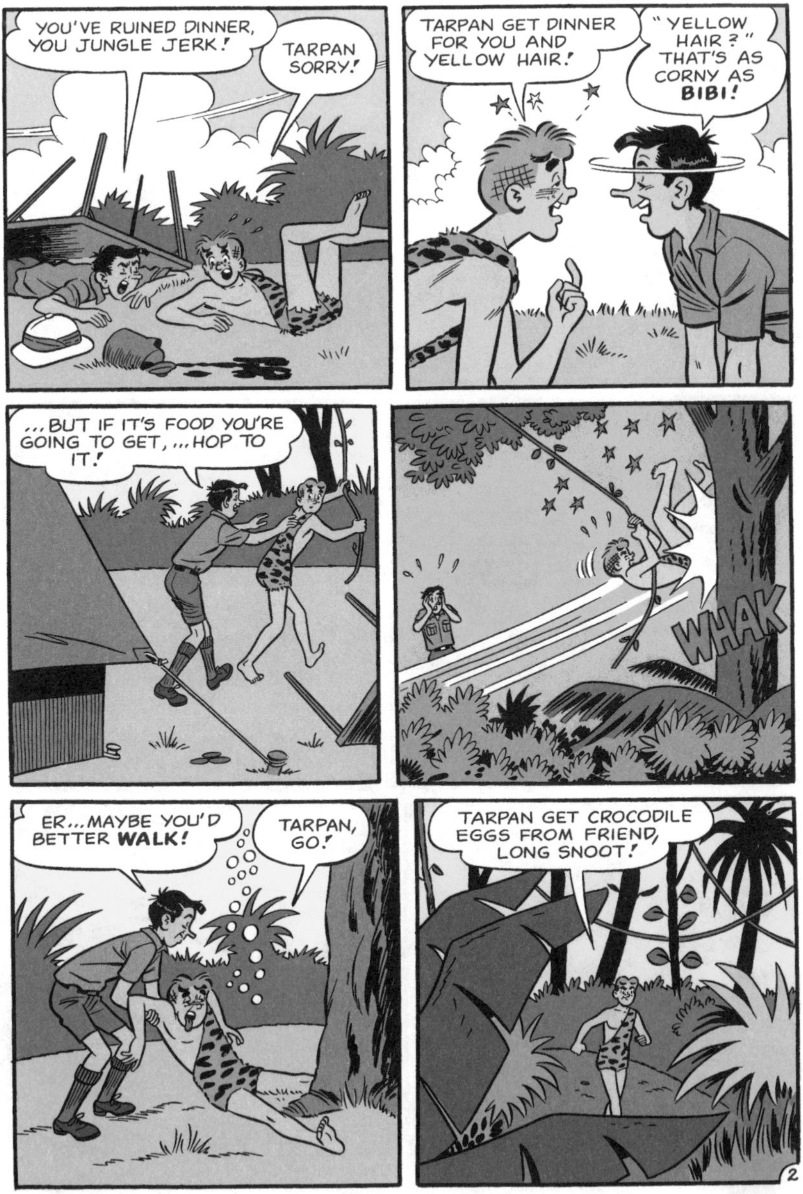
YOU'VE RUINED DINNER, YOU JUNGLE JERK!
TARPAN SORRY!
TARPAN GET DINNER FOR YOU AND YELLOW HAIR!
"YELLOW HAIR?" THAT'S AS CORNY AS BIBI!
...BUT IF IT'S FOOD YOU'RE GOING TO GET, ...HOP TO IT!
WHAK
ER...MAYBE YOU'D BETTER WALK!
TARPAN, GO!
TARPAN GET CROCODILE EGGS FROM FRIEND, LONG SNOOT!
2

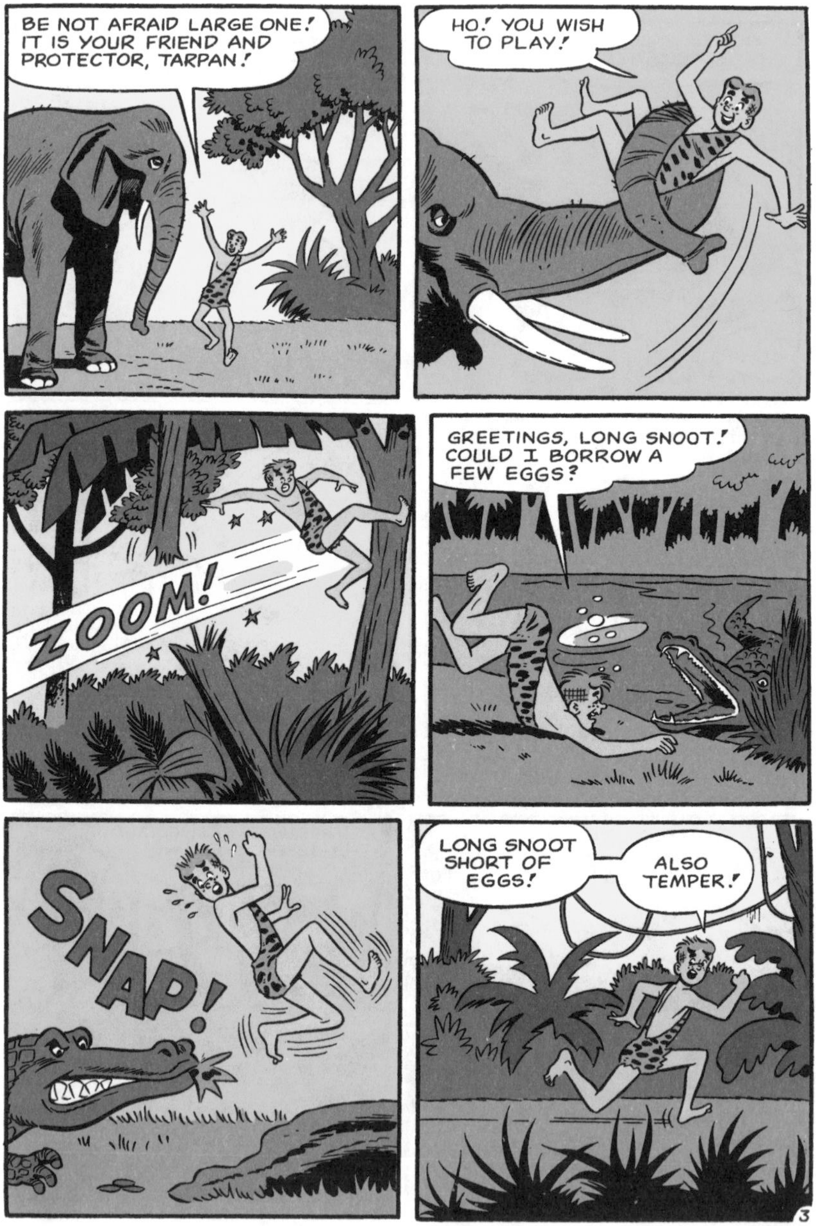
BE NOT AFRAID LARGE ONE! IT IS YOUR FRIEND AND PROTECTOR, TARPAN!
HO! YOU WISH TO PLAY!
ZOOM!
GREETINGS, LONG SNOOT! COULD I BORROW A FEW EGGS?
SNAP!
LONG SNOOT SHORT OF EGGS!
ALSO TEMPER!
3

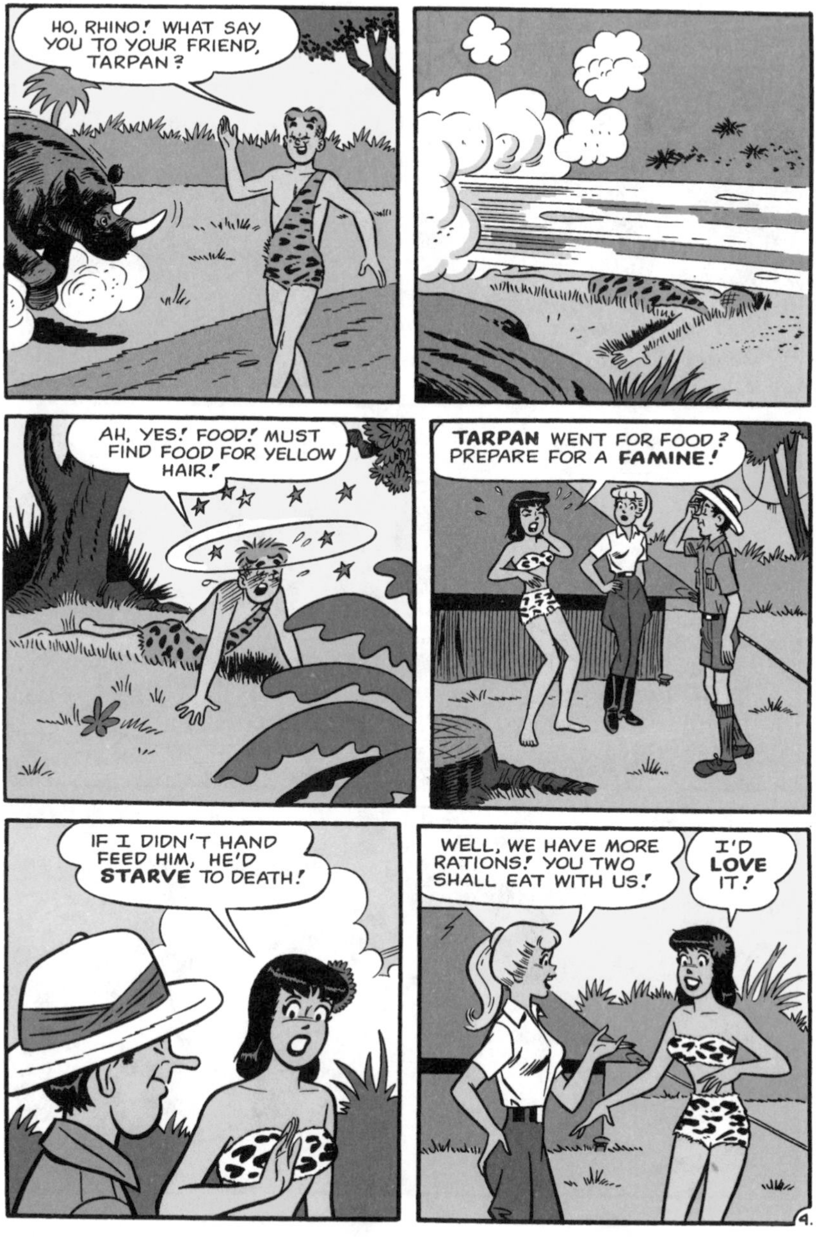
HO, RHINO! WHAT SAY YOU TO YOUR FRIEND, TARPAN?
AH, YES! FOOD! MUST FIND FOOD FOR YELLOW HAIR!
TARPAN WENT FOR FOOD? PREPARE FOR A FAMINE!
IF I DIDN'T HAND FEED HIM, HE'D STARVE TO DEATH!
WELL, WE HAVE MORE RATIONS! YOU TWO SHALL EAT WITH US!
I'D LOVE IT!
4.

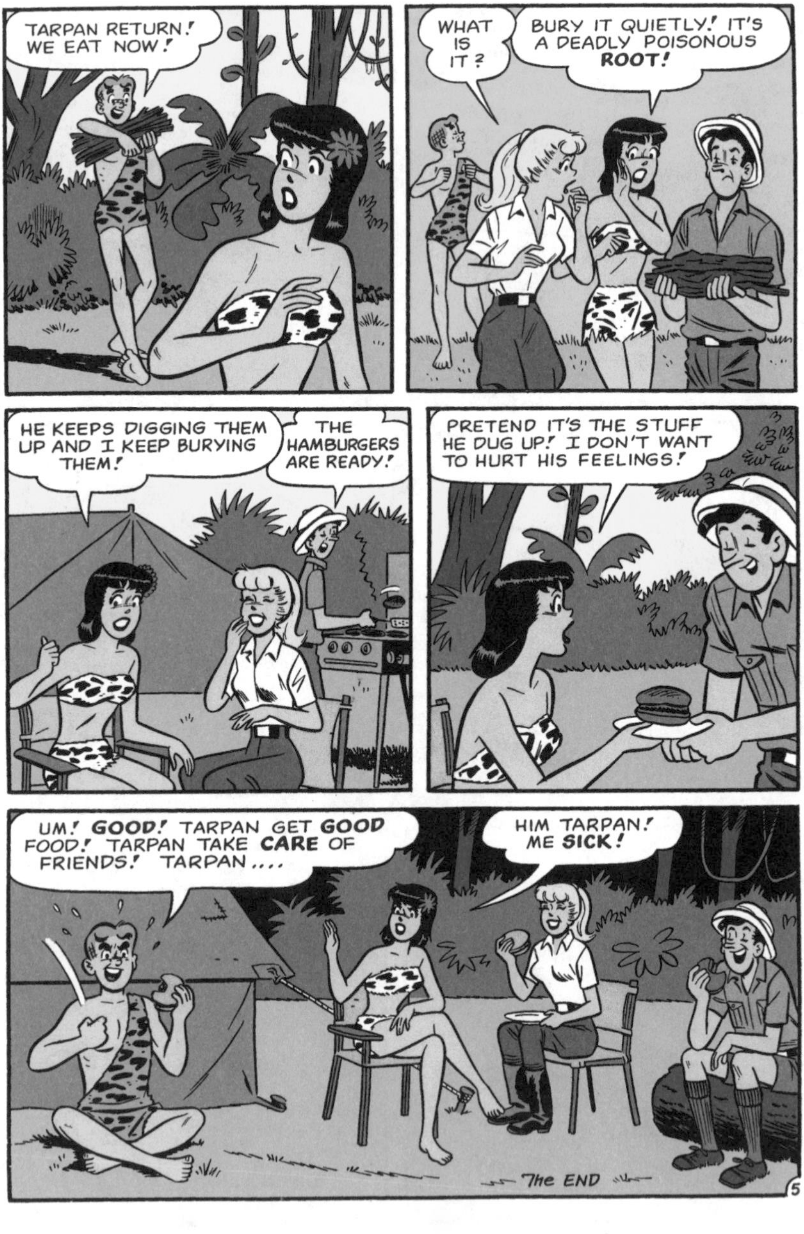
TARPAN RETURN! WE EAT NOW!
WHAT IS IT?
BURY IT QUIETLY! IT'S A DEADLY POISONOUS ROOT!
HE KEEPS DIGGING THEM UP AND I KEEP BURYING THEM!
THE HAMBURGERS ARE READY!
PRETEND IT'S THE STUFF HE DUG UP! I DON'T WANT TO HURT HIS FEELINGS!
UM! GOOD! TARPAN GET GOOD FOOD! TARPAN TAKE CARE OF FRIENDS! TARPAN....
HIM TARPAN! ME SICK!
The END
5

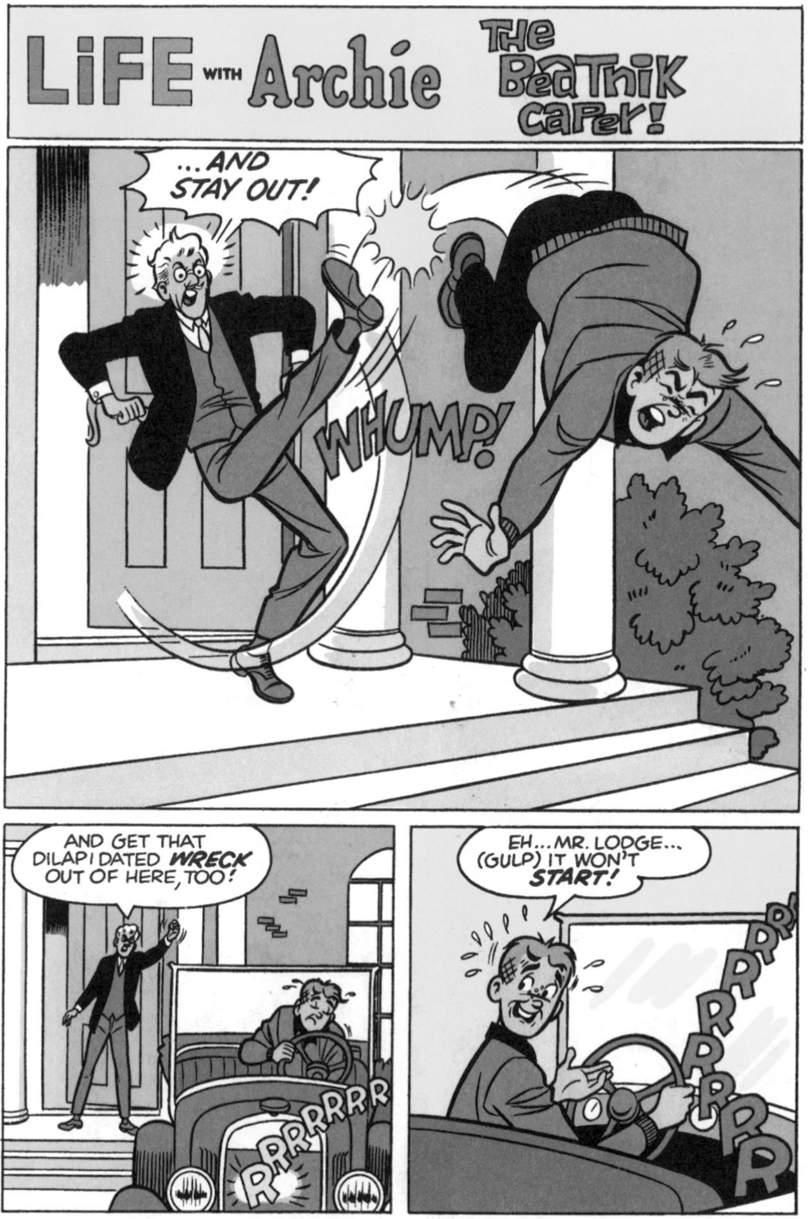
LIFE WITH Archie
THE BEATNIK CAPER!
...AND STAY OUT!
WHUMP!
AND GET THAT DILAPIDATED WRECK OUT OF HERE, TOO!
RRRRRRR
EH... MR. LODGE... (GULP) IT WON'T START!
RRRRRRRRR

Story & Pencils: Bob White Inks & Letters: Marty Epp

Originally printed in LIFE WITH ARCHIE #34, February 1965

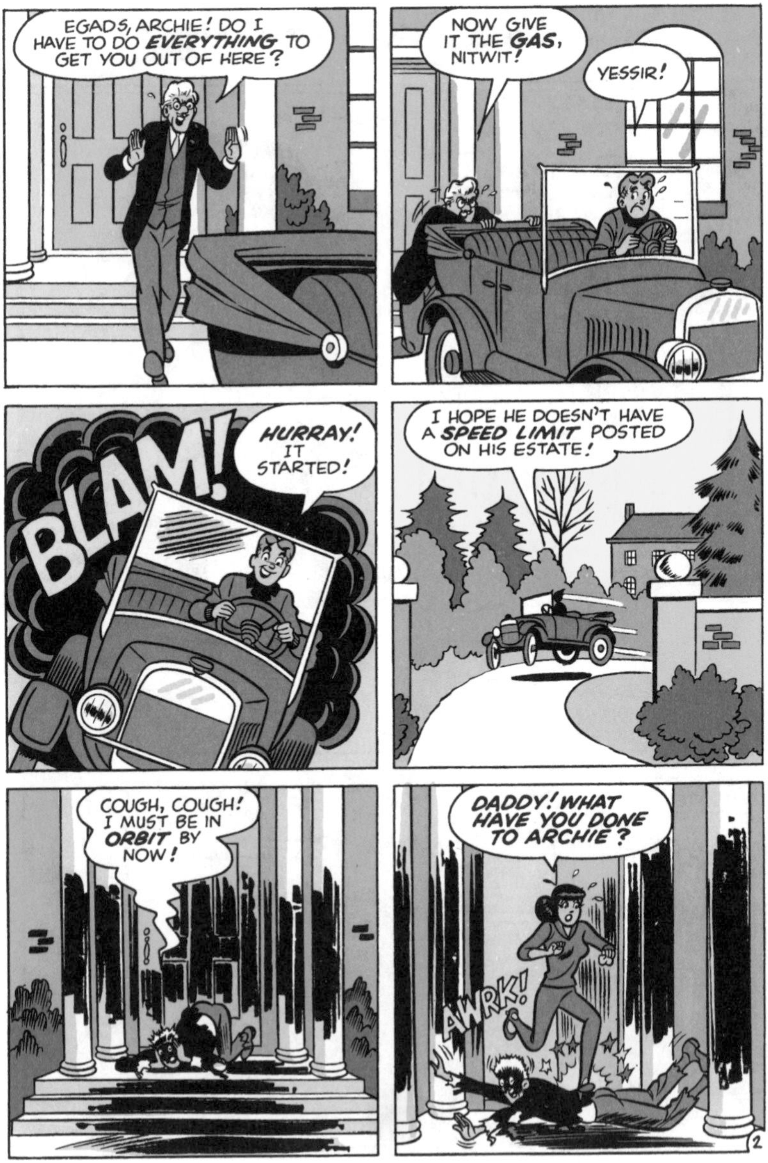
EGADS, ARCHIE! DO I HAVE TO DO EVERYTHING TO GET YOU OUT OF HERE?
NOW GIVE IT THE GAS, NITWIT!
YESSIR!
BLAM!
HURRAY! IT STARTED!
I HOPE HE DOESN'T HAVE A SPEED LIMIT POSTED ON HIS ESTATE!
COUGH, COUGH! I MUST BE IN ORBIT BY NOW!
DADDY! WHAT HAVE YOU DONE TO ARCHIE?
AWRK!
2

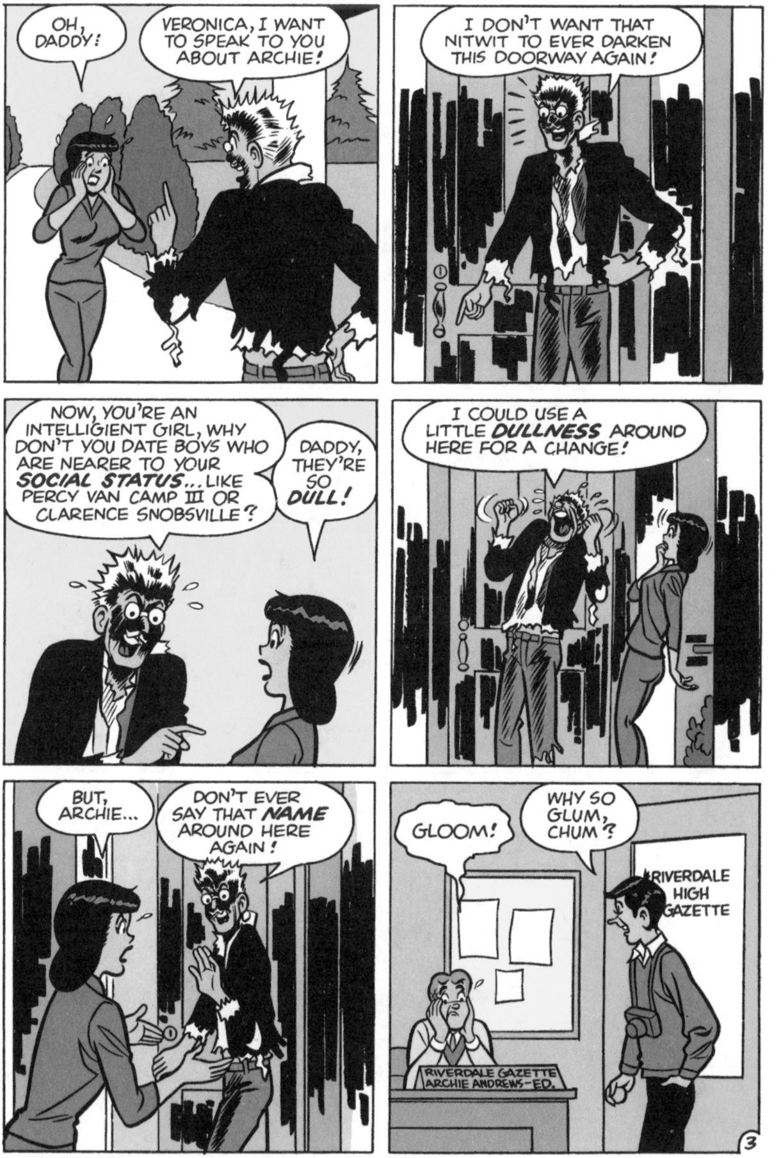
OH, DADDY!
VERONICA, I WANT TO SPEAK TO YOU ABOUT ARCHIE!
I DON'T WANT THAT NITWIT TO EVER DARKEN THIS DOORWAY AGAIN!
NOW, YOU'RE AN INTELLIGIENT GIRL, WHY DON'T YOU DATE BOYS WHO ARE NEARER TO YOUR SOCIAL STATUS... LIKE PERCY VAN CAMP III OR CLARENCE SNOBSVILLE?
DADDY, THEY'RE SO DULL!
I COULD USE A LITTLE DULLNESS AROUND HERE FOR A CHANGE!
BUT, ARCHIE...
DON'T EVER SAY THAT NAME AROUND HERE AGAIN!
GLOOM!
WHY SO GLUM, CHUM?
RIVERDALE HIGH GAZETTE
RIVERDALE GAZETTE ARCHIE ANDREWS-ED.
3

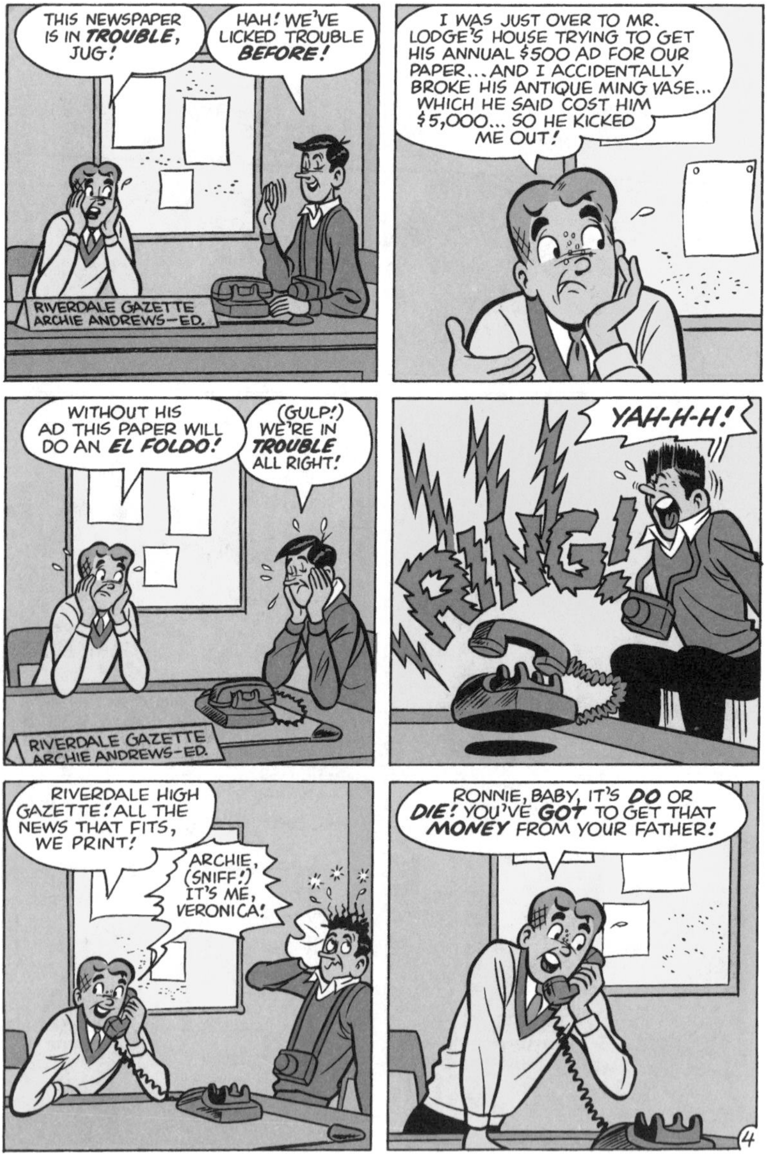
THIS NEWSPAPER IS IN TROUBLE, JUG!
HAH! WE'VE LICKED TROUBLE BEFORE!
RIVERDALE GAZETTE ARCHIE ANDREWS—ED.
I WAS JUST OVER TO MR. LODGE'S HOUSE TRYING TO GET HIS ANNUAL $500 AD FOR OUR PAPER...AND I ACCIDENTALLY BROKE HIS ANTIQUE MING VASE... WHICH HE SAID COST HIM $5,000... SO HE KICKED ME OUT!
WITHOUT HIS AD THIS PAPER WILL DO AN EL FOLDO!
(GULP!) WE'RE IN TROUBLE ALL RIGHT!
RIVERDALE GAZETTE ARCHIE ANDREWS—ED.
YAH-H-H!
RING!
RIVERDALE HIGH GAZETTE! ALL THE NEWS THAT FITS, WE PRINT!
ARCHIE, (SNIFF!) IT'S ME, VERONICA!
RONNIE, BABY, IT'S DO OR DIE! YOU'VE GOT TO GET THAT MONEY FROM YOUR FATHER!
4

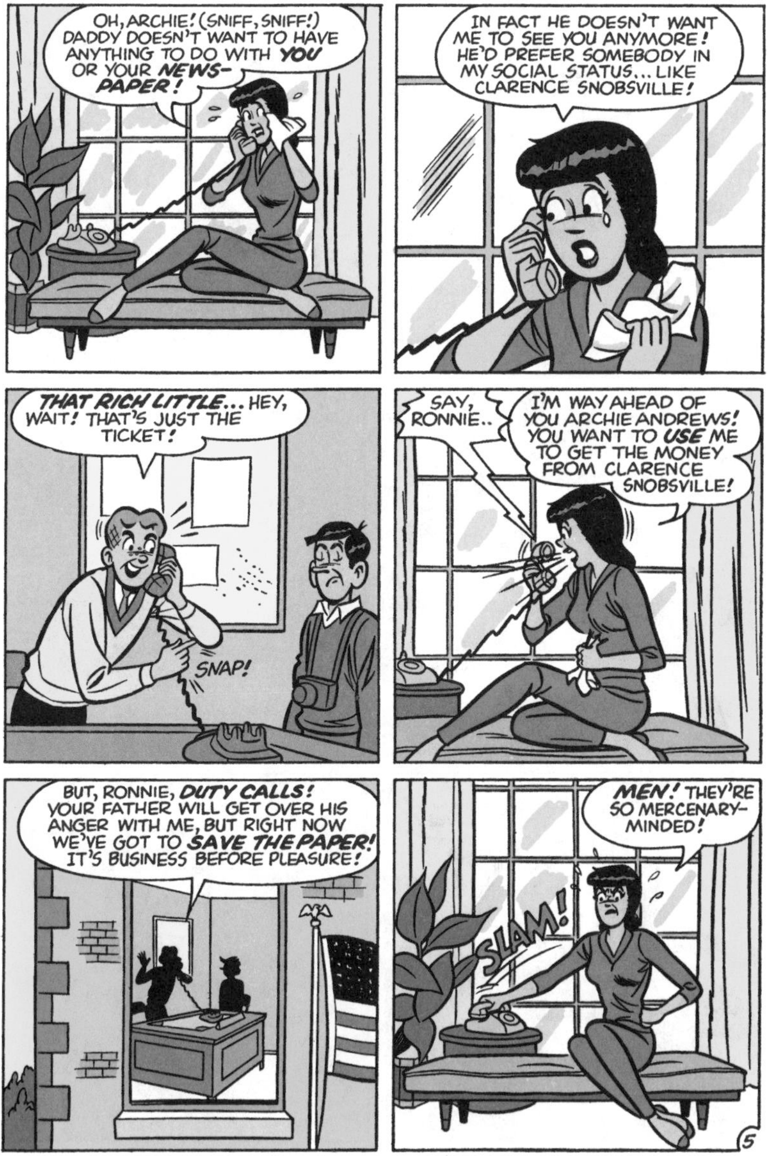
OH, ARCHIE! (SNIFF, SNIFF!) DADDY DOESN'T WANT TO HAVE ANYTHING TO DO WITH YOU OR YOUR NEWS-PAPER!
IN FACT HE DOESN'T WANT ME TO SEE YOU ANYMORE! HE'D PREFER SOMEBODY IN MY SOCIAL STATUS... LIKE CLARENCE SNOBSVILLE!
THAT RICH LITTLE... HEY, WAIT! THAT'S JUST THE TICKET!
SNAP!
SAY, RONNIE..
I'M WAY AHEAD OF YOU ARCHIE ANDREWS! YOU WANT TO USE ME TO GET THE MONEY FROM CLARENCE SNOBSVILLE!
BUT, RONNIE, DUTY CALLS! YOUR FATHER WILL GET OVER HIS ANGER WITH ME, BUT RIGHT NOW WE'VE GOT TO SAVE THE PAPER! IT'S BUSINESS BEFORE PLEASURE!
MEN! THEY'RE SO MERCENARY-MINDED!
SLAM!
5

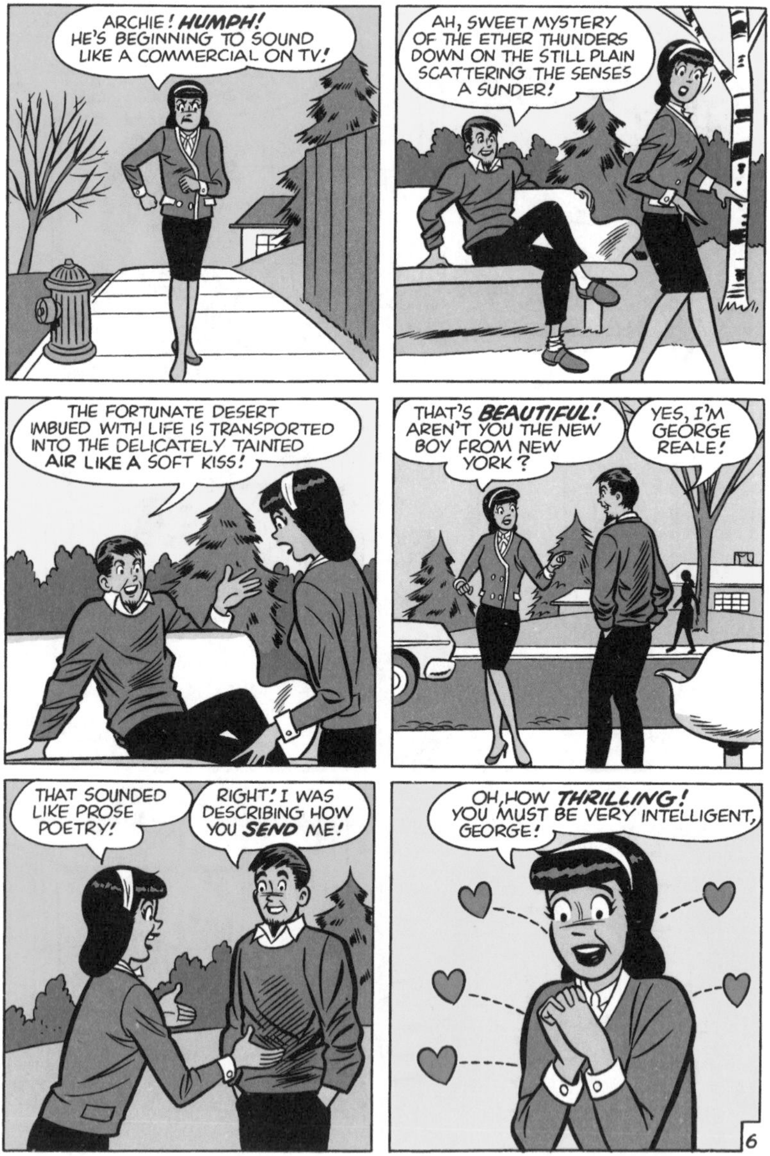
ARCHIE! HUMPH! HE'S BEGINNING TO SOUND LIKE A COMMERCIAL ON TV!
AH, SWEET MYSTERY OF THE ETHER THUNDERS DOWN ON THE STILL PLAIN SCATTERING THE SENSES A SUNDER!
THE FORTUNATE DESERT IMBUED WITH LIFE IS TRANSPORTED INTO THE DELICATELY TAINTED AIR LIKE A SOFT KISS!
THAT'S BEAUTIFUL! AREN'T YOU THE NEW BOY FROM NEW YORK?
YES, I'M GEORGE REALE!
THAT SOUNDED LIKE PROSE POETRY!
RIGHT! I WAS DESCRIBING HOW YOU SEND ME!
OH, HOW THRILLING! YOU MUST BE VERY INTELLIGENT, GEORGE!
6

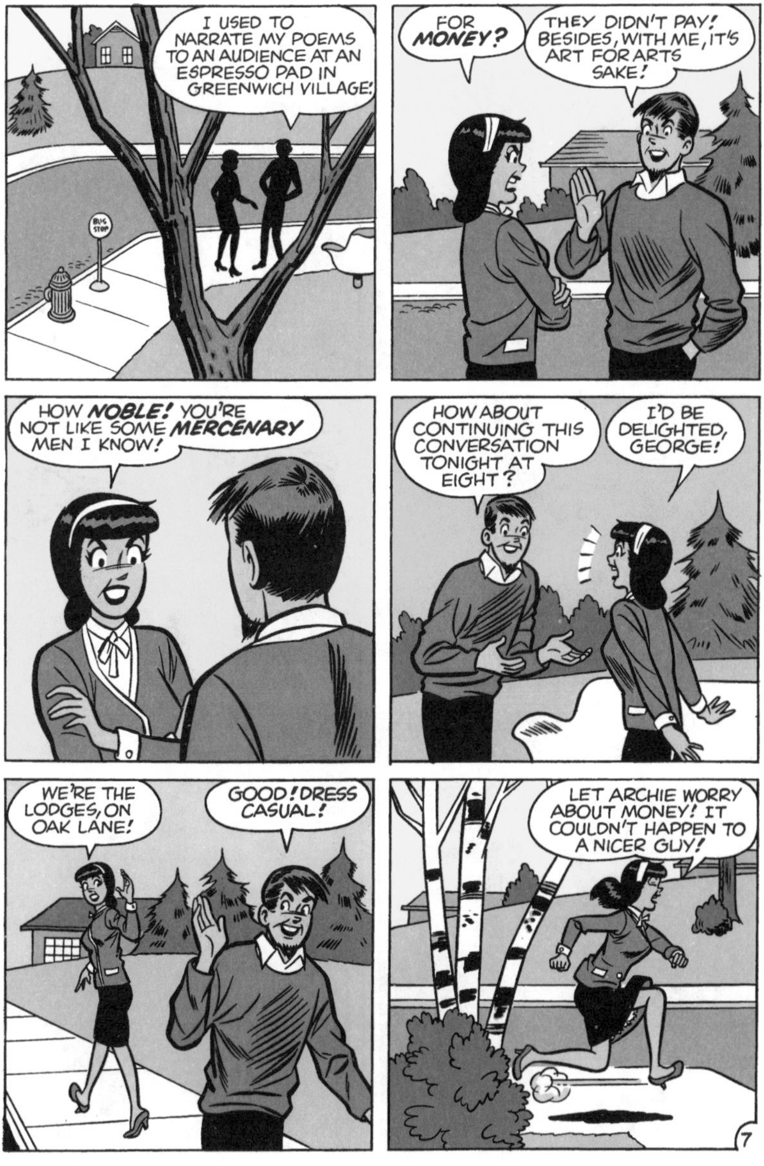
I USED TO NARRATE MY POEMS TO AN AUDIENCE AT AN ESPRESSO PAD IN GREENWICH VILLAGE!
BUS STOP
FOR MONEY?
THEY DIDN'T PAY! BESIDES, WITH ME, IT'S ART FOR ARTS SAKE!
HOW NOBLE! YOU'RE NOT LIKE SOME MERCENARY MEN I KNOW!
HOW ABOUT CONTINUING THIS CONVERSATION TONIGHT AT EIGHT?
I'D BE DELIGHTED, GEORGE!
WE'RE THE LODGES, ON OAK LANE!
GOOD! DRESS CASUAL!
LET ARCHIE WORRY ABOUT MONEY! IT COULDN'T HAPPEN TO A NICER GUY!
7

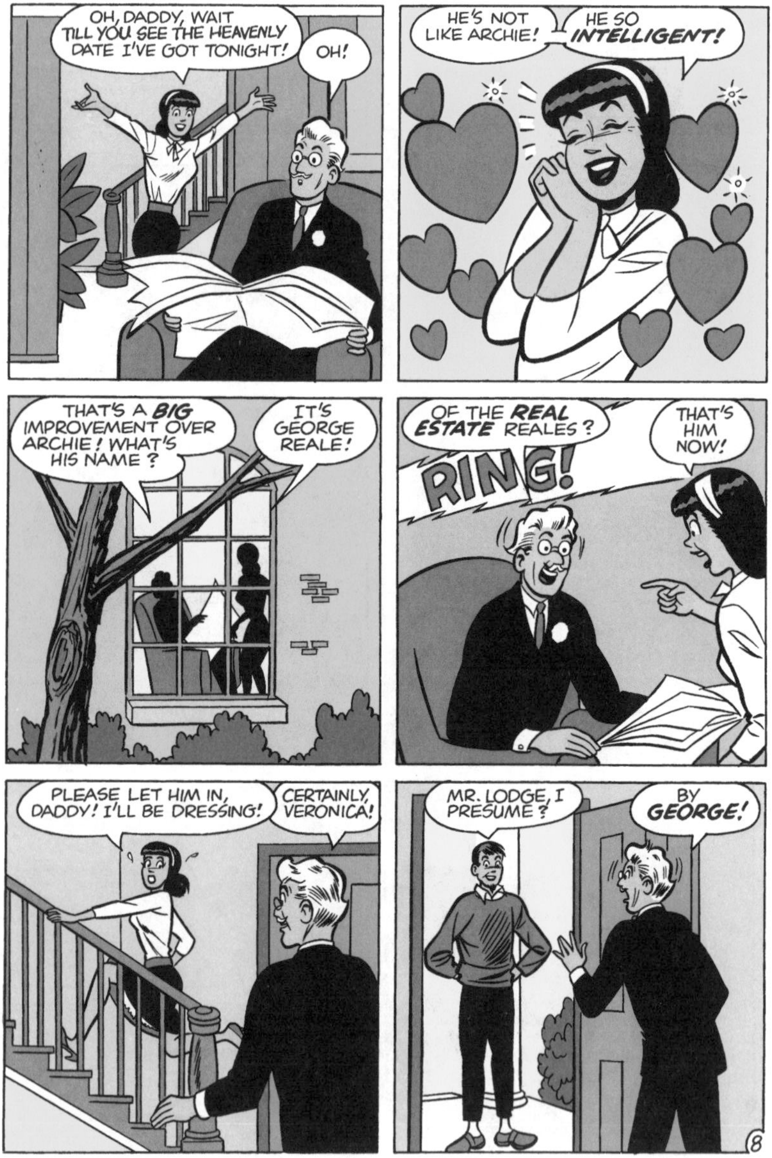
OH, DADDY, WAIT TILL YOU SEE THE HEAVENLY DATE I'VE GOT TONIGHT!
OH!
HE'S NOT LIKE ARCHIE!
HE SO **INTELLIGENT!**
THAT'S A **BIG** IMPROVEMENT OVER ARCHIE! WHAT'S HIS NAME?
IT'S GEORGE REALE!
OF THE **REAL ESTATE** REALES?
RING!
THAT'S HIM NOW!
PLEASE LET HIM IN, DADDY! I'LL BE DRESSING!
CERTAINLY, VERONICA!
MR. LODGE, I PRESUME?
BY **GEORGE!**
8

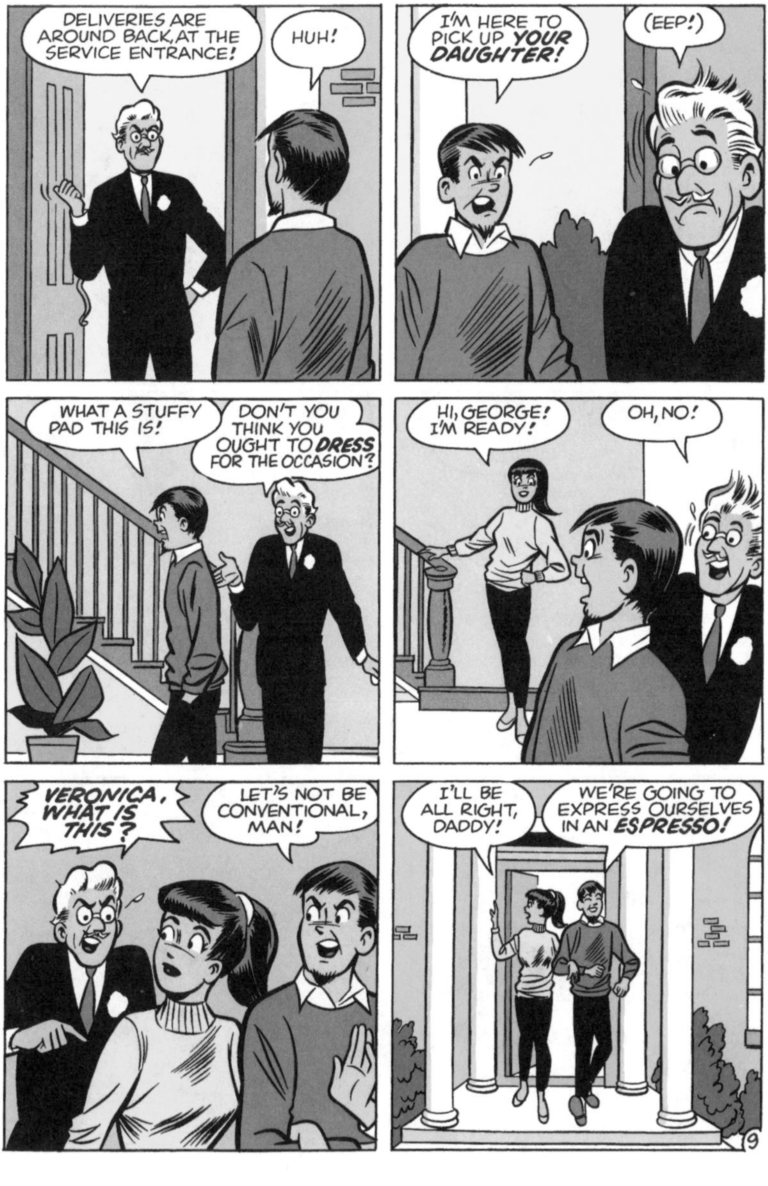
DELIVERIES ARE AROUND BACK, AT THE SERVICE ENTRANCE!
HUH!
I'M HERE TO PICK UP YOUR DAUGHTER!
(EEP!)
WHAT A STUFFY PAD THIS IS!
DON'T YOU THINK YOU OUGHT TO DRESS FOR THE OCCASION?
HI, GEORGE! I'M READY!
OH, NO!
VERONICA, WHAT IS THIS?
LET'S NOT BE CONVENTIONAL, MAN!
I'LL BE ALL RIGHT, DADDY!
WE'RE GOING TO EXPRESS OURSELVES IN AN ESPRESSO!
9

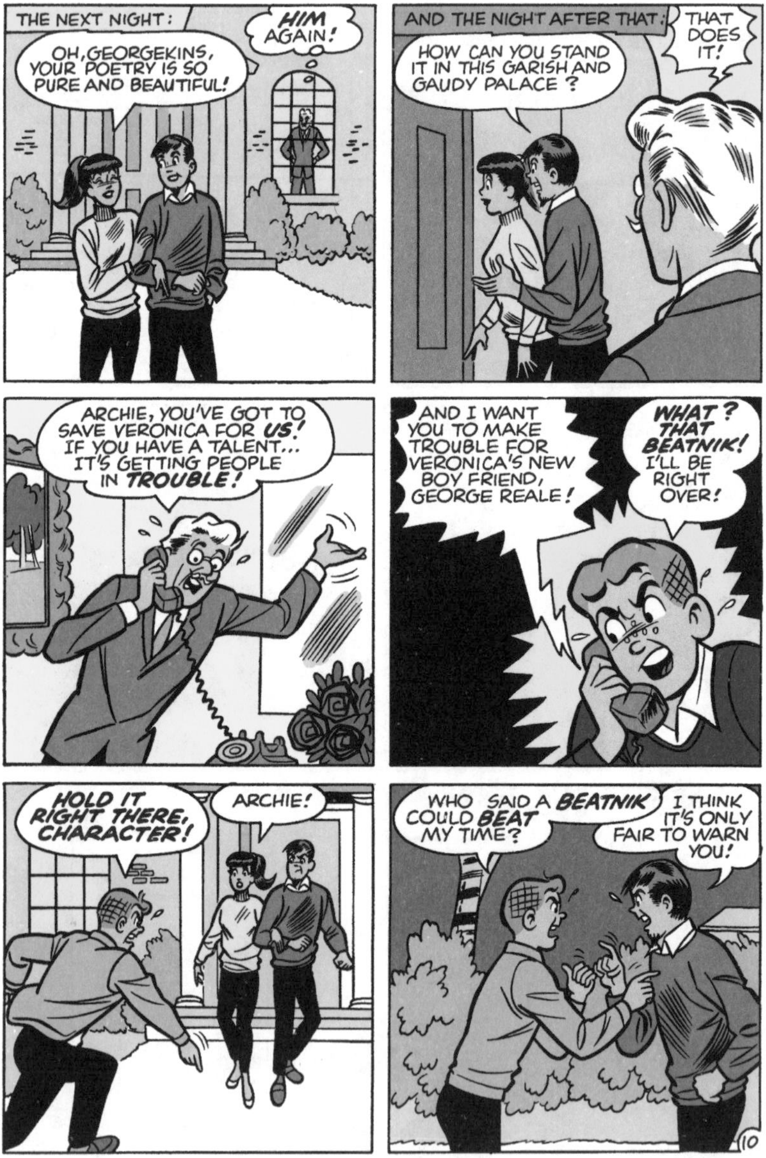
THE NEXT NIGHT:
OH, GEORGEKINS, YOUR POETRY IS SO PURE AND BEAUTIFUL!
HIM AGAIN!
AND THE NIGHT AFTER THAT:
HOW CAN YOU STAND IT IN THIS GARISH AND GAUDY PALACE?
THAT DOES IT!
ARCHIE, YOU'VE GOT TO SAVE VERONICA FOR US! IF YOU HAVE A TALENT... IT'S GETTING PEOPLE IN TROUBLE!
AND I WANT YOU TO MAKE TROUBLE FOR VERONICA'S NEW BOY FRIEND, GEORGE REALE!
WHAT? THAT BEATNIK! I'LL BE RIGHT OVER!
HOLD IT RIGHT THERE, CHARACTER!
ARCHIE!
WHO SAID A BEATNIK COULD BEAT MY TIME?
I THINK IT'S ONLY FAIR TO WARN YOU!
10

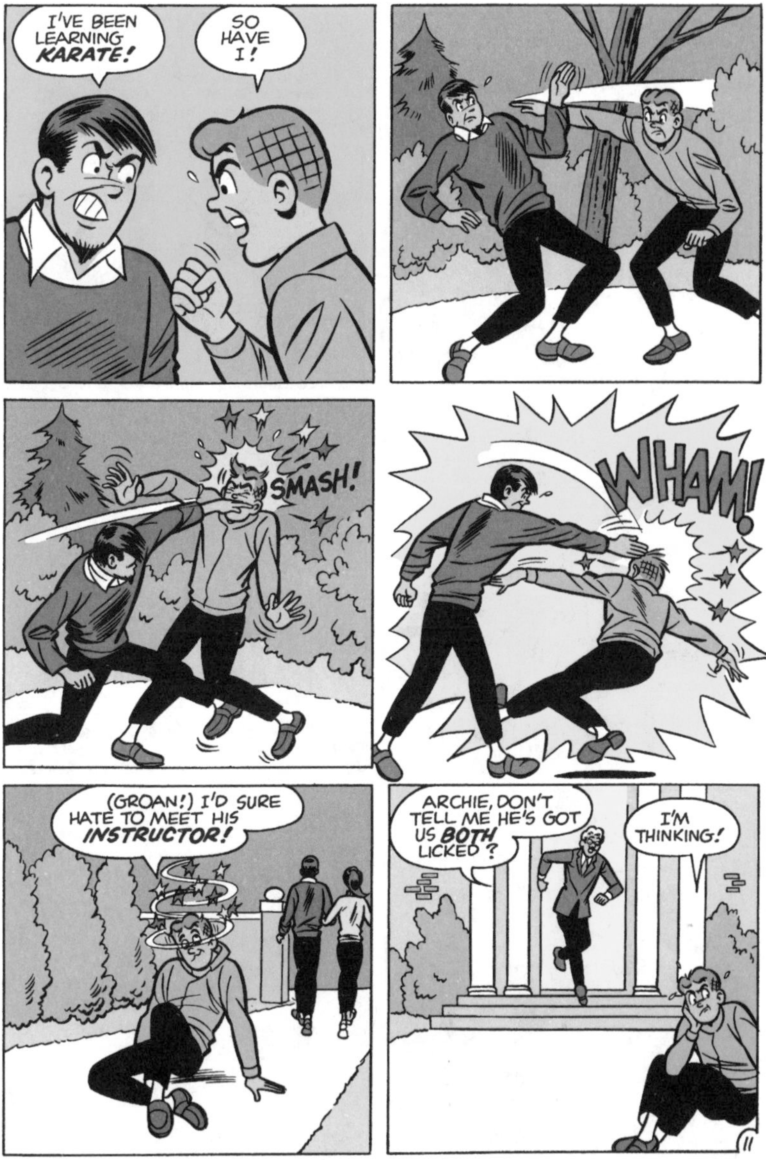
I'VE BEEN LEARNING KARATE!
SO HAVE I!
SMASH!
WHAM!
(GROAN!) I'D SURE HATE TO MEET HIS INSTRUCTOR!
ARCHIE, DON'T TELL ME HE'S GOT US BOTH LICKED?
I'M THINKING!
11

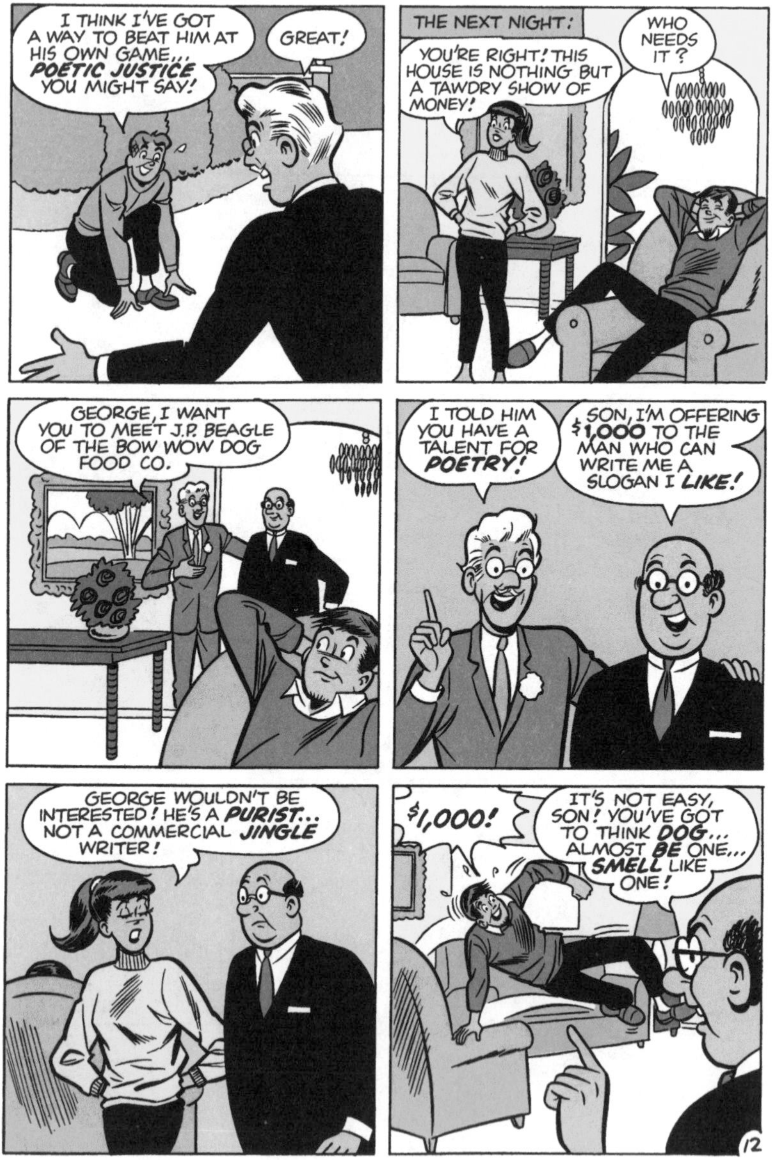
I THINK I'VE GOT A WAY TO BEAT HIM AT HIS OWN GAME... POETIC JUSTICE YOU MIGHT SAY!
GREAT!
THE NEXT NIGHT:
YOU'RE RIGHT! THIS HOUSE IS NOTHING BUT A TAWDRY SHOW OF MONEY!
WHO NEEDS IT ?
GEORGE, I WANT YOU TO MEET J.P. BEAGLE OF THE BOW WOW DOG FOOD CO.
I TOLD HIM YOU HAVE A TALENT FOR POETRY!
SON, I'M OFFERING $1,000 TO THE MAN WHO CAN WRITE ME A SLOGAN I LIKE!
GEORGE WOULDN'T BE INTERESTED! HE'S A PURIST... NOT A COMMERCIAL JINGLE WRITER!
$1,000!
IT'S NOT EASY, SON! YOU'VE GOT TO THINK DOG... ALMOST BE ONE... SMELL LIKE ONE!
12

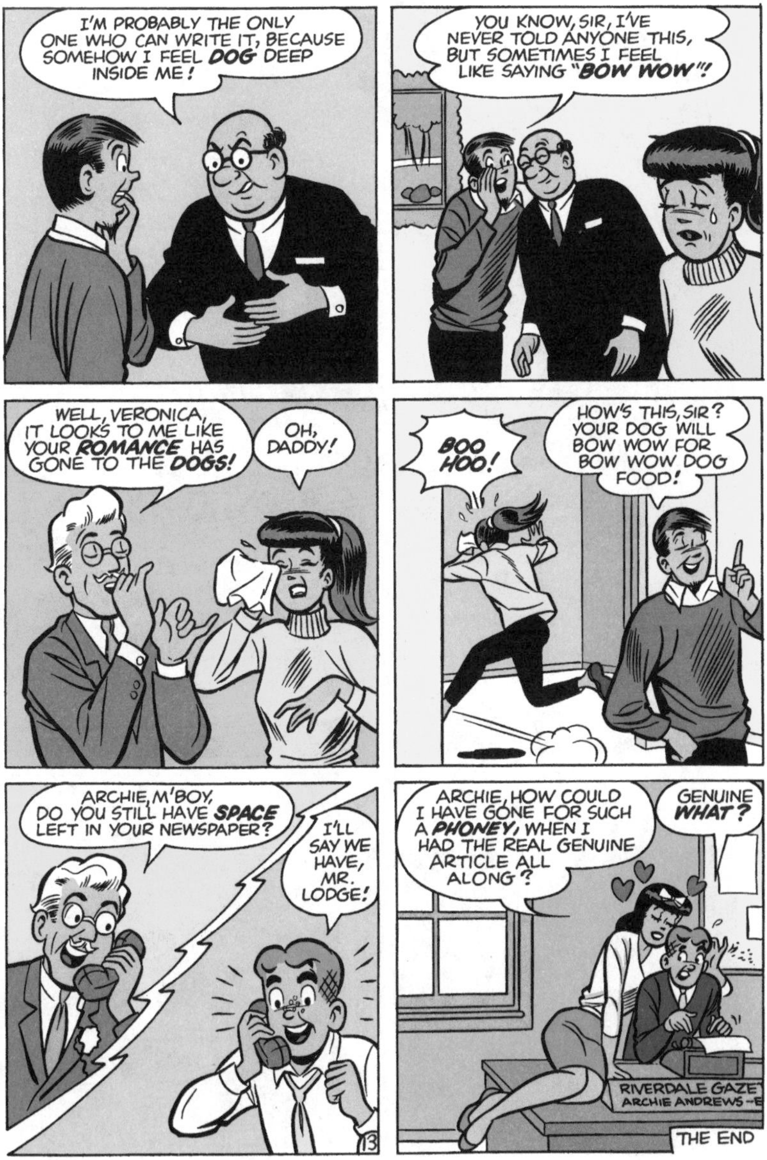
I'M PROBABLY THE ONLY ONE WHO CAN WRITE IT, BECAUSE SOMEHOW I FEEL **DOG** DEEP INSIDE ME!
YOU KNOW, SIR, I'VE NEVER TOLD ANYONE THIS, BUT SOMETIMES I FEEL LIKE SAYING "**BOW WOW**"!
WELL, VERONICA, IT LOOKS TO ME LIKE YOUR **ROMANCE** HAS GONE TO THE **DOGS**!
OH, DADDY!
BOO HOO!
HOW'S THIS, SIR? YOUR DOG WILL BOW WOW FOR BOW WOW DOG FOOD!
ARCHIE, M'BOY, DO YOU STILL HAVE **SPACE** LEFT IN YOUR NEWSPAPER?
I'LL SAY WE HAVE, MR. LODGE!
13
ARCHIE, HOW COULD I HAVE GONE FOR SUCH A **PHONEY**, WHEN I HAD THE REAL GENUINE ARTICLE ALL ALONG?
GENUINE **WHAT?**
RIVERDALE GAZE
ARCHIE ANDREWS -- E
THE END

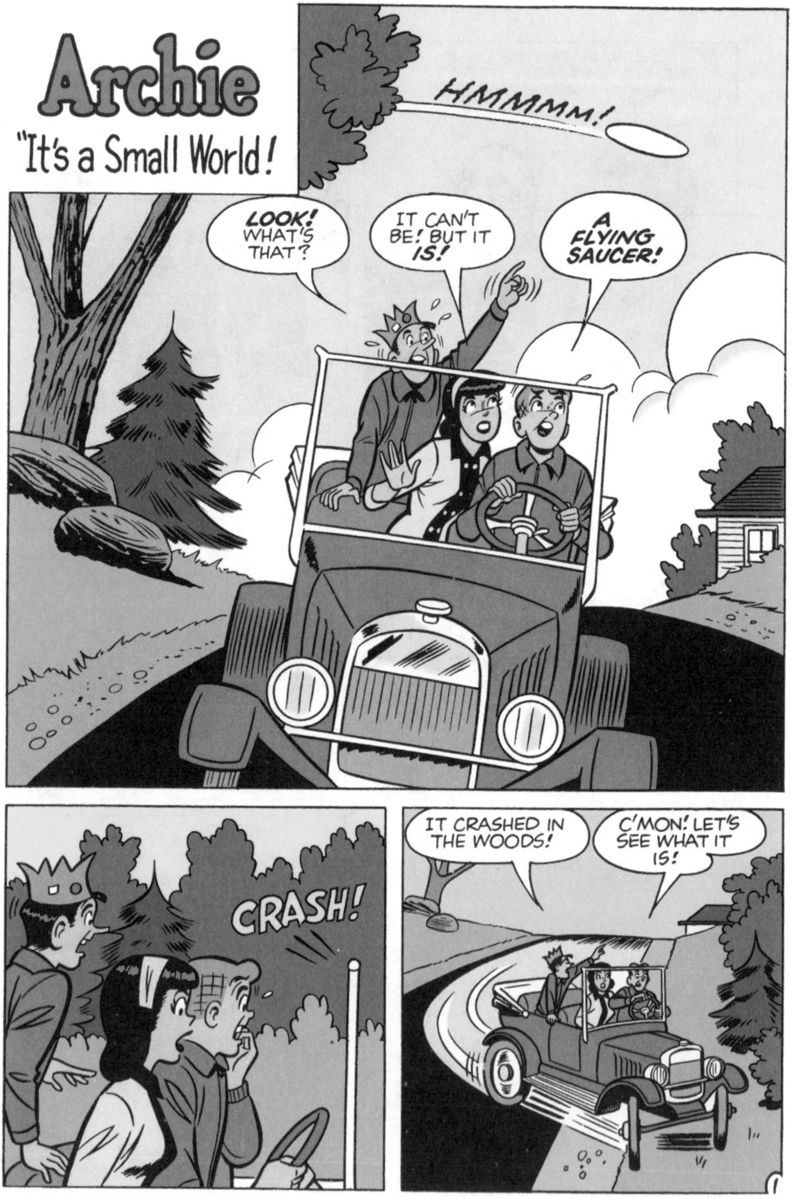
Archie
"It's a Small World!
HMMMMM!
LOOK! WHAT'S THAT?
IT CAN'T BE! BUT IT IS!
A FLYING SAUCER!
CRASH!
IT CRASHED IN THE WOODS!
C'MON! LET'S SEE WHAT IT IS!

Story: Frank Doyle Pencils: Bob White Inks & Letters: Marty Epp

Originally printed in LIFE WITH ARCHIE #35, March 1965

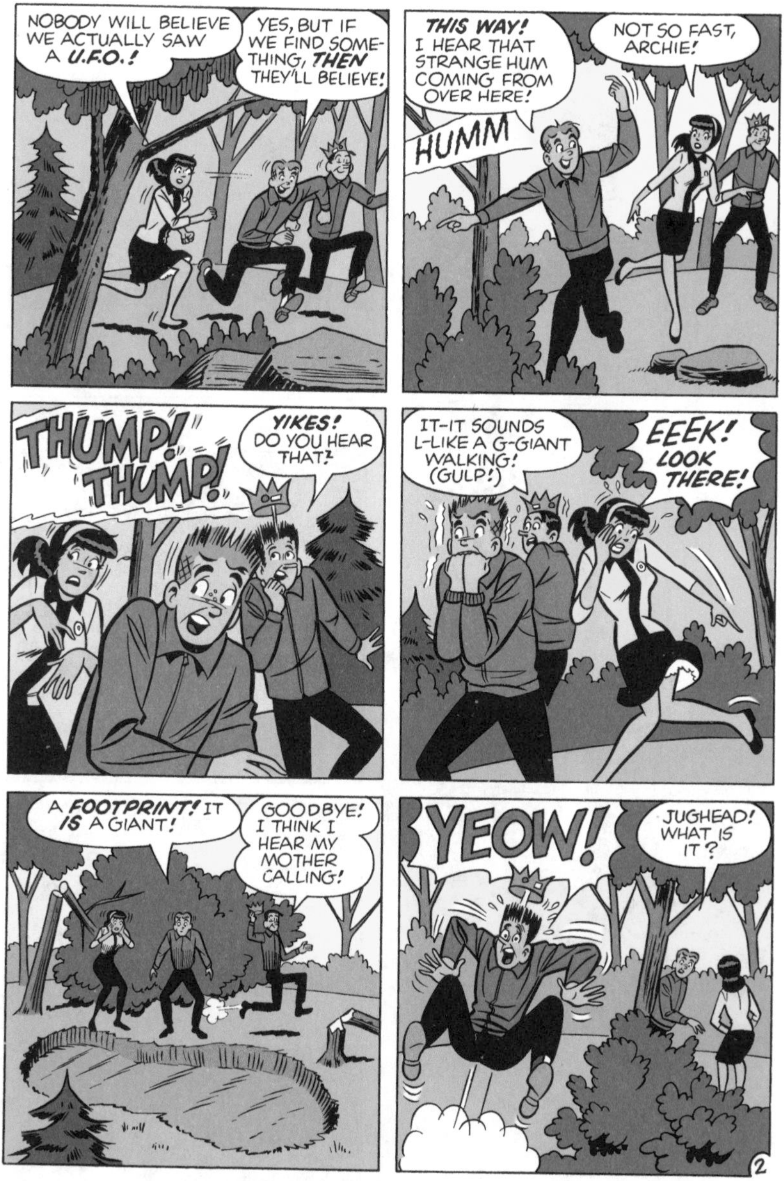
NOBODY WILL BELIEVE WE ACTUALLY SAW A U.F.O.!
YES, BUT IF WE FIND SOMETHING, THEN THEY'LL BELIEVE!
THIS WAY! I HEAR THAT STRANGE HUM COMING FROM OVER HERE!
HUMM
NOT SO FAST, ARCHIE!
THUMP! THUMP!
YIKES! DO YOU HEAR THAT?
IT-IT SOUNDS L-LIKE A G-GIANT WALKING! (GULP!)
EEEK! LOOK THERE!
A FOOTPRINT! IT IS A GIANT!
GOODBYE! I THINK I HEAR MY MOTHER CALLING!
YEOW!
JUGHEAD! WHAT IS IT?
2

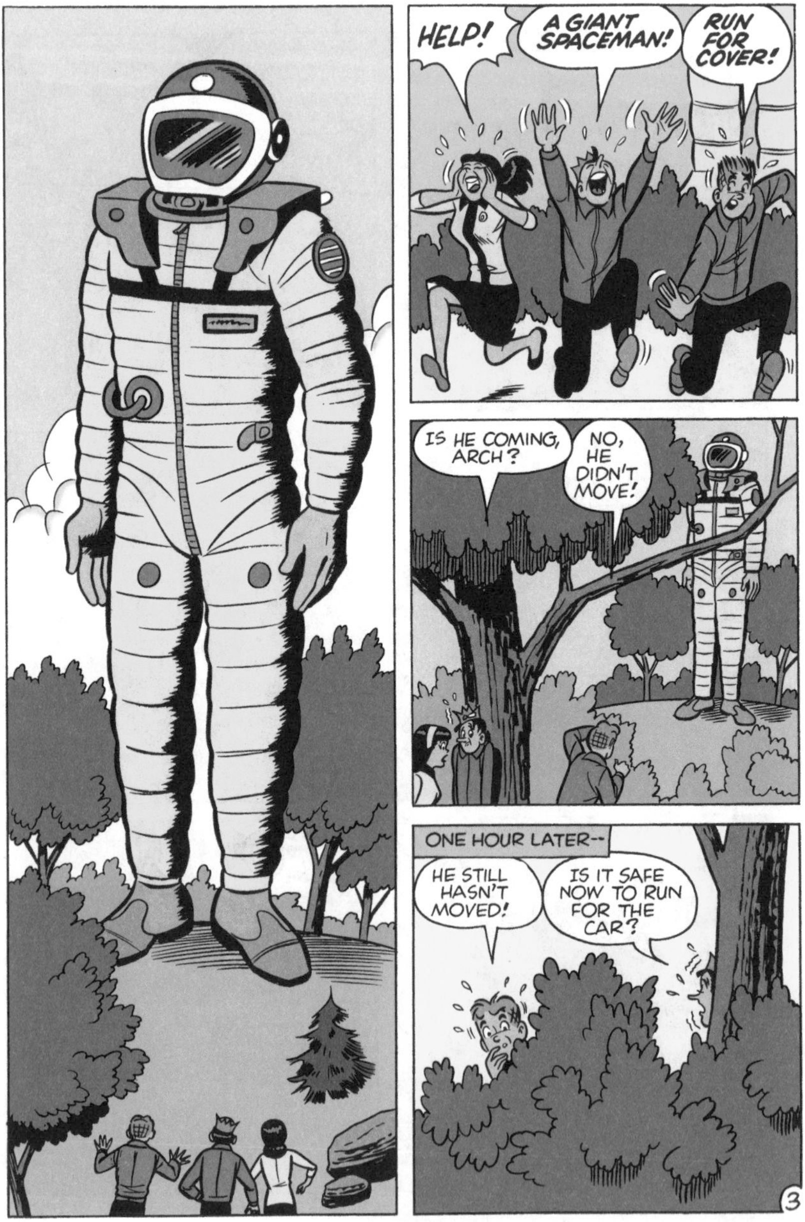
HELP!
A GIANT SPACEMAN!
RUN FOR COVER!
IS HE COMING, ARCH?
NO, HE DIDN'T MOVE!
ONE HOUR LATER--
HE STILL HASN'T MOVED!
IS IT SAFE NOW TO RUN FOR THE CAR?
3

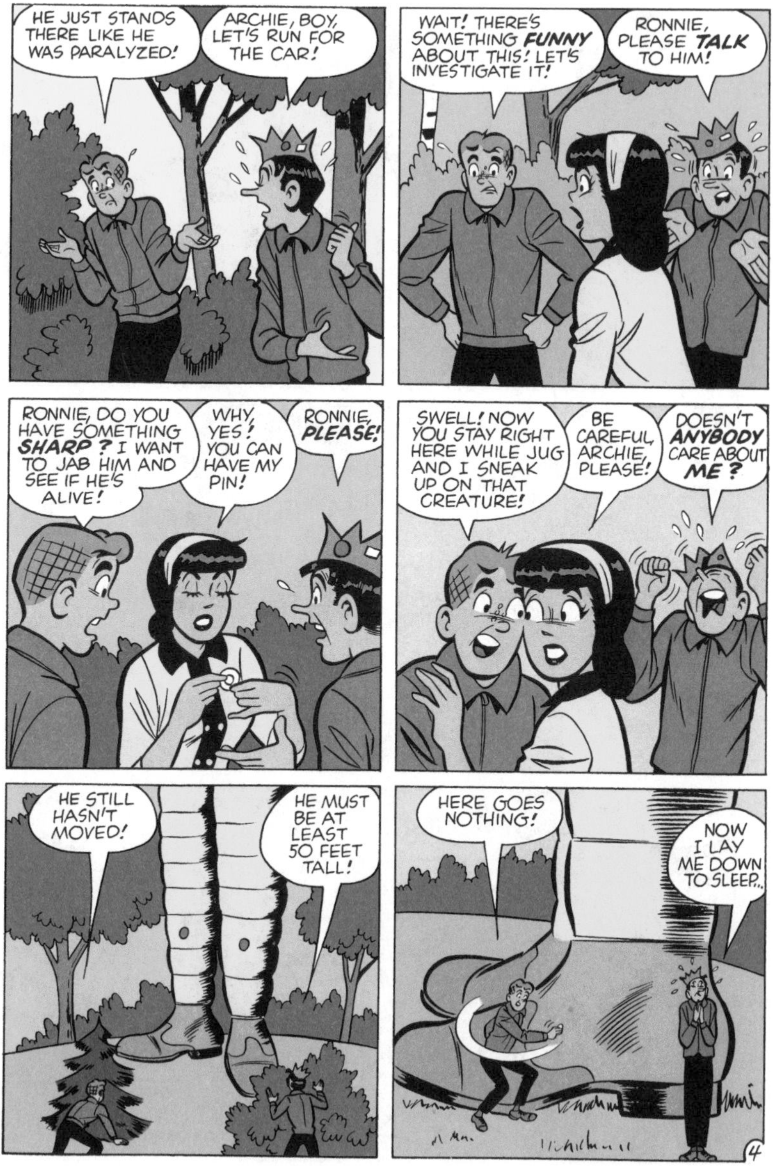
HE JUST STANDS THERE LIKE HE WAS PARALYZED!
ARCHIE, BOY, LET'S RUN FOR THE CAR!
WAIT! THERE'S SOMETHING FUNNY ABOUT THIS! LET'S INVESTIGATE IT!
RONNIE, PLEASE TALK TO HIM!
RONNIE, DO YOU HAVE SOMETHING SHARP? I WANT TO JAB HIM AND SEE IF HE'S ALIVE!
WHY, YES! YOU CAN HAVE MY PIN!
RONNIE, PLEASE!
SWELL! NOW YOU STAY RIGHT HERE WHILE JUG AND I SNEAK UP ON THAT CREATURE!
BE CAREFUL, ARCHIE, PLEASE!
DOESN'T ANYBODY CARE ABOUT ME?
HE STILL HASN'T MOVED!
HE MUST BE AT LEAST 50 FEET TALL!
HERE GOES NOTHING!
NOW I LAY ME DOWN TO SLEEP...
4

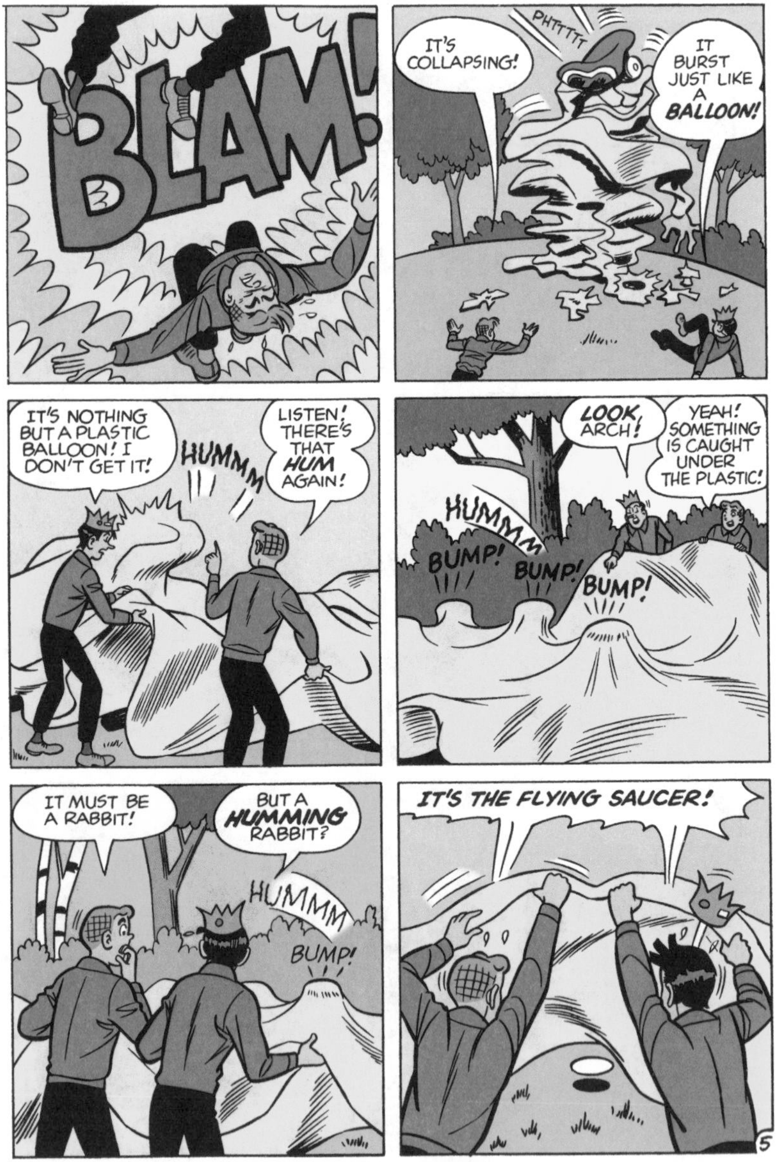
BLAM!
PHTTTTT
IT'S COLLAPSING!
IT BURST JUST LIKE A BALLOON!
IT'S NOTHING BUT A PLASTIC BALLOON! I DON'T GET IT!
HUMMM
LISTEN! THERE'S THAT HUM AGAIN!
LOOK, ARCH!
YEAH! SOMETHING IS CAUGHT UNDER THE PLASTIC!
HUMMM
BUMP!
BUMP!
BUMP!
IT MUST BE A RABBIT!
BUT A HUMMING RABBIT?
HUMMM
BUMP!
IT'S THE FLYING SAUCER!
5

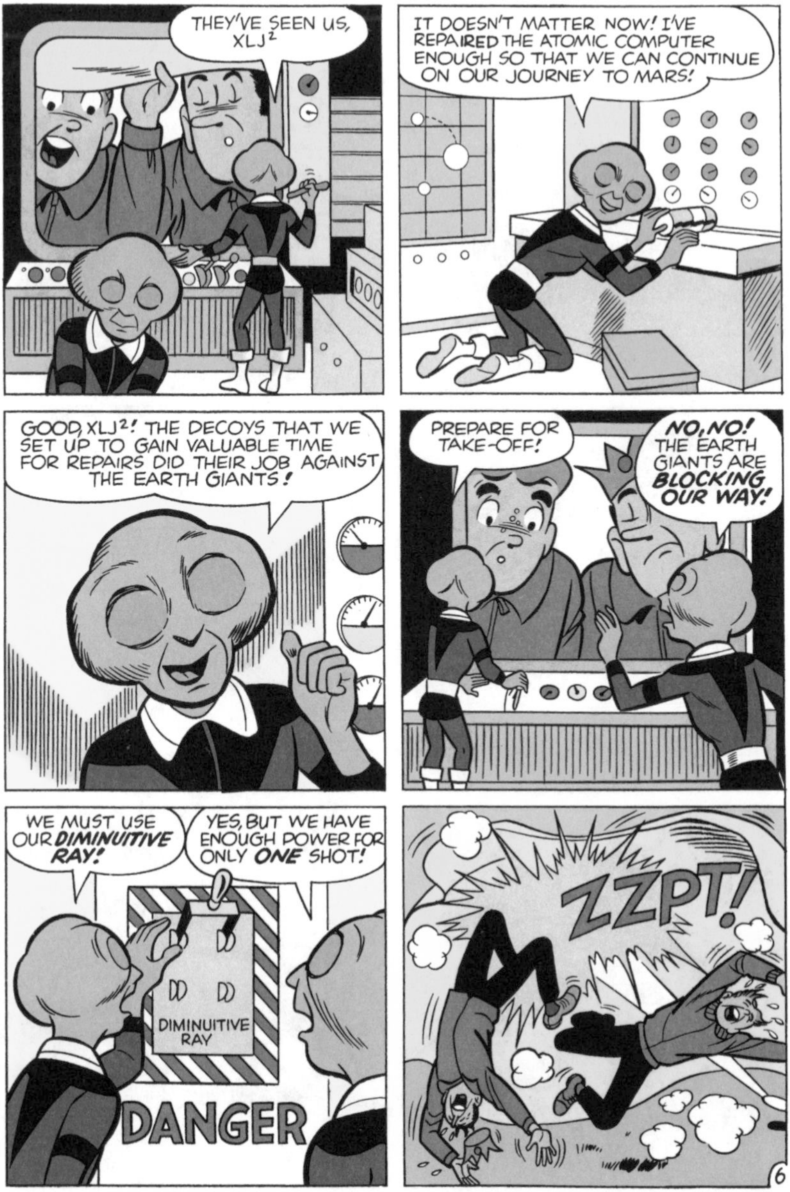
THEY'VE SEEN US, XLJ²
IT DOESN'T MATTER NOW! I'VE REPAIRED THE ATOMIC COMPUTER ENOUGH SO THAT WE CAN CONTINUE ON OUR JOURNEY TO MARS!
GOOD, XLJ²! THE DECOYS THAT WE SET UP TO GAIN VALUABLE TIME FOR REPAIRS DID THEIR JOB AGAINST THE EARTH GIANTS!
PREPARE FOR TAKE-OFF!
NO, NO! THE EARTH GIANTS ARE BLOCKING OUR WAY!
WE MUST USE OUR DIMINUTIVE RAY!
YES, BUT WE HAVE ENOUGH POWER FOR ONLY ONE SHOT!
DIMINUTIVE RAY
DANGER
ZZPT!
6

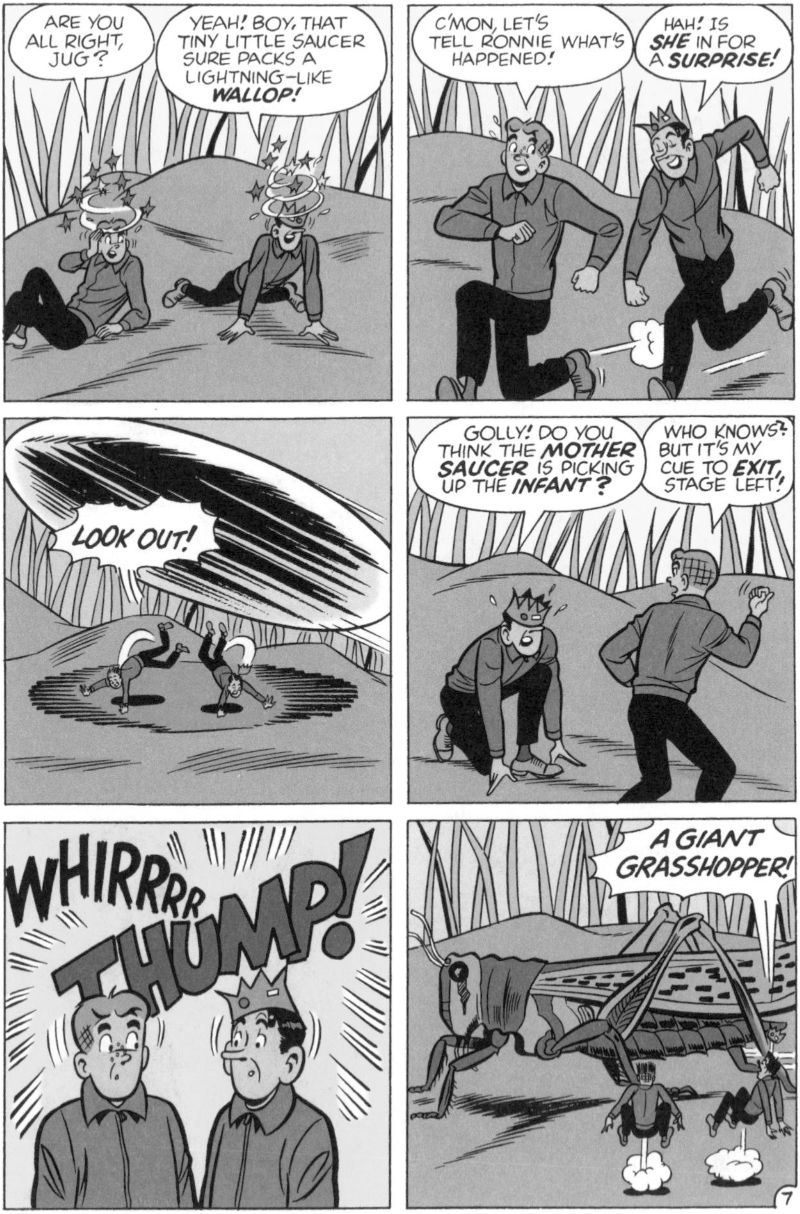
ARE YOU ALL RIGHT, JUG?
YEAH! BOY, THAT TINY LITTLE SAUCER SURE PACKS A LIGHTNING-LIKE WALLOP!
C'MON, LET'S TELL RONNIE WHAT'S HAPPENED!
HAH! IS SHE IN FOR A SURPRISE!
LOOK OUT!
GOLLY! DO YOU THINK THE MOTHER SAUCER IS PICKING UP THE INFANT?
WHO KNOWS? BUT IT'S MY CUE TO EXIT, STAGE LEFT!
WHIRRRRR
THUMP!
A GIANT GRASSHOPPER!
7

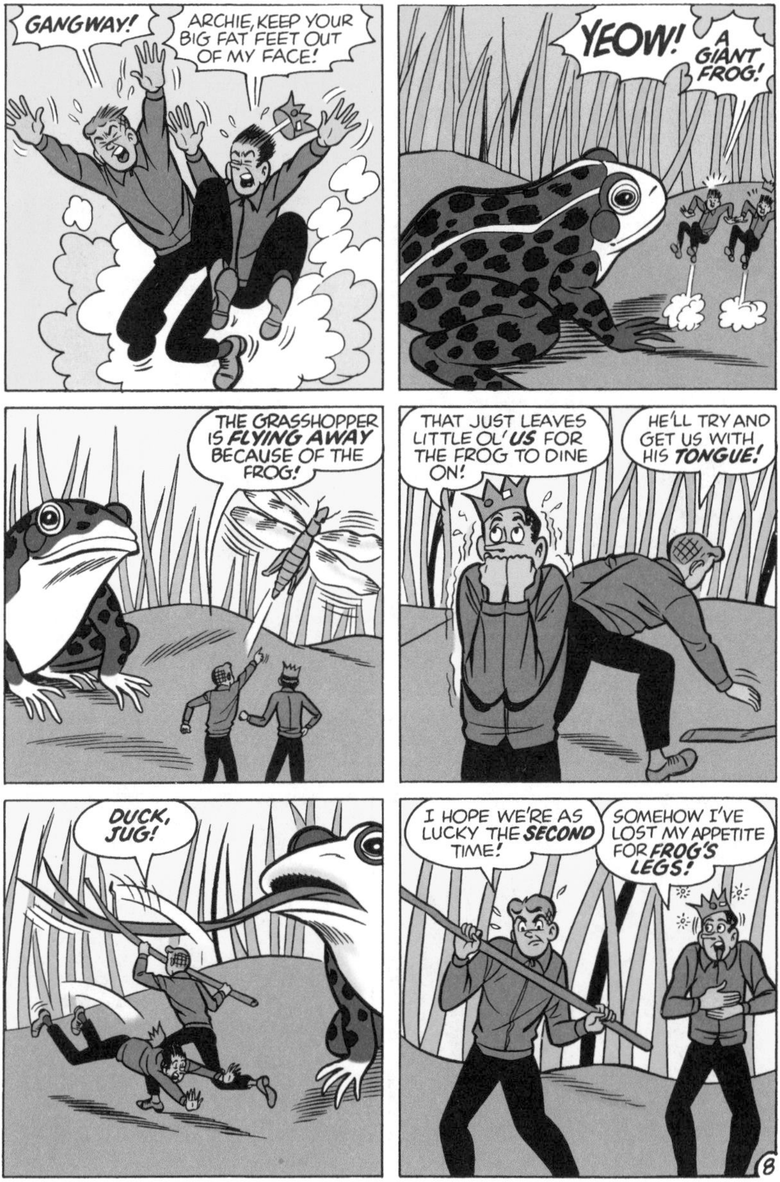
GANGWAY!
ARCHIE, KEEP YOUR BIG FAT FEET OUT OF MY FACE!
YEOW!
A GIANT FROG!
THE GRASSHOPPER IS FLYING AWAY BECAUSE OF THE FROG!
THAT JUST LEAVES LITTLE OL' US FOR THE FROG TO DINE ON!
HE'LL TRY AND GET US WITH HIS TONGUE!
DUCK, JUG!
I HOPE WE'RE AS LUCKY THE SECOND TIME!
SOMEHOW I'VE LOST MY APPETITE FOR FROG'S LEGS!
8

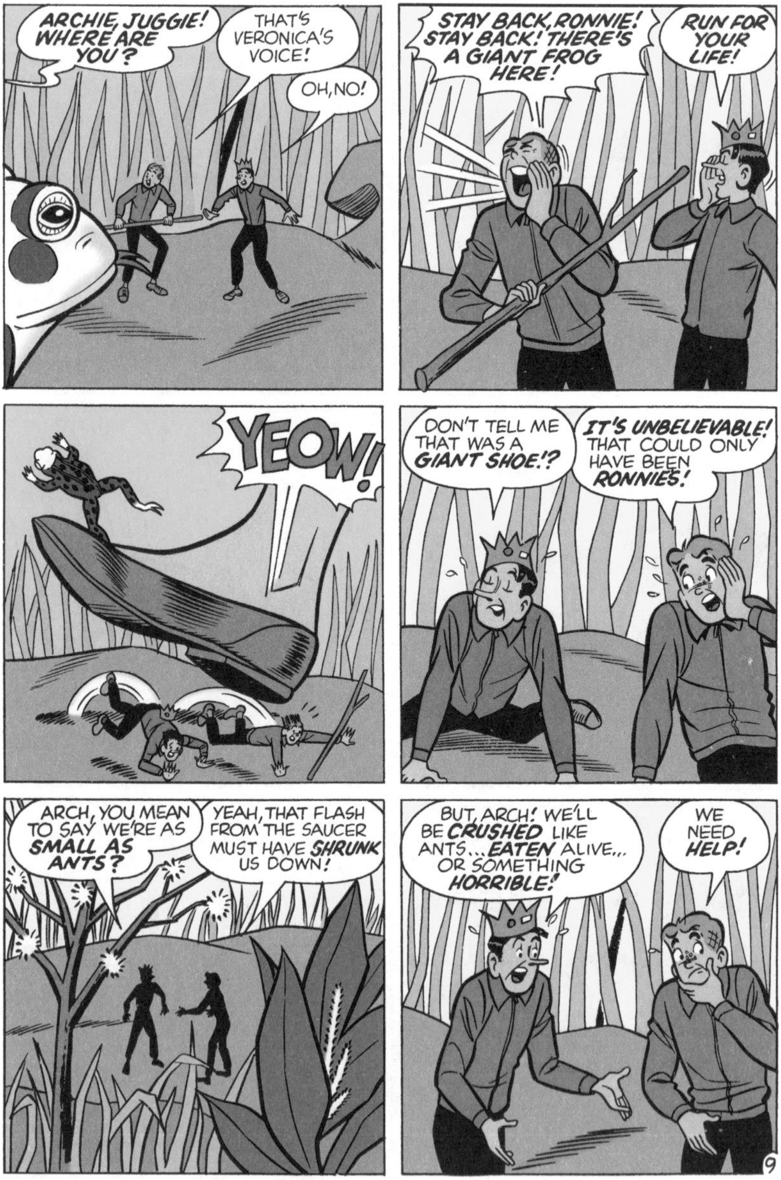
ARCHIE, JUGGIE! WHERE ARE YOU?
THAT'S VERONICA'S VOICE!
OH, NO!
STAY BACK, RONNIE! STAY BACK! THERE'S A GIANT FROG HERE!
RUN FOR YOUR LIFE!
YEOW!
DON'T TELL ME THAT WAS A GIANT SHOE!?
IT'S UNBELIEVABLE! THAT COULD ONLY HAVE BEEN RONNIE'S!
ARCH, YOU MEAN TO SAY WE'RE AS SMALL AS ANTS?
YEAH, THAT FLASH FROM THE SAUCER MUST HAVE SHRUNK US DOWN!
BUT, ARCH! WE'LL BE CRUSHED LIKE ANTS... EATEN ALIVE... OR SOMETHING HORRIBLE!
WE NEED HELP!
9

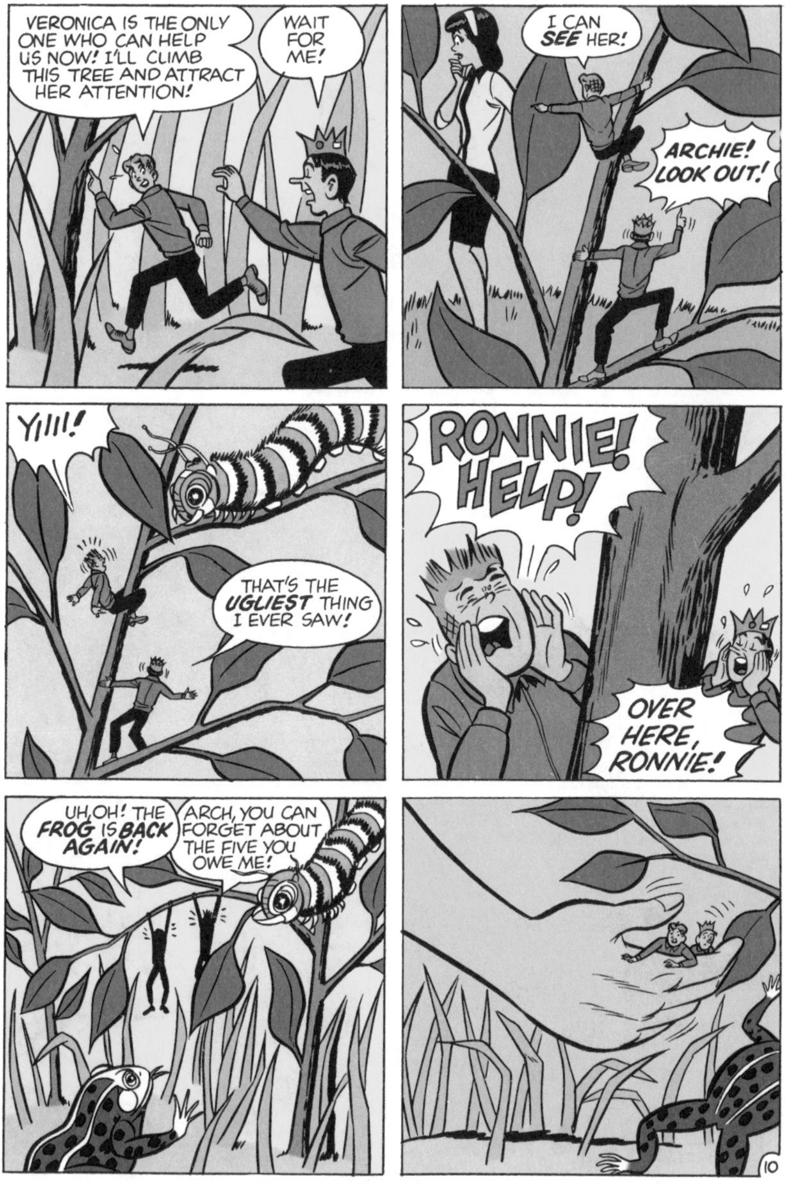
VERONICA IS THE ONLY ONE WHO CAN HELP US NOW! I'LL CLIMB THIS TREE AND ATTRACT HER ATTENTION!
WAIT FOR ME!
I CAN SEE HER!
ARCHIE! LOOK OUT!
YIIII!
THAT'S THE UGLIEST THING I EVER SAW!
RONNIE! HELP!
OVER HERE, RONNIE!
UH,OH! THE FROG IS BACK AGAIN!
ARCH, YOU CAN FORGET ABOUT THE FIVE YOU OWE ME!
10

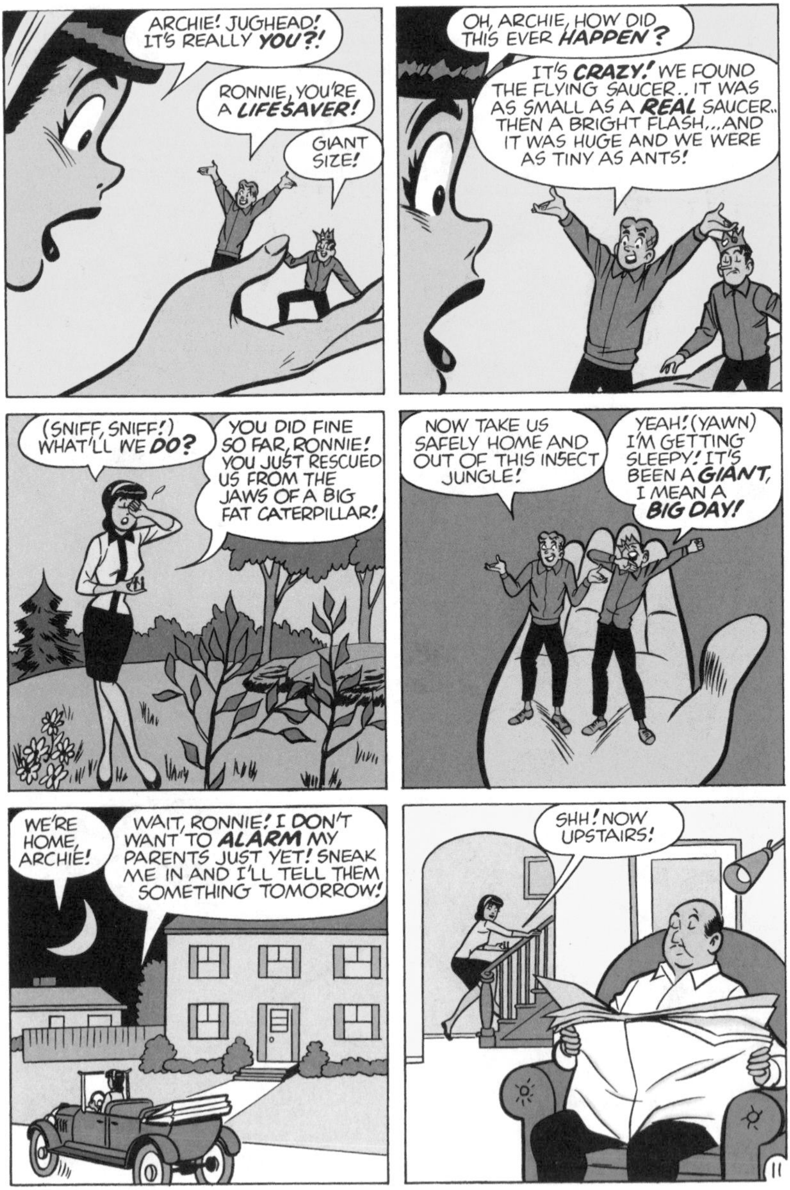
ARCHIE! JUGHEAD! IT'S REALLY YOU?!
RONNIE, YOU'RE A LIFESAVER!
GIANT SIZE!
OH, ARCHIE, HOW DID THIS EVER HAPPEN?
IT'S CRAZY! WE FOUND THE FLYING SAUCER.. IT WAS AS SMALL AS A REAL SAUCER.. THEN A BRIGHT FLASH,..AND IT WAS HUGE AND WE WERE AS TINY AS ANTS!
(SNIFF, SNIFF!) WHAT'LL WE DO?
YOU DID FINE SO FAR, RONNIE! YOU JUST RESCUED US FROM THE JAWS OF A BIG FAT CATERPILLAR!
NOW TAKE US SAFELY HOME AND OUT OF THIS INSECT JUNGLE!
YEAH! (YAWN) I'M GETTING SLEEPY! IT'S BEEN A GIANT, I MEAN A BIG DAY!
WE'RE HOME, ARCHIE!
WAIT, RONNIE! I DON'T WANT TO ALARM MY PARENTS JUST YET! SNEAK ME IN AND I'LL TELL THEM SOMETHING TOMORROW!
SHH! NOW UPSTAIRS!
11

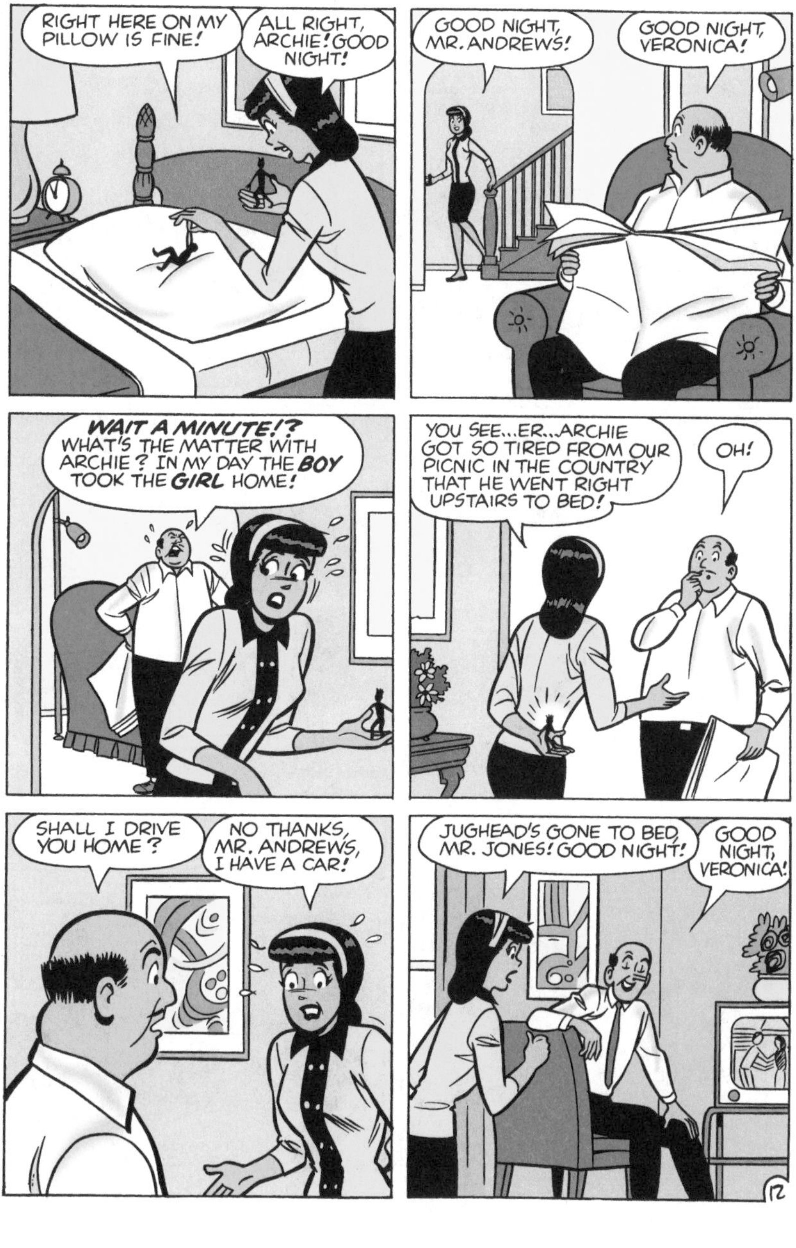
RIGHT HERE ON MY PILLOW IS FINE!
ALL RIGHT, ARCHIE! GOOD NIGHT!
GOOD NIGHT, MR. ANDREWS!
GOOD NIGHT, VERONICA!
WAIT A MINUTE!? WHAT'S THE MATTER WITH ARCHIE? IN MY DAY THE BOY TOOK THE GIRL HOME!
YOU SEE...ER...ARCHIE GOT SO TIRED FROM OUR PICNIC IN THE COUNTRY THAT HE WENT RIGHT UPSTAIRS TO BED!
OH!
SHALL I DRIVE YOU HOME?
NO THANKS, MR. ANDREWS, I HAVE A CAR!
JUGHEAD'S GONE TO BED, MR. JONES! GOOD NIGHT!
GOOD NIGHT, VERONICA!
12

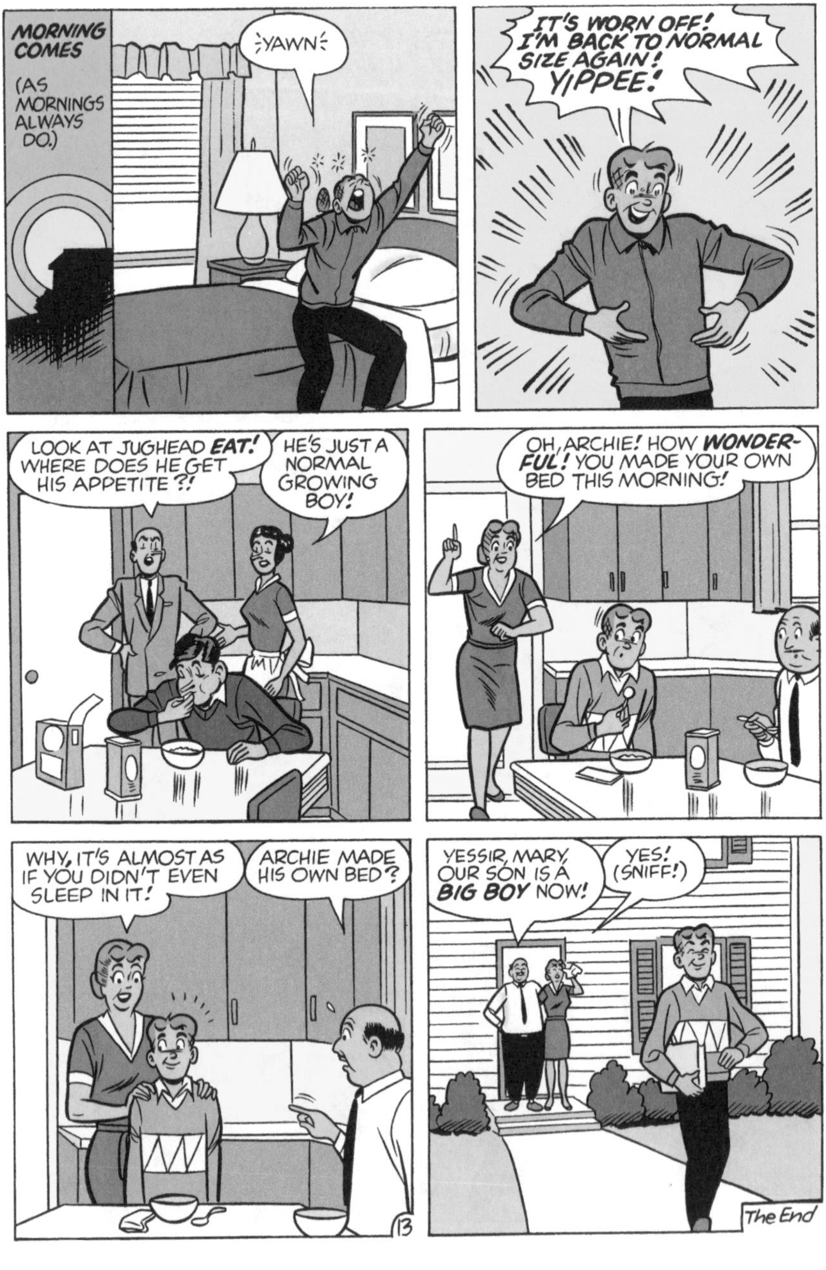
MORNING COMES
(AS MORNINGS ALWAYS DO.)
YAWN
IT'S WORN OFF! I'M BACK TO NORMAL SIZE AGAIN! YIPPEE!
LOOK AT JUGHEAD EAT! WHERE DOES HE GET HIS APPETITE ?!
HE'S JUST A NORMAL GROWING BOY!
OH, ARCHIE! HOW WONDER-FUL! YOU MADE YOUR OWN BED THIS MORNING!
WHY, IT'S ALMOST AS IF YOU DIDN'T EVEN SLEEP IN IT!
ARCHIE MADE HIS OWN BED?
13
YESSIR, MARY, OUR SON IS A BIG BOY NOW!
YES! (SNIFF!)
The End

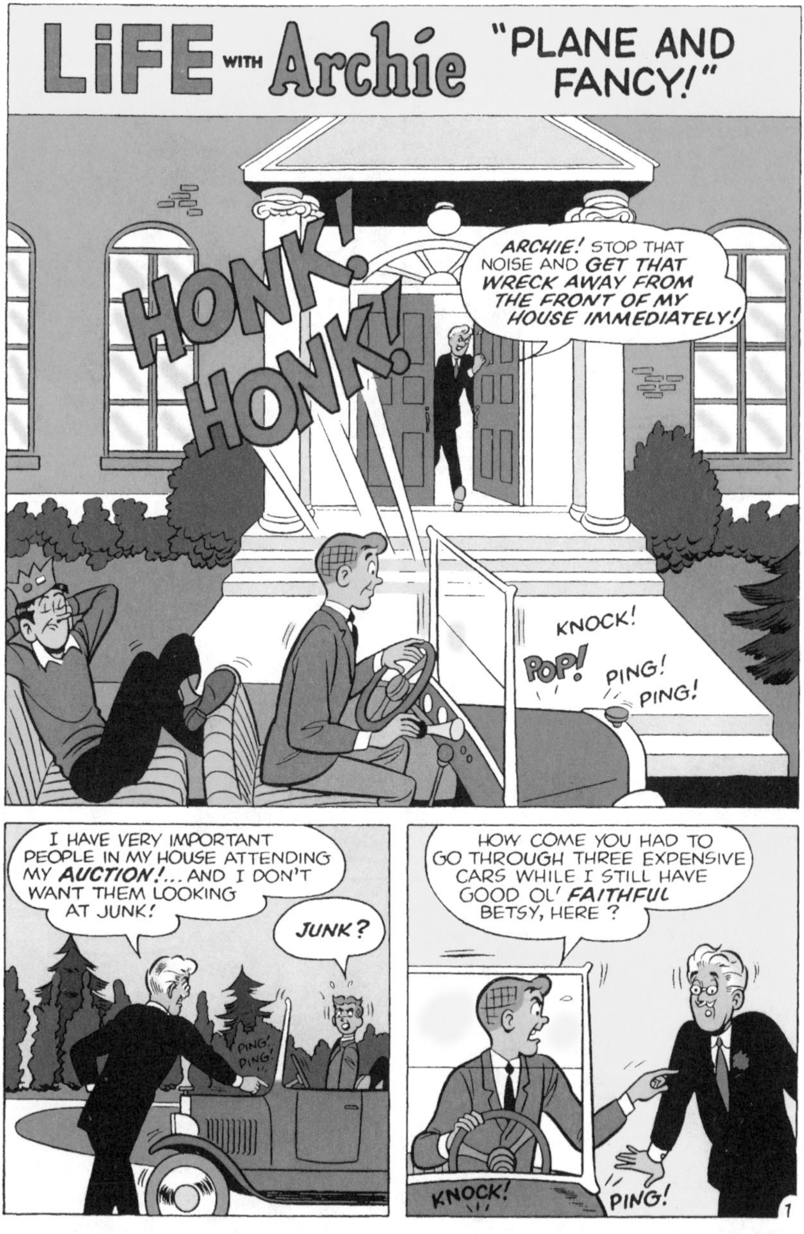
LiFE WITH Archie
"PLANE AND FANCY!"
HONK! HONK!
ARCHIE! STOP THAT NOISE AND GET THAT WRECK AWAY FROM THE FRONT OF MY HOUSE IMMEDIATELY!
KNOCK!
POP!
PING!
PING!
I HAVE VERY IMPORTANT PEOPLE IN MY HOUSE ATTENDING MY AUCTION!... AND I DON'T WANT THEM LOOKING AT JUNK!
JUNK?
PING! PING!
HOW COME YOU HAD TO GO THROUGH THREE EXPENSIVE CARS WHILE I STILL HAVE GOOD OL' FAITHFUL BETSY, HERE ?
KNOCK!
PING!
1

Story: Frank Doyle Pencils: Bob White Inks & Letters: Marty Epp

Originally printed in LIFE WITH ARCHIE #35, March 1965

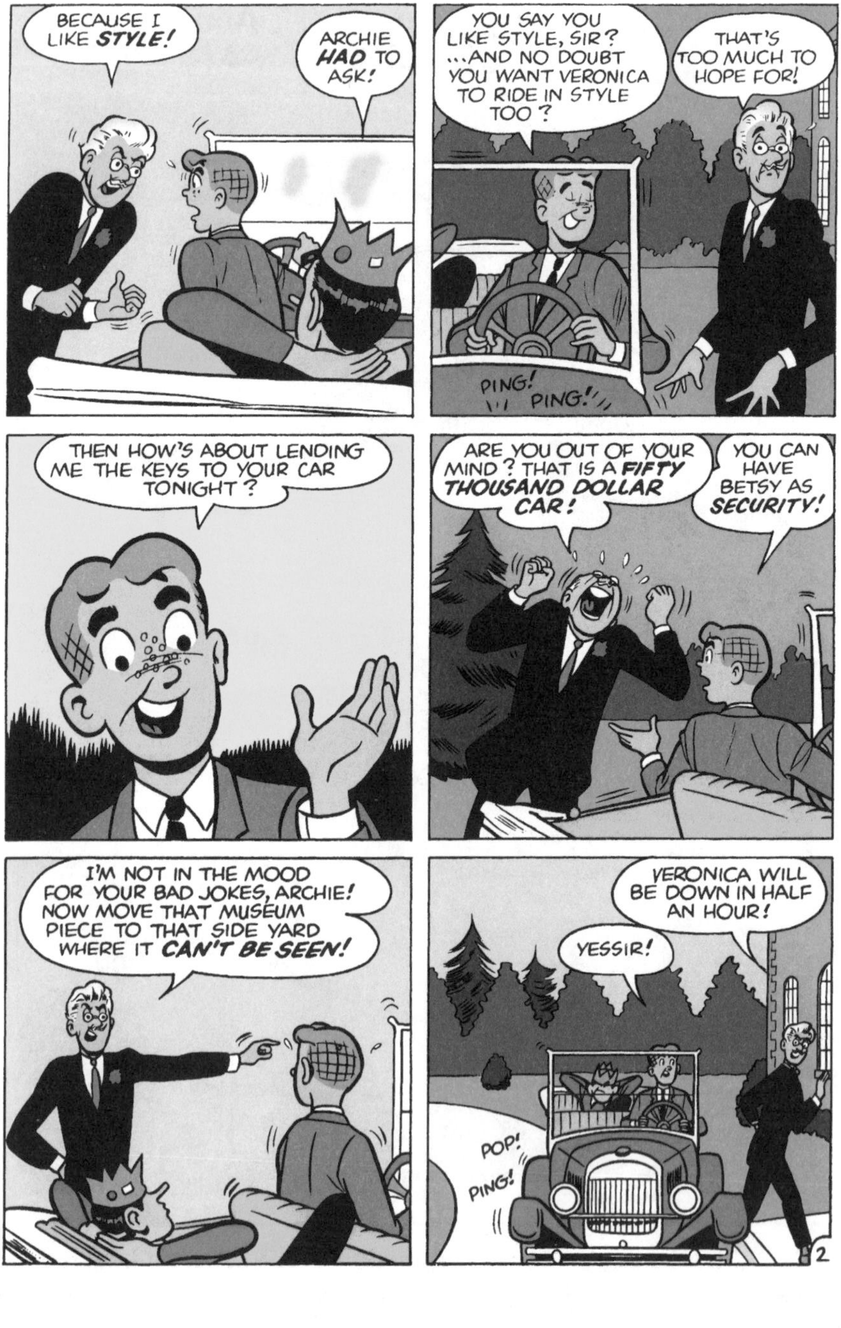
BECAUSE I LIKE STYLE!
ARCHIE HAD TO ASK!
YOU SAY YOU LIKE STYLE, SIR? ...AND NO DOUBT YOU WANT VERONICA TO RIDE IN STYLE TOO?
THAT'S TOO MUCH TO HOPE FOR!
PING! PING!
THEN HOW'S ABOUT LENDING ME THE KEYS TO YOUR CAR TONIGHT?
ARE YOU OUT OF YOUR MIND? THAT IS A FIFTY THOUSAND DOLLAR CAR!
YOU CAN HAVE BETSY AS SECURITY!
I'M NOT IN THE MOOD FOR YOUR BAD JOKES, ARCHIE! NOW MOVE THAT MUSEUM PIECE TO THAT SIDE YARD WHERE IT CAN'T BE SEEN!
VERONICA WILL BE DOWN IN HALF AN HOUR!
YESSIR!
POP!
PING!
2

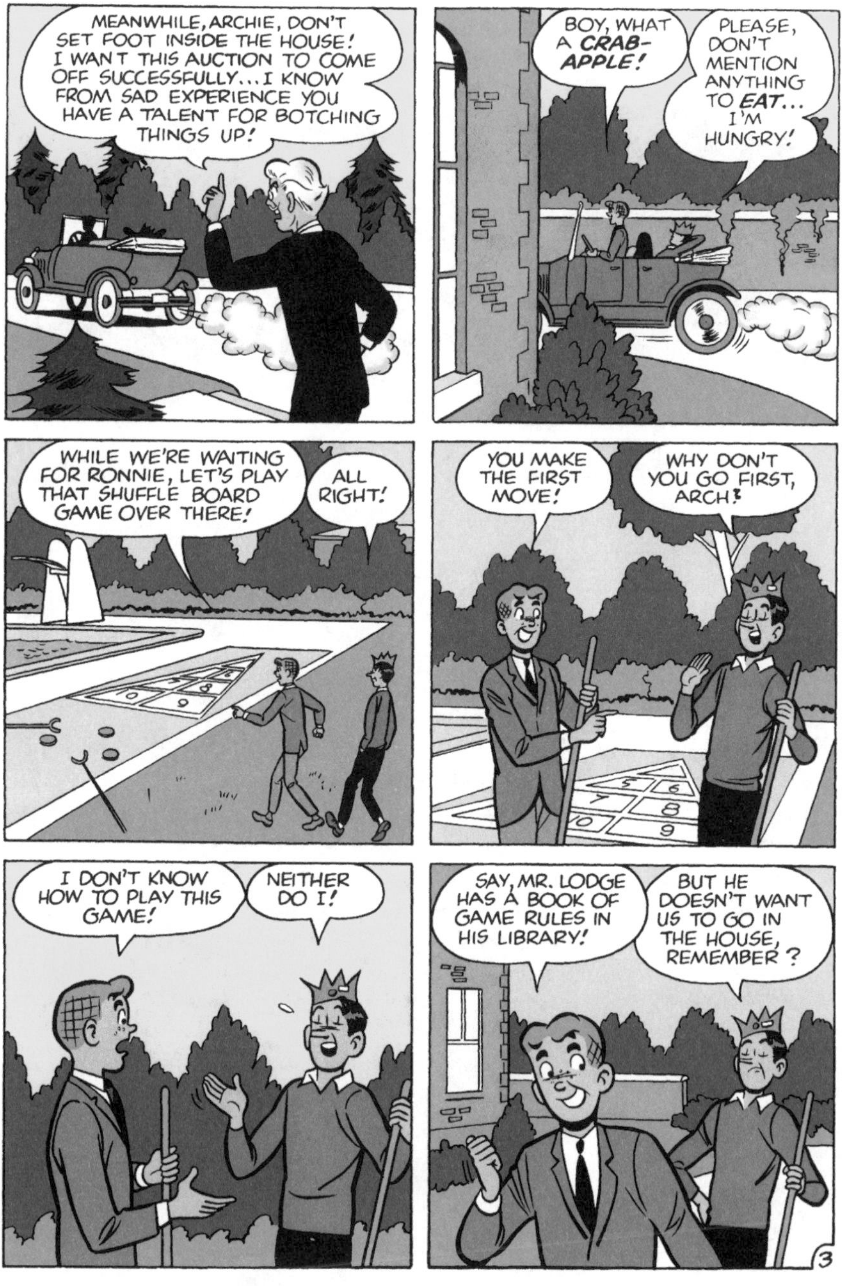
MEANWHILE, ARCHIE, DON'T SET FOOT INSIDE THE HOUSE! I WANT THIS AUCTION TO COME OFF SUCCESSFULLY... I KNOW FROM SAD EXPERIENCE YOU HAVE A TALENT FOR BOTCHING THINGS UP!
BOY, WHAT A CRAB-APPLE!
PLEASE, DON'T MENTION ANYTHING TO EAT... I'M HUNGRY!
WHILE WE'RE WAITING FOR RONNIE, LET'S PLAY THAT SHUFFLE BOARD GAME OVER THERE!
ALL RIGHT!
YOU MAKE THE FIRST MOVE!
WHY DON'T YOU GO FIRST, ARCH?
I DON'T KNOW HOW TO PLAY THIS GAME!
NEITHER DO I!
SAY, MR. LODGE HAS A BOOK OF GAME RULES IN HIS LIBRARY!
BUT HE DOESN'T WANT US TO GO IN THE HOUSE, REMEMBER?
3

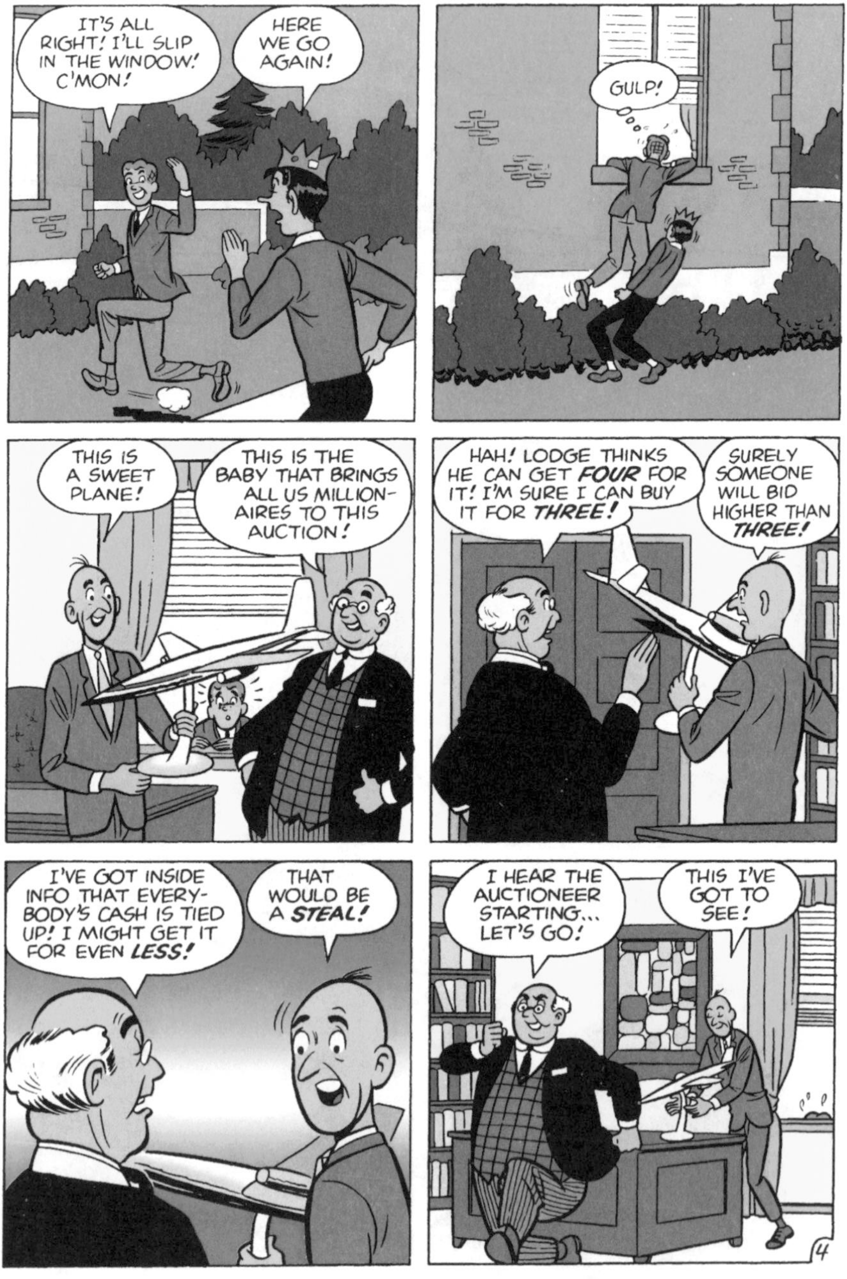
IT'S ALL RIGHT! I'LL SLIP IN THE WINDOW! C'MON!
HERE WE GO AGAIN!
GULP!
THIS IS A SWEET PLANE!
THIS IS THE BABY THAT BRINGS ALL US MILLION-AIRES TO THIS AUCTION!
HAH! LODGE THINKS HE CAN GET FOUR FOR IT! I'M SURE I CAN BUY IT FOR THREE!
SURELY SOMEONE WILL BID HIGHER THAN THREE!
I'VE GOT INSIDE INFO THAT EVERY-BODY'S CASH IS TIED UP! I MIGHT GET IT FOR EVEN LESS!
THAT WOULD BE A STEAL!
I HEAR THE AUCTIONEER STARTING... LET'S GO!
THIS I'VE GOT TO SEE!
4

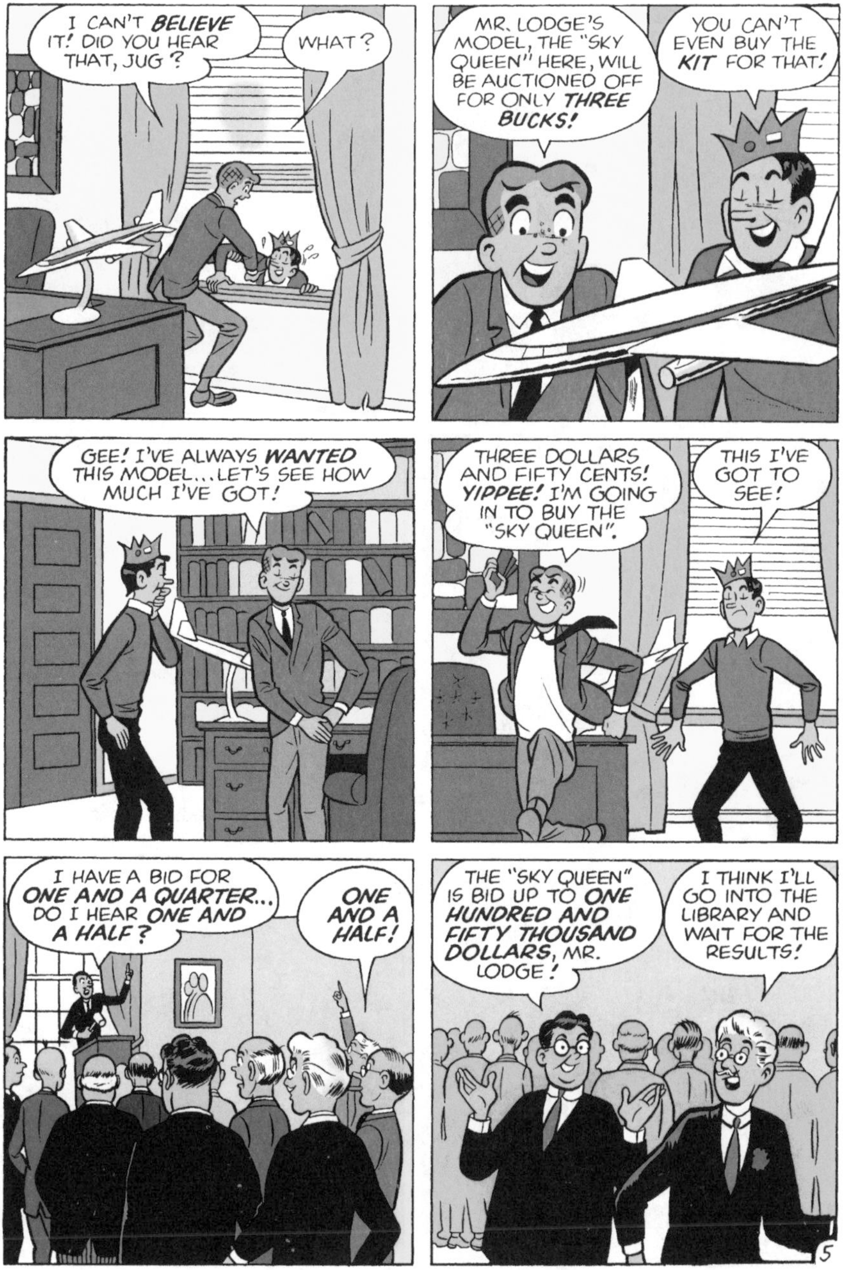

I CAN'T BELIEVE IT! DID YOU HEAR THAT, JUG?
WHAT?
MR. LODGE'S MODEL, THE "SKY QUEEN" HERE, WILL BE AUCTIONED OFF FOR ONLY THREE BUCKS!
YOU CAN'T EVEN BUY THE KIT FOR THAT!
GEE! I'VE ALWAYS WANTED THIS MODEL...LET'S SEE HOW MUCH I'VE GOT!
THREE DOLLARS AND FIFTY CENTS! YIPPEE! I'M GOING IN TO BUY THE "SKY QUEEN".
THIS I'VE GOT TO SEE!
I HAVE A BID FOR ONE AND A QUARTER... DO I HEAR ONE AND A HALF?
ONE AND A HALF!
THE "SKY QUEEN" IS BID UP TO ONE HUNDRED AND FIFTY THOUSAND DOLLARS, MR. LODGE!
I THINK I'LL GO INTO THE LIBRARY AND WAIT FOR THE RESULTS!
5

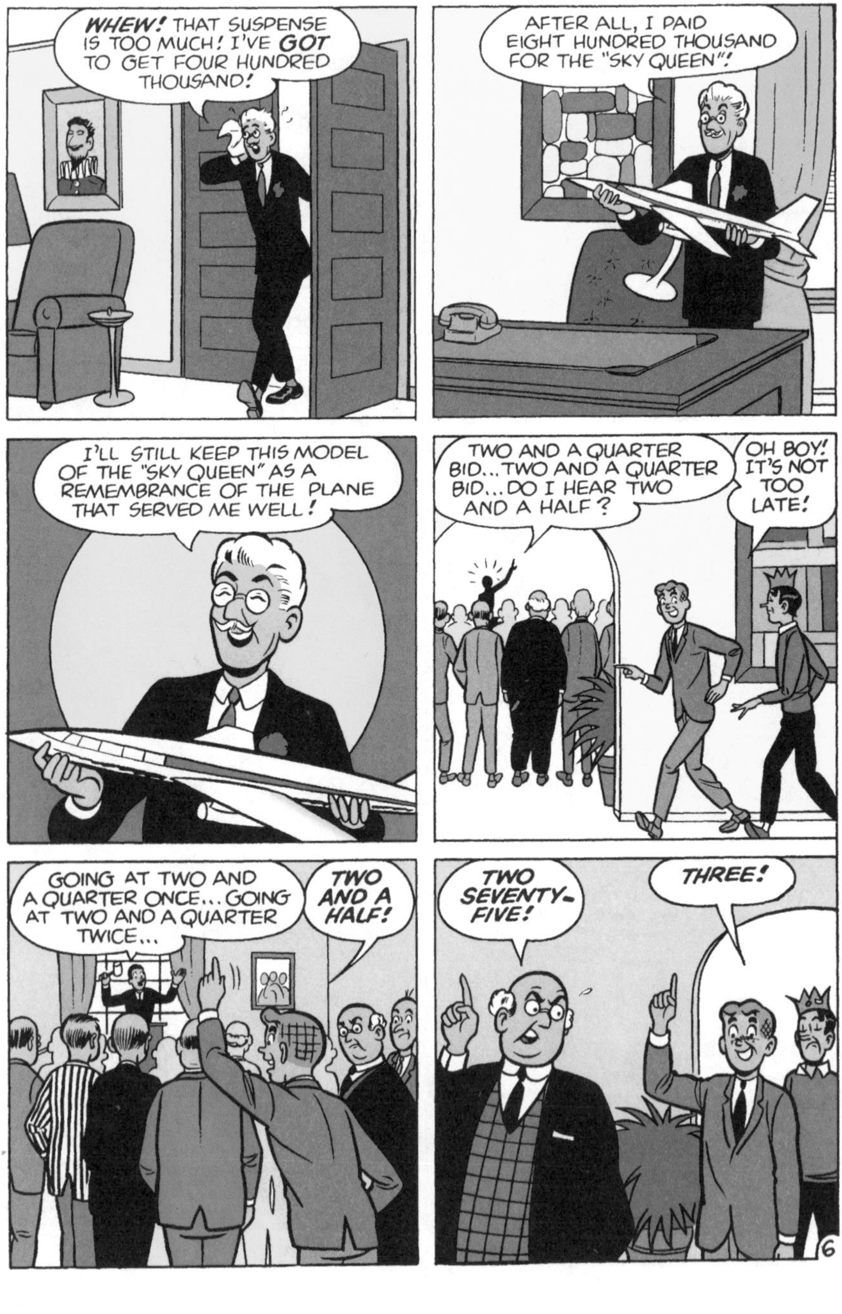
WHEW! THAT SUSPENSE IS TOO MUCH! I'VE GOT TO GET FOUR HUNDRED THOUSAND!
AFTER ALL, I PAID EIGHT HUNDRED THOUSAND FOR THE "SKY QUEEN"!
I'LL STILL KEEP THIS MODEL OF THE "SKY QUEEN" AS A REMEMBRANCE OF THE PLANE THAT SERVED ME WELL!
TWO AND A QUARTER BID... TWO AND A QUARTER BID... DO I HEAR TWO AND A HALF?
OH BOY! IT'S NOT TOO LATE!
GOING AT TWO AND A QUARTER ONCE... GOING AT TWO AND A QUARTER TWICE...
TWO AND A HALF!
TWO SEVENTY-FIVE!
THREE!
6

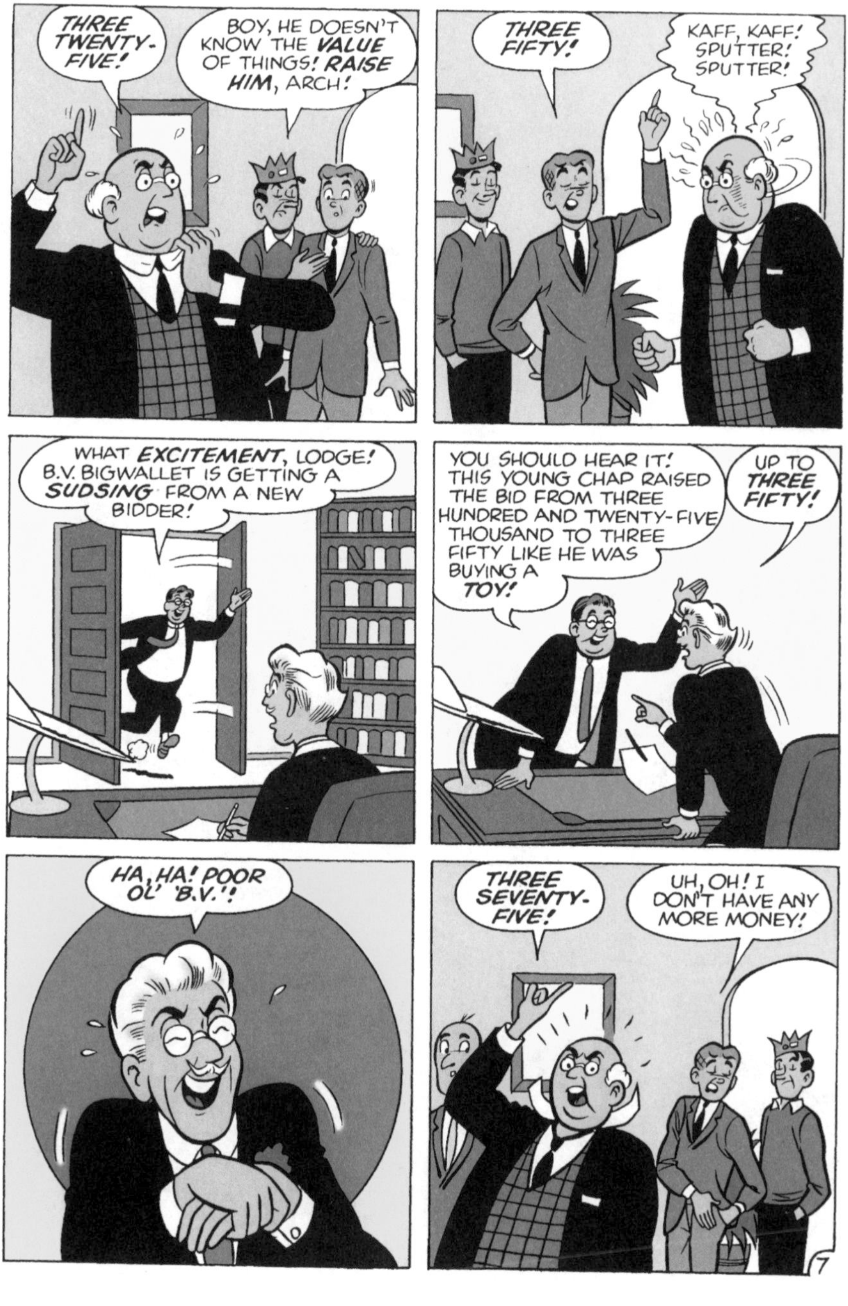
THREE TWENTY-FIVE!
BOY, HE DOESN'T KNOW THE VALUE OF THINGS! RAISE HIM, ARCH!
THREE FIFTY!
KAFF, KAFF! SPUTTER! SPUTTER!
WHAT EXCITEMENT, LODGE! B.V. BIGWALLET IS GETTING A SUDSING FROM A NEW BIDDER!
YOU SHOULD HEAR IT! THIS YOUNG CHAP RAISED THE BID FROM THREE HUNDRED AND TWENTY-FIVE THOUSAND TO THREE FIFTY LIKE HE WAS BUYING A TOY!
UP TO THREE FIFTY!
HA, HA! POOR OL' 'B.V.'!
THREE SEVENTY-FIVE!
UH, OH! I DON'T HAVE ANY MORE MONEY!
7

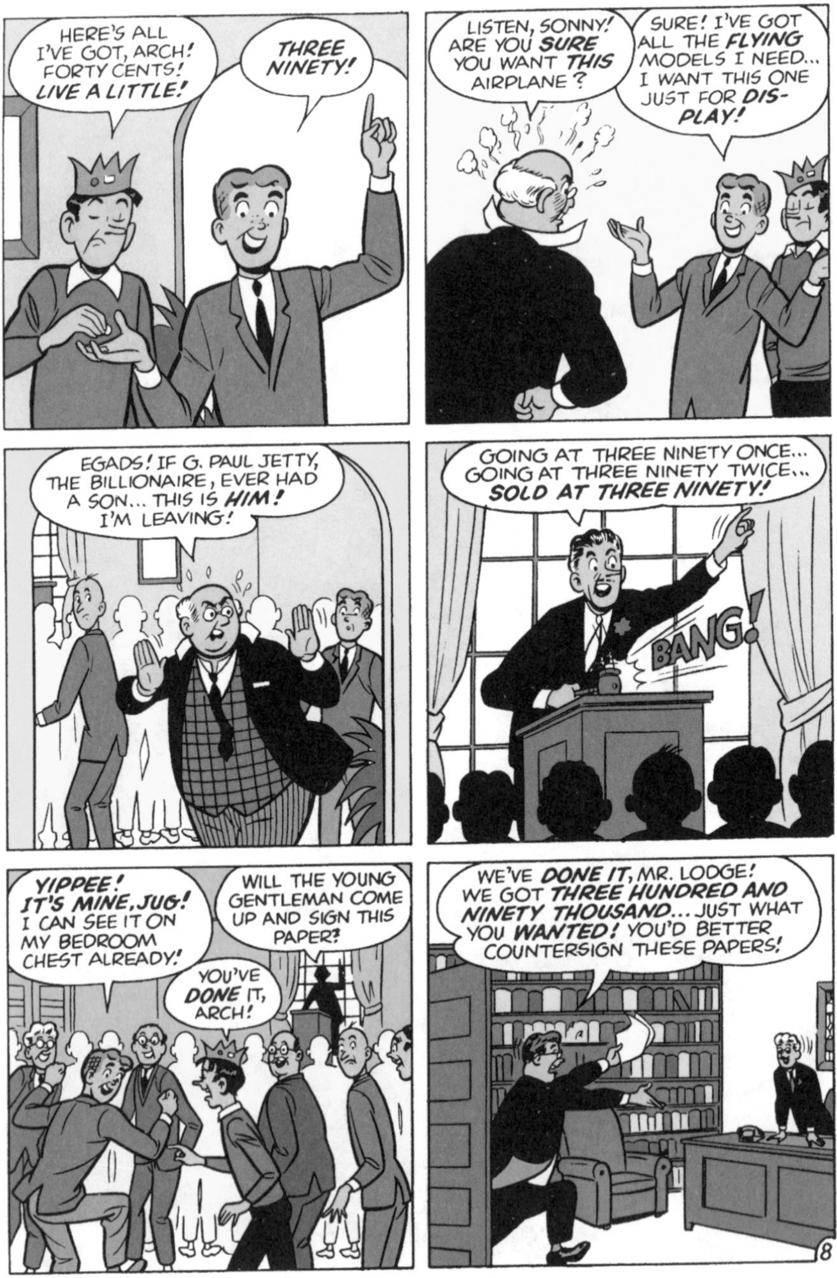
HERE'S ALL I'VE GOT, ARCH! FORTY CENTS! LIVE A LITTLE!
THREE NINETY!
LISTEN, SONNY! ARE YOU SURE YOU WANT THIS AIRPLANE?
SURE! I'VE GOT ALL THE FLYING MODELS I NEED... I WANT THIS ONE JUST FOR DIS-PLAY!
EGADS! IF G. PAUL JETTY, THE BILLIONAIRE, EVER HAD A SON... THIS IS HIM! I'M LEAVING!
GOING AT THREE NINETY ONCE... GOING AT THREE NINETY TWICE... SOLD AT THREE NINETY!
BANG!
YIPPEE! IT'S MINE, JUG! I CAN SEE IT ON MY BEDROOM CHEST ALREADY!
WILL THE YOUNG GENTLEMAN COME UP AND SIGN THIS PAPER?
YOU'VE DONE IT, ARCH!
WE'VE DONE IT, MR. LODGE! WE GOT THREE HUNDRED AND NINETY THOUSAND... JUST WHAT YOU WANTED! YOU'D BETTER COUNTERSIGN THESE PAPERS!
8

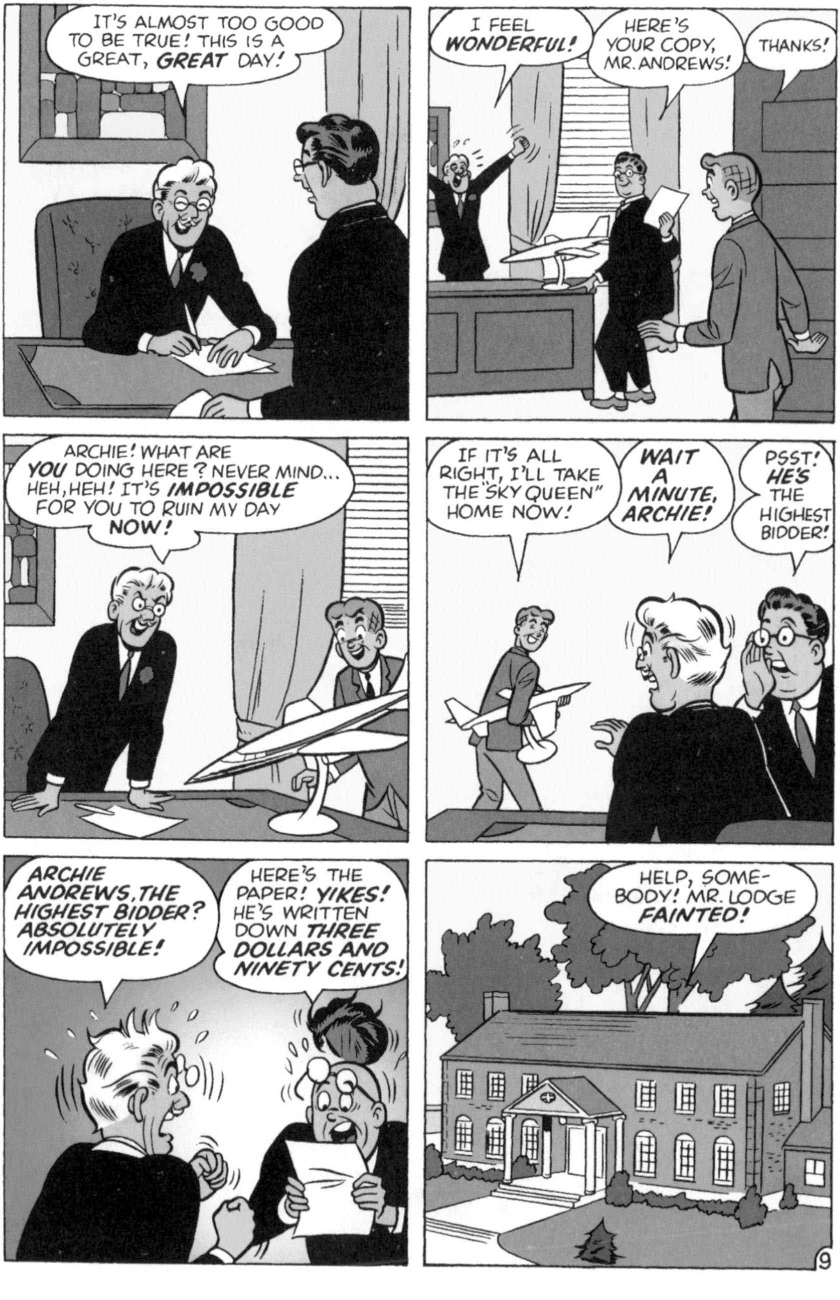
IT'S ALMOST TOO GOOD TO BE TRUE! THIS IS A GREAT, GREAT DAY!
I FEEL WONDERFUL!
HERE'S YOUR COPY, MR. ANDREWS!
THANKS!
ARCHIE! WHAT ARE YOU DOING HERE? NEVER MIND... HEH, HEH! IT'S IMPOSSIBLE FOR YOU TO RUIN MY DAY NOW!
IF IT'S ALL RIGHT, I'LL TAKE THE "SKY QUEEN" HOME NOW!
WAIT A MINUTE, ARCHIE!
PSST! HE'S THE HIGHEST BIDDER!
ARCHIE ANDREWS, THE HIGHEST BIDDER? ABSOLUTELY IMPOSSIBLE!
HERE'S THE PAPER! YIKES! HE'S WRITTEN DOWN THREE DOLLARS AND NINETY CENTS!
HELP, SOME-BODY! MR. LODGE FAINTED!
9

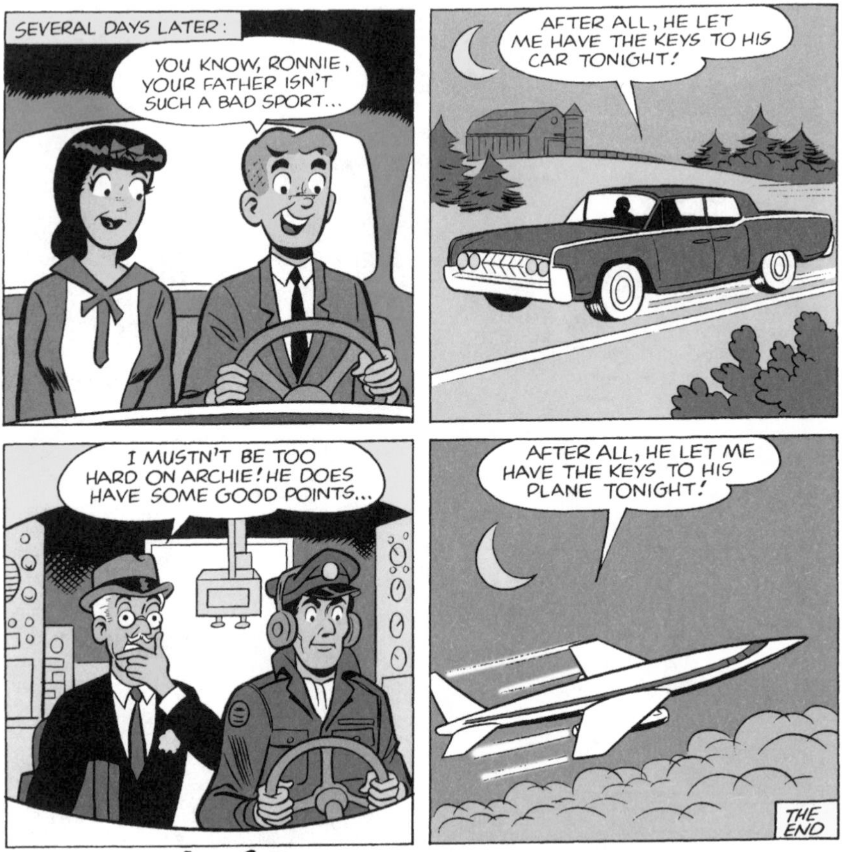
SEVERAL DAYS LATER:
YOU KNOW, RONNIE, YOUR FATHER ISN'T SUCH A BAD SPORT...
AFTER ALL, HE LET ME HAVE THE KEYS TO HIS CAR TONIGHT!
I MUSTN'T BE TOO HARD ON ARCHIE! HE DOES HAVE SOME GOOD POINTS...
AFTER ALL, HE LET ME HAVE THE KEYS TO HIS PLANE TONIGHT!
THE END

Archie in "SITTING PETTY"

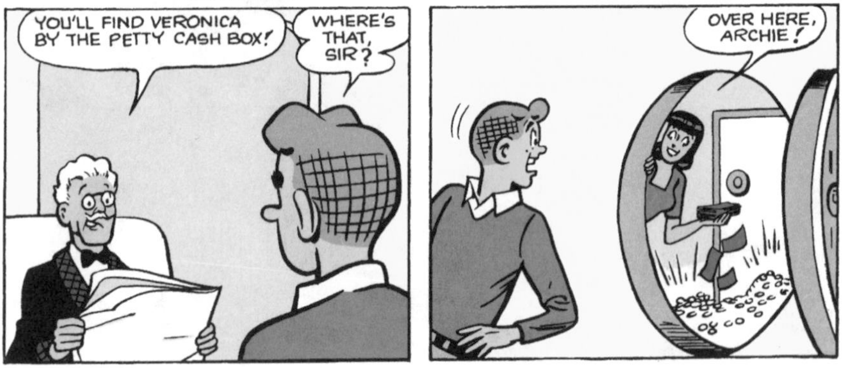
YOU'LL FIND VERONICA BY THE PETTY CASH BOX!
WHERE'S THAT, SIR?
OVER HERE, ARCHIE!

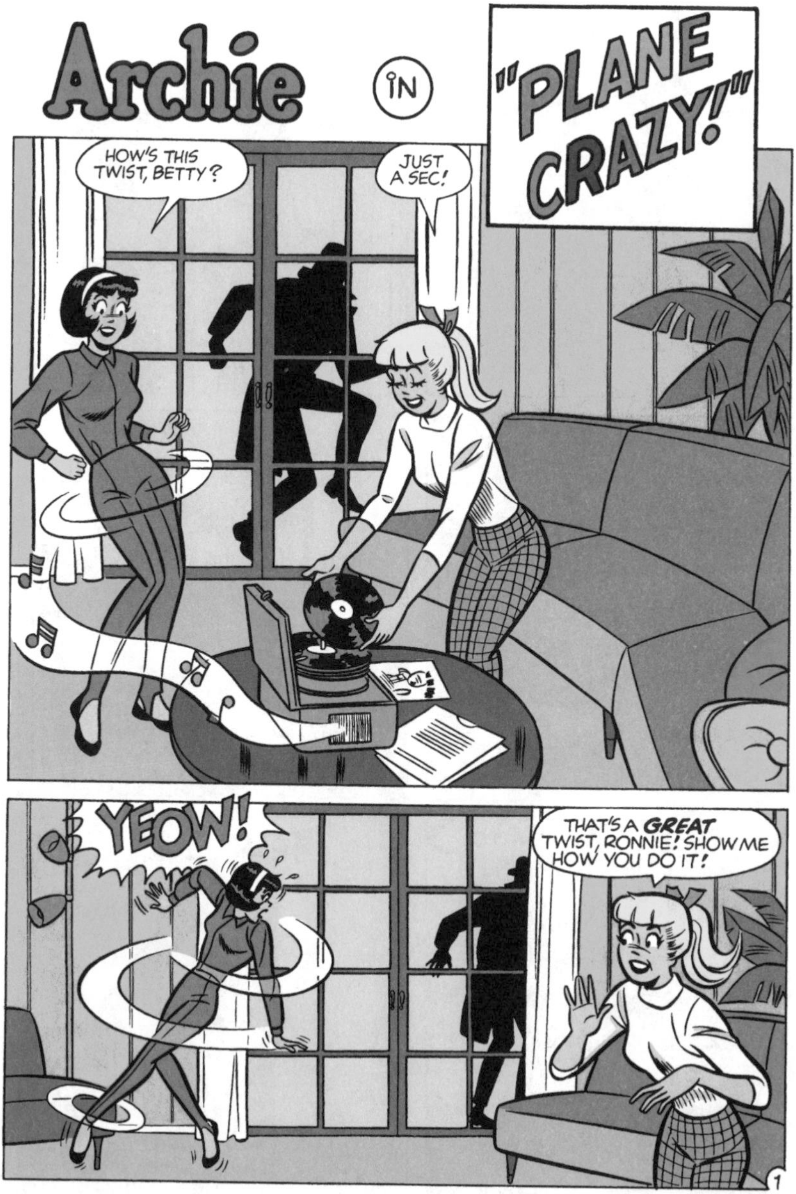
Archie
IN
"PLANE CRAZY!"
HOW'S THIS TWIST, BETTY?
JUST A SEC!
YEOW!
THAT'S A GREAT TWIST, RONNIE! SHOW ME HOW YOU DO IT!
1

Story: George Gladir Pencils: Bob White Inks & Letters: Marty Epp

Originally printed in LIFE WITH ARCHIE #37, May 1965

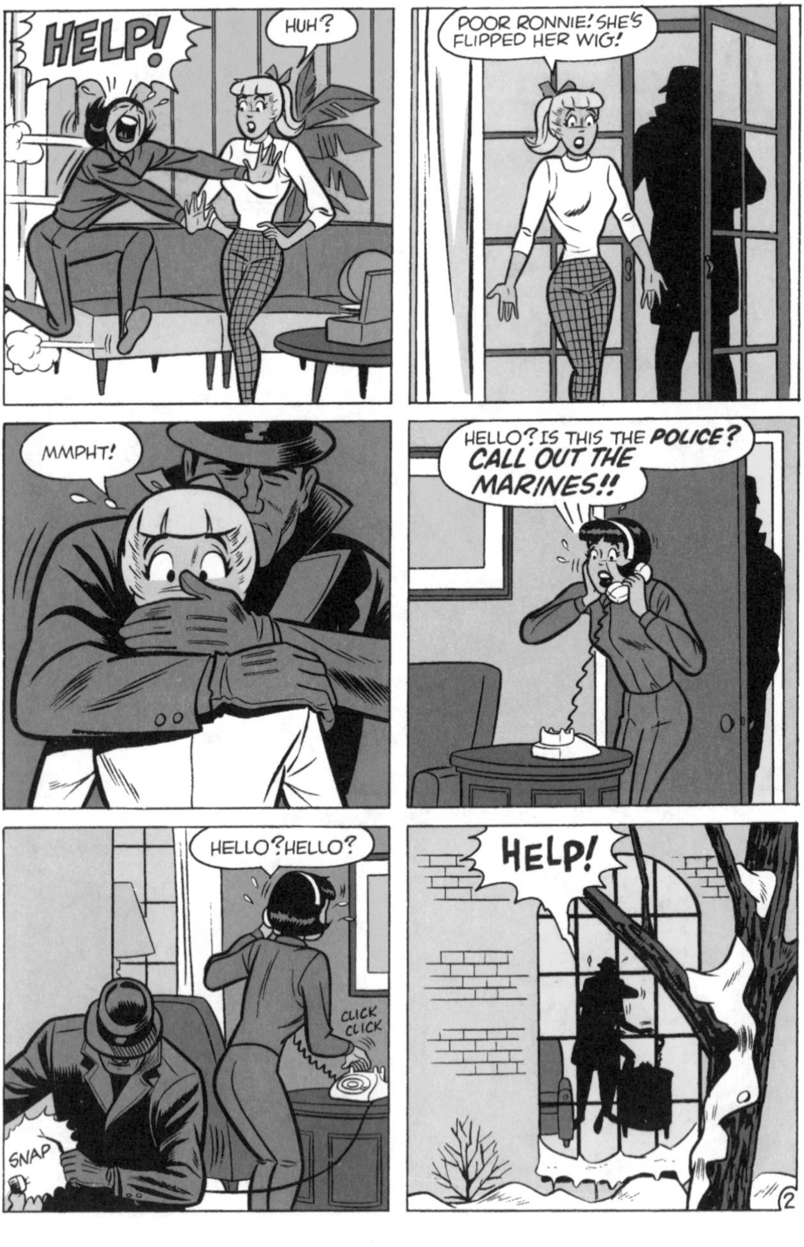
HELP!
HUH?
POOR RONNIE! SHE'S FLIPPED HER WIG!
MMPHT!
HELLO? IS THIS THE POLICE? CALL OUT THE MARINES!!
HELLO? HELLO?
CLICK CLICK
SNAP
HELP!
2

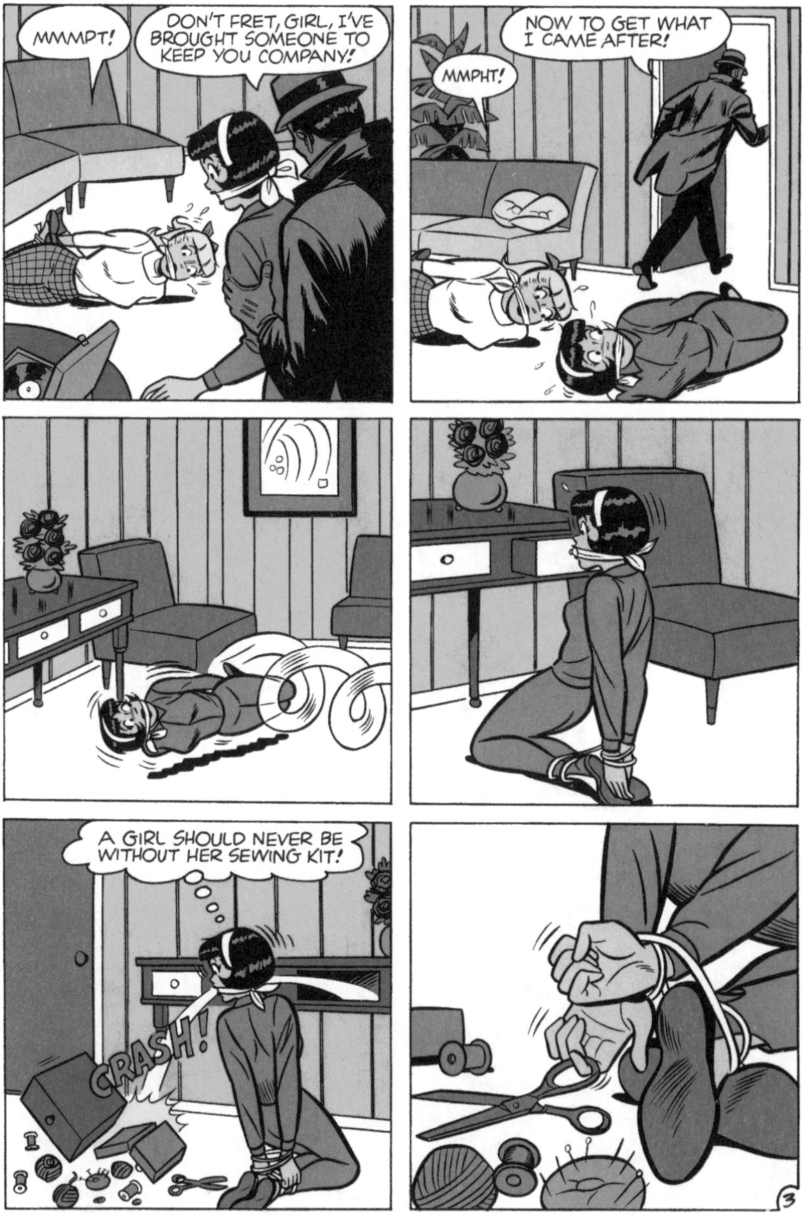
MMMPT!
DON'T FRET, GIRL, I'VE BROUGHT SOMEONE TO KEEP YOU COMPANY!
NOW TO GET WHAT I CAME AFTER!
MMPHT!
A GIRL SHOULD NEVER BE WITHOUT HER SEWING KIT!
CRASH!
3

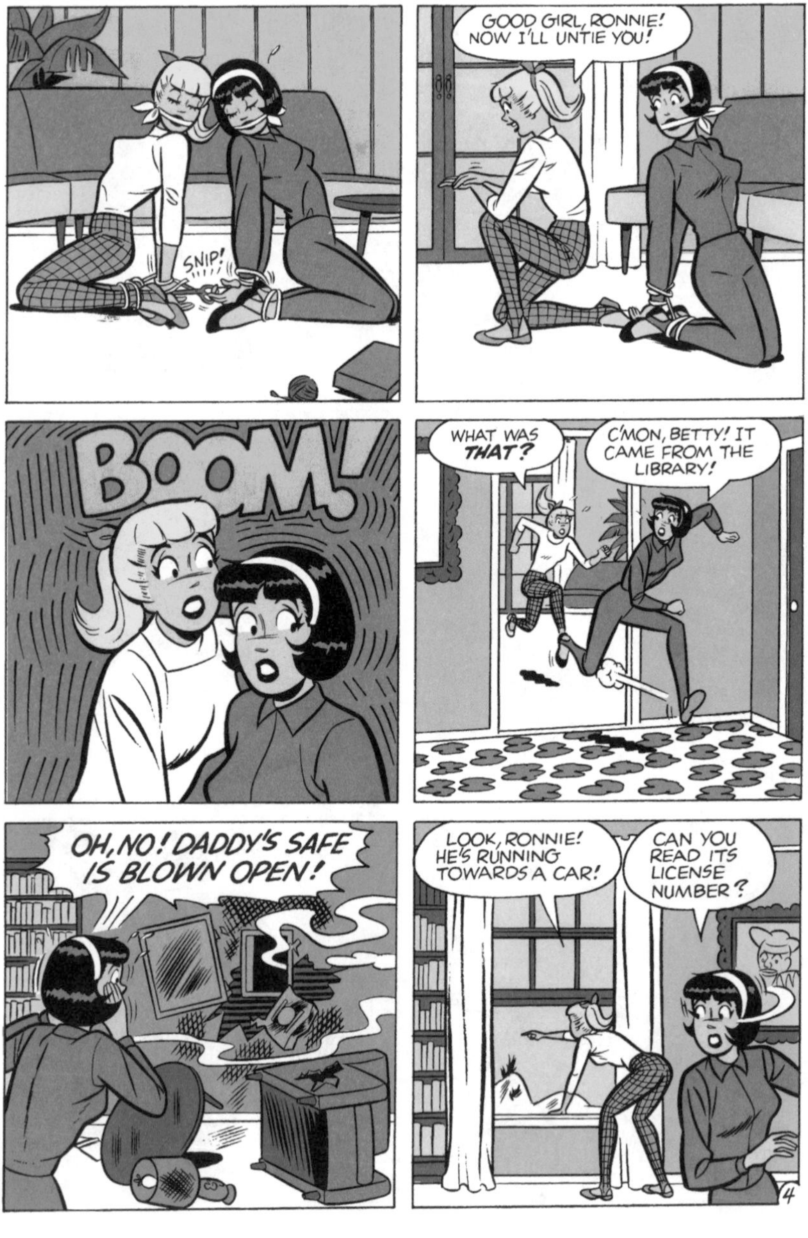
SNIP!
GOOD GIRL, RONNIE! NOW I'LL UNTIE YOU!
BOOM!
WHAT WAS THAT?
C'MON, BETTY! IT CAME FROM THE LIBRARY!
OH, NO! DADDY'S SAFE IS BLOWN OPEN!
LOOK, RONNIE! HE'S RUNNING TOWARDS A CAR!
CAN YOU READ ITS LICENSE NUMBER?
4

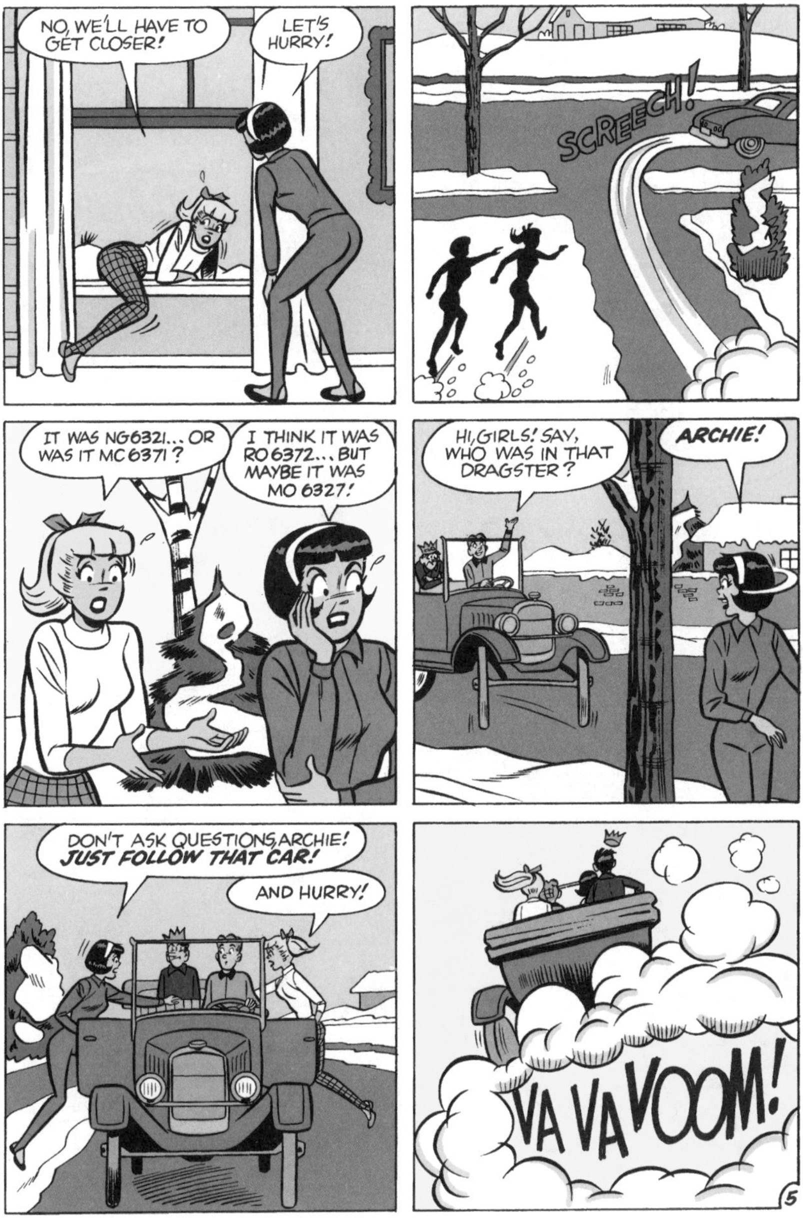
NO, WE'LL HAVE TO GET CLOSER!
LET'S HURRY!
SCREECH!
IT WAS NG6321... OR WAS IT MC6371?
I THINK IT WAS RO6372... BUT MAYBE IT WAS MO6327!
HI, GIRLS! SAY, WHO WAS IN THAT DRAGSTER?
ARCHIE!
DON'T ASK QUESTIONS, ARCHIE! JUST FOLLOW THAT CAR!
AND HURRY!
VA VA VOOM!
5

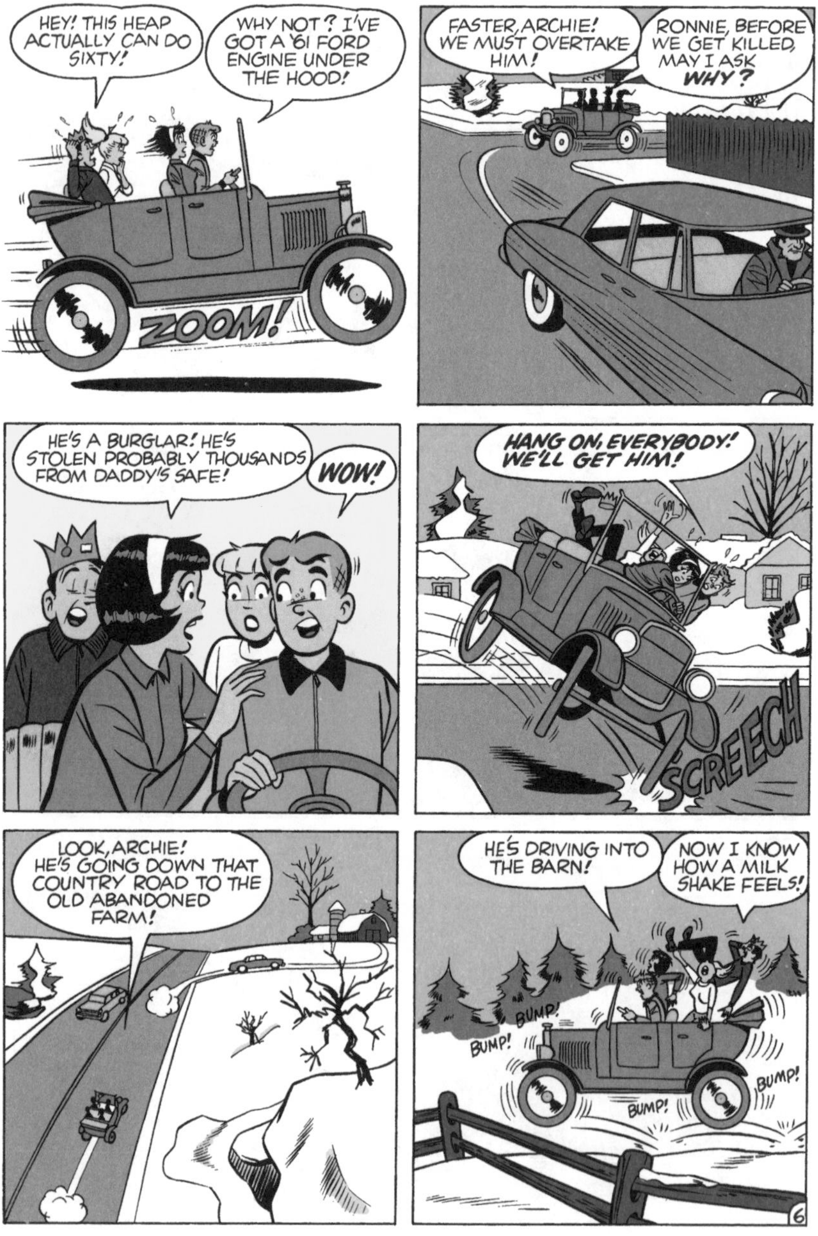

HEY! THIS HEAP ACTUALLY CAN DO SIXTY!
WHY NOT? I'VE GOT A '61 FORD ENGINE UNDER THE HOOD!
ZOOM!
FASTER, ARCHIE! WE MUST OVERTAKE HIM!
RONNIE, BEFORE WE GET KILLED, MAY I ASK WHY?
HE'S A BURGLAR! HE'S STOLEN PROBABLY THOUSANDS FROM DADDY'S SAFE!
WOW!
HANG ON, EVERYBODY! WE'LL GET HIM!
SCREECH
LOOK, ARCHIE! HE'S GOING DOWN THAT COUNTRY ROAD TO THE OLD ABANDONED FARM!
HE'S DRIVING INTO THE BARN!
NOW I KNOW HOW A MILK SHAKE FEELS!
BUMP!
BUMP!
BUMP!
BUMP!
6

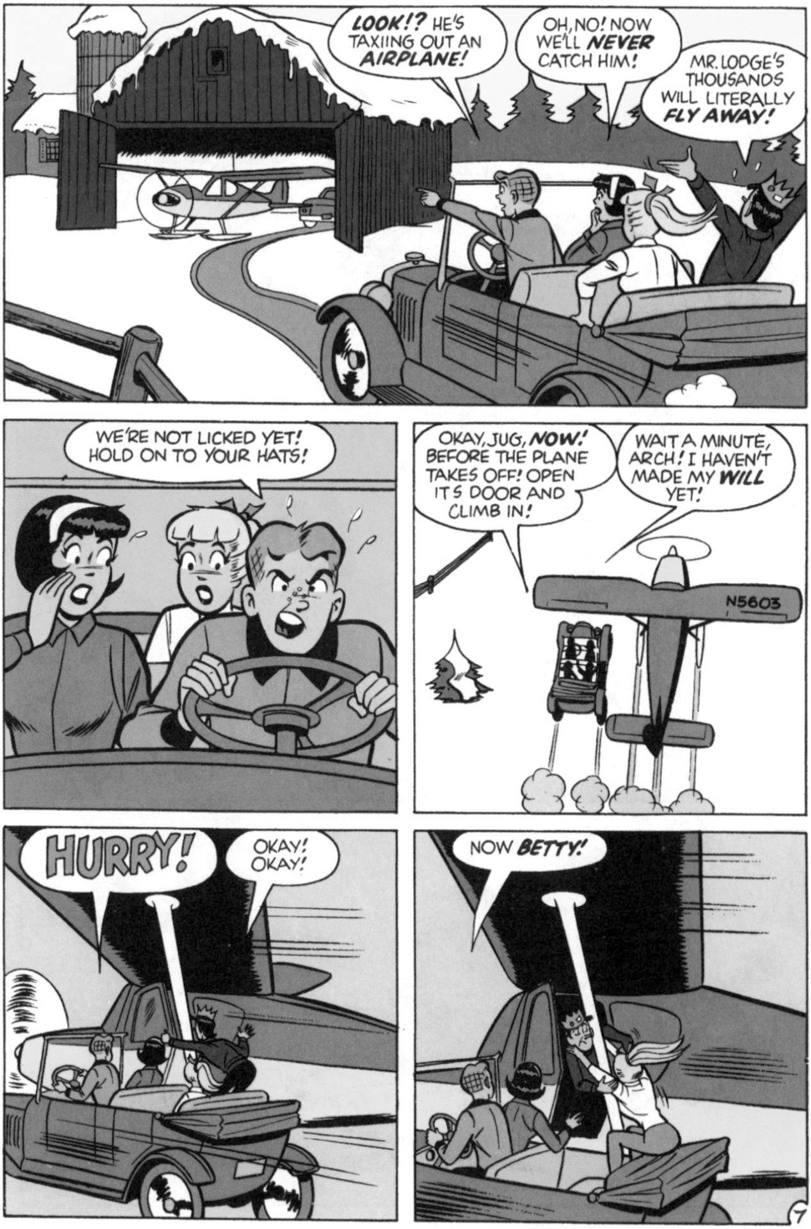
LOOK!? HE'S TAXIING OUT AN AIRPLANE!
OH, NO! NOW WE'LL NEVER CATCH HIM!
MR. LODGE'S THOUSANDS WILL LITERALLY FLY AWAY!
WE'RE NOT LICKED YET! HOLD ON TO YOUR HATS!
OKAY, JUG, NOW! BEFORE THE PLANE TAKES OFF! OPEN IT'S DOOR AND CLIMB IN!
WAIT A MINUTE, ARCH! I HAVEN'T MADE MY WILL YET!
N5603
HURRY!
OKAY! OKAY!
NOW BETTY!
7

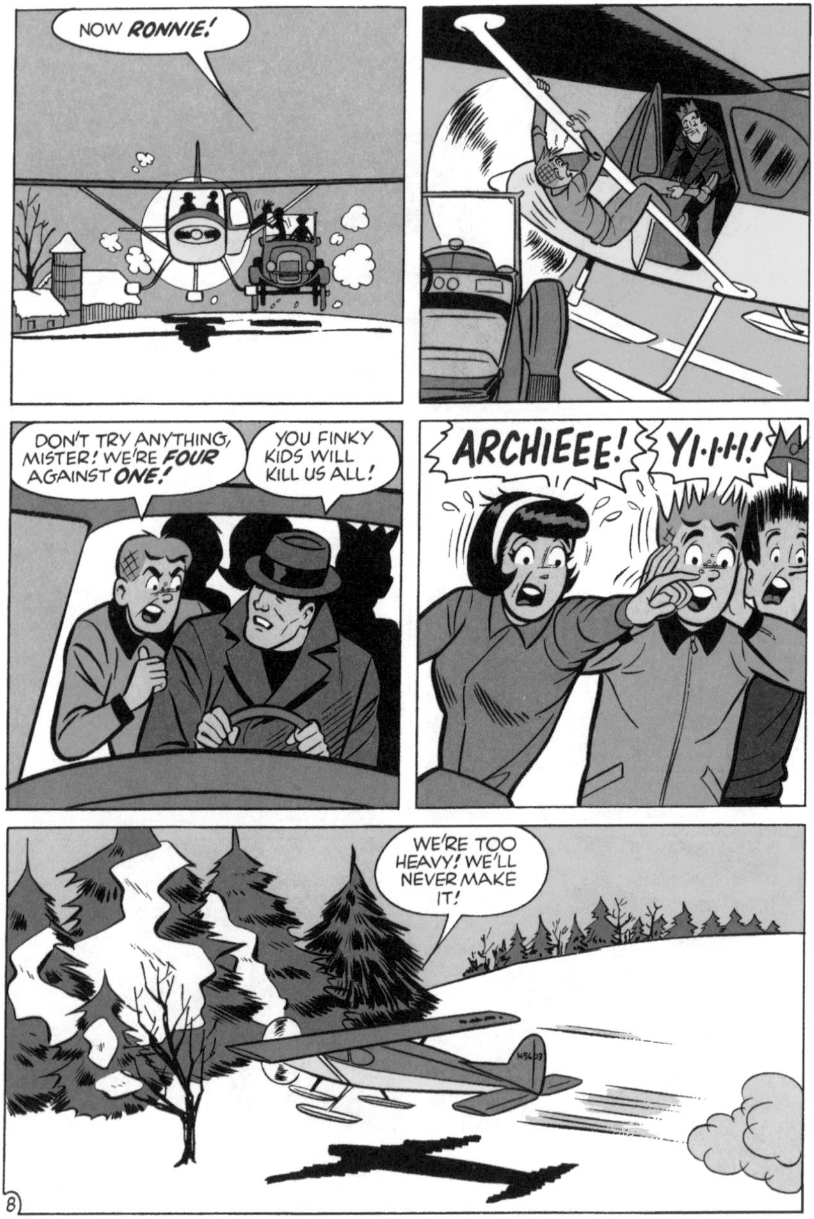
NOW RONNIE!
DON'T TRY ANYTHING, MISTER! WE'RE FOUR AGAINST ONE!
YOU FINKY KIDS WILL KILL US ALL!
ARCHIEEE!
YI-I-I-I!
WE'RE TOO HEAVY! WE'LL NEVER MAKE IT!
N5403
8

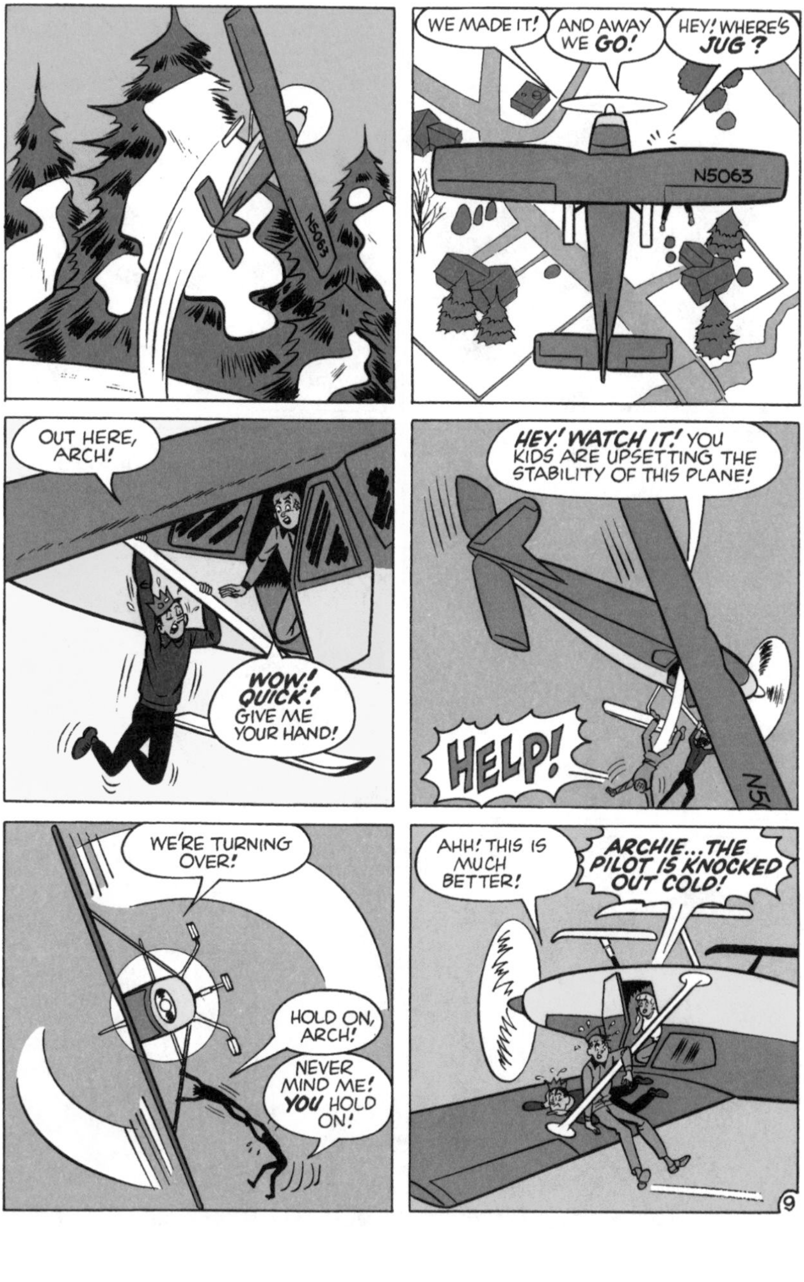
WE MADE IT!
AND AWAY WE GO!
HEY! WHERE'S JUG?
N5063
OUT HERE, ARCH!
WOW! QUICK! GIVE ME YOUR HAND!
HEY! WATCH IT! YOU KIDS ARE UPSETTING THE STABILITY OF THIS PLANE!
HELP!
WE'RE TURNING OVER!
HOLD ON, ARCH!
NEVER MIND ME! YOU HOLD ON!
AHH! THIS IS MUCH BETTER!
ARCHIE...THE PILOT IS KNOCKED OUT COLD!
9

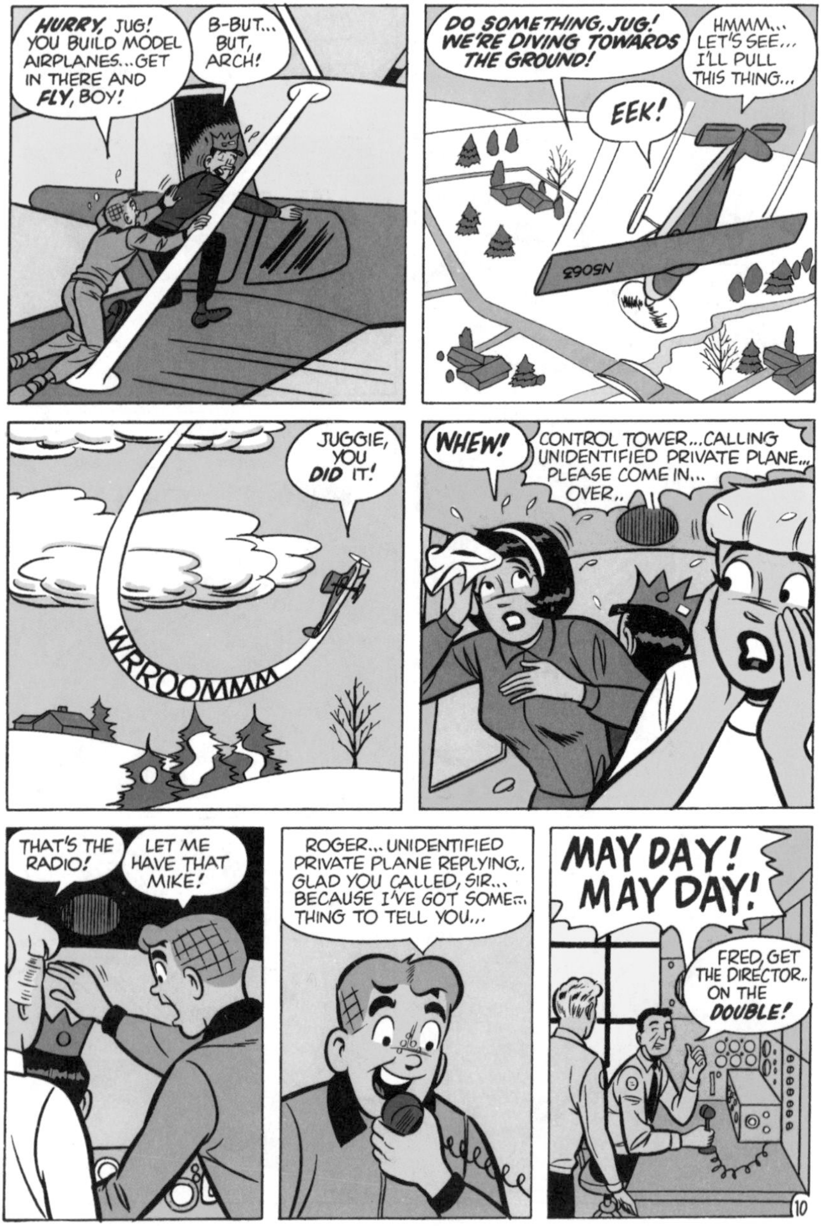
HURRY, JUG! YOU BUILD MODEL AIRPLANES...GET IN THERE AND FLY, BOY!
B-BUT... BUT, ARCH!
DO SOMETHING, JUG! WE'RE DIVING TOWARDS THE GROUND!
HMMM... LET'S SEE... I'LL PULL THIS THING...
EEK!
N5063
JUGGIE, YOU DID IT!
WRROOMMM
WHEW!
CONTROL TOWER...CALLING UNIDENTIFIED PRIVATE PLANE... PLEASE COME IN... OVER..
THAT'S THE RADIO!
LET ME HAVE THAT MIKE!
ROGER... UNIDENTIFIED PRIVATE PLANE REPLYING.. GLAD YOU CALLED, SIR... BECAUSE I'VE GOT SOME-- THING TO TELL YOU...
MAY DAY! MAY DAY!
FRED, GET THE DIRECTOR.. ON THE DOUBLE!
10

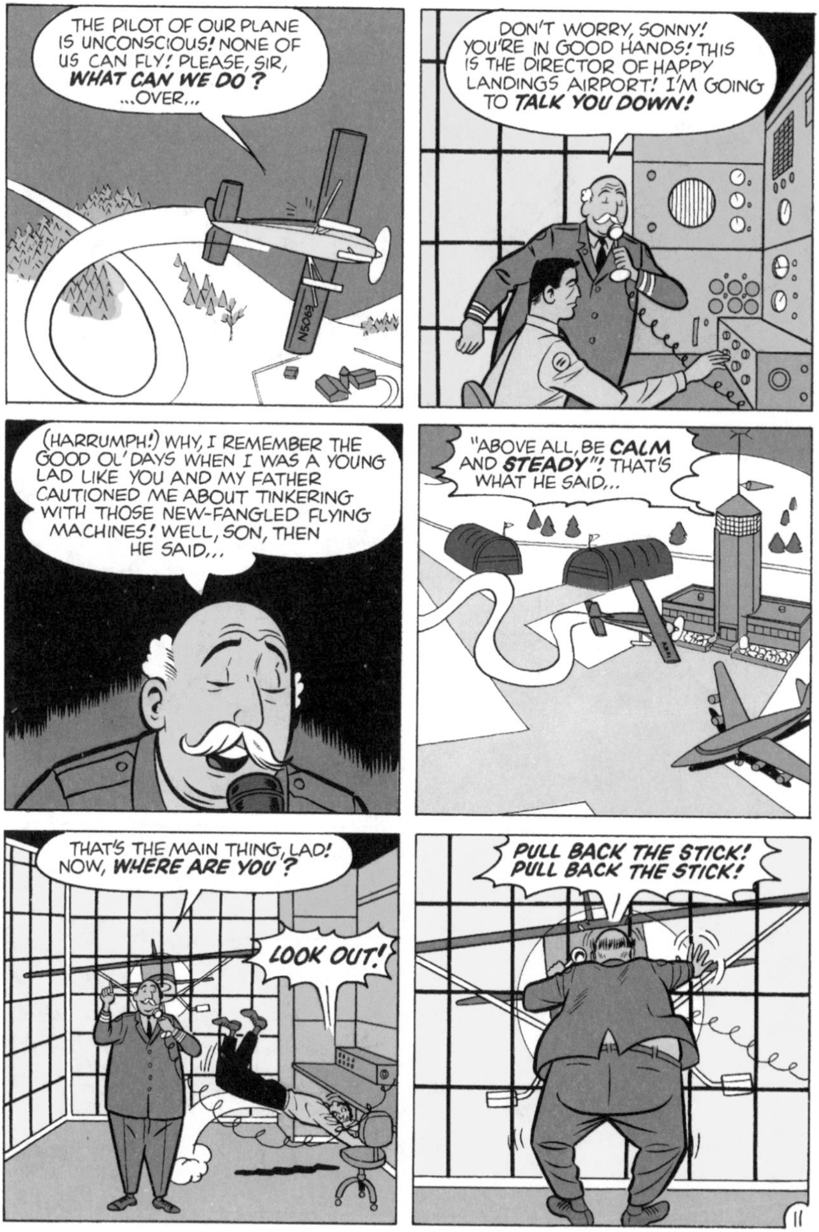
THE PILOT OF OUR PLANE IS UNCONSCIOUS! NONE OF US CAN FLY! PLEASE, SIR, WHAT CAN WE DO? ...OVER...
N5063
DON'T WORRY, SONNY! YOU'RE IN GOOD HANDS! THIS IS THE DIRECTOR OF HAPPY LANDINGS AIRPORT! I'M GOING TO TALK YOU DOWN!
(HARRUMPH!) WHY, I REMEMBER THE GOOD OL' DAYS WHEN I WAS A YOUNG LAD LIKE YOU AND MY FATHER CAUTIONED ME ABOUT TINKERING WITH THOSE NEW-FANGLED FLYING MACHINES! WELL, SON, THEN HE SAID...
"ABOVE ALL, BE CALM AND STEADY"! THAT'S WHAT HE SAID...
THAT'S THE MAIN THING, LAD! NOW, WHERE ARE YOU?
LOOK OUT!
PULL BACK THE STICK! PULL BACK THE STICK!
11

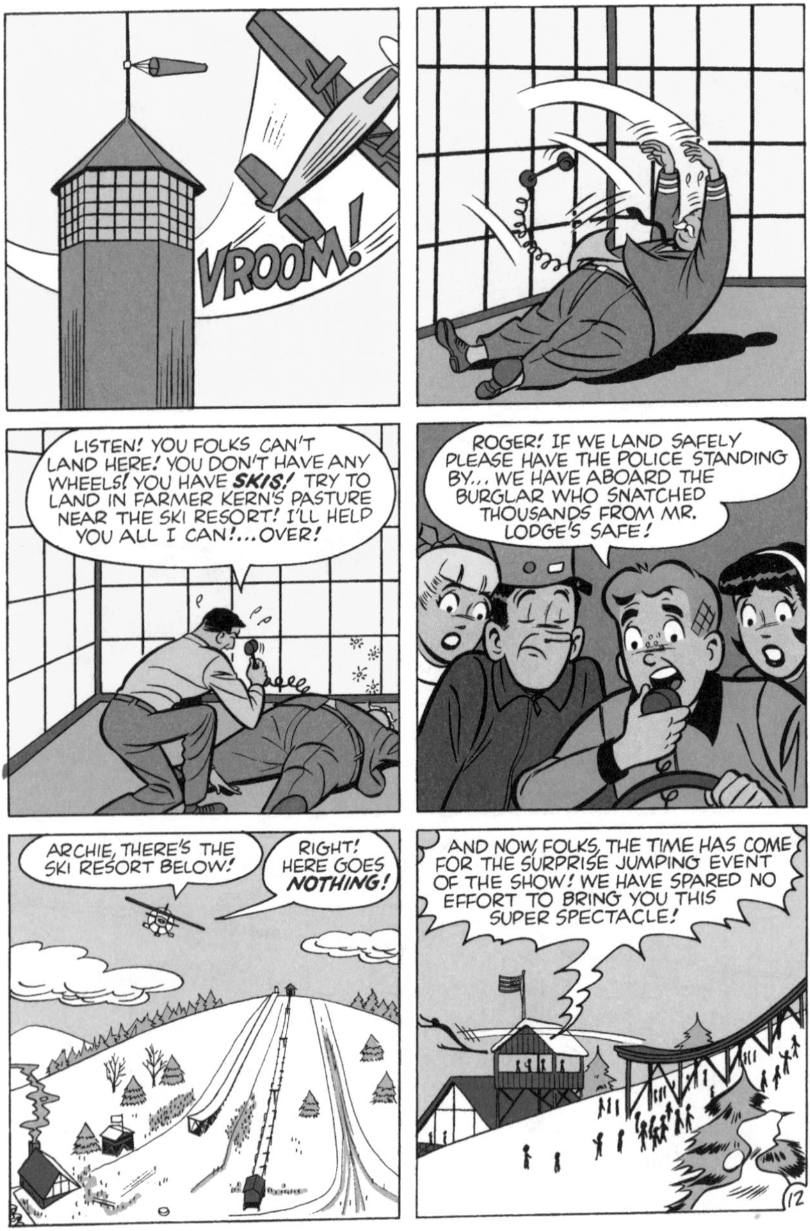
VROOM!
LISTEN! YOU FOLKS CAN'T LAND HERE! YOU DON'T HAVE ANY WHEELS! YOU HAVE SKIS! TRY TO LAND IN FARMER KERN'S PASTURE NEAR THE SKI RESORT! I'LL HELP YOU ALL I CAN!...OVER!
ROGER! IF WE LAND SAFELY PLEASE HAVE THE POLICE STANDING BY... WE HAVE ABOARD THE BURGLAR WHO SNATCHED THOUSANDS FROM MR. LODGE'S SAFE!
ARCHIE, THERE'S THE SKI RESORT BELOW!
RIGHT! HERE GOES NOTHING!
AND NOW, FOLKS, THE TIME HAS COME FOR THE SURPRISE JUMPING EVENT OF THE SHOW! WE HAVE SPARED NO EFFORT TO BRING YOU THIS SUPER SPECTACLE!
12

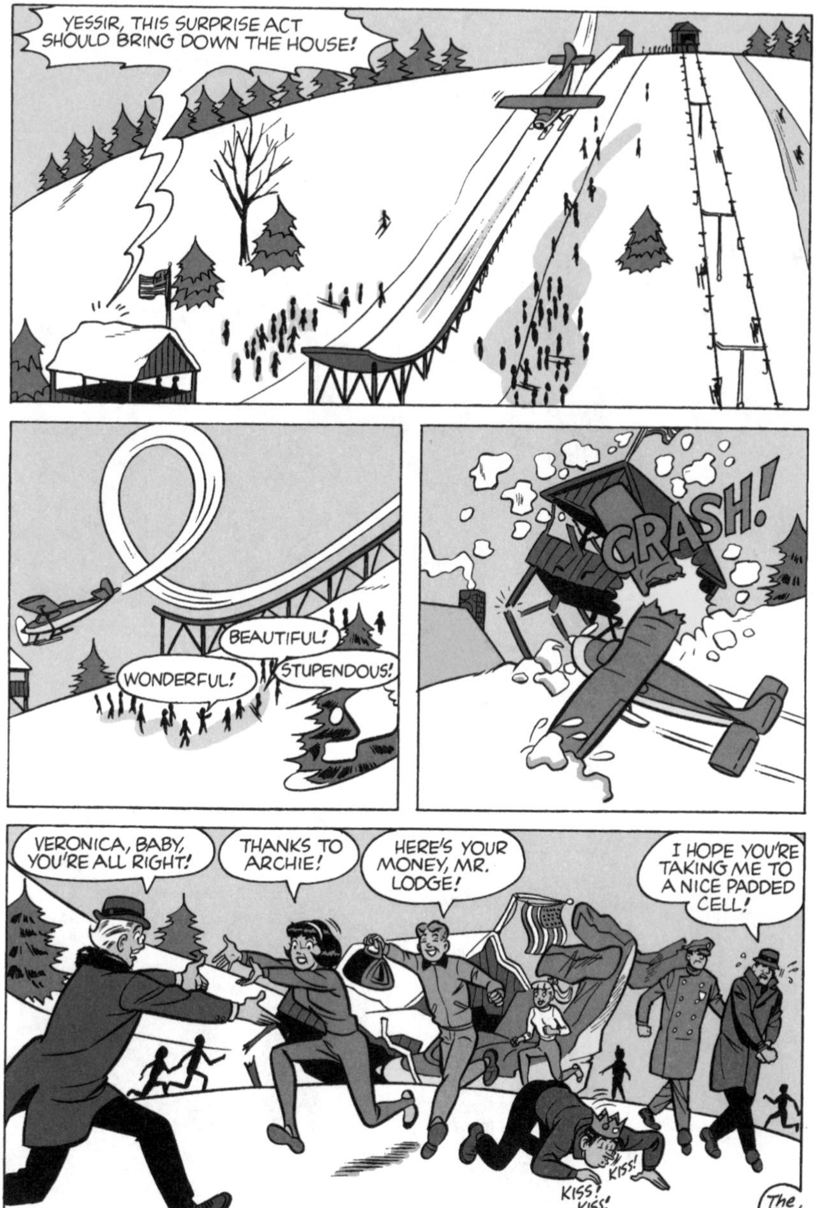
YESSIR, THIS SURPRISE ACT SHOULD BRING DOWN THE HOUSE!
BEAUTIFUL!
WONDERFUL!
STUPENDOUS!
CRASH!
VERONICA, BABY, YOU'RE ALL RIGHT!
THANKS TO ARCHIE!
HERE'S YOUR MONEY, MR. LODGE!
I HOPE YOU'RE TAKING ME TO A NICE PADDED CELL!
KISS! KISS! KISS!
The End

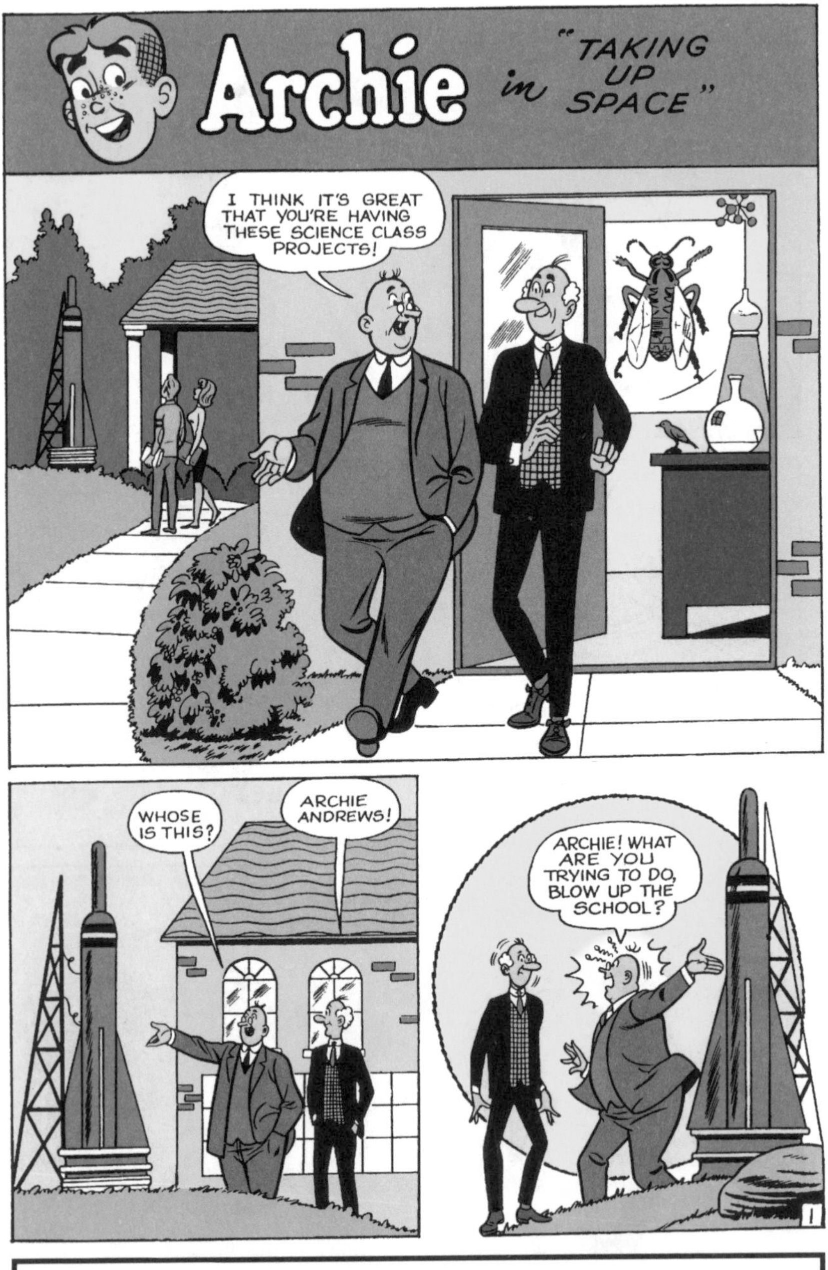
Archie in "TAKING UP SPACE"
I THINK IT'S GREAT THAT YOU'RE HAVING THESE SCIENCE CLASS PROJECTS!
WHOSE IS THIS?
ARCHIE ANDREWS!
ARCHIE! WHAT ARE YOU TRYING TO DO, BLOW UP THE SCHOOL?
1

Story & Pencils: Bob Bolling Inks: Mario Acquaviva

Originally printed in LIFE WITH ARCHIE #39, July 1965

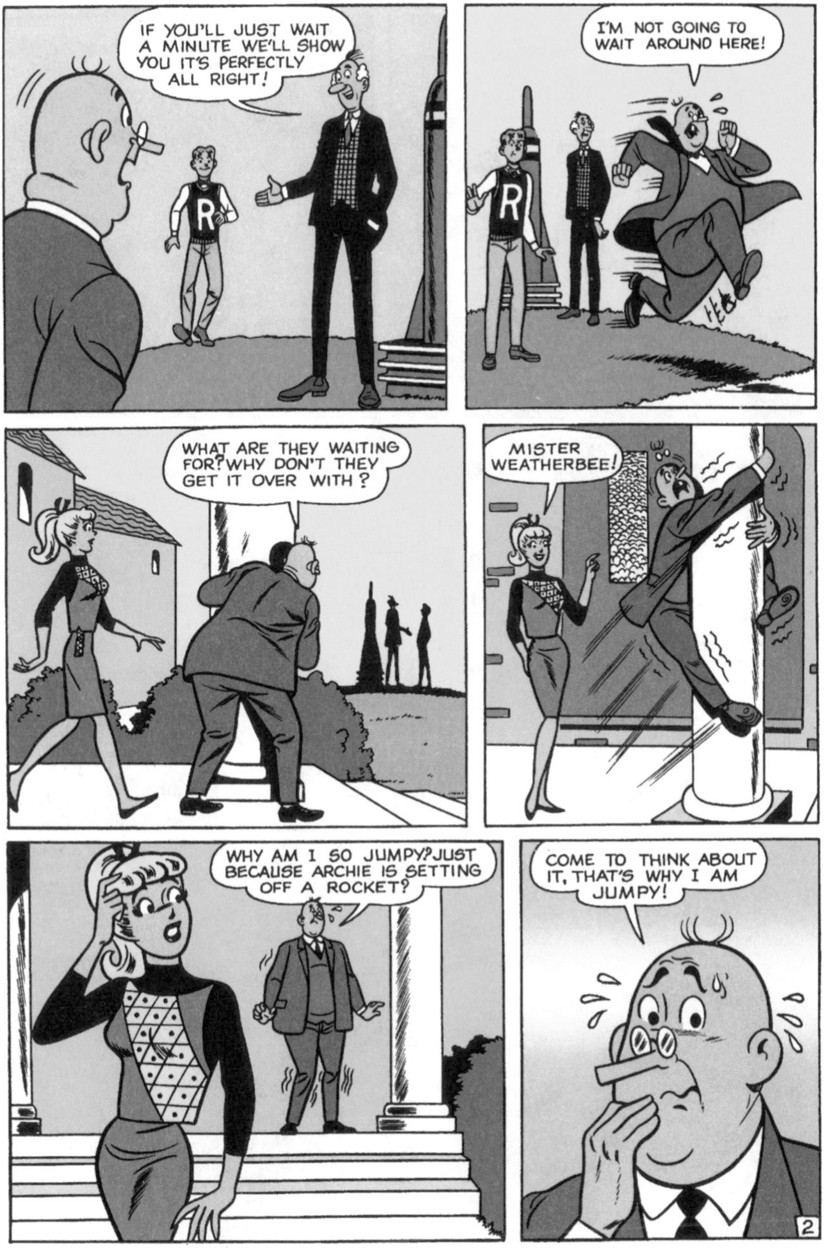
IF YOU'LL JUST WAIT A MINUTE WE'LL SHOW YOU IT'S PERFECTLY ALL RIGHT!
I'M NOT GOING TO WAIT AROUND HERE!
WHAT ARE THEY WAITING FOR? WHY DON'T THEY GET IT OVER WITH?
MISTER WEATHERBEE!
WHY AM I SO JUMPY? JUST BECAUSE ARCHIE IS SETTING OFF A ROCKET?
COME TO THINK ABOUT IT, THAT'S WHY I AM JUMPY!
2

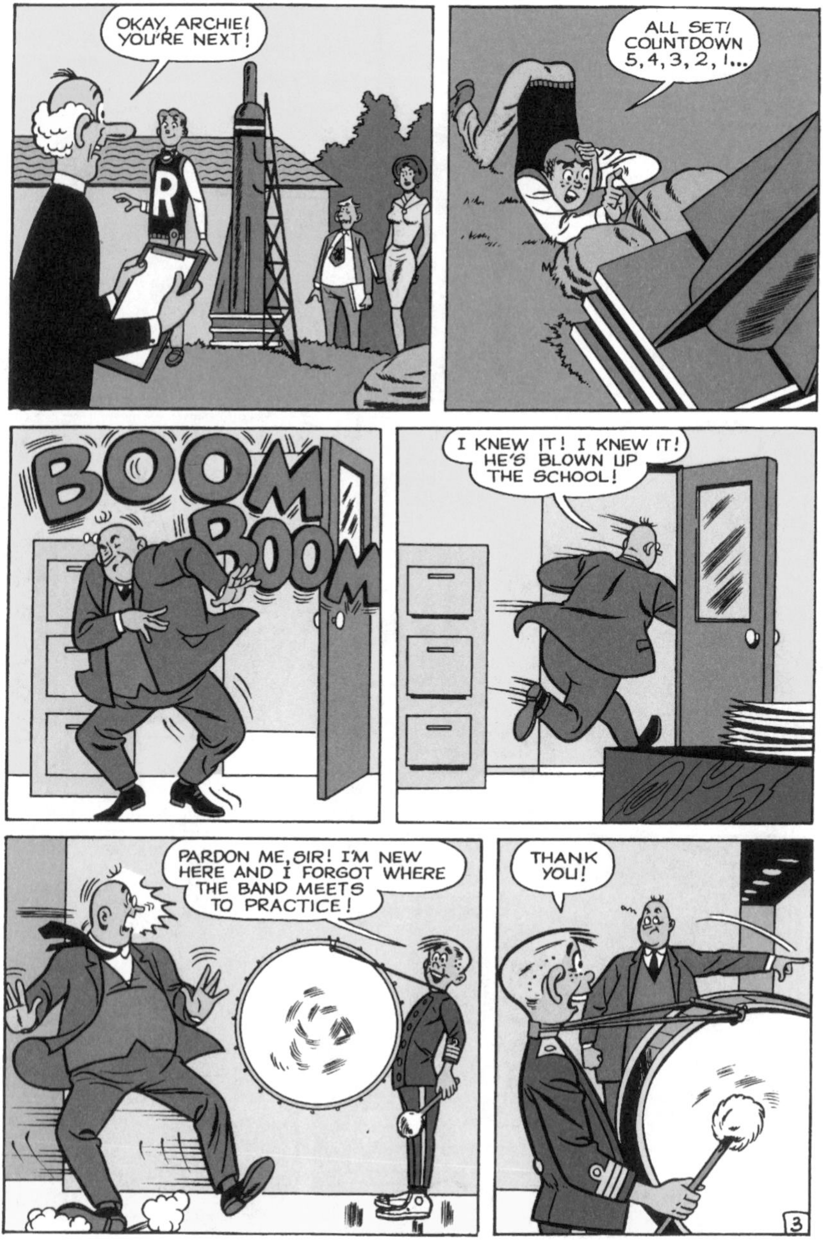
OKAY, ARCHIE! YOU'RE NEXT!
ALL SET! COUNTDOWN 5, 4, 3, 2, 1...
BOOM
BOOM
I KNEW IT! I KNEW IT! HE'S BLOWN UP THE SCHOOL!
PARDON ME, SIR! I'M NEW HERE AND I FORGOT WHERE THE BAND MEETS TO PRACTICE!
THANK YOU!
3

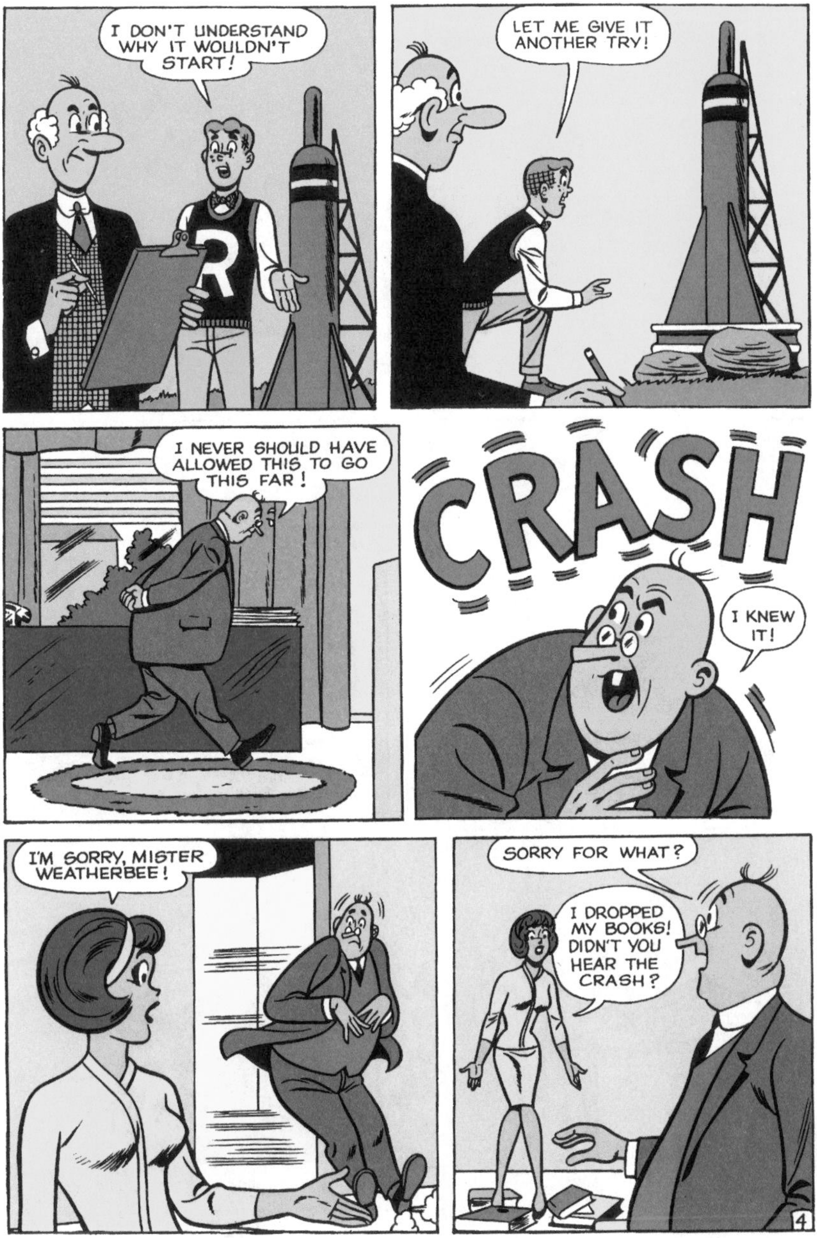
I DON'T UNDERSTAND WHY IT WOULDN'T START!
LET ME GIVE IT ANOTHER TRY!
I NEVER SHOULD HAVE ALLOWED THIS TO GO THIS FAR!
CRASH
I KNEW IT!
I'M SORRY, MISTER WEATHERBEE!
SORRY FOR WHAT?
I DROPPED MY BOOKS! DIDN'T YOU HEAR THE CRASH?
4

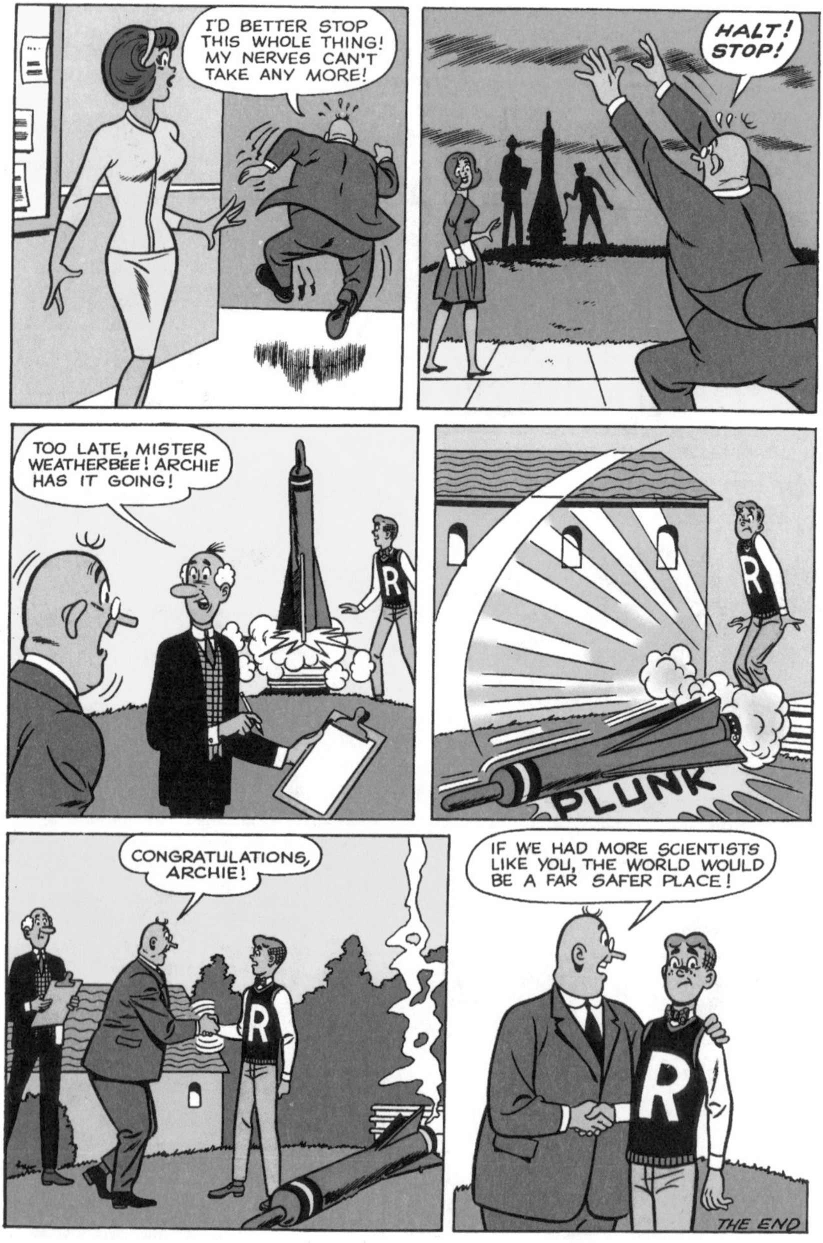
I'D BETTER STOP THIS WHOLE THING! MY NERVES CAN'T TAKE ANY MORE!
HALT! STOP!
TOO LATE, MISTER WEATHERBEE! ARCHIE HAS IT GOING!
PLUNK
CONGRATULATIONS, ARCHIE!
IF WE HAD MORE SCIENTISTS LIKE YOU, THE WORLD WOULD BE A FAR SAFER PLACE!
THE END